The Autopsy

Best Weird Stories of Michael Shea

The Autopsy

Best Weird Stories of Michael Shea

Edited by Linda Shea and S. T. Joshi

Hippocampus Press

New York

Published by Hippocampus Press
P.O. Box 641, New York, NY 10156.
www.hippocampuspress.com

Cover art © 2022 by Tom Brown.
Cover design by Daniel V. Sauer, dansauerdesign.com
Hippocampus Press logo designed by Anastasia Damianakos.

First Edition
1 3 5 7 9 8 6 4 2

ISBN 978-1-61498-383-5   trade paper
ISBN 978-1-61498-384-2   ebook

Contents

Introduction

Michael Shea (1946–2014) began writing weird fiction—as well as fantasy fiction and science fiction—in the mid-1970s. He achieved immediate success: "The Angel of Death" (1979) was a finalist for the Nebula Award; "The Autopsy" (1980)—now adapted for Guillermo del Toro's *Cabinet of Curiosities* on HBO—was a finalist for both the Nebula and Hugo Awards and also appeared in David Hartwell's landmark anthology *The Dark Descent* (1987), among many other volumes; and "Polyphemus" (1981) was a finalist for the Hugo Award. A number of these stories appeared in the *Magazine of Fantasy and Science Fiction,* whose editor, Edward L. Ferman, was particularly keen on the distinctive melding of genres that Shea's work embodied. Other stories of that era appeared in Stuart David Schiff's *Whispers* as well as in anthologies compiled by Ellen Datlow, Karl Edward Wagner, John Pelan, and other notable editors.

Shea's tales were gathered in the collections *Polyphemus* (Arkham House, 1987), in a large Centipede Press omnibus, *The Autopsy and Other Tales* (2008), and in *Demiurge: The Complete Cthulhu Mythos Tales of Michael Shea* (Dark Regions Press, 2017), and several other volumes; all but *Demiurge* are out of print, so the present volume—which includes two unpublished stories, "Ghost" and "Feeding Spiders"—fills a real need in presenting the full array of Shea's short fiction.

The fusion of genres is indeed a signature trait of these tales. "Polyphemus" appears to be a straightforward science fiction story, complete with a spaceship populated by a diverse array of male and female characters voyaging to another planet; but the crew's encounter with a titanic creature dwelling in a lake—the title derives from the entity's "titanic eye" (clearly meant to evoke Polyphemus, or the Cyclops, from Homer's *Odyssey*) into which some of the human figures fall—quickly becomes an excursion into terror. And while the technical scientific language in parts of the tale might seem to inhibit the emotional intensity of the narrative, the meticulously precise descriptions of the creature's anomalous physical characteristics creates a grimly tactile sense of unnatural horror.

"The Angel of Death" also has a science-fictional premise, even though it takes place largely in the world we know. But it soon becomes apparent that the protagonists of the tale are two alien entities who look upon the human race with the same clinical detachment with which we ourselves would consider the denizens of some remote corner of the universe. Even "The Autopsy"—which outwardly seems to be the ultimate exposition of body horror in a coroner's dissection of the bodies of miners who perished in an explosion—gains a science-fictional element as it proceeds.

More purely in the realm of weird fiction is "The Horror on the #33," where a man observes a homeless woman—derisively referred to as a "trashbagger"—turn into something unthinkably alien. In "Water of Life," the baleful proprietor of a liquor store, known only as A-Rab, proves to be something much more sinister. "Ghost" is perhaps the most superficially conventional weird tale in this volume, but it is far more than an account of a simple apparition.

Michael Shea was born and bred in California, ending his days on an expansive plot of land in the state's wine country in Sonoma County. His tales richly display the unique culture of the nation's most populous state, with its endless freeways ("Fill It with Regular") and its broad distinctions of race, class, and wealth ("Upscale"). Shea had a particular sensitivity toward the prostitutes, drug dealers, and the other refuse of society whom the bourgeoisie would like to render invisible. This indeed is the focus of "The Horror on the #33" and also of "Tollbooth," a Golgotha of horror involving drug dealing as well as an ancient Native American as a figure of vengeance. In "Ghost" we find a Californian seemingly out of his element in the very different culture of the East Coast.

The theme of psychic possession or displacement is a recurring one in Shea's tales, as can be seen in "Salome" (where a man's personality momentarily enters the body of a cat), "The Autopsy," "The Angel of Death," and others. In these latter two stories one might suspect the influence of H. P. Lovecraft's "The Shadow out of Time," where an alien entity possesses the body of a human being in order to learn about the culture of that individual; "Polyphemus," with its observation that "Polyphemus was an earthquake," brings Lovecraft's "The Call of Cthulhu" to mind. Shea's work was infused with Lovecraftian elements from beginning to end, as the novel *The Color out of Time* (1984) and the stories in *Demiurge* attest.

"Feeding Spiders" is one of a quartet of unpublished stories Shea wrote in recent years. Their focus on children or adolescents as protagonists might seem to evoke the nostalgic realm of Ray Bradbury's fiction, but these narratives are far more horrific than was generally the case with the work of Shea's fellow Californian. Other unpublished tales remain in Shea's corpus of writings, and they add their bit to our overall picture of the author's output.

Michael Shea will be remembered for his contributions to fantasy literature (notably the Nifft the Lean series of novels), his ventures into science fiction, and his extensive work in weird fiction. It is rare for authors to exhibit such range, and even rarer for them to show such skill and panache in this multiplicity of genres. But Shea's work is distinctive not only for its diversity of subject-matter but for its effortless elegance of style, its powerful scenes of terror and gruesomeness, and perhaps most of all for the deep empathy that saw a value and significance in every human—or non-human—creature all apart from that creature's status in society. It is that profound insight into human motives and emotions that will render his work eternally vital.

—S. T. JOSHI

The Horror on the #33

Of those grim events I find it difficult, even at this late date, to write. Strictly speaking, they did not even involve me, but Knavle, my dear friend, from whose voluminous correspondence alone I know of them. But we are close in soul, Knavle and I, and through his accounts, hellishly circumstantial as they were, I can say that I too, in a manner, lived those moments of horror with him.

When that first dread encounter befell him, Knavle had been a wino for almost exactly a year. He was in fact observing the anniversary month (he had already lost his memory for exact dates) of his choosing that bibulous career.

I must confess that all of us who knew him sought to discourage him from following this alcoholic vocation. Even I, his closest confidant, had been so unsupportive as to call his choice of lifestyle a "downward path." He had mildly replied that his was no smooth downhill way; that it was far easier, in fact, to be a short-order cook (for example) or a bank president than to be a wino; that, moreover, in being an object of compassion he was performing a vital moral service for those more fortunate than himself who would otherwise, lacking such flagrant specimens of misery, pity only themselves.

Fortunately, over the months Knavle's happiness and dedication persuaded me of the narrowness of my prim response, and by the time I write of, our breach was well healed. In the last letter I had from him before the one detailing his encounter, my friend had written with calm gaiety of his simple rituals of anniversary: apart from drinks cadged from others' bottles, over whose nature he had no control, he was drinking, throughout the month, only Santa Fe White Port—his first "poison" (so he fondly called it) as a fledgling sot.

Ah, the contrast of that letter with the next! The former closed with an airy reference to von Schecklestumpff's remark that religious faith lies more in small observances than grand beliefs, and in the postscript Knavle put the bite on me for five dollars. But even as I was sealing my reply, with a two-dollar money order, his next letter was dropped through my door slot, thick with Knavle's scrupulous detail. About its pages hung—not the festive fragrance of Santa Fe—but the light stink of sweating fear!

Knavle is slight and short—in general, large-bodied winos don't survive well. Knavle was one of those who could fold themselves out of sight to take their doses of oblivion. An important concomitant of this skill is the habit, on waking, of lying perfectly still until one has rediscovered one's surroundings. This Knavle did on the night in question.

He climbed up out of the chasm of two quarts of White Port to find himself folded up, vibrating. He lay on a taut surface of ocher-colored plastic whose texture parodied skin, and which had a scorched smell. He was, he realized, on a bus. That it was late at night, he judged from its being interiorly lit, and from the absence of voices. And by the fetid hum beneath him Knavle knew he was over the bus's motor, at the rear of the great rattling fluorescent barn of a vehicle. Knavle turned his face up and looked above.

He could see the contents of the bus without sitting up, because it was a new model, with yard-square windows that, when it was dark outside and light within, formed facing walls of mirrors. Out either side, the bus's interior, in hologram, lay adjoining itself. Thus Knavle saw all just by twisting his head slightly, and the image quality was excellent, even down to the striates of the red rubber aisle-mat and the felt-tipped graffiti on the aluminum screen up front concealing the driver.

As plainly mirrored were the bus's two other passengers, closer to the front. One was a small elderly Oriental man, sitting motionless, wearing a suit and tie, his skull appearing as soft as the thin ashen hair slicked down across it. And the other, some seats behind him, was an old woman, a trashbagger.

She was, with her three bulging handbags and two doubled grocery sacks of junk, one of the shopping-cart crazies, the trashcan scavengers who wheeled their wealth, mumbling, through just such parks and public squares as Knavle frequented. This one he had never seen. Her hair was a frozen yellowish thornball, like tallow radiating in spikes from her dirty nut-hard face. Even as Knavle studied her, she rose and carried her baggage up the aisle to the little Oriental gentleman's seat, muttering to herself as she went. He turned up to her, inquiringly, his smooth bulged brow suggesting infant frailty; the frecklings of age around the deep orbits of his eyes gathered into the constellations of a painful smile. The old woman plumped down beside him and began mumbling with more purpose, almost audibly to Knavle where he lay.

My friend watched, expecting the old man's attempt to extricate himself. The little person made none. His mouth widened—a smile now of absorption in what the old she-crazy was saying. Tenderly, absently, he almost touched the careful knot of his tie and replied something. The white spike-radiating head rocked, nodding.

Knavle's neck was cramped, and he was just deciding to sit up when he saw the old woman throw a look round the bus. There was something in the alert competence of the look that chilled him. He felt sure she had not seen him, and that look made him know that she must not. The bus increased speed, plowing down a long slope between sparse lines of streetlamps just visible through the interior reflections in the windows. The motor went into a higher, sighing key, and the boom and hustle of the great chassis erased all traces of what the trashbagger was now saying to her seatmate.

As she spoke she began actually to touch the little man, to groom him here and there—pat his tie knot, smooth the hair like fine dead grass at his temples, stroke his lapels. While she did these things, the man's head drooped forward, he gaped at her and seemed to want to deny something that she was saying.

Then all at once the old woman shifted in her seat and went straight to work on him. She unknotted his tie, dragged it out of his collar, and wadded it into one of her bags. She reached down, seemed to fumble obscenely for a moment, then sat up, tucking one of his shoes into a different bag. Lastly, she rousted the comb from one of his back pockets and snagged it decoratively in her waxy locks. The old man gazed at her, rapt, with the expression of one who wants to smile politely, but finds what has been said a bit too difficult, or shocking.

As what seemed a finishing stroke in this senseless touch-up, the trashbagger tilted the man's head slightly to one side. Then she set all her parcels down in the aisle, reached up and took hold of her own throat with both hands, and stripped her face clean off her skull. However, it was not a skull that was revealed, but the head of some huge wasp, or great carnivorous fly. Its merciless oral machinery sank into the old man's neck. For perhaps fifteen seconds, the trashbagger fed.

Then she pulled her face back on, swept up all her goods in one arm, and supported the little body like some drunken crony on the other. Staggering down the aisle to the head of the bus as the vehicle suddenly slowed for a stop, she tendered a small something to the unseen driver. The doors gasped open, and the spiky head descended.

Knavle could not resist sitting up to peer outside. They were at an in-town park he knew, at an intersection where the neon of an all-night coffee shop added to the light of the signals, set to idiotic pulsations of red and yellow. From the intersection, he knew he was on the #33 bus.

She set the small gentleman's body on a bus-stop bench backed by the park's dark wall of foliage. She walked on toward the crosswalk, leaving him sprawled in a slovenly way that the neatness of the man himself would never have tolerated. Knavle looked at him and saw that across the street a bored waitress, leaning at her counter in the coffee shop, stared at him too. Then he glanced back at the corner and saw that he himself was being studied by the trashbagger. She had paused in her hobbling departure and now looked Knavle straight in the eyes. They stared at each other a long moment across the disjointed figure that slouched in the poison-candy-colored light. Then the bus pulled away. With a groan my friend shrank back down in his seat. Alas! In a world of glass, where can a man lie hidden?

2

A person without experience of the wino perspective could easily miss the peculiar dismalness of Knavle's position. He and his caste inhabit the waste corners of the world and have therefore the least power to hide of any class of men. Only a man who possesses things has any power to rear-range his life, to avoid or defend; as for the resolutely destitute, they are already clinging to crannies and last possibilities. There are only so many places to sleep for free, or to get a morning's work distributing supermar-ket advertisers, and to these places Knavle had to go.

In his account of the day following the incident his style was firm and factual, but the activities he reported betrayed how disturbed he was. In the first place, around noon, he bought and ate, not only two hot dogs, but an order of fries as well. In the second place, after his meal he went and reported the murder on the bus to the police.

The food alone was very telling—any serious wino dislikes buying it. Wine is a corrosive that reduces and disposes of one's time. Nothing is ex-pected of it, it commits one to nothing—its purchase expresses not even the bare assumption that the morrow will dawn. How different the act of buying food, a stark confession of belief in the future! I needed no more than this to tell me that Knavle was contemplating positive action and might even go so far as to try to save his life in a coherent and serious way.

But of course I *had* further and far more startling evidence of this. To go to the police! Knavle! He was himself shocked that he had gone to this extreme, as his letter ended by expressing. Here follows Knavle's own ac-count:

I went to the central station, McPittle, instead of one of the local tanks where I'm known, because I reasoned that such heavy news should go straight to the heart of the organization, for promptest action.

The central station is a square glass building at least twenty-five stories high. It's a mirror-shaft, it reflects everything around it—sky, neighboring buildings, street traffic.

Inside the building, though, total transparency takes over. There are some floors where you can see the entire width of the place through hundreds of glass cubicle dividers. A forest of heads bobs in and out of view among the window-maze, round black heads as numerous as the acres of little round black holes in the ceilings. These, like a field of boringly orderly stars, are hung with ugly fluorescent moons—square aluminum grids like ice-cube trays. The slightly chilled air has a mausoleum smell, I think from the presence of so much underarm deodorant.

The first man I saw asked me if I had a record. I expected this, what with my good suit off at the cleaners, and having left my shave and my shine in my other pants. I said I had a record, but I hadn't done anything lately and that I had come to report a murder I'd witnessed last night after midnight on the #33 bus, Airport to Flanders Heights. The murder was of an elderly Japanese or perhaps Chinese gentleman, and by an even more elderly woman of a vagabondish, addled appearance. The man I spoke to turned to his partner and said, thumbing at me: "Get this individual's name and data. I've got a feeling he has a record."

The partner took my name and data, and I waited for about an hour on a cushioned bench without a back. Finally the report came up from downstairs that yes, I did have a record. They gave me my file number and sent me up two floors to see a detective. All the detectives were busy, so I waited in the detectives' waiting room for about two hours. At last they called me to the bench. The girl asked for my file number. I had lost it.

They telephoned downstairs, but the file-number department was closed. They told me to come back in the morning, and I left, blessing my luck, for I'd managed to work out of my system this strange compulsion to report this thing and without having actually to do it. More important still, I'd thought about the trashbagger through all those hours waiting and come to realize something about her: she would never let herself get caught, and no human power would ever take her against her will.

After this, Knavle's fatalism returned—or so *I* believed. His letters pointedly excluded mention of the incident, and the life they reported, divided between the usual parks and missions and neighborhoods, was his old life unaltered. It would have been tactless to applaud the stoic bravery of this. We both knew that he had confronted an entity of the direst kind, which now knew him as a witness to its act. But to live on in spite of this, to make, after his initial excited folly, no move to hide or defend himself—this was no more than his wino's code of honor required. To praise an integrity that he would want his friends simply to assume him to have, would have insulted him.

But I was misled, and his behavior was in fact *not* perfectly fatalistic. After several letters he "let slip" that, not only had he not cut down on his bus riding—he had increased it and had begun to ride the #33 with especial frequency. This was a converse species of betrayal of his ethics. I wrote him so at once, my real concern, of course, being greater for his life than his code of behavior. But I stressed this point—to seek the inevitable was as mad as to flee it. What had happened to his sot's detachment? I knew his desert-fringed city well enough to realize that he could get around it quite adequately without using the #33 line, and told him quite forcefully that this he ought to do. His reply was rather airy. He insisted the #33 had always been one of his entertainments. Aside from its offering, if taken round-trip, three hours of warm lodging, its cross-town course gave one an excellent panorama of the city—from its spectacular glass-and-girders heart, through successive ethnic zones, through the outlying bean fields, orchards, and eucalyptus windbreaks on the town's fringe, out to the airport. Moreover, he added, he never took it at night anymore. Small protection! For Knavle's second encounter was soon enough in coming. And it happened on the #33 in broad daylight, at high, glorious noon!

On the #33's return ride from the airport, the farmland is succeeded by a black-and-Latin ghetto whose streets are broad, their asphalt striped with grass-tufted seams, and on whose plank fencing or raw cinder-block walls *cholo* writing jostles the styleless black graffiti. The land rises into minor hills after this, where the streets are crowded with taller, more Victorian frame structures. Chinese, Korean, and aged white people live here. And here, as the bus topped a rise, the cloud cover that had dimmed the whole first half of Knavle's ride broke up before a fresh breeze. Tons of honey-colored sunlight were poured upon the steep shingled rooftops; the winter-scoured pavements glowed white and dry. My friend rejoiced in the sight and wondered if his sole fellow-passenger did likewise. She was a little chicken-necked biddy, wattled with age, and wearing a small round Sunday hat *cum* non-functional fragment of blue veil. She sat near the front, Knavle the rear; he could not determine if she even saw beyond the window glass beside her. The bus, just past the rise, pulled into a stop, its big new-model brakes making barely a squeak. The door wheezed and clapped. A thornball of tallowish hair rose, like a malign jerky sun, from the step well. Paying nothing, the old leather-faced trashbagger mumbled up the aisle as the bus pulled away. Had there been a hum of revolution from the roll of identifying plaques set in the bus's brow? Perhaps to not in service?

Oddly, Knavle did not feel directly endangered, though he was perfectly visible. Without knowing why, he felt sure from the first that the biddy was to be the old vagabond's prey. Just so. The trashbagger gasped to a seat just two aft of the biddy. She sat mumbling, rummaging without system among her multiple tacky baggage. Knavle watched, with no slightest concern to conceal the focus of his attention. The crone had not met his eyes as she came up the aisle.

Now she got up and advanced to the lady's seat—she sat, as many of them like to do, on its aisleward edge. The old nomad stood there in a bearish slouch, hugging her bags and sacks of trash, muttered down, and made a vague uncouth movement with her head. The biddy looked up at her, and Knavle could feel, though not see, how her knobby hands fretted with the gloves they doubtless held in her lap. Yet with the disquiet, there was also in that biddy's brow the same knit of fascination Knavle remembered from the little Japanese gentleman. Her thrifty, bony chin hung slack an instant, then she positively smiled, tightening the threads of age across her lean jaw. She moved in to the window, and the trashbagger plumped herself down in her place.

The she-tramp set her bundles down in the aisle, then leaned forward to massage her legs, speaking in a steady rumble the while. The biddy, whom Knavle saw in profile, wore as she listened a beaming church-social smile that he was sure was the liveliest in her repertory. She nodded to some remark, then lifted her hand with a little gesture that suggested the sliding-aside of some intervening panel. Leaning close to this aperture of special confidence she had created, the biddy murmured an eager sentence to the trashbagger, who, sitting up from rubbing her ankles, nodded deliberately.

They sat bent in closer conference. The spiky head spoke; the biddy's; again the spiky. And as she spoke, the trashbagger casually reached up and plucked one of the biddy's earrings off of her earlobe and pocketed it. The biddy nodded dazedly—seemingly more at something said than done. The trashbagger muttered and plucked down the second earring.

Knavle, for no clear reason, expected the old vagabond to take the Sunday hat as one of her trophies, but she did not. She took the coat of the biddy's blue knit suit off her with surprising address and, as with the Japanese gentleman, a shoe last of all. Knavle had been asking himself if he would watch to the end. Now he sat powerless to look away as the crone seized her own throat and wrenched off the rubbery bag of face and scalp, freeing the huge insect head with its black nodular eyes and the compact surgical apparatus of its mouthparts.

It was not the busy, multiple scissoring movement of these that Knavle watched as they sank into the biddy's neck—but rather the eyes. Since each of them was a hemisphere and they faced opposite directions, he knew that they had wraparound focus and saw the bus's whole interior. Nevertheless he had the overwhelming feeling that they were aimed at himself, centrally and exclusively, in the manner of a human gaze.

For fifteen seconds he and the immense arthropod stared at each other while the latter fed. The exuberant unpent sunlight poured through the

all-admitting windows and lit those compound eyes with a rainbow corus-
cation. Knavle marveled at the radiance fractured on those hundred thousand lenses; the creature seemed gilded with immortality in those
moments, with the gorgeous streets and sky passing outside.

Then the trashbagger was pulling back on the wigged sack, shoulder-
ing the biddy and her bundles on either side, and shuffling out, as the bus
sighed curbward for its first stop since she had gotten on. She tendered
something at the driver's stall and got off. She set the biddy on the bus-
stop bench and shuffled away, round the corner, gone. The biddy sat
askew—coatless in her lace-throated blouse, but still wearing her Sunday
hat—and seemed to sleep with a faintly abandoned air, publicly, shame-
lessly, like an old wino in a park.

3

After receiving Knavle's account of this second confrontation, I awaited
his next letter with dread. I hoped he would decide to abandon that city,
but had too much reason to expect him—not only to stay—but to seek out
the Trashbagger again.

When his next letter came, it brought not only the disappointment of
seeing my fears justified, but a more subtle unease as well. I present that
brief epistle in its entirety. Knavle's unsettling degree of intuition about the
Trashbagger, the particularity with which he surmises the Trashbagger's
aims and her laws, strongly suggested to me that my friend was already to
a critical extent subject to a kind of hypnotic influence exerted by the creature. I subjoin the document:

March 17

To Mr J. Bradley McPittle
Dear McPittle:

A wino is a frontiersman, a romantic. He lives squarely in the wasteland that most men so furiously deny, though it surrounds them. For all
our best mirrors and lenses, aimed star- or atom-ward, tell the same tale:
motes of matter wheeling in gulfs of black space.

Anyone who takes a walk on the desert at night, on a clear night, can see this truth without lenses. I've often insisted, McPittle, on the fact that my city stands on a desert. Even lacking this, any big city at night is in itself a good facsimile of a desert, and a good wino is the official desert rat of all such wastelands.

Any wino who is not merely a timeserver inhabits the desert out of pride, because it is the truth, or at least the truth's image. He scorns the glass mazes of responsibility, wherein so many well-upholstered heads bristle and bob and keep the ever-deepening streams of data creeping through the crooked course of systems!

But I digress. I'm on the bench at the park stop of the #33 line. It's late afternoon now—near rush hour. I'll stay on the bus all night if need be. I distributed advertisers yesterday—endless miles of advertisers! I have with me both fare and provisions. In a nice stout paper bag I have a quart of Santa Fe White Port, a quart of Italian Swiss Tawny Sherry, a quart of Thunderbird, and a pink bottle of Pagan Pink Ripple. I've got three packages of cracker-and-peanut-butter sandwichettes, fifty cents' worth of beef jerky, two Three Musketeers bars, and a package of Beer Nuts. Also, in a separate bag made out of red plastic netting, I have five pounds of oranges.

For the past half-hour I was wondering why I got the oranges, which I don't like—but I just remembered that we used to take them with us as kids when we rode the bus to the beach.

I'm petrified. But I am also strangely sure of one thing: it's in that last conversation you have with the Trashbagger that all is won or lost. Only if she outtalks you there, only if she hypnotizes you, does her face come off. If you outthink her and resist her will, you win your freedom.

I wish I had a gun! I couldn't even afford a kitchen knife!

There's something else I know too, McPittle. I'm convinced I'm not the only man in this city to have witnessed the Trashbagger's crimes. And I feel that her other witnesses have been as powerless to testify as I was, perhaps through fear of madness, or torpor of the will. How many of those people in that coffee shop across from me, eating there doggedly, docilely, on display, how many of them have seen and are saying nothing? Their fat, freckled earlobes, their veiny noses, move slightly in mastication. Their neckless profiles are a trifle stiff with the pretense of invisibility to the roaring street . . .

Whatever else, I won't hide. I won't—the bus, two blocks off. Must seal and send. May luck sit on my shoulder!

Yours,

Knavle

4

I intended to present a digest of Knavle's subsequent letter—the last he ever wrote. But despite the vagaries of my friend's style, and the rather baroque imagery to which he was addicted, I feel it would be unfair of me to interpose myself between the reader and what must be the sole firsthand account of the Trashbagger extant.

I here present then, with the most poignant feeling, the letter itself, intact as before, despite its length:

March 1_?

Dear McPittle:

Taking the #33 at rush hour is a kind of drowning, an immersion in breathless waiting men. Children, or an occasional addled vociferous type, will send ripples of response through the mass, but then all our engines return to *idle.* The feel of all those idling psychic dynamos around one causes at moments an unbearable suffocating suspense. How can we all wait like this, you think, packed, paralyzed? You think of the thousand unguessable impulses that any one of us could explode with at any moment. The fact that we don't, that we all sit and stand, drowned in silence—it becomes amazing, awe-inspiring in itself.

As the light fails in the sky and the interior lights come on, then we, a fluorescent-lit thicket of the drowned, go more minutely on display to the sidewalks we pass. We are they, shown them as plainly as are the manikin displays in plate glass. We flee, a little copse of shadows, across the concrete. Perhaps we look like an exhibit in some future museum of our culture. We are quietly posed, seemingly intent, unaware that our world lies buried a millennium deep in time past.

We were all agreed to sit and wait in silence. Most of the other passengers had other agreements going, such as about taking baths and
washing their clothes. They resented anyone's waiting in silence with
them, who had not entered these other covenants too.

Therefore, since I was already in bad odor with the company to begin
with (so to speak), I didn't aggravate matters by sneaking any sips. I ate
my cracker sandwichettes, and then an orange, as quietly as possible in
the window seat I had gotten. I waited.

Around eight it was safe to start getting a gloss on, and I did so. I
wasn't yet afraid, because I really expected nothing until the post-eleven
thin-out of riders. Now I nursed my wine and enjoyed the sense of being
on a cruise. A bus has the same rock and surge as a boat, and at night it
contains you in an alien element—the dark—just as a boat does. I peered
through my reflection at the streets outside, or followed the easy-paced
changes of the faces of my fellow-travelers—augmented at one door,
eroding away at the other. I did the latter discreetly by watching the windows. I had the contented feeling, as I did this, of guaranteed distraction,
such as watching TV can give—though this, of course, had far more va-
riety than TV.

My wine ran out at about ten-thirty. Since we were nearing the out-
bound end of the run, I decided to get down at the last intersection before
the bus entered the airport. I could replenish at the liquor store that stood
there and get the bus again as it came back out of the airport.

Just after I got down, I realized I hadn't gotten a clear look at the
driver's face. I hadn't remembered to do this on the previous encounters
and had told myself to keep track of the drivers this time out.

But when I got back on, I was startled by the bus's being completely
empty, and when I took my seat a ways back, I still hadn't noticed the
man behind the wheel.

The bus almost never left the airport without someone aboard—not
before midnight, anyway. The implication of its being empty did not escape me. I sat literally on the edge of my seat, meaning to face the Trashbagger standing if she got on. This was irrational. I knew she could only
be escaped through debate and that no physical dodging could save my

life, failing in this. Still I sat poised.

But absolutely no one got on. Not at the lonely stops in the rural stretch, where the dead light of the brown-vapor highway lamps lay on the black rank and file of identical orange trees. Not in the ghettoed hills, where the intersections were lit by the Coors sign of a ten-stool bar, the traffic signals, and an old-fashioned streetlight on a pseudo-Corinthian column of cement. And not in big-money downtown, in whose glass-box megaliths the ceiling lights formed shapeless mosaics, hanging like white larvae in hives. Not for over fifteen miles. We got onto the freeway for the last short stretch to our turnaround downtown.

This was nothing short of impossible. It was a minor order of impossibility, but it was one nonetheless. Not once did the bus pause to fall back into the schedule that it must surely be getting ahead of, barreling stopless on, as it was. The longer I delayed saying something to the driver—going up, for instance, and making a jocular remark about its being a busy night—the more powerless I was to speak. The bus spun through the turnaround in the downtown terminal and roared back out and onto the freeway again.

The certainty—panicky and insistent—that if I pulled the cord, the driver would not let me off, almost drove me to try, though I was resolved so fiercely to come face to face with my enemy, and though this was so clearly a premonition of our confrontation. We roared through the recrossing of the city. Once more, absolutely no one got on.

I got numb enough to my suspense to open the bottle of port I had bought when I got off. We turned through the airport without a pause and, with a deepening hum of gears, charged out on our return. I heard a snort, a cough, and a stir behind me.

I turned. Six seats back, near the rear, a tousled unshaven face—toothless though relatively unsenile—sprouted into view, scrubbing gummy eyelids with a blackened hand whose dirtiness was so deep-lying that it was glossy. It was a fellow-wino, just ending a nap that must have been going on for hours. As I stared at him, as blank as his own scarce-wakened mind, the bus braked with a whistling gasp, and its door clapped open.

I will relive that moment of waiting for as long as is left me. We sat in that weird triptych of the interior adjoined by its differently tilted selves on either side. There we were, six winos, waiting, amid six rows of chrome arcs on the empty seat-backs, like shiny rib cages. Up from the doorwell rose, dodderingly, the spiky tallowish planet. The Trashbagger passed the driver without paying, and waddled toward me—*me* now, I was sure!—as the bus pulled out. I could not move. My nerves cried *rise* to my legs, but the electric impulse fell down into a bodiless gulf where no legs were.

Her body was a squat mass of dowdy brown overcoat, a matronly nonshape. Over this her burst of electric hair—like a dirtied dandelion seed-puff—and her brown face as etched with lines as an oak's bark, floated with a faint tremor that suggested inner voltage, fierce, secret meditation. I looked at my reflection in the window beside me, asking myself why I did not rise, stand ready, fight, or flee.

But as she stood near my seat, looking at me, I found that I feared not so much for my life, as lest I should make a mistake. It was something like stage fright that I shook with, an overawing sense that in this interview I must make my ultimate and all-determining account of myself and that my subsequent fate should be precisely as good as my performance now. The urgency of escape was muffled by this dread. The Trashbagger set her parcels down on a seat across the aisle and, with a whispery concussion, dropped onto the seat next to me. With the panic of a nervous child who blurts the first thing he can think of, I asked her:

"Do you push around a shopping cart?" For I had seen many like her who did.

The old face aimed itself at me—the hair gave off a whiff of something like shoe polish with the movement. The walnut-shell topography of skin gullied and rivered more deeply with the tightening of a smile:

"Yes. You bet I do."

"Why?" I croaked.

"Why, to collect everything that's mine."

"And what . . . is yours?"

"All trash."

I nodded. I did not want to ask my next question: "And what's trash?"

"Why, don't you know that? It's everything, sooner or later." Her answers came with serene clarity. Yet I could not be sure, as I stared in her face, if her lips in fact moved, or even if she used a voice.

And each answer astonished me. Not in itself—but simply that I had received it. Without expecting for an instant that she would spare my life, I felt a mellow pang of faith in her. Her aura irresistibly inspired it. For despite her poverty and dirt, her agedness had taken on a wild-old-wicked-man quality. Hers, I felt, was the crusty, careless age of genius—Einsteinian, Whitmanesque, vital and bookish and humane.

It struck me then. To the old gentleman she had surely seemed benevolent, Confucian. To the biddy she must have been deaconish, and oozed a pastorly unction.

But realizing this did not free me from the spell. I found it impossible to recall what her head looked like when stripped of its living mask. I felt, and could only feel, that she was wisdom itself, that she was the very center of my hope and held the key to my salvation.

"But listen, ma'am," I said—carefully, hushedly—"I am not trash."

She shook her head very slightly. "But you will be."

"Tell me," I said, "just give me a hint. What must I argue? What line of defense must I take? I only want a clue."

"But what *can* you argue?" she said. My heart moved with a despairing assent to this. I saw through the reflection in the window that in this seeming-short time we had almost recrossed the city and were not far from the freeway stretch. In my stomach I felt an antlike crawliness. I remembered the maggots I had found, with horror, in the belly of a dead cat I had turned over as a boy.

"I think I understand you," I said. "All lives are chance-formed electrochemical engines, vastly isolated in space. Then entropy . . . atrophy . . . death . . . trash . . ."

Each word I said sank me deeper in fear, till I felt I was suffocating in my speech. Conversations with the Trashbagger led to a single end. I'd seen it. This conversation too was a brief maze leading to the same door.

"But isn't there something more, something else, that doesn't become trash?" I cried. It took great effort to say this. She exerted a kind of gravity, causing the mind to fall into her mode of thought. It was like physical toil to formulate an idea alien to her. The words came out of my mouth stillborn. Her old eroded face was a desert my question got lost in.

"Something more? Something else?" she echoed, with remote sad humor. Again I wondered—had she spoken with her voice, or had her eyes answered, cold black stars above her desolation of a face? She leaned forward and scratched at a varicosity through a hole in her filthy socks. "Motes in space," she sighed as she sat up, "wound up by accident, running down by necessity."

I might have been speaking myself, so simple and direct was my assent to what she said. I heard a concluding note in her tone and sensed our talk was ending, but could not for my life deny what she had said.

"You've got to tell me," I blurted. "Are you going to take it off?"

She bent to scratch her other leg. "Take what off?" she asked me.

"Your face."

"My face?" she asked, sitting up. She looked into my eyes for a long moment. "Yes," she said, putting her hands to her throat.

I saw the seam in the skin—crosswise to the esophagus—split cleanly, like withered lips parting. A thinner neck was unveiled within, bristling with black chitinous hairs and barbs. This could not be. There was, however, no other reality—only these three bus interiors and, outside, the arc-lit sixty-mile-an-hour emptiness of the freeway, which we had just entered. With a flabby friction the empty bag of the old woman's face slid completely off the instrument-cluster of the Trashbagger's feeding apparatus, and off the vast compound eyes.

I looked in the window beside me and beseeched my image to move, not to sit there and die, but somehow to rise. My image did nothing. Behind me the black multilensed planets, lit by a fluorescent sun, loomed near.

I did the impossible. I tore myself loose from my reflection. It remained still, stupefied, looking on, while I wrenched myself round to face the immense hymenopterous head. I felt as powerless to move as if there were no space around me, or as if I had become completely insubstantial.

But with the same furious blind contradictiveness, I *did* move. I heaved, and brought upward arms and hands that held something. With this something, desperately, I smote the Trashbagger.

It was my plastic bag of oranges. It weighed several pounds, and the flexible neck of the bag made blackjack-like blows possible. The fruit had a meaty sound against the stiff and surprisingly tough globes of the Trashbagger's eyes.

It was a groggy-enough blow, given her mass and strength, but it had enormous effect. The Trashbagger rocked back on the seat, and in the same moment the bus swerved sharply; this, combined with her recoil, dumped her straight out of the seat. I had a glimpse of the wino staring on round-eyed from the rear, and then the sudden emergence of the driver's head from behind his aluminum screen brought me around.

He was a young black man with a goatee and a half-length natural.

The bus still roared forward down the freeway, and yet he had brought his head and shoulders completely around, to stare back at me in outrage and shock.

"Are you crazy, man!" he shouted. "What you doin'? Don't you know who that *is?*"

"Jesus Christ!" I screamed back. "Look out!!"

The freeway poured toward us through the windshield behind the driver's head, and there I saw a big two-trailer truck drop sluggishly from an on-ramp and into our lane ahead. It was barely doing thirty yet, and we were at sixty-five.

The driver looked around and, in slow motion, it seemed, pulled himself back behind the screen. Both trailers of the truck were heaped with oranges. As the vehicle struggled toward forty with dinosaurian effort, and as we began—too late, I saw—to brake and swerve aside, it seemed I saw each individual orange—dewy, porous, luminous in the freeway's arc lights. Our wheels locked before we could quite pull out of the lane, and the bus skated sideways against the trailers of the frantically accelerating fruit truck.

A rain of oranges drummed on our roof, and then our whole long rattling frame whirled through a half-circle and crashed rear-first against one of the legs of an overpass.

I clutched the seat through the impact, which sent the Trashbagger rolling down the aisle to the rear of the bus. Then we were motionless, and with a cough the pneumatic doors flapped open. I sprang up, crossed the aisle, and jumped out onto the freeway. I took three running steps toward the on-ramp the truck—now sprawled ahead of us—had entered by. From behind the bus the Trashbagger stepped out and stood in my way. I stopped and lifted my sack of oranges again.

One of her antennae was bent, half-folded sideways. In the arc light her great eyes seemed to brim with sight, each one of them like a cosmos of individuals—lenses innumerable as the tiny relentless lives of coral in an acre of archipelago. I realized with astonishment that, save for the orange truck beyond the bus, the freeway was perfectly deserted.

"There is no place to run," the Trashbagger said. Unmistakably, it was a voice, the creature's true voice—a dry chitinous whisper that made clicks and slotting noises serve for its consonants. "No place. Not in time. Not in space. Nowhere. Are you quite mad?"

"Yes!" I shouted, desperately eager to agree. "Yes! Stand back! Stand back, or I'll hit you again!"

The Trashbagger's mouthparts, a black and green bouquet of rasps and pliers, worked, clicking and twiddling with a curious energy. As if she did not have wraparound focus, she tilted now one and now the other globe of lenses at me, with a movement like a bird's, or a mantis's delicate head-cocking. Her shoulders shook. She made a low pneumatic commotion. I realized that she was *laughing.*

That laughter raised every hair on my body. It had the nasty final sound of a quarter falling into a glass box. It had some of that blind wild energy, that booming clatter, of an empty bus doing seventy on a midnight freeway. The locking tomb was in it too, the gasp of the closing door. I ran past her—she made no move to stop me. I ran straight up the ivied slope of the embankment, through the lamp-lit smog-oily leaves, cold and wet with the fog. At the top there was a chain link fence. I climbed over it, and I ran. My God, McPittle, how I ran!

Knavle

5

Knavle never wrote another letter, as I have mentioned. He said it was a morbid habit, and abandoned the practice.

He also abandoned the wino's life. He has become an itinerant juggler, and as a result I see him much more frequently. And though he speaks wistfully of his days as a drunkard, he realizes that their attraction is largely a matter of that fortuitous beauty all things have when they are past. He is sincerely devoted to juggling, the art of which he first assayed using those same oranges that saved his life that night.

He was here just recently, for an engagement at the local Senior Citizens' Center, and he spoke of his new calling:

"Juggling, McPittle," he told me, "has given me something I never had as a wino. It is a defiance of gravity of the most beautifully direct kind. Everything that lives is a defiance of gravity! Everything has a dance in it which it is my joy to liberate, and I mean to specialize in precisely this, until my next meeting with the Trashbagger. Everything must dance, you see—everything—until it winds up in her shopping cart, that rattling jail!"

Salome

Rod hadn't been pronging Courtney for half a minute—not even ten seconds—when astonishment filled his mind like a flood of light. He was himself again! He'd been someone else for almost a year without quite realizing it, and all it took was easing himself into Courtney's ginger-tufted pubic patch (more girlish than Barbara's glossy black pelt), smelling Courtney's scent (more delicate, flowery, than Barbara's rich musk), tasting Courtney's tongue (slenderer, slicker, shyer than Barbara's)—all it took was a few seconds of boning another woman, and he felt himself come back to himself with a rush. This was Rod Norse, also Rod Wadd of X-rated fame, a man who had slid himself into a new pink—at least one new pink—every day of his adult life, or damn near.

He had known something was wrong, of course. A year's fidelity to one woman, even a breathtaking, volcanic she-beast like Barbara Sauciere, was, for a stud of Rod's caliber, alarming. It was dysfunctional. And his growing sense of wrongness, of dysfunction, was the reason he and Courtney were here now, in Barbara's bed under the big skylight on the second floor of her Bel Air mansion.

But knowing something was wrong, and feeling this kind of total rightness, were a world apart. When Courtney, Barbara's Best Friend, called this morning, saying she was thinking of dropping by, wondering if Barbara was in, it was not the first time she had dangled this sly bit of bait for Rod. And it had filled Rod with the same strange flood of indifference that every bit of pink, winking at him from the sidelines of the straight-and-narrow, had filled him with this past year, since his moving in with

Barbara. Inertia chilled his loins. A bored voice muttered in him: too many moves for too slight a return.

But this grotesque fidelity had to end. The thought it might be known, and laughed at, tortured Rod increasingly of late. With a sharp effort of conscious will, he had taken Courtney's bait. Had said, "Does Barbara *have* to be here for you to drop by, Court?" It was surprisingly hard to do. He scarcely managed a suave tone, hearing a tremor in his voice, and as soon as he'd hung up he went to the kitchen to build a stiff Bloody Mary. Incredible, this flutter in his guts! It was almost like . . . anxiety.

He had a second Mary in him by the time Courtney arrived and defiantly took her, of all the bedrooms the house offered, here to the big round bed he and Barbara had shared these past twelve months.

And now, no sooner was he socketed in Courtney's newness than he knew his old self again. Unshackled, he sheathed himself in her silky skin, jockeying her like his Jag up, up, up through the curves to her peaks, shooting her off of them, piloting her down like a glider through orgasm's freefall. Free! Free at last!

It was not that Barbara left him hungry. Barbara Sauciere, enigmatic millionairess, was a force of nature, devouring him with endless appetite, ferocious glee, and Rod had early on discovered, amazed, that his appetite for her was equally unflagging. She only had to give him that slanty look from her hot dark eyes, and his balls flared alight like match heads raked by a thumbnail. She had him performing far past himself, past even his adolescent levels. But it was this sense that she contained him—that was what this fidelity translated to, that he was turning into someone unknown to himself, who lived only within and for Barbara's dark beauty and fierce will.

He came in Courtney for the fourth time, his spirit jetting far and free with his seed, jetting out of Barbara's thirty-room manse, jetting high over the swimming pool, the tennis courts, the acres of lawn, high and away out over Beverly Hills, Hollywood, far and gone above the ccitied plain.

He went down to make them some drinks, leaving Courtney sprawled voluptuously on Barbara's black silk sheets. Women. He loved their sinuous simplicity. So many curves and indirections to them, so few and simple their key desires. Here was Courtney nested in Barbara's sheets, goal scored, touchdown, every lax line of her body proclaiming contentment: she had Barbara's bed, and Barbara's man. She had bested her Best Friend.

The kitchen tiles were cool to Rod's bare feet, and, making the drinks, feeling the house's big emptiness around him, haunted by Barbara's betrayed spirit, he found his thoughts taking a cool and shivery turn. Here was that . . . unease again. Bizarre! Was it that he felt Barbara might . . . take vengeance? Like, hire some muscle to break parts of him? Rod knew just what everyone else knew about where Barbara's money came from: absolutely nothing. This kind of personal invisibility was impressive; it certainly made criminal connections seem plausible. Was this it? And had a half-conscious sense of this danger been working on him all along?

No. The idea simply didn't fit Barbara. Paying to have his legs broken just didn't *feel* like her. Betrayal would enrage her . . . but Barbara's rage would be more personal, it wouldn't take the form of hired muscle. She owned him and relished owning him; that wild, glittery-eyed smile of hers told Rod this at odd moments. They might be dining, or driving somewhere, or dancing, or fucking, and he would look at her and there it would be this smile. She relished him, gloated over him in some gleeful, private place in her mind. But Rod now realized that what she was thinking, feeling when she looked at him like this, was absolutely dark to him.

Rod was no talker. He left it to the women to make the conversation, and they were always talkative in their delight to have him, in their eagerness to captivate him. But Barbara never needed to fill the silences Rod made. Easy and smiling, she could sit all through dinner with him and not say a word, her eyes, when his sought them, showing him her affection, her secret merriment.

He took the drinks back upstairs. Pronging Courtney was easier than this probing in the shadows Barbara cast. Courtney was here and now.

They drank, and Courtney talked. She said, "I'd rather die than hurt

Barbara—she's like a sister to me," and all the earnest bullshit that went with this. Rod poured a dollop of his drink into her bellybutton, and sucked it out. He slid his tongue up her middle, and sucked her little *café au lait* nipples till they were hard and pebbly. Gently he nudged her labia with the cushy mushroom of his glans until they were fat and sopping. He entered her inchingly, inexorably, feeling the wavefronts of pleasure roll through her, one after another, up the countless branchings of her nerves. She gripped him with all she had, with fingers, arms, legs, cunt, mouth— he wore her body as snug as a glove and pumped her fuller and fuller of his will till her lips and tits were swollen taut with it. This was going to be the best one yet, he was going to go off like a geyser this time, and Barbara was mixed in it now, he was smelling Barbara's peppery musk from the sheets, flashing on her opulent body even as his eyes feasted on Court-ney's. One of Barbara's faintly funky teddies hung from a bedpost above them, haunting their cheaters' fuck like a sexy ghost, or a slutty angel, and the orgasm that was almost on him now was for both women at once, he was fucking them both now and loving it, each silken, socketing impact blowing starbursts of neural fire out of the backs of his eyeballs, dazzling his brain, making him tingle down to his footsoles. Soon now, oh, soon.

Salome, Barbara's pampered Calico cat, leapt onto the bed with them, causing Rod's rhythm to falter with guilty shock. Salome liked to join Rod and Barbara at just such moments as these—to Barbara's unfailing delight and Rod's poorly masked annoyance. How had the beast gotten in? How-ever she had, she was true to her usual form in delaying her entrance until the humans were so far along towards climax that they were powerless to eject her. Then here she came, slinky-sinewy, purring, eyes half closed and sultry, threading herself between them in their rutting, rubbing and nuz-zling in that obscene, shameless participation that cats seek when they find their humans mating.

The little monster's pumping paws and kneading claws worked on Rod's sweating flanks; her rough, hot, shocking little tongue raked his ribs. Rod loathed it but was too far gone to stop now. Courtney wailed and came, and Rod came, too, and just as he did, Salome unleashed the hissing shriek of a banshee and slashed her claws across his buttocks.

He bellowed, stunned by an explosive ejaculation. Belatedly he lashed out, and his hand met only air. The animal was gone.

They lay gasping a moment—it seemed to Rod he had never come so hard in his life. But then they realized that he was bleeding abundantly, and it galvanized them with a sudden panic not to mark Barbara's bedclothes with bloodstains. Courtney stanched his scratches with the nearest things at hand—her bra and underwear. In the bathroom they bandaged him properly and then Courtney had a wild whim—exquisite, upper-crust Courtney! She put on her underclothes, gaudily splashed with his gore. "Just another casualty of love," she grinned, archly posing.

Perhaps it was delayed shock from his wound, but Rod's stomach turned violently to see her spattered costume. His face broke sweat and he barely fought down his urge to vomit; he had to cover it as a spell of dizziness, and joke about love's excess.

As they stepped out the front door, Courtney squealed and stumbled, almost fell. Salome had bolted out of nowhere right under her feet. As Rod steadied Courtney, the cat jumped onto the hood of his black Jag—a Valentine's Day present from Barbara—and crouched there, ears flattened, hissing at them, its yellow eyes moving from Rod to Courtney and back to Rod. The beast's air of challenge so unnerved them they stood frozen for a heartbeat, till Rod's wound flared, and anger with it, and he stooped for a rock from the plantings. When he turned again, arm cocked, Salome was gone.

The lovers drove their separate ways when they reached the Strip. Rod cruised, waiting to feel some afterglow, at least some pride in his emancipation from fidelity. Instead he found a nagging anxiety. He would need some story to explain his wounded buttocks to Barbara. It was a grotesque dilemma, a joke, really, but its seriousness grew the more he considered it. The claw marks were like a branding; Barbara's instant inference, on seeing the wounds, would be that Rod had been fucking.

The day was cool and overcast—saying he'd been sunning nude by the pool was out. Could he say he'd been in the rec room, lying naked on a towel after the jacuzzi? It was something he never did. And the gist of it wouldn't go away: Salome never touched him, never approached him, unless he was having sex with Barbara.

His sense of entanglement in this petty problem became intensely aggravating. He grew more convinced by the minute that his best course might actually be to leave town for a few days and let the scratch heal before facing Barbara. At least a trip would give him scope to invent some pretext for the wound.

It burned him even now. He could feel each claw track distinctly, five hot slashes. The same number of times he'd pronged Courtney. Five.

He could leave and say he'd been to the desert, to Hot Springs for the spa, for example, and make up something with a cactus. Were there actual cactuses out there . . . ?

In any case, there was no way he would tell Barbara it was Salome. If she knew it was the cat that had scratched him, then she'd instantly know *why*. In fact, one of Barbara's odd little jokes recurred to him now with a ridiculous kind of relevance; sometimes, in her infrequent bursts of playfulness, Barbara would stroke Salome on her lap and say things in the beast's ear aimed archly at him. "I know this man of mine's behaving," she would tell the cat. "My sweet little Salome would tell me if she saw him being bad. My sweet little Salome helps me out when I need it, doesn't she? She does just what I tell her . . ." And the two females, human and feline, would look at him, their unlike eyes glinting with the same feral gleam.

In the end Rod got sick of his own queasy brooding. If Barbara found out, worst case, he'd be thrown out. Big deal! He'd start boning some other rich pink, and have her give him a different color Jag. Because it was time to get a grip! What kind of wuss was he turning into here? What had the bitch been doing to him? Some kind of fancy drug in his food, maybe? Hypnosis? Look how he was sitting here sweating things, brooding and worrying like some twist on the rag . . .

Rod stopped for a Martini or three, his drink of choice in the afternoon. He drove back to Bel Air feeling no pain, and most definitely feeling no anxiety, making the Jag's engine race and the tires squeal on the curves up into the hills. He didn't have to explain shit to Barbara about scratches on his ass or anything else. At the same time, he also knew he was getting home soon enough to throw a few things together and be gone somewhere before Barbara got home.

He built a drink in the kitchen, and carried it, sipping, on a quick tour of inspection for overlooked clues of the morning. Then he went to the phone and checked the messages.

He replayed only the first one on the tape: a call from the Emergency Room at Memorial Hospital, telling him Barbara was in Intensive Care after an auto accident a little after noon today—just about the time, some voice whispered to him, that he and Courtney were having their last wild fuck.

He wasn't allowed near Barbara's bed; there, high-tech hookups dominated, and high-priced doctors. He could see her in there, an oblong shape of white linen webbed in tubes. Barbara was all still, icy whiteness, except for one tress of her raven-black hair that escaped the bandage on her head, and excepting too her vivid red lips, proud and sensual.

Rod found something queenly in the sight. All unconscious, still Barbara could conjure up all this medical sorcery. Of course her mere wealth—wherever it came from—would do as much: let her be stricken, and doctors sprang up on all sides of her. But Barbara had something more, had an aura about her. The medicos moved with a hushed, devotional air, and a kind of radiance shone from her stillness. Her coma faintly hummed with power, like a dynamo.

A junior doctor superciliously explained to Rod that, in essence, every scan known to man was being done. The doctor's awareness that Rod, though an intimate of the patient's, had no connection with her money hung almost palpably in the air between them. The doctor had spoken, was turning away, when Rod blurted, "So what are her chances? I mean for recovery?"

"Well, as I think I indicated, with certain key reservations, I'd say they were good—all subject to the outcome of ongoing tests, of course."

"Of course."

A strangeness hit Rod then, as he stood looking into that room. There was something about this whole scene, Barbara lying in state, her red mouth and lock of black hair the sole touches of glamour amid all the gowns of white or drab green, amid consoles and LCDs and tubing—there was something theatrical about it all. Staged.

This feeling lodged like a particle of glass in his brain, and he couldn't dislodge it. He drove back up into the hills, night falling now. Could it be he was getting a little screwy? Maybe drinking too much? So vivid that sensation was, almost like hallucination! That powerful sense he had that Barbara wasn't truly lying in the deep-freeze of coma; that she was lying in state, and all those doctors—courtiers—were just milling around, awaiting her further orders . . .

Back home again, Rod wandered from room to room, feeling taut and touchy, like a balloon that might pop if he accidentally bumped into something sharp. He was coming down from the morning's fucking and all the drinks.

He made a tall, stiff vodka and tonic, and dropped in twists of lime. The bruised green rinds sank into the vodka's chill like drowned swimmers at peace with their fate. He took the drink to the rec room and got into the Vibra-Lounge. He set the chair back to horizontal, what he thought of as NASA lift-off mode, for star-traveling. He used the remote box to kill the room lights and turn on the floodlights and the airjets in the vast jacuzzi, to get a kind of tropical background of hissing water and ripply, aqueous underlighting that shuddered on the shadowy ceiling.

He lay in the half-dark, taking the vodka with a Flex straw, only having to lift his head a little. The illusion of escape was achieved. This was some Pacific Paradise, the ferny bank of a moonlit stream.

He reflected that right now Barbara lay supine as he did. On being shown the accident report (by a cop with a polite face and mean, mocking eyes) Rod had learned that she'd rolled off the highway just about exactly when he and Courtney were getting launched on number five. *It was utterly casual,* Rod told Barbara in his mind. *And I was thinking of you the whole time. It sounds phony, but I really was!* He sipped vodka, thinking: *It's all right. She does not know. The scratches will be healed by the time she is well.*

She will never know.

He drained his glass. Spikes of icy Stolichnaya stilettoed down through his nerves, nailing him with delicious numbness to the chair that cradled him. But he found himself picturing the redness of Barbara's mouth again, the blackness of that crow's wing of her hair that escaped the bandages. Somehow these vivid details spoke a secret, crazy language of fear to him. Barbara knew of his infidelity. She knew, and she had not really been struck down, she had withdrawn to lie in state in that hospital. Strategically withdrawn from him, knowing his crime . . .

Craziness, pure and simple. Time to go mix another drink. It was then Rod discovered that he could not move. He could . . . not . . . *move!* Not a foot. Not a finger. He could not even raise his head.

He could not even *try* to move, could not even cause a tightening in the least of his muscles! His will hung in a bubble, connected to no part of him.

Was this some freak alcohol overdose? Would his lungs freeze up next? Would he suffocate? Not possible, not with—what? Seven or eight drinks in the course of a day? Ten at the most? Anyway, his breathing was fine, and he wasn't numb. He could feel things. Could feel, for instance, a slight breeze from the door to the hallway as it creaked gently open.

He lay in terror, still as stone. Was someone coming in? He couldn't lift, or even turn, his head to look. He heard no footsteps. It was probably just a breeze pushing the door open. Dear Christ, why couldn't he *move?*

Something gripped him by the ankle. His heart gave a wallow of terror in his unmoving chest, and his bladder would have let go if it had still been connected to his consciousness. Little clawed pads got a purchase on his pant leg and vaulted up. He could not tilt his head even enough to see his own feet, but he knew it was the compact and sinewy tread of a cat that now moved along his leg and crossed his midriff.

Salome—now he could see her calico muzzle—advanced across his chest. Her face was the most extravagant nightmare he'd ever had, seen from this angle, this victim's vantage. Her opalescent, upslanted eyes, the bristly caves of her radaring ears, were pure terror to a man who could not move a finger. There was a . . . a strut to her gait, a swagger of ownership. She stood on his throat and lowered her face to his and he could smell her carrion breath. She put her forepaws to his lips and pried, with padded strength, his jaws apart. Glaring into his eyes, she opened her mouth and hissed. A gust of pure Barbara welled into his throat and nostrils—her musk, her sweat, her perfume. Rod was gorged with Barbara's mingled essences. And then the beast lowered her muzzle further, more intimately deep into his mouth, and inhaled. Her little lungs with surprising power pulled the air out of Rod's own. His lungs collapsed in the vacuum. His thoughts were snatched from his brain by that terrible, blinding, annihilating suction.

Rod saw a wolf spider crossing the patio's flagstones—a big one, as big as his paw. Only faint light from the house's windows dusted the spider's bristly abdomen and busy legs, and yet Rod, seeing the creature through Salome's eyes, found it abundantly visible, seething with movement in the dark.

The cat was wired to leap at such a sight, and Rod couldn't restrain the taut little body imprisoning him. He and the animal sprang, their tail unfurling to balance the leap, and their paw stunned the spider with a swipe. They sniffed the prey and then neatly bit off the soft, oozy raisin of the spider's abdomen; its silken pus was surprisingly pleasant to Rod's raspy tongue. Not unlike seafood, he thought.

The cat licked her chops, feral drives discharged for the moment. Such pauses were opportunities to control the animal. Rod exerted his will, sending the pulse of his desires through the alien tissue. In the hour since he'd wakened to his transplantation, Rod was only now fitfully managing to steer the beast. He was learning to move it by radiating raw bursts of his wishes through this meat-machine that had dragged him into its cogs, into this unimaginable nightmare through which he prowled lithely on all fours. He'd been able to discover this trick of concentration only after subduing his panic, subduing his fear, which was a thrashing, mad giant in his mind that seemed it might thrash him to pieces.

But now Rod knew how to go *with* his body, even when his body had been switched on him. He fought down the terror of it, to be padding around inside a tiny panther, seeing everything through inhuman eyes, seeing the neon-and-smog-stained sky in hues of hemorrhage and bruise that he had never imagined . . .

Now, by concentrating, he could move the animal when it wasn't strung tight on some drive. In a way, it was like boning a pink, fucking her scientifically along, running his current through her wiring. But it was *trickier* than boning. It was like pulling on a glove that kept melting off your hand. Control unpredictably vanished, and the carnivore swallowed him up in her will again.

Rod got Salome, sated by spidermeat, to pad her way past the pool, heading around back, toward the one-story bathhouse near the mansion's east wall. He got her moving at a slight trot, building momentum, his hopes rising as the cat-body kicked in to his intent, for here at the bath-house wall they must *jump,* claw right up the trellis of vines, get on the roof. Salome, with a slight lag of confusion in her movements, nonetheless made the climb, her claws biting the soft redwood lath and tearing down a rain of leaves.

Where was the conscious devil who had sucked Rod out of his body? That leering monster that had opened his mouth and thrust her whiskered snout inside it? This animal imprisoning him was mindless, automatic— seemed unaware she contained him.

Once on the bathhouse roof, Salome must stop to wash herself, the in-stinctive feline display of nonchalance after a flawed athletic performance. Rod had learned there was no way he could prevent her doing this at fre-quent intervals, much though he loathed the careful licking the animal always gave her asshole.

When the lickdown was done, he was able to move her again, thrusting in her, cat-fucking her forward to jump up onto a low-thrust eave of Spanish tile, and climb up onto the roof of the house itself. Again the beast was faintly awkward, perhaps feeling jockeyed now, and half balking at it. Salome performed a second, briefer lickdown.

But then, just a little farther was all he had to nudge her, up to the skylight over the rec room, the last place he had been when he was still in possession of his body. He had to see what was going on in there—know his rightful body's separate fate.

He humped the animal harder, faster, for the skylight, praying the furry little bitch would stay with it, move to his pumping.

Salome slammed to a halt and froze in a crouch. They'd run into the smell of danger, into a blast of pheromones riddling them like radioactive sleet. Down there on the eave, just above the rain gutter, was a huge, tattered gray tomcat. A twenty-pounder at least, the monster crouched, ears flattened, eyes hot amber, frozen in mid-advance with one paw foremost. Aggression welled in freezing molecular fronts from the tom's glands, and cascades of adrenaline rippled through Salome's muscles in response. Dear God, Rod thought, was that thing going to fuck them?

The beast looked big as a tiger to Rod, but Salome, even in terror, growled, radiating the scent of her hate against the interloper. It held the brute at bay. The tom flattened his ears a notch, a feral hint of accommodation. Now Salome, working her own will, edged up the rest of the way to the skylight, taking the nearest high ground.

She crouched on the skylight and stared down into the tom's eyes, and the game of cat-patience began, the big tom waiting, yellow-eyed, for the first sign of crumbling, of concession in the she-cat's posture. And with a chill Rod understood that this tom was not here about fucking. He was here about clawing. He was here about killing.

At least now Rod could see down into the Activity Room, where he had last possessed his own beloved body.

Down in the rec room, the main lights were on, the Vibra-Lounge empty, the jacuzzi turned off. Just beyond the jacuzzi, recessed in the wall, was the dazzlingly pink-tiled bath, with mirrors that multiplied a forest of many-colored bottles and jars. In these mirrors there were fragments of movement. Someone was there, at the makeup counter in a corner he couldn't see from this skylight. Rod must get to the next one over.

So violently did he thrust his will into Salome that it made her start. It marred her perfect poise and, because it looked like fear, this launched the tom's attack. He came whirling up the tiles, a blizzard of claws. The bitch-cat fell on one side and rabbit-clawed his belly with her hind claws as his rush dragged her under. Razors slashed Rod's ears and furry flanks. They rolled, twisting and kicking, and Rod and Salome kicked the tom off. They went into a new crouch on the next skylight over, while the tom circled sullenly, driven back, but not far back.

And now Rod could see who was in the half-bath. Rod could look down and see himself sitting at the makeup counter.

His stolen self sat down there at the tiled counter, leaning close to the mirror-wall, doing something to his face, doing some careful and minute work on his face . . . in that moment madness was a black whirlpool sucking down on Rod, the true Rod, cat-imprisoned. His sanity almost fell, kicking and screaming, into the impossible distance he saw now, this heart-freezing gulf between himself and himself.

What was that little tool that he—that Rod there!—was applying to his mouth? Was it a file? Was that what he was doing down there? *Was he filing his teeth?*

It was after a moment impossible to doubt: the Rod-body (Not himself now! Someone else! Something else!)—the Rod-body was leaning his face up close to the mirror and minutely, patiently, with tiny, self-caressing thrusts, filing his front teeth down to points. Rod could just hear the filing sound, like a muted cricket, through the heavy glass of the skylight.

The cats sat utterly still, adrenaline bombs watching each other for the signal to blow.

In the house below, the phone rang. Rod could just hear its multiple chirr from all eight of the extensions. He watched himself set down the file. He saw by the file's red handle that it was the one he used to keep his buck knife sharp. He saw himself set down the file and pick up the phone.

He watched himself speak in a voice easy and intimate, just below audibility. He watched himself smile as he spoke, displaying the little triangles of darkness he had created between his teeth. His grin looked ragged, cheerfully insane.

Instantly Rod knew who his fanged pseudo-self was talking to. He watched himself hang up the phone, and a clock began ticking in his mind: Courtney already hurrying out and tucking herself into her Beemer. Courtney sliding out of her drive and beginning to thread the route through the hills, the lights of the Valley blazing below her . . .

Rod must escape the roof. He had to get down to the driveway and somehow be positioned to keep Courtney from entering the house. Megavolts of fear hummed through him; he hammered at the bitch-cat's body.

Salome resisted him for an endless time, but she was worn down by the duel of stares, and in the end she got up, carefully, carefully, growling low. She raised her head and showed her fangs.

(Now Courtney would be cruising the last couple miles, the Beemer's top down probably, her scarfbound hair twisting like dark, pent flames in the wind . . .)

Salome began to move, a slow, prowling step along the roof's ridge line. The tom was up too. There seemed less murder in him somehow—something still dangerous, but also gamesome in his yellow eyes. He matched her, paralleling her, or perhaps edging just an inch closer. Rod's panic hammered at Salome and she began another slow step, laterally along the roofpeak, her growl getting louder, her tail beginning to lash and slash.

Courtney was entering this street! Rod knew that Beemer's pitch, and wasn't that it out there, gearing up for the last slope to Barbara's hilltop? Another slow step, matched by the tom, which was—yes—edging closer. Then another, slightly less slow step, and there came Courtney's Beemer, nosing to a stop in front of the house, and Salome broke and ran, and the tom launched itself after her, a claw-tipped comet of fur.

Their claws crackled across the roof tiles; they streaked down the ridge line, the bigger cat two strides behind, holding tight for all the she-cat's desperate speed. Acres and acres of roof, it seemed, and there was the *thunk* of the Beemer's door . . . the opening of the front door . . . voices . . . Salome reached the front of the house and leapt, hanging tiny in the gulf of empty air.

They were still falling, Salome and Rod, as Courtney's voice rose: "How awful! Is she going to be all right?" Then they crashed down into cushiony blackness, the convertible's back seat, as the front door closed and cut off her excited voice. They sprang out of the car just as the tom came hurtling down to strike where they had been. It was out a beat behind them, and instantly in close pursuit. The yellow-eyed devil drove them hard, zigged them and zagged them. They were running full out, and had to veer exactly as the demon steered. Back to the bathhouse it ran them, and again up the trellis, and again up onto the bathhouse roof, and thence back onto the roof of the house.

And once on the roof, it drove them—just where it wanted them—onto another skylight. This was the skylight that looked down on Rod's and Barbara's bed. Here the tom, when he had treed them on the glass, backed down a step, crouched, and waited.

Approaching the glass, Rod had heard harsh sounds within the house, muffled barks of pain. As he looked down through it, these cries exploded into screams.

Rod beheld red carnivorous horror. He could look straight into Courtney's stunned, up-staring eyes, already turning glassy with shock. Rod understood what was happening. Understood who was making this nightmare for him. As Rod and Courtney had feasted on one another in this bed this morning, so again now—except that now, only Rod feasted.

And as Rod had the thought, his own fang-mouthed face, smeared red, turned to look up at him with a fierce, lascivious humor. Rod felt Salome grow liquid around him, or felt himself grow denser and begin to leak out of the crude weave of the cat's tissues. Rod felt himself sinking out of the cat, falling from her belly, and his powerless will clutched desperately to grip its inhuman refuge. It failed and Rod fell, fell back to himself. Fell back down to himself grinning up at his fall with Barbara's eyes.

Groggily, as after a long upward fight through drunkenness, Rod opened his eyes, possessed himself again. What was that sound outside, like banshees in the street? Police vehicles? His body felt like an intolerable burden, a gross excess of bone and muscle. His eyes focused, and he came woozily up on all fours and saw what shared the vast mattress with him, abundantly splashing it with color. Rod understood his sense of heaviness was not mere contrast with his recent littleness. His human belly, hugely swollen, bulged under him. His jaws ached, and he was wet all over.

He remained there, still on all fours, dizzied by the reek of blood, struggling sluggishly inside his skull to shed this hideous nightmare he was now embedded in. It seemed that calls had been made, yes, for here were vehicles and loud radios and voices out front, and hammerings of doors, and more voices and the drumbeats of many approaching feet. Dear God! Mouthed and lion-paunched like this, what denial, endlessly reworded, could save him now?

The first officer who came in, nine millimeter at the ready, flak jacket on, saw naked Rod, all blood, lurch up from beside the horror of his human meal, and launch himself, fangs bared in a snarl. When the officer squeezed three rounds into Rod's forehead, it seemed a mercy to all concerned.

Polyphemus

The sunlight falls bright and strong on the wastes of Firebairn at noon, but the wind is fresh and cuts through the warmth of it. Consequently, murmions usually sun themselves in the lee of the buttes and the eroded volcanic cones that stud those plains. In the lee of one such cone—more like a ragged ringwall really, no higher on the average than a hundred meters, but more than four kilometers in the diameter of its enclosure—a murmion luxuriated on a patch of red sand.

The creatures are rather like baby seals in shape, though a bit smaller, which still makes them among the largest of Firebairn's terrestrial fauna. The lakes (such as the one in the crater behind this murmion) and the sea contain the overwhelming majority of the planet's animal life and all its most impressive forms. Indeed, the colonists there had recently established that the murmion evolved from an aquatic line, the same order to which the economically important and much larger delphs belonged. Members of this order were sometimes called "mammalian analogues," based on their reproductive systems, lungs, and vascular organization, but there was something of the arthropod in all of them, perhaps most noticeably in this little pioneer of the dry land. It had a smooth chitinous hide and primitive eyes—ommatidia, really—like small black knobs, while its "flippers," fore and aft, were rigid and three-jointed, though of an oarlike flatness that proclaimed their ancestral function.

This murmion had chosen an unfortunate spot for its nap. It was dark blue in color, and the reddish sand put it in sharp relief. This had not gone unnoticed by a second organism that now crouched upon the crater's rim, still dripping from the lake within, whence it had just emerged. This, known colloquially by the colonists as a "gabble" (*Sturtis atrox thom-*

sonia), was batrachian in form, though morphologically a far simpler organism than any frog, being in fact more analogous to an immense rotifer or roundworm in its internal structure. Moving on four pseudopodia, it was a green viscid mass with a vast slot for a mouth and, above the mouth, a freckling of rudimentary eyes reminiscent of a spider's. It found prey by a subtle discrimination of color contrasts, and since it frequently left the water to forage along the land fringes, one could not help feeling the murmion's sunbathing habits were maladaptive. The gabble was easily four times the size of the murmion, and swift and silent as liquid—properties it now demonstrated as it leapt and flowed down the side of the crater toward the sleeper. Its final lunge came from so high that the force with which it smacked down on the murmion imparted a paralyzing shock to the prey.

The gabble stepped daintily back from the stunned creature, bobbed and weaved, seemed to shudder with delicate anticipation, and swallowed the murmion whole.

The gabble settled down for a digestive nap on the warm red sand. Had it possessed more highly evolved eyes, it might have been alarmed, for something of immense size was already quite near, grinding its slow way across the desert toward the crater. Perhaps not. The gabble had no natural land-dwelling predators larger than itself.

The wastelands of Firebairn would have inspired awe in anyone susceptible to nature's grandeur. The genesis of this continent—and of the planet's only other one—was now well understood. Both were immense tables of volcanic outflow produced by several primary magma vents in the sea floor, and augmented by a multitude of lesser vents.

The period of active vulcanism was a hundred million years past, and there had long been established a global weather cycle that seasonally scoured the land with hurricane winds and hammering rains. Erosion had burnished the buttes and cones, scoured the obsidian fangs and claws off them, till now they shone like glazed ceramics in the sun. Of the once-towering volcanic cones, only the stumps remained, like twisted pots and cauldron rims. Everything was red, black, olive green, ocher, and orange—not just the buttes and the glassy ramparts of the worn cones, but the rain-polished sands and gravels too. These formed threads, ribbons, whole fabrics of color, all woven and braided by the millennial winds.

And bejeweling this already jeweled terrain were the numberless lakes. Most of the lakes were in the craters, but many were on the flats as well, where their stark, cruel blue shone impossibly intense, framed by the polychrome mosaics of the plains. It was a world of inexorable beauty, through which a man might go in rapture, but only if borne in steel, only in a juggernaut harder than the harshness of that stern paradise.

The sand-hog was such a craft, a great tractor-transport, tank-treaded, that chewed across the gravel, gnawing it with a continuous fifty-ton bite. It bore three boats in its undercarriage, nine men and women in its upper decks. In its middle was a holding tank, a belly that whole schools of delphs could be swallowed into and carried off to sate the hunger of the growing colony. It was now farther from the colony than it had ever gone, not due to any shortage of delphs in the colony's immediate vicinity, but in order to combine forage with exploration and mapping of the continent. As the vehicle drew near the landmark its captain had selected for inspection, Penny Lopez, watching from one of the ports, said:

"Look. There's a gabble."

Several of the others joined her at adjacent ports. The presence of a gabble indicated that the crater indeed contained a lake. More than this, it portended that the lake would contain delphs. Delphs and gabbles were ecological associates. Both inhabited only "ocean-rooted" lakes—those whose surrounding craters had still-open vent systems that connected their waters with subcontinental oceanic influxes.

"Why is it wobbling like that?" asked the group's cartographer, Japhet Sparks. Nemo Jones, one of the two armorers, smiled within his ragged beard.

"He ate something nasty, I expect." Penny looked at him sharply. The uncouth armorer had been a suitor of hers at one time. Repulsing his attentions had not sufficiently expressed Penny's dislike of him, and the power of even his most innocent-seeming remarks to irritate her was a source of open humor among the colonists. But Orson Waverly, who was the expedition's biologist, glanced at Nemo and shared his smile.

Indeed, the gabble did not look well. Pseudopodia spread, it seemed to be trying to brace itself, while spasms and tremors made it quake like a shaken plate of jelly. One of its sides bulged. From the bulge, something sprouted that looked like a blue, crooked knife blade, and even as it did so, a second identical one erupted from the creature's opposite side. With a synchronized sweeping motion, like oars plied by a boatman, these blades began to cut two jagged incisions through the flanks of the gabble.

"Captain Helion," said Waverly, "would you go at one-third for a moment for a field observation?"

The formality of the request was necessary, for the captain, a tall and statuesquely handsome man, disliked modification of any of his procedures. He arched an eyebrow, nodded coolly, and cut speed.

The observation required little time, for as the gabble ceased its impotent quiverings of resistance, a second pair of angled blades thrust from its sides. With an undulating swimming motion (not unlike a baby seal's) these four trenchant protrusions completed a circuit of the froglike belly. Head and forelegs flabbily collapsed, and from the bloody-edged barrel of the gabble's hindquarters the snout of a murmion poked into the sunlight. It was a brief exulting gesture, such as a dolphin might make, breaking the surface out of sheer exuberance to dive again—and this the murmion did, greedily, into the nourishing pot of its prey's stomach.

Penny gave the smiling Nemo Jones a brief scowl. She went over to the piloting console, where Helion was already steering a course along the crater's perimeter, seeking an access to its interior negotiable by the tractor treads of the fishing craft the hog carried. She asked him the chances of finding such a break, and he cocked an eye at the crater and murmured a judicious reply. The captain's normal manner of stalwart composure was always faintly heightened by Penny Lopez. To Waverly, who was making a journal entry, Jones said:

"You rarely see that happen on dark sand. Murms always lie upon red or yellow, to show up better for the gabbles."

"Don't tell me," put in Jax Giggans, his fellow-armorer, who was readying the rifles. "You've hunted murmions on Katermand. Katermandian murmions. And you know all their tricks. And when they can't find sand the right color to lie on, they make use of special polychromatic piss glands they have to dye it yellow."

Nemo gave a single bark of laughter, practically a cachinnation from this rather solemn and formal man. Jax's joke might have been offered by any of the colonists. The backward jungled planet of Jones's origin, and his endless repertory of woodsman's tricks and lore, were a favorite target for humor. Nemo's normal reaction, however, would have been a courteous blankness—perhaps a blink of bafflement so straight-facedly feigned that many at first believed him slow-witted. But with Jax, he actually laughed, and riposted:

"No. They always piss green. Diet of gabbles."

"A joke!" said Sari, one of the pilot-gunners. "Nemo Jones has made a joke! Check the ports—the sky may be falling." There was a bitter edge to this sneer that was a little surprising to everyone who heard it, perhaps even to Sarissa Wayne herself. She didn't like the way it rang; it made her sound jealous of Jax's friendship with the Katermandian—which she was.

Sarissa considered punching Jones in the face. No, she would probably have to use some heavy blunt instrument to hurt him enough to get things started. In any case fighting him, as Jax had done, seemed to be the only way to get close to him.

Nemo Jones had been less well liked during his first year on Firebairn. For one thing, when he offered solutions to problems arising in the field, they were often bewilderingly irrelevant to the courses of action everyone else was debating—and just as often, they proved to be the best solutions. Combined with his curious solemnity and the definiteness of his opinions, this was an irritating pattern. And for another thing, while he obeyed most orders (though sometimes with an air of stoic compliance that subtly pronounced them stupid), he would every now and again immovably *refuse* an order. And not always a significant order—sometimes quite a routine one. But he could not be argued out of these strange fits of stubbornness and had spent quite a few weeks in the detention cubicle.

Senior staff had soon determined that his usefulness outweighed his recalcitrance and generally allowed him his quirks. And his fellow-colonists in general quickly worked out the same equation on the social level—but not before Jax Giggans, overhearing Jones refuse some commonplace order, had gotten "fed up with the hairy little primadonna." Helion had been the officer in charge and had allowed the fight.

Jax was bull-bodied, over six feet tall. He shaved his scalp, and his head looked like a battering ram. Jones was a hand'sbreadth shorter, and lighter by fifteen kilos. He was not unimpressive—lean, wide-shouldered, his knot-muscled arms roped with veins, hairy as a goat. But still the smaller man by far.

It was an eventful fight, though not a long one. Jax lost an upper canine, had his nose broken and a rib cracked, and received a multitude of astonishingly large and vivid bruises all over his body. He was a man of courage and picked himself up no less than four times, but he fell five.

Afterward, he would unabashedly describe the fight to anyone who asked. He told Nemo that anyone who could fight as hard as he could had to have good and sufficient reasons for whatever he did.

And there they were—friends now in a way that Jones was with no one else. Sarissa was not averse by temperament to punching Jones in the face, but was ruefully aware that in any case she wanted something more than Jax had with him. First she wanted his friendship, his respect, and then she wanted to mate with him. The crazy phrase was his own, for ironically Jones had first made his suit to her. Back then, before she had known what to make of him, she had rejected his grotesquely formal gestures of courtship. He had gone on, in his methodical way, to woo the more conventionally beautiful Penny Lopez—with a similar lack of success.

"We're approaching a likely entry point. Pilot-gunners below-decks, please." Helion, ever official, used the intercom, though he might have spoken over his shoulder and been heard by all. Sari went below with her friends Angela and Norrin, to check the chemical balance of the quarry tanks and see to their harpoon guns. Nemo helped Jax lay out the field kits of the party's other weaponry while Orson Waverly and Japhet Sparks stood behind the captain, watching the terrain from the pilot's port.

Erosion had broadened a crack in the cone wall, creating a gravel-floored defile that could be reached by a few meters' climb from the desert floor. Helion stopped the sand-hog below the defile. "Reconnaissance party stand by to disembark," he said, again through the intercom. He thumbed a switch. The door coughed open and the gang ramp creaked outward, downward to the bright sand. He gave the controls to Penny, took his rifle from Jax, and preceded Jax and Nemo down the ramp. The three of them set out to reconnoiter.

The defile appeared more than adequate for the boats. Before they were halfway through it, they saw the lake: a vast, brilliant arena of water, steep-shored save for a small beach at the defile's foot. Near the water's center, perhaps two kilometers offshore, was a small craggy island.

"There's delph here. No doubt of it," Nemo muttered. As was often his way on unknown ground, he moved tautly, "ready to drop to all fours" as Sarissa had once expressed it. Helion disregarded him, but Jax looked at his friend with an air of inquiry, not so much for the remark as for an undertone of unease he had heard in it.

The boats' access assured, they climbed to the crown of the rim and moved along it. The island seemed to be a volcanic plug, an upwelling of magma that had succeeded the cone's formation by a long time, for it was far less eroded than the wall they stood on, to a degree for which the wall's shelter could not account. They had gone less than a mile when a deep cove in the island's flank was revealed.

"Shit," Jax growled in awe. The cove teemed with delphs, by far the biggest school the men had ever seen. Even at that distance they didn't need the glasses to see the beasts—scores of them sunning in the shallows, their backs bulging above the water looking like a nestful of silver eggs, and scores more where the cove deepened, playing the leaping game of tag characteristic of the younger members of the species. Helion gazed in silent satisfaction. Nemo Jones said:

"There's something wrong with the way the water moves. Have you noticed it?"

The captain's face changed as if a sourness had touched his palate. Jax asked, "How do you mean? Where?"

"Out in midwater, this side of the island. Twice now it's looked jittery in a way the winds don't account for."

Helion sighed. "For God's sake, Jones. *Jittery?* There's some wind chop, a little swell, the sun dazzle . . . Just what kind of ominous subtleties do you think you're seeing?"

"It *is* subtle, Captain, and it's not happening right now. But I've seen it twice since we've been up on the ridge here. Subtle but definite. At the least it means some kind of deep current."

"Jones, you may be sincere, but you are also compelled to concoct frontiersman's intuitions about even the most straightforward good luck. I've been watching the lake, and I saw nothing. What about you, Jax?"

"I can't say I did, but I don't make light of Nemo's eye for things."

"Nor do I make light of it, Jones. It'll go in the log if you wish. Meanwhile our job here seems strikingly clear to me, and I think we'd better get to it."

The Katermandian shrugged, staring not at the captain, but at the lake. "Maybe it's meaningless—how can I say? But it wasn't intuition. It's something I saw."

He didn't immediately follow the other two back toward the sandhog. He watched the water a few minutes more, then tensed. "Again," he murmured. "Yes, I see you. A convective eccentricity, from some magma vent? I think you're too erratic for that . . ."

He spat on the ground for luck and hurried to catch up to the others.

The boats, moored at the little beach, rode the soft heave of the waters, their armor-glass cockpit bubbles flashing in the sun. The expeditioners stood on the shingle. Nemo squatted a bit apart from the group, watching the lake, meditatively grinding his rifle butt against the gravel. Captain Helion stood facing the other seven. His stance was more erect than usual, almost truculent.

"Captain, I have to question this," Orson Waverly was saying. "If you make a special Command Override of it, naturally I'll obey, but it seems needlessly—"

"Needless, Waverly? We don't need delph roe? We don't need fresh breeding stock for the pens at base? Maybe we should radio home and have our surpluses destroyed. Perhaps we should just relax, have a swim, and go back."

"But, Captain," Jax said, "two boats or three—what's the differential?"

"You tell me the differential, Giggans. With three boats out there, we can dye the cove and drive damn near the whole school to shore in one sweep. With two, we might get a third at the first sweep, and then we could go back cruising and gunning all day and not get more than another third from the scatterers."

"But that's just it," Waverly said. "More than two-thirds of a school that size would put the hog near overload. With the tanks that full, half the live take could die on the ride home. It's roe we need more than meat."

Helion's proposal was a distinct departure from his normal style, undeniably unorthodox. Colony procedure was quite explicitly prescribed on this point: one fishing craft was to remain onshore at standby during any maneuver in unexplored environments. The captain's numerical assessment of the situation was not wrong. For a few minutes after a school had been blinded by a dye grenade, it was panicked enough to be moved en masse if the boats' ultrasonic pulsars could effectively bracket it with their crossfire. Here, three boats might handle it, but two could not. Meanwhile, blinded delphs rapidly reoriented to a sightless defensive pattern—sounded shallowly and dispersed—and individuals that eluded a first sweep would have to be painstakingly stalked and harpooned one by one.

But considering the probable yield of even the two-boat deployment, Helion's insistence on the three-boat plan was unreasonable—gluttonous. Waverly saw that his objection hadn't moved the captain, and he added:

"Listen, sir. I respectfully suggest that you're excited by the size of the find. You want to make a record catch. You're letting pride bend your judgment. I'm not rebuking—it's normal, healthy ambition, but—"

"Thank you, Waverly. Now that you've spit out your bit of malice, we'll proceed. We'll start in Formation Delta, assignments as follows . . ."

Nemo Jones crouched silent throughout the briefing, somberly grinding his rifle butt against the sand. But as the group dispersed to their boats, he rose and touched Penny Lopez's shoulder.

"Penny, I want you to take special warning. This lake is dangerous. It . . . smells wrong. Stay especially alert."

Penny scowled. It was hard for anyone to blame her for shortness of temper. Jones had importuned her with his embarrassingly formal attentions long past the time when anyone else would have understood her answer to be an emphatic NO. She turned to Helion. "Captain, Armorer Jones reports a negative olfactory observation on reconnaissance. Should it be entered in the log?"

Perhaps Jones was finally starting to get the message—he sighed and turned away. Sarissa was more hurt by the exchange than he was, though only her fellow-pilot Angela Rackham observed it. Sari was dark, slight, and lean—always tautly poised. Anger in her produced an almost visible vibration in this tautness, like a plucked string, and seeing this vibration now, Angela threw an arm across her shoulders and detained her furious departure with a brief, discreet hug.

"Hey. Sari. The sap's slow-witted. He still thinks he's her official suitor! He's riding with you—why would he see the need to give *you* a warning?"

Sari shrugged off Angela's arm, uneasy over being so accurately understood—but then gave her a kiss before getting into her boat. She hated being splenetic and jealous like this, but she was getting intensely fed up with Jones's dense inability to see that she'd thought him over and changed her mind. When he and Japhet Sparks had climbed into their seats behind her, she thumbed shut the bubble with a bang and pulled out onto the water without a backward glance.

The three boats—domed ellipsoids—moved out in a triangular formation, sliding noiselessly across the water's softly breathing blue. Their wakes were so slight they scarcely marred the waters, wherein the colossal wall containing them, all glossy carmine marbled with jet black, was repeated.

Japhet Sparks sat amidships, between Sarissa and Nemo. He had a true cartographer's love for physical creation, and he turned his bony face greedily upon the scene surrounding them.

"By God, look at it! I've never seen such a gorgeous lake. A marine vent for sure—probably along the magma vent at the root of that island. And talk about recent vulcanism—if that island's a day over ten million, I'll eat it. Oh, for a week to check it out with a lung!"

Without turning, Sarissa asked, "How does the water smell to you?"

Sparks grasped the allusion, but only granted the gibe an irritated shrug.

Nemo stared at the back of their pilot's head. "I didn't say it in jest, Sarissa. What it meant I don't know, but—"

"You gave that stiff-necked bitch a special warning. What about *me*, you brainless idiot?"

Deep in the grotto of his shaggy beard, a glint of surprise Nemo's eyes. Sari was so infuriated by the plaintive sound of her own outburst that she jerked the joystick, launching their craft on a wide, extravagant excursionary curve away from their prescribed formation.

The island lay between them and their quarry-filled cove on its farther side. Her gesture didn't compromise their mission, though she knew that it was going to enrage Helion. Even so, when his raging voice burst from the intercom, it angered her further. She had been pulling back in, but now she cut even more widely back out. Then with insolent leisure—

rubbing in the redoubled insubordination—she began a slow return to formation, all the while enjoying Helion's furious diatribe in the manner of a musical obbligato to her grand gesture.

When Jones moved, it took both her and Japhet Sparks completely by surprise. He sprang from the stern seat and dove for the communicator, whose reply-switch he threw repeatedly, signaling the captain that he wished to cut in.

Helion was ordering Sarissa to dock at the nearest shelving of the island's shore, toward which he already had the other two boats putting in, and there to yield her helm to Japhet. Nemo's signals, far from inducing him to open the line, made him flood it even more furiously.

But in Sarissa's boat he now went unregarded. Both she and Japhet had just seen what Nemo had seen. With a moan of horror she accelerated to catch up, zigzagging wildly as she did so, trying to set up a watery commotion that would draw the eyes of their friends behind them. The two lead boats were now at half engine as they neared the island. And just astern of them, a huge shape bulged beneath the surface of the lake.

It was not a turbulence, but a coherent pallid mass that glided after the boats perhaps a fathom down in the water. Subtler, but as horrific, was the wake it left—a greasy surface boil hundreds of meters broad, bespeaking a bulk far vaster than was visible, though that blurred globe was many times the size of all three boats combined.

The two advance craft were scarcely a hundred meters from the island, and their pursuer half as far behind them, when Helion's boat accelerated explosively, a full-drive leap that should have run it straight up onto the shoal. Instead, its thrust snagged and slowed to the leaden crawl that shackles flight in nightmares. Black grass sprouted from the water, engulfing both the boats.

Grass that writhed like snakes as it grew, its every fibril clutching and raking the air with a blind and busy greed. Angela's boat was completely enmeshed, its stern cocked high above the water, turned weightlessly in the shuddering weave as a bug is turned by the spider wrapping it. Helion's boat, however, was gradually tearing shoreward from the net, whose grip its burst of speed had half foiled.

And now Sarissa had reached them. At ninety knots she swerved obliquely to the uncanny meadow and plowed across its fringe. A shock wave, as of pain, rolled through the field. Helion's boat lurched free, roared through the shallows and plunged, spraying sparks, up onto the island. Sarissa's drive had slowed to fifteen knots before she herself fought free into the shoals that fringed the isle and which the monstrous growth had not invaded. She swung parallel to the shore and tucked the boat into an inlet.

The colonists jumped from their vessels and gathered on the shore. Jax and Nemo broke out the rifles, but those they gave them to held them helplessly, standing in a rapture of horror, watching the struggle. Then, near the meadow's center, the pale bulb rose and swelled up from the water.

It was a titanic eye—a transparent orb of gold, intricately veined within, the pupil a scarlet rhomboid into which five sand-hogs could have driven abreast. Deep in the yellow ichor, black shapes moved, whole constellations of them swarming through the kelplike jungle of veins; while outside the globe, round its base, a collar of huge tonguelike tentacles stirred, stretched, and licked the air. With cyclopean sloth the whole orb rolled within this tentacular calyx and aimed the red vent of its pupil upon the captured boat.

And now a dreadful purpose entered the action of the fibrils. Variously, testingly, they turned and tilted the craft, probing and caressing it in every orientation. There was a grinding noise. As a man might open a jar, the creature twisted off the boat's cockpit bubble, inverted and shook its hull. Norrin and, a moment later, Angela Rackham tumbled down into the black seethe. The fibrils heaved and catapulted the boat away. It crashed on the island's shore.

All that the watchers did was as a dream. Jax and Nemo pumped explosive shot against every part of the eye and its corolla. The grenade slugs produced only negligible tatterings of its gelatinous substance. Sarissa struggled to free a coil of harpoon line from the wrecked boat's equipment locker, while Helion and Penny helped Sparks lift Orson Waverly—the only surviving occupant of the captured boat—from the space beneath the control panel where he had wedged himself and where he now lay bleeding and comatose. But all these were ghostly acts, performed in stupefaction, while every man and woman did but one thing—watch Norrin and Angela, and the thing that had them.

The black meadow undulated still, but less chaotically, with an insistent peristaltic surge that brought the victims toward the eye. Like castaways caught in a hideous slow surf, they struggled in the snakish grip—clutched, stroked, raised, and dipped, but always eased inexorably nearer the eye. The colonists saw now Norrin's arm clawing sunward, festooned with serpents, now Angela's back and shoulders, bucking to wrench her head free of the nauseous swell.

The tentacles nearest the victims began an obscene elongation, till finally two of them plunged down and plucked the captives free. Swinging them high, the tentacles brought the women inward and poised them above the alien pupil, which moved below, as with a savoring gaze. The tentacles uncoiled. The women plunged into the red vent and sank kicking down within the golden ichor.

In the eye blink of their vanishing through that red chasm, they entered another world and were transformed to different beings. Drifting down, they came within the eye, dancing the drowning agony in a tempo surreally slow, an almost comic pantomime of life's wrenching-free from its frame. Their faces and limbs were bloated, corrupt of color in the amber light. Angela's hair bannered wantonly, slow-motion, while those on the island could see her eyes—black holes in a gape-jawed mask—aimed downward on the swarming deep she sank to. Webbed veins, huge crooked roots now partly screened their fall, which showed in glimpses as the overall organic movement within the eye began to boil with a new energy.

Those on the island watched what followed with an amazement so complete it looked like rapture. At one point, responding no doubt to some impulse to avert his own eyes (though he never did so), Nemo Jones cried out:

"Don't look away! Remember details! We've got to know it to kill it."

His companions needed these exhortations as little as Nemo himself did.

Forgetting even to attend to Waverly's serious head injury, they watched as if the universe and all time contained no other thing to see. And there were many details to be remembered.

The group sat in a circle around the camp's field stove. Helion sat closest to its light, more visible, more erect, than the others. But there was less pride of rank in his posture than an air of pained self-presentation, as if in response to a tacit charge lodged against him by the others slouched tiredly in the shadows. He had been arguing with Nemo for the last five minutes. Throughout, his normal inflexibility had been accompanied by an uncharacteristic calm. Now he shook his head definitively, rejecting in the gesture not only all the Katermandian had said, but all that he might say. When he spoke, it was formally, his eyes sweeping the whole group by way of preface.

"You will all, as a body, formally depose me and place me under arrest, to which I willingly accede, or you will do this as I prescribe, and with the personnel I have designated. There is no more to say, Jones. Take it or leave it."

The Katermandian squatted on his hams. The light escaping the shadow pools over his eyes was baleful, and this the captain saw; but it was also—and this Helion did not see—compassionate. He set his words out carefully:

"Listen, I beseech you, Captain. You have all the good of pride, as well as the bad of it. You want to atone for our danger, but you've done no real wrong. If you've been foolish, why, everyone's a fool! I've been one thousands of times—it's a wonder I'm alive! It's my plan. Do you want to throw on me the guilt of having someone else take the risk of it? You *know* that Jax and I are our best swimmers . . ." He gestured awkwardly, breaking off. He read his failure in the captain's sour smile before he heard the man's answer.

"The plan was yours. The log already so witnesses. Our need for it, our predicament here, is wholly my doing, and the log testifies this as well. My decision is as before."

Nemo stood up. He nodded and stepped out of the circle. The wind was freshening, but he left the shelter of the hollow they had camped in and climbed up to the island's saw-toothed crest and found himself a seat overlooking the delph cove, some hundred meters below. He had not been there long when his fellow-armorer joined him. They sat in silence for a while, watching the stars in the molten black mirror of the lake.

"After we fought—remember?" Jax said smiling. "When I said you had good and sufficient reasons for doing things your own way? I was taking that on faith, just because you could fight so well. Well, now I know I was right. I could've sat down for a solid year and never come up with anything like this plan of yours."

"Jax." Nemo clamped a hand on his friend's arm, as if he had been waiting for this opening. "I'm having bad second thoughts. I'm afraid of this plan now. I think it will fail, if Helion goes. You have to dig your heels in—refuse to go unless you're teamed with me. He has no hunch-nerves. He's brave, but he has no *luck.* Your dissension would have more weight with him than anyone's. Force him to use me."

Jax was smiling, shaking his head. "What a storm of words! You're turning downright chatty lately. I'm sorry, Nemo. I know what you mean about his luck. But if he's denied this chance to redeem himself, it'll break him. He'll be good for nothing after this. And I've always liked the poor stiff-neck."

"Shit." Nemo said this mournfully, looking now more directly below their perch to the cove. Only eyes that had watched the school at dusk, when the beasts found berths in the fissures of the shore and emptied their flotation sacs to sink to their rest, could have found them now in the moonlight—vague torpedoes of silver just under the heave of the black water.

He scowled at them. His expression might have been that of some deity gravely with what he had wrought. It was Firebairn that had made the delphs, of course; Nemo had made only an escape plan that enlisted them. He looked again at Jax, his eyes bitter, refusing to reiterate his request, but also refusing to withdraw it. For answer, his brawny friend turned his face, wryly, to the island's northern quarter, where all explanation of the morrow's insanity lay.

It looked like an immense planktonic toadstool now, the pale orb still exposed, though half sunk from its former elevation. The field of cilia was similarly contracted. Only the tips of the tendrils showed, bristling the moon-polished waters, a field of thorns. The two men stared at the thing for a long time.

"It is watching us," Jax said, speaking his decision in the debate that both had pursued internally. All useful speculations had long ago been traded, mutual conjecture exhausted. "So huge it is, and so sharply *aware* . . ."

"It had to be Orson blinded," Nemo mourned. "Something this big—it has to be marine, from up this vent. If we knew how it worked, there might be . . ."

"Be what?"

Nemo shrugged helplessly. "Who's that?" Someone was climbing toward them.

"Sari," the pilot-gunner answered, choosing her handholds on the crag as easy and sure as someone gathering shells from a level beach. "Orson's fully conscious," she told them. "He took some broth. He wants us all to have a talk while the captain is still asleep." Nemo heard the shade of pity in this—Sarissa usually called him "Helion." They followed her back down to the camp.

It was past midnight when Captain Helion was wakened. Jax and Japhet told him the group's proposal. Any innovative consensus among his subordinates could now only strike the exhausted man as veiled mutiny. He gave Jax an *et tu, Brute* look, and stared disgustedly into the glowing coils of the camp stove.

"It's clear you'll all do what you want. Kindly trouble me with no further parades of obedience. Spend the time any way you please between now and tomorrow."

"No! Someone bring me out to him. Captain!"

As surprised as Helion, Jax turned to help Sarissa and Nemo carry Orson Waverly's camp chair into the center of the circle. The biologist's eyes were bandaged. Some few tears of blood had escaped the bandages and tracked his cheeks.

"Captain?" The face scanned, hunting a voice-fix on Helion.

"I'm here, Waverly."

"Listen, Captain. Don't slacken now. Give us strictness here, where we need it. This will have to be a systematic information-pooling, using the log. Make it official to make it strict. This thing is epochs ahead of us in its adaptation to this world. We had better evolve a very sharp and efficient group mind to fight it with, and do it pretty damn fast, or else we're all going to die, and you've seen how we're going to die."

The captain rose to the occasion, but only just. He nodded. "Wake me when it's my turn." He went back to his bed.

It was almost dawn. Nemo and Orson Waverly sat by the stove. Everyone else was asleep. Waverly had just turned off the log, which he'd had on playback, and now he sighed. The two men's ears still rang with all the perplexities the tape had woven round their weary minds.

"Dear God, Nemo. What I wouldn't give for an image of the thing, a five-second look at it to give me a nice solid, detailed picture. I'm awash in all these words. My brain is a knot, and all I'm visualizing is a cartoon, a caricature."

"So give it back to me—this caricature."

Waverly sighed deeply. "Two distinct groups of carnivores, patrolling the interior of a huge transparent sphere. The sphere also contains thick growths of kelp. The kelp is rooted in a layer of basal muck that floors the sphere, and the two breeds of cruising carnivores—I see them as sharks and squids—are also rooted in that muck, or at least connected to it by long slender flexible tethers of translucent material, sort of like delicate umbilici that issue from their caudal extremities and trail down behind them to the floor of the sphere."

"Mmmm. What's kelp, and what are sharks and squids?"

When Waverly had explained these terrene forms, Nemo granted the general accuracy of the caricature. "Of course," the biologist went on, "the things you've all described have more tentacles than squids, and a greater variation in tentacle size, and the others, except for the teeth, sound as much like delphs as they do like sharks . . . You know, I find myself wondering about those tethers. Both groups in constant restless movement—even the ones still waiting their turn to feed—and all that dense growth in there. What kept those caudal umbilici of theirs from getting tangled, snagged—even breaking?"

"Orson! Yes! Now that you say it, I remember I saw exactly that. One of those squids, while they were all circulating, waiting their turn, as you say . . ." Nemo paused fractionally here, and Waverly's head lowered—remembering two young women, full of life. "Its tether snagged on a kelp stalk. I think it sensed it—it instantly reversed itself. But not in time, and the tether broke. It stopped cold, and then corkscrewed straight down to the bottom, and I lost sight of it. Actually it's amazing that didn't happen more often. But then their movements were so intricately patterned, so fluid . . ."

Waverly said nothing, pursuing some thought, and Nemo sat motionless like cupped hands cherishing a young flame to life within their stillness. But at length the biologist sighed again.

"I keep thinking their tethers could be some sort of alimentary connection with the larger structure containing them. But how could such an important pipeline be so delicate? The whole feeding relationship of the parts to the whole—I'm damned if I can get a handle on it. I want to hear Japhet again."

Nemo keyed up Japhet's testimony from the log. They skimmed through the first few minutes of it, seeking the juncture Waverly wanted. In the snatches of Japhet's voice they heard his anguish, slightly miniaturized by the reduced volume. Angela and Norrin had been well loved by all, and not least by Japhet. Then the biologist nodded, Nemo turned it up, and they listened. First Waverly's voice:

"OK, Japhet. Now let's move to what happened to them on the inside."

"They were still alive—kicking and fighting, but slower moving than you'd expect. Bloating, I think. Swelling a little—like maybe those fluids in there were some kind of enzymes? When they'd sunk to the top of all that . . . seaweed, those first things hit them. Fish-shaped, big saw-toothed mouths. Black eyeknobs set in stripe patterns—a little like delph eyes except for their having so many of them.

"Anyway, they hit them first. Started tearing chunks out of them. Swarmed on them thick as ants, till they looked like just two wriggling clusters of them. Their blood . . ."—the ghost of a groan was recorded here—". . . their blood came out in clouds. Like smoke. It hid what went on."

"I'm sorry, Japhet." Now Waverly's mouth made wry corners at the feebleness of his own apology. "Did they keep sinking as they were being fed on?"

"Not much. The feeding activity buoyed them up. And then all those things broke away. Pretty suddenly. For a couple seconds their . . . remains just hung there, then started sinking again. Then the other things—"

"I'm sorry, Japhet, but I need you to tell me just how much—"

"All the flesh gnawed off!" It was a burst of rage evading intolerable pain. "All the skin, major muscle. Just skeletons, held intact by scraps of tendon, ligament. Some of the larger internal organs left . . ."

"So then the others fed? And they were just as numerous?"

"Yes."

"So you've all said. You must forgive my putting it like this. I have to. But this arrangement seems to leave so small a share to feed on to this multibrachiate group."

There was a silence before Japhet answered, not loudly. "I meant yes, they were just as numerous. But I don't think they were *feeding* on them at all. It was more like they embraced them and clung in a slightly pulsating way. Because Norrin's face, I remember . . . most of it . . . was left intact by those first things. Then the second ones covered her face, like a fur of wiggling feelers—and yet there she still was, looking out at me, when those octopoid ones cleared away."

And now Orson and Nemo sat surrounded by the same kind of silence that could be heard on the tape. During that silence the biologist groped his hand across the log's keys and cut it off before the catechism continued. After a moment he raised both his hands to adjust his blood-crusted bandage, resettling it gingerly against his maimed eyes. When he had done this, he let out the pain of the maneuver in one long breath.

"It may be that they're detritivores—the tentacled things. You all report organic debris in the basal muck—the trash-heaped hard parts of larger, presumably bathic, prey. Yet none of you saw the squids penetrating the muck. On the other hand, both Helion and Penny saw sharks down there penetrating the muck—these sharks, already amply nourished by their lion's share of prey.

"I'm done for the night, Nemo. Right now my brain is a goddamned square wheel. I can't get any kind of interpretation *moving*. It's stupefying, this bizarre complexity. The field of prey-snaring cilia, the central mouthed dome of intestinal structures, surrounded by a calyx of major cilia—there are pseudo-coelenterates they've found over at Base Two that have these features. They're littoral-benthic-zone dwellers—one meter across at the biggest, goddamn it, and with nothing like this kind of endosomatic complexity. There might be bathic varieties that are bigger, but the things are sensorially impoverished; slow, groping, tactile hunters. You say this thing tracked our boats toward the island and is now hemming us in, dodging laterally to catch any move we try to make from shore. This thing sees or smells or hears or all three. Monstrous. Incomprehensible. I need more medicine. I need some sleep. Maybe the answer will come in a dream. But I'll give you one thing to dream on, Nemo. If this thing does in some way follow the model of those little pseudo-coelenterates they've found—if it hangs proportionally deep in the water and is able to expand as broadly in the lateral dimension—then its tail end hangs down into this lake for at least half a kilometer, and its field of cilia is able to hug this is-land's whole perimeter, or damn near it, in its loving embrace.

"Take me to my cot, Nemo. Helion and Jax are going to die tomor-row. I'm sorry, but this seems to me a simple fact. I've told them what I'm telling you, but I couldn't change their minds. So I say to you now, brutal though it is—choose vantage points from which you can see down into this thing from all possible angles. Have the log's microphone run out on an extension, and issue field glasses. When they die, I want it to pay off with every scrap of sight and sound that can be gotten out of it. If Poly-phemus takes their lives, it's going to betray itself to us in the process. Wake me an hour after dawn, and don't fail me. By the time they set out, I'll have a list of specific questions I want answered and some final ar-rangements I want made."

Just after dawn, Sarissa Wayne climbed to the ridgetop where Jax and Nemo had sat the night before. She settled down and watched the prepara-tions, already well along, being made in the delph cove below. She and Penny had begun them. The roll of metallic net that each craft carried had been taken from its spool in the stern of Sarissa's boat and brought over to the cove. One end of it was anchored to the cove's southern spur, and then she and Penny had swum it across the cove mouth.

They had made marvelously silent work of it, and only partly for fear of waking the delphs, which Jax and Helion were already edging up on with the tranquilizer guns. Polyphemus—as Waverly, without explana-tion, had bitterly dubbed their persecutor the night before—Polyphemus had already demonstrated how swiftly it could pour itself around the is-land's perimeter. The previous afternoon the colonists had done some ex-perimenting. They had driven Helion's boat—only slightly damaged—to the opposite side of the island, choosing a launching spot more than four hundred meters upshore from Polyphemus's visible limit of extension. They detached its harpoon winch, anchored this ashore, and tethered the boat to its cable. They set it on autopilot with just enough fuel in the tanks for a few hundred meters' run. It was making thirty-five knots within the first four seconds of its launching and was snared by the giant's sudden-sprouting tendrils less than seventy meters offshore.

The capture was not resisted—cable was paid out as the titan wrestled its prey toward its central orb. But the craft never reached that organ. Well before the cilia had brought it within the grasp of the larger feeding tentacles, they froze, still gripping it. A few seconds later they flung it into the air, and by the time it had struck the water it had vanished from beneath it. The colonists hauled the boat ashore, feeling themselves, if potentially wiser, no less baffled and terrified.

Swimming in the black predawn waters with this recollection of the giant's speed, its inscrutable responsiveness, had been the closest thing to a lived nightmare in Sarissa's experience. Her legs could still feel that ticklish expectancy of Polyphemus's caustic, sticky first touch, through every second it had taken to string the barricade.

But her mind was now detached from these bodily memories. It was not the scene below that so distracted her. The tranquilizer darts used on captured delphs to prevent their panicking and crushing one another during their transport in cages to the sand-hog had paralyzed six of the creatures in the cove. The men had collared them with cable in two trios, staggered so that the middle delph of each trio was positioned half a length in advance of its flanking fellows. The trios had been tethered to shore, and though the beasts were just waking and getting restive, Jax and Helion were able to slip into the undercarriages they had rigged and test their fit. Their boot heels were just visible through the water, kicking for purchase under the tails of the delphs. Their recirculating respiration packs made no more than a faint boil in the water, and this the delphs' motion, once they were goaded forward, would obliterate.

Sarissa's own life, and those of all the others, depended on this grotesque rehearsal, which did not alter her staring inattention. Her preoccupation was elsewhere, its focus revealed when her eyes narrowed at Nemo Jones's reappearance in the cove. He came down from the knoll that flanked it, where he had been helping Japhet make the two harpoon-gun emplacements she had requested the evening before. He went straight to Penny Lopez, who was working on a release mechanism for rolling back a segment of the cove barrier when it was time for Jax and Helion to make their sortie. Whatever Nemo said to Penny caused her to straighten and face him.

He talked to her for perhaps a minute, and when, with a queer formal bow, he left her, Sarissa's eyes didn't merely fail to follow him—they refused to. Thereafter, she didn't watch anything in particular so much as she avoided watching that sector of the crag that lay between herself and the point from which Nemo had left her view.

"Sarissa. Sarissa. I have something important to say. Will you talk with me?" The question seemed necessary to Nemo, as she had not looked up when he saluted her. Still not looking, she said:

"Whether or not I'll talk to you depends on what you have to tell me."

Nemo nodded at this and sat down at a discreet distance from her so she would not have to strain to keep him out of her field of vision. He looked at the sky a minute before saying, "I've just given Penny Lopez my apologies and told her I was withdrawing my suit for her. To disappoint a woman is always grave, so no lying should go with it. I confessed to her—"

Sarissa snorted, shook her head, and, visibly in spite of herself, began to laugh. Nemo looked at his knees and waited humbly. Sarissa had to make several attempts before she could speak her retort:

"Nemo, I swear to you. I was watching your exchange with her. After you walked away from her, that poor woman literally jumped into the air and clicked her heels together."

"I agree her feelings are mixed. But I have never entirely displeased her. Once I had stated my case to her, last summer—"

"What did you confess to her?"

"She started out not entirely disliking me. I confessed to her that the woman I first chose, first desired—that I did not pay suit to this woman only because she *did* entirely dislike me."

Sarissa looked at him now. She studied him with wrath, perplexity, relish. "What was this woman's name, this first choice of yours?"

"Sari Wayne."

She sat there, grinning a grin of sardonic vindication, nodding slowly, the picture of one who bitterly acknowledges an idiocy she has long struggled with.

"Me. Right. And I remember your first tender gesture."

New movement down in the cove distracted them momentarily. Helion and Jax had begun to goad their "mounts" through some elementary paces. They did not use the sonic pulsars designed for delph herding—all too probably detectable by Polyphemus—but small electric prods that Jax had improvised. The method seemed to be working, though it produced an uncharacteristically jerky movement in the beasts. The sun's edge kindled on the eastern crater rim. Sarissa and Nemo faced each other again. She resumed reminiscingly.

"It was that enormous hydra I harpooned on Gamma. A superlative shot. But not like your thirty-meter dive from the ringwall! Nor your herculean amputation of the major tentacle—even as it thrashed in its deaththroes. Being upstaged like that was not enough, of course. You had to drag the amputated member to me afterward!"

"It was a declaration! Such marksmanship was once-in-a-million marksmanship! Could I do less and fitly show my love? I did it for your entertainment."

Sarissa had what in an earlier era had been called the Aha Experience. Why, she asked herself, were women so slow to identify irony or deadpan humor in men? Obviously, she answered, because they unavoidably deemed men to be a little dimmer than they sometimes were in fact. She gave a long sigh.

"Well, that may be true," she admitted—both to what he had said and to what she had thought—"but you're still a miserable idiot. Embarrass them enough and anyone will run. But after that you should have seen how I came to feel. I want you to pay suit to me, and love me, and make love to me, and not to anyone else. Now hasn't that been plain enough, you backwoods dolt? And whether it has or not, well, what about it? Here and now, once and for all."

Nemo nodded energetically, but though his mouth opened, nothing came out of it. Apparently, this ardent inarticulacy conveyed an answer to Sarissa that she found satisfactory. She wrapped her arms around his waist and pressed her face against his chest. He held her, looking over her head toward the sunrise, and clearer than the happiness his face showed was his amazement. All in his world had been craft, the stalking, second-guessing, and teasing-out of quarry from the hostile complexities of its habitat. To have Sarissa, whom he had thought irreversibly inimical to him, holding him with such single-mindedness, was to him in the nature of a prodigy. It was as if, in his native rain forest, an archidand—that wily, toothsome biped, splendid-winged and brazen-taloned—had leapt from its cover in the dense warpvine and sparx and—far from dodging away with invisible speed—had ambled up to the astonished hunter and dipped its head to nuzzle at his hand. The pair did not notice the two figures approaching them until they were in speaking distance and one of them, Japhet Sparks, hailed them.

Sparks was leading Orson Waverly. The lovers broke their embrace—not out of shame, but from a chilling of their hearts. They knew Waverly's errand. Sarissa helped him to a seat. She, Nemo, and Japhet—all those who must be Waverly's eyes—now looked only at him, not down toward the cove, not at each other.

"I've already briefed Penny. I wanted to do it while they were still in the water. They know what I'm doing and approve, but it's pointless to sicken them with the sight of my actually doing it. So let's be quick. The captain will be assembling us for his own briefing in a little while, as soon as he and Jax make some last adjustments to their undercarriages. Sarissa?"

"Here, Orson."

"The guns from Helion's and Angela's boats are set up. Japhet's wound double cable on the winches and got the guns anchored where you wanted them. Give them both the field glasses, Japhet. Hang these around your necks now. Get them focused for Polyphemus immediately, then you take up your positions. I want you on the knoll across the beach from Sarissa's, Nemo—Japhet has it worked out. You'll be on the other side of the thing from her and almost as high above it. Penny and Japhet will be shoreside, watching it from different angles. They'll both have mikes we've rigged to the log. I want to get any sound any of us makes correlated with a running account of its moves. We want all its behavior, and every possible synchronicity of that behavior with what happens around it.

"Because of course we can't assume it sees, just because it looks to us like an eye. It twisted our boat open like—someone unstoppering a specimen bottle. If it does see, I don't think Jax and Helion have a prayer.

"Here are my specific questions. First and foremost, how precisely does it track us? Every detail of its behavior that we can correlate with any detail of its *prey's* behavior—" Waverly's mouth moved speechlessly a few times. He resumed more quietly. "If we can relate these two spheres of activity in any new way, we may get a key to how to dodge it. Killing it seems to me as good as impossible. Nevertheless, it *has* occurred to me that if we understood its feeding mechanism, we could conceivably poison it. Its whole alimentary setup is one of the things that confuses me most. These quasi-independent packs. By the time they're through with the prey, it's just a carcass. If they are the digestive apparatus itself, how are they transmitting the nutrients they absorb to the macro-organism? Polyphemus itself is a kind of huge detritivore, nourished by the sharks' and squids' carrion leavings. But then why the gross volumetric disproportion? Why does Polyphemus get forty percent, at most, of every kill, and these . . . predacious saprophytes sixty or more?

"But to test this, study the basal areas all you can—Sarissa and Nemo especially. That's why I've got you high. Look for . . . feeding debris, its relation to the inner landscape of Polyphemus. What's the structure down there? Japhet and Penny will be studying the packs more particularly, but I want all of you to be constantly checking the whole.

"With the squids and 'sharks' two things. Watch for waste excretion in any form. They could be producing usable wastes that Polyphemus absorbs. Second: you all seemed to agree that the squids didn't consume nearly as much as the sharks, if indeed they actually *fed* at all. Precisely what were they doing? Study that closely.

"That's it. As far as productive guesses go, I've got next to nothing to offer at this point. This thing is completely incredible. God help us to think effectively together, because, so far, I am truly in the dark."

Midmorning on Firebairn is, next to sunset, its most golden hour. The jumbled colors of the igneous wastes blaze, melt, smolder under the sky's brilliance as if the land were still in its molten nativity. And in this particular place the young sun kindled a special jewel even more dazzling than the vast ringwall or the waters contained by it. As Nemo climbed the knoll assigned him, he looked upon that jewel with loathing and wonder. Within the sphere of lustrous amber, the patrolling packs wove their own distinct colors through the black-and-purple jungle. Those that Waverly called "sharks" were especially striking. Their torpedo bodies had streaks of pigmentation that flashed iridescent as the things cruised through the filtered sunlight. Nemo thought of the cove—invisible to him now beyond the ridge Sarissa stood on—from which he had just come. Helion, grim and businesslike, had turned directly from the briefing to the water and slipped under, snuggling himself out of sight beneath his harnessed beasts. But Jax had paused by the brink so that Nemo could take his hand. Nemo had said:

"Lucky fellow. In an hour you'll be in the sand-hog, radioing air rescue."

The big man had smiled, glanced at the binoculars hanging against the fur on the Katermandian's chest, drawing their owner's eyes upon them, filling his heart with wretchedness. But Jax had grinned:

"That's right. Use these, and when I climb ashore you can see me waving to you."

Nemo had reached his position, but before he signaled to Sarissa he looked down on their enemy. He pressed his clenched fist against his chest, which is the way the hunters of Katermand take oaths, and he said:

"Hear me, Polyphemus. My name is Nemo. Nemo Jones. And I am going to rip the life right out of you. We together will find the way, but it's me that's going to do it to you."

He raised his arm and signaled to the short, slight figure manning the guns on the next knoll over. Even as he had turned his eyes away, a detail had snagged at their periphery. He caught up his glasses and trained them on the orb, at a point deep within the anchorings of the "kelp."

Sarissa hesitated. Japhet, Penny, Nemo—all were stationed now, but for a moment she found herself unable to pass on the go-ahead to the cove. She checked the welded cable moorings Japhet had rigged for the guns and for the third time reassured herself that the crag she stood on would break before they did. She looked down into the cove, where Orson waited for her word, the barriergate's pull-cord in one hand. Jax and Helion held their beasts ready—not near the gate, but by the shore of the inlet, for before they emerged themselves they would drive out a large part of the school ahead of them and thereafter keep as many of these as possible around them as they penetrated the dangerous waters offshore.

The delphs had swum unmolested past Polyphemus; some of them had even cruised through its peripheral field of cilia. It was one of the first observations they had made the previous afternoon, once some measure of organization had succeeded their initial trance of horror. The plan had seemed good. Now, without any of Waverly's biological training to reinforce her pessimism, she felt a gloom as deep as his. It was not going to work. It would fail because Sarissa now had everything to lose—not just her life, but Nemo as well. Whenever the heart prayed entirely for luck, that was when luck failed. She cupped her hands by her mouth and, in a tone scarcely louder than conversational, said:

"Now."

Orson, seventy meters below, pulled the cord. When Jax and Helion saw the opening, they launched prearranged converging drives on the gate that cut out about two-thirds of the school and herded it before them. "Close it," Sarissa said. Orson relaxed his grip on the cord and let the gate spring back. If the sortie failed, its survivors would need food.

The shepherding of a protective screen of free-swimming delphs did not start well. The trios were bulky enough to exert a local dominance on their unharnessed fellows, but too awkward of movement to work the group as a whole into any formation. As the teams edged past the sheltering horn of the cove, the school began to dissolve before them, individuals and couples—game-some with the unpent tensions of their confinement—dispersing swiftly. Sarissa watched the two men's cover bleeding away, branching out into the lake in quick, silvery trickles. She ground her teeth and looked to Polyphemus.

The giant was half the island away—the knoll she stood on walled off the cove from its vision, if vision it had. And with the captain and Jax angling sharply away from the giant as they penetrated the open waters, they would be three-quarters of the island's length distant from it before the shoreline ceased to mask them. It was not conceivable that two men, the subtlest shadows of men, really, clinging to the undersides of living screens twice their size, could be detected at such a range. And still Sarissa groaned at the steady shrinkage of the school. As the lure of open water grew stronger, the clumsy goading of the two trios came to seem itself a force of dispersal, an irritation even the nearer members of the school began to flee.

And then it seemed the two men abandoned the attempt to herd the rest of the school and began to make smoother progress outward. They were already a hundred meters offshore, and she watched them make the next fifty as quickly as they had that first stage. As if in illustration of her thoughts about luck, a fair-sized cluster of delphs, uncoerced now, cohered, and stayed just ahead of the escapees.

Sarissa realized that for perhaps the last full minute the men had been out in the zone of Polyphemus's unimpeded survey. Her head snapped round toward the colossus. The swarming globe was as before—though perhaps a shade farther out from its sector of the shore? She swung her eyes back to the two little silver blurs, the escaping trios, but even before she focused on them she had swept her gaze halfway back toward Polyphemus. Out there, between the monster and the hidden men, some hundred and fifty meters offshore from where she stood, a narrow boil of movement scarred the water. It was the surface track of an underwater thrust whose rate was perhaps thirty knots, and precisely aimed to intercept the trios.

Sarissa stepped over to the gun whose emplacement commanded the coveward sector of the water, kicked up the muzzle for a long shot, and trained it on the spot where the surface scar and the delph trios would impact. Touching the gun, which always calmed her, helped little—her heart was all hollowness and terror. The two men must have seen what was approaching them. The trios veered sharply about three seconds before it struck, and the water all around them sprouted Polyphemus's viperous cilia. Within another two seconds, she had already fired her first shot.

It was well over two hundred meters, at the very limit of the harpoon's effective striking power. Only her elevation made it even feasible. The line's silver arc sang out and down. She held her breath, as she always unconsciously did when she feared to disturb the plunge of a long shot that she already knew, as soon as it had left the cannon, was good. The medusa-tangle had meanwhile gripped the lead trio and propped the silver beasts upward, like three bright tombstones against the sun, while other cilia worked for what was under them. It was the delicate, discriminating motion of a man lifting a trapdoor to pluck something out from beneath it. The line's arc crumpled, shuddered through its 220-meter length as the spear impacted, transfixing the lead delph of the trio. With one hand Sarissa flicked on the automatic winch, and the line pulled straight—one puny machine engaging Polyphemus in a tug-of-war. Her other hand had already re-aimed the gun.

The second trio, while equally entangled, was not held so clear as the first. She fired and knew in the instant of doing it the shot was bad. She writhed through the seconds' wait before she could fire again. From under the trio she had hit, a struggling weave of cilia and human limbs fought its way round to the backs of the beasts. A snake-wrapped arm sought and seized the shaft of the harpoon.

"Yes!" Sarissa screamed. "That's it! Climb the line!" Her second shot dove short of its mark. The instant the cable had ceased to pay out and cleared the feed-out spools, she fired again, and again knew she had it. A tremendous expectancy filled her. To beat this titanic enemy, rob it—never had she felt that the delicate geometry, the fleet calculus of her art, an art of parabolas and pin-sharp steel points, could achieve so much. Far away, a tiny Laocoön, the man wrestled half his body onto his trio's backs, having to fight the panicked heave of the beasts as well as the great leeches woven round his frame. It was Jax. His shaven head, stripped of its respiration helmet, fought clear. Now he had the shaft by both hands.

Her third shot struck, and she winched in the line. As it tautened, she saw the trio come loose and thrash freely against its pull—utterly untethered by any cilia. She knew in that sickening instant what she would shortly see—*did* see seconds later: Helion's struggling shape making the now-familiar storm-heaved progress through the black tentacular field, passed from cilium to cilium, moving Eye-ward—for now a field of that black grass sprouted in a long swath, a pathway back to Polyphemus.

Sarissa howled with rage and concentrated furiously on the one she might save. Switching to her magazine of untethered harpoons, she began to pump them down upon the zone surrounding Jax, hoping to scythe down just enough cilia to give him a fighting chance.

And the armorer fought indeed against the giant—himself a giant of relentless will, his big muscles sharp-cut in the morning light with the strain. His struggle had tilted the trio toward him, and he had worked his grip up to the harpoon line itself. Sarissa's shots rained around him, as close as she dared put them, and suddenly it seemed he had several fewer cilia round his chest. He surged up, working two handspans higher up the line—but the cilia had not withdrawn, merely shifted their grip to his shoulders. They bowed him backward, folded him impossibly. Sarissa saw his hands let go before the sharp sound of his breaking back reached her. He collapsed into the meadow, like a wearied man throwing himself back on the grass for a rest. His trio was now also winched easily shoreward. The swath that bore Jax and, farther along, Helion now began a swift contraction, without submerging. Round the island's shore the two were swept, while the huge orb rolled languorously and turned what she could not help but feel was a lusting gaze upon them as they drew near, the red rhomboidal pupil-mouth contracting and dilating in anticipation.

"When is she coming down?" Orson Waverly asked. "I need everyone's report. It just doesn't cohere yet. What's she doing?"

The other three traded looks.

"She's crying, Orson," Nemo Jones said. "Let her be, just a while yet. She thought for a minute she had saved them."

The biologist sighed. "All right. Let's rake through it again. Penny and Japhet agree they saw both squids and sharks excrete—eject large clouds of fine sediment of considerable volume, that drifted down to the base of the orb. Meanwhile, early on, Nemo caught sight of some kind of large carcass, a cetaceanoid he thinks, being actively swallowed down, by minute movements, into the basal stratum. Cetaceanoids are bathic lake dwellers, and Polyphemus hasn't left the surface for the last two days. Conclusions: first, it is a giant detritivore; second, it's hunting and feeding from deep down even as it sits here, my guess being that it hunts with structures similar to those it uses up here and probably engulfed the cetaceanoid last night. Fine. At this point I see no way those things help us.

"Now to the packs. Very little that's new, essentially. Both Japhet and Penny now agree that when the squids fasten to their prey they show a shuddering movement that might be the reverse of peristaltic. But as to what they might be pumping into the bodies, you caught no clues. What would it *be?*" Waverly sounded petulant, exhorting his own imagination rather than the others. "Digestive fluids? Then what feeds the squids themselves if they just soften up the prey for Polyphemus—and if nourishment flows from it to them, how does it do so? And this about the sharks. You all three now say you saw them dive to the bottom even when their tethers had not been broken—saw more than one of them worming themselves belly-down against the basal stratum and then rejoining their packs above. Were they grazing on some of the detritus there? No one saw them using their jaws down there?"

All shook their heads, and Nemo answered for them: "No."

"Shit! It's too much to cope with! Was there nothing else new, no change in the pattern of the packs' collective behavior, for instance? In the way each group acted together, or the way the two groups interacted?"

"Well . . ." All faces, including the blind one, turned toward Penny. "Look. This is nothing certain, but I had the *feeling*, at least, that the packs, both kinds, were concentrated a little more heavily at one side of the globe just before . . . just before Sarissa started firing." She had started weeping, though she struggled stubbornly against letting her voice break. Nemo laid a hand on her forearm, and she clutched it. She let herself go then, cried in slow, quiet gasps, which Waverly didn't seem to notice. His mind had snagged on something.

"They concentrated on the side nearest the prey? Penny? On the side nearest the prey?"

"Yes. They . . . always kept *cir*culating . . . circulating so much it was hard to say. But, yes. I think so."

Waverly nodded. His face had tightened. His teeth ground slightly, busily, behind his closed lips, a sign of thought in him. The faded blood tracks on his cheeks ceased to resemble tears, looked more like war paint now.

"Japhet. Tell me again about the movement of the squids' tentacles— not while they were on the prey, but well before that."

"But what can I say that I haven't already—"

"Try this on. You've all reported that their tentacles show size differential—some quite short and fine, others thicker and considerably longer. All, you've more or less agreed, 'vibrated all the time.' But are you sure? Absolutely? Did anyone notice, for instance, that sometimes it was the smaller, finer tentacles doing most of the vibrating, sometimes almost exclusively the larger ones, and only sometimes all of them together?"

Nemo's eyes immediately came up, to meet Japhet's. These were similarly kindled. Japhet said:

"Yes. That's precisely right. Nemo saw it too."

Waverly's back straightened, and his palms rested carefully on his thighs. "And the sharks. Someone on the log, Jax I think, said their eyes were reddish-black, in three triangular clusters that tapered back to sharp points on the dorsum. And you, Japhet, said they reminded you of delph eyes. There are three clusters instead of two, but what would you others—"

"Look," Nemo said. "Sarissa. She's seen something."

Even Waverly turned his futile gaze toward the knoll where the gunner stood. Her body was taut, and she had her glasses trained on Polyphemus. She lowered them, raised them again. Then she let them drop to her chest, spun around, and rushed to her as-yet-unused gun, the one trained on Polyphemus's sector of the lake.

Sarissa sighed and wiped her eyes. She had cried this way once before, at the training camp on Cygnus IV. She had been just seventeen and had failed her first gunnery finals. Failed. She had placed third in the class (of over a hundred)—not first. She had gone into the sand dunes fringing the lake where the finals were given each year and thrown herself down like a piece of trash discarded in the wasteland. Then she had mourned her shipwrecked pride and mourned two target floats, grazed but unpunctured, that had bobbed back up to mock her after she had fired on them. Now, two faces grieved her, and these would not bob back up from the water they had slipped into an hour and a half before. She faced Polyphemus and spat toward it, feeling hate enough to make her spittle caustic, to make her eyes spout laser beams. She saw what looked like a deep crease forming down in the muddy floor of the giant's interior.

She trained her glasses on it. It was not a stable feature of the stratum. It had not been there before, and now she could see it deepen, as if the whole layer were contorting for some unguessable effort. A few seconds more, and a shudder passed through the titan that made the crystalline walls through which she spied blur in the magnified field of her vision. The puckered place at once began to smooth out again.

Perplexed, she took the glasses from her eyes and it was then, viewing Polyphemus as a whole, that she saw a boil of motion to one side of the globe, halfway out amid the circumambient field of cilia. She brought up the glasses again.

As she focused on the turbulence, its cause popped to the surface: a glassy, opaque ellipsoid, perhaps half the size of one of the fishing boats. One end was more tapered than the other, and at this end two flagella, perhaps three meters long, were attached. With a slow, labored thrashing, they drove the organism out of the black meadow that fringed the parental hemisphere.

Once the thing had been a few moments in progress, it seemed that it hugged, preferentially, the shallows fringing the isle, for it began to make its way round toward a point just off the knoll Sarissa stood on. The perception and the reaction came in the same instant. She rushed to the nearer gun, swept its muzzle downward, and waited. It was already within range, but she waited for the shot to become absolutely sure, and waited too for the slightest sign of divergence from its course as her signal to fire. She heard the others hailing her but spared no fraction of her attention for a response. This little piece of her enemy she could take from it, and she meant to do so.

It was within a hundred meters when she saw bubbles appearing around its flanks and realized that it had begun to sink even as it thrashed onward. She fired. The line hissed vindictively, the barb plunged to the little orb's center, fierce as a viper. The flagella continued to thrash impotently, but not, it seemed, particularly excitedly. She noted that the main part of the orb was tough only in its sheath and that its contents were ge-latinous. So she set the winch going on the first line and planted her sec-ond shot at the base of the flagella, where she reasoned a greater muscular rigidity should give her barb a firmer bite. Her aim was surreally true— she saw where the lance would lodge well before it did so, and almost set the winch on the line before it had even struck. She was already hauling her catch along the surface of the lake by the time the others reached her.

"Polyphemus ejected it—its basal stratum seamed up and squeezed it out somewhere on that side, just below the water level."

The winches had dragged it directly below them now and began to lift it from the water. The flagella, with a brainless mechanicity, did not cease to flail as the blubbery mass floundered up the rock wall. Out of the group's watchful silence, Nemo muttered:

"Polyphemus can see it—if it sees. Can hear it—if it hears. But it's not interfering."

"Polyphemus sees and hears," Orson Waverly said. "But it doesn't think. That thing isn't prey if it came out of the giant's body. And what isn't prey our greedy, mindless friend doesn't bother with."

The five people stood around the thing, watching its flagella's movement weakening gradually. Their knolltop group might have been a scene of an-cient sacrifice. The things Waverly had called for when the organism had first been lashed to the rock promoted the illusion. Japhet, Nemo, Penny, and Sarissa all held flensing knives, and Japhet had used the little industri-al lasers the boats carried to good effect on the plastic oars their emergency rafts contained. A large scoop, fork, and oversized pair of tongs had been fashioned, and a large sifting screen improvised from cable. The log was set up on a rock near the blunt prow of the sacrificial beast. The recorder's console might have been the abstracted face of the deity this druidic cult had gathered to appease: the Group Mind's memory-amplifier. Into this, the blindfolded priest meant to feed each scrap and nuance of the offering he could not see, hoping to purchase with this rite the greater insight that he and his fellow-supplicants sorely needed.

The warm wind washed over the sacrifice, and the propulsive energy slowly metronomed out of its black stern-whips. Its smooth envelope had been faintly translucent, but now had grown waxier and begun to wrinkle. Out of the silence Sarissa said:

"I think it's weak enough to cut. Let's open it."

"Remember," said Waverly. "First the integument. If it has a distinct structure, flense me out sections and separate it as neatly as possible from what's under it."

At first, once their giant scalpels had been at work a few minutes, everyone was reporting that no clearly defined integument existed, but this proved an error. A distinct outermost layer did exist, but it was more than two feet thick. It was a gelatinofibrous material. Its fibrosity was attenuated at the outer levels, but the deeper into the stratum one went, the more sharply articulated, and more darkly pigmented these fiber-bundles became until, at the stratum's interface with the subincumbent tissues, it looked like a tightly packed surface of black-tentacled sea anemones. An embryonic Meadow of Medusa—all question of the thing's identity was settled here.

Within the cavern-urn lined with this dark pile of fibril-tips was a smooth, elongate capsule perhaps twice the size of a man. Its surface was of a thin, tough material of linked hoop-shaped plates, so that the whole suggested a giant pupal case. The celebrants of the rite exhumed the whole upper surface of this sarcophagus shape. They worked with gusto, scattering the black, blubbery rugs of tissue about them on the sunlit stone, until the core of this biological torpedo lay upon a supporting remnant of the integument—lay on a crude-cut altar hewn from its own protective material.

Waverly, considering a moment, decided, "Cut in thirds, carefully and gradually, along seams in the plating. Be looking for clear structures, and also be checking with each other as you cut to see how far along the length of the thing those structures run. Then, when you've cut halfway down through it, open it lengthwise, along a lengthwise seam if you can find one."

His vatic crew raised their drenched blades and returned eagerly to work. Their concentration was complete. Their victim could have been as huge as its parent—their every move expressed an unconditional will to sift its secrets out of it. But revelation was quick to come. The pupal case proved thin, easily cut, and all reported that a dense, very delicately fibrous gray tissue underlay the sheath. It was macroscopically featureless, and after they had gone some thirty centimeters down, it began to look like the sheath's sole content. Then Sarissa's blade scraped on something hard.

Japhet and Penny joined her with knives. They scooped a hollow round the object, shaved it free from webs of tissue, pried it out. It was a human skull, which the tissue packed within as it had without, filling its orbits with gray gelatinous pseudo-eyes. Sarissa held it up in the light of the noon sun. Her eyes stared into its jellied gaze, and her face worked as if she was struggling to read a message in its masklike expression. She said:

"It's . . . fresh. There's still some cartilage in the . . . nose hole."

Nemo came up behind her. He reached around, took it gently from her hand, gave it to Japhet, and gripped her shoulders. His hands strained, as if by the firmness of their grip he could throttle—as with a tourniquet—the grief and horror rising in her. Face blank, she let Nemo steer her to a seat on the rock. She watched the lake.

Waverly was deeply excited by the find and made them bring him to the site of discovery. His hands, tremulous and lustful as a gloating miser's, caressed the socket the skull had lain in, palped the surrounding tissue. A blind augur, he did a thorough divination from the alien entrails.

"It's deep inside a highly specialized structure. It didn't just wander in. Saw it open. Comb out the tissues packed inside it."

The skull had hardly been opened before something was found: thumb-sized white ovoids, nearly a score of them, embedded in the tissue. Penny helping him, Waverly cut one open, fingered its contents with exquisite thoroughness. "Listen," he said. "Improvise a large comb, fine-toothed as possible. Start with the fork we made while Japhet makes something finer. Anywhere in this tissue, whether it's encased in fragments of prey or not, look for anything that might be an egg—smaller than these, larger, I don't know—but probably on a similar scale and, hopefully, of a recognizably different form. Nemo and Penny on that. I'm going to open a few more of these. Sarissa, I want you to help me with knife and tweezers, but first help me rig a little table. Sarissa?"

Not speaking, she came up, touched him. The augurs went to work.

A bit later, they all sat together on the knoll. Waverly sat at his little bench, where he and Sarissa had unraveled the innards of three more of the objects found in the skull. On the same bench were four black pellets, half the size of those from the skull, which Japhet had just combed from the tissue of the sarcophagus. He had cried, "Orson! I found some. They're black. They're a little like delph roe. Smaller, harder, separate, but shaped like roe." Waverly had straightened then. He had called them all around him, but once they had gathered, had sat quiet a long time.

They waited, the bright, bulky tatters of their butchery scattered all about. The chunks and gobbets of alien blubber surrounded them like the debris of some bizarre biological sculpture they had lately joined in finishing. In a way, this was true. They had hewn out the features, the intelligible form, of the being that imprisoned them. Waverly's face came up, and he smiled slightly, as if with pleasure at the flood of sunlight that bathed him. His mouth groped for speech, but luxuriatingly, as if his mind were rummaging through a wealth of utterances.

"Delph eyes have the incredible motion-detective power of a jumping spider's, and we've recently confirmed to our satisfaction that their resolution of image and detail—of the very subtlest gestalts—that it probably surpasses our own. Polyphemus doesn't eat delphs."

This might have been the gloating introduction of a very hot paper read at an academy meeting. Waverly paused, visibly trying to sober himself. "I think the reason is that independent organisms, evolved more or less directly from the delphinid order, have become functioning saprophytes in the systems of Polyphemus's kind. These delphinids have first crack at their host's prey, and they function as their host's eyes." He talked faster now, rushing to include his fellows in his new overview. "My guess is that the sharks' ancestors were engulfed by polyphemids as food, enjoyed some natural resistance to their digestive enzymes, and learned to thrive on their captors' meals. If polyphemids resembled the smaller littoral analogues I mentioned, they had only tactile sensibilities, with perhaps some primitive olfactory discrimination. Any one of them whose saprophytes could start cueing it to their visual recognitions of prey would surely eat better than its blind fellow-hunters. And the saprophytes, evolutionarily speaking, would feel a great stimulus to providing such cues.

"And I'm convinced the squids are similar in their history. Their tentacle activity is discriminative in just the way the cilia of our own organs of Corti are. When the smaller tentacles vibrate, higher frequency sounds are being registered; and when the larger, the lower frequencies, while all are usually in some kind of motion, as would be expected from the mixture of frequencies in most environmental noise. The squids are the giant's ears—grotesque though it sounds, I have no doubt of it. Both these captured species have evolved a caudal nerve-link with the giant's own major ganglia, which I am certain are in that basal stratum. The kelp is part of its own neural system, and perhaps respiratory and alimentary as well. If what's in this egg's yolk is at all analogous, and I think it is, then the giant's basal stratum is a dense neural tangle, the plane of intersection for Polyphemus and its two breeds of saprophyte, as well as being its zone of absorption for nutrients. And when those sensory cooperatives breed, their reproductive packets are planted in that same stratum. The squids embed their eggs in the carrion before it is absorbed there. Quite possibly, they don't feed at all as adults and take in their life's nourishment during some kind of larval phase. The sharks go down and lay their eggs directly in the stratum. These genetic packages are then apparently well located to be included in that of the host itself, and the tidy partnership is perpetuated, while those that are not entrapped in the material of Polyphemus's spores no doubt hatch endosomatically to replenish the adult host's sensory packs.

And as for the nutritive disproportionality between host and saprophytes, it's even less than I thought, for as the individual adult sensories die, they surely fall to the basal stratum and feed their master with their own corpses."

Waverly stopped, but with an air of cutting himself short. He sat, a small canny smile on his face, as if challenging his friends to see what he did.

Nemo said:

"Then if those sharks are still close enough to being delphs—if their eyes are built the same—our dyes could blind them."

Waverly cackled—it was the most blatant hilarity that any of his fellows had heard from him. Then all five of them were talking at once. But when the first gusts of jubilation and (often fantastic) strategy had subsided, the biologist said:

"Listen. I think we can do it. And if it works, it's surely a start, a great satisfaction if nothing else. But it may not be enough. Because if blinding fails to drive it away, its auditory mechanism may be all it needs to kill us. I've got one or two specific suggestions to add to all you've said. Let's get down to the beach, finalize our plan, and get to work."

The work that began that afternoon lasted most of the night, and decorated the island with a small, unsteady constellation of lights. Japhet welded harpoon line into three-strand cables, Nemo and Sarissa toiled by camp lanterns modifying rifle ammunition, Orson and Penny converted the tough hides of freshly slaughtered delphs into a hundred meters of tubing, Orson scrolling the material and holding it for Penny to fuse with the bright needle-fine laser beam.

Just after sunrise, the boat that Polyphemus had rejected once already set out from the island's shore. It was, as before, tethered to a rock, though even more strongly than before. But this time it had passengers: two rather rigid figures with heads of stuffed cloth, painted features, and stuffed wetsuits for bodies. A system of wires, guyed to one of the boat engine's flywheels, imparted a jerky agitation to the lifeless shapes.

Polyphemus reached for the craft the moment it was offshore. As soon as the creature took hold, Japhet stepped up the winch paying out the cable, to facilitate the giant's speedy taking in of the prey. A quarter of the island's circumference away, Polyphemus's mouth opened.

And when that red-rimmed trapezoid dilated, there came a series of twelve explosive barks. They sounded from the knoll Sarissa had been stationed on the day before. Their noise, eerily gradual, traveled out to cross and fill the lake's whole vast arena, and before the second had sounded, their effects began to appear: a series of twelve splashes in the lake of ichor bordered by the mouth's rim. Violently expanding clouds of yellow smoke began to bloom within the orb, some near its surface, others deeper down. The coalescence of these roiling masses had stained the contents of the entire globe within a minute and a half. Sarissa and Nemo, whose rifles had launched the missiles, stood with field glasses trained on Polyphemus.

The giant's overall movement had suffered a marked change. The steady peristaltic surge of the cilia faltered—the entangled boat ceased to flow so smoothly toward the orb. It paused, was joggled as by choppy seas. The fibers enmeshing it grew frenetically active, but somewhat less purposive.

"It's groping the boat," Penny shouted up to the two on the knoll. She stood on the beach, the nearest of them all to the captive bait. "It's not pulling it in nearly so fast!"

Nemo and Sarissa probed the thinning mists of dye for clues to the fate of the giant's eyes. The pigment was dispersing according to its normal behavior in lake and seawater, the bulk of it settling out in a harmless precipitate within three minutes of going into solution. The orb's inner jungle melted back into visibility. Sarissa said, thick-voiced as with desire:

"They're scrambling. Panicking."

"Yes. It's their normal patrolling motion, speeded up. Can you make out the eye color?"

"Yes! Red! Check that pack to the lower left." In both delphs and Polyphemus's visual sensories, the eyes' normal color was blackish-red in most light. And now the eyes on the "eyes" of Polyphemus flashed deep ruby as they boiled in their kinetically heated-up patrol movements. This was the color of dye-blinded delph eyes, once the chemical had converted their chromatophore molecules to an isomer that the impingement of photons could not reconvert—that is, once the eyes' retinal substances had been permanently bleached.

"But they're not colliding," Sarissa said. The joy in her voice had diminished several degrees. "Getting snarled more often, but still coordinated. I think they can still hunt and kill . . ." Nemo knew that the foreboding in her tone related not to this part of their assault, but to a secondary phase of their plan that everyone hoped would not need implementation, but he pretended not to understand this.

"So what? They can't show it the way to its food, that's all we care about."

"The boat!" Penny called. "It's started bringing it in again!"

The action of the cilia, though different in quality, more searching and gradual, was smooth again. The craft wallowed and toppled onward.

And it was, some moments later, consumed by the giant. There was no opening of it, no shaking out of the tasty nutmeat and discarding of the husk. The cilia brought it to the feeder-tentacles, which plucked it up, crushed it like a large shellfish, and hurled it whole into the mouth. As it sank, the sharks, clearly endowed with fine directional control and some form of sensitivity to mechanical vibration, swarmed on it. All took their turns, assaulting hungrily, retiring unsatisfied from the metallic morsel. The squids too took their futile turns, and at length the craft settled to the basal muck, with Japhet still paying out cable to allow its sinking.

The day's agenda was completed a short while later, executed by five rather taut, silent people. A respirator, rigged to a float so that it rode some six feet under water, was set adrift from the cove. A hundred meters of improvised air hose linked it to the shore, where Nemo and Japhet worked a crude bellows of delph hide to produce continuous aspiration in the device. Polyphemus struck it with violent accuracy a short distance offshore.

*   *   *

Sarissa Wayne tilted the muzzle of the harpoon gun a little higher. This brought the grappling hook strapped to the underside of the harpoon up to her eye level. She reached out and touched one of its needle-sharp points, looked at the hook with distaste and unease.

"It's ludicrous," she said. "The more I think about it. How did we ever convince ourselves that it was rational? All of Orson's goddamned *inferences . . .*"

These words were addressed to no human shape, but to a grotesque manikin, half-beast, half-machine, that stood beside her on the flank of the knoll. The body was a squamous hulk, ensheathed in overlapping plates, shingles, and greaves of a dark leathery substance. The head that crowned it was a metal-and-glass bulb with insectoid mechanical mouthparts, while on its back something like an engine was mounted on a shoulder frame.

This Caliban replied in an eerie remnant of a voice, filtered by the respirator mask:

"Don't start doubting it now, Sarissa—you won't function as effectively if you do."

"Horseshit! I'm getting you out of there if I have to spear you and fish you out. Function effectively! You think I'm going to let you down, Jones? All this shit about trusting me, everything you said to me in bed last night, all lies, right?"

Nemo knew she was not really concerned with his words, that essentially she needed to hold him again before he went down. He shook his head, shifted his feet wretchedly in their delph-skin boots, his queer expeditionary armor a torment bottling up his answering need to hold her.

"Dearest love. I'm going in, and I'm coming out."

"Coming out," she said quietly. "That's just it. You won't have any trouble getting *in . . .*"

They looked at the cable that belted the entire hummock they stood on. From a point just under their feet it dove in a shallow arc to Polyphemus's mouth-corner. Within the orb the cable dangled through the kelp. Down on the neural mulch their eyes could just pick out the wreck of their decoy boat. Sarissa stepped over to the second gun and checked its angle, speaking in a tone so carefully constrained it sounded absent. "If this thing wants to pull away, submerge, all our lines together won't hold it. If it's aroused while you're . . . *deafening* it—if it reacts, it will take you down."

"Listen, sweetness, if we let ourselves go over it all again, we only lose what time we have to talk about our love."

"Talk about our love!" She whirled on him. "Jones, you fool, with all your courtships and vows and declarations. I don't want to talk about our love, I want to *have* it."

Japhet Sparks called from the beach: "It's ready!" He and Orson had slipped their bait into the water. It was the engine of their most seriously damaged boat, mounted on a cut-down raft and anchored to the rock by a length of tripled cable. Sarissa went round the knolltop and called to Penny down in the cove. She sat in the helm of their escape craft—their one good boat, driven in the shallows around the island and hooked to a trailer raft for the two riders who would not fit inside.

"Penny! Bait's up! Here we go!" "Hit it! I'm standing by!"

Nemo raised his gloved hand to Sarissa. She stood still and nodded, staring him straight in the eyes through his faceplate. Nemo took from the ground a large heavy hook with a handle-gripped bar attached. He eased down to the lower ledge cut for him to stand on, just under the cable where it began its plunge to the giant's mouth. He checked the weaponry in the side racks of his back-frame. The motor the frame supported was one of the small ones with which each boat's emergency raft was supplied. Nemo switched it on briefly for a final assurance of its stability on its improvised mount, and switched it off. Then he hung the hook on the cable above his head and gripped the bar with both hands.

"OK, Sarissa."

She called down to Japhet: "Now!" The noisy little bait-raft fired on and chugged out toward the black meadow.

It was seized by the fibrils and tumbled orbward. Polyphemus's mouth began to open—and then the raft hit the limit of its tether. The cilia began to toil, frustrated, roused. The mouth, as if impatient, gaped fully open. Nemo jumped from the ledge.

As he dove, he felt metamorphosed into a kind of bomb. He wore two wet-suits, and to the outer one his delph-hide armor was sewn with steel wire. A padded, capsuled thing, his body was surreally snug and remote from the dreadful vision into which he plunged. The veined opacity of the orb's wall loomed into sharper focus, and the teeming amber lake in the giant's lips rushed to him. Nemo brought his feet up and locked his knees. With the sense of exaggerated mass his gear gave him, it seemed when his heels impacted that he struck a titanic hammerblow on the bell of his own doom. The true proportionality of the matter was that he was like a sparrow touching down on the flank of a large hill. Even so, when he freed his hook and hacked it for purchase into the orb wall, the suicidal blatancy of the act horrified him. The material was tough, pierceable only with fierce blows. He worked his way up from the mouth- corner along the giant's lip, a swollen, scalloped border of tissue shot with purple fibrosities. He gained his feet and began to stalk along the border of the golden tarn.

From his rack he took a crooked scythe welded from the blades of three flensing knives. He stuck its razor tip into the ichor and vigorously slashed up its surface. Sharks, as fast as rockets, rose and converged on the spot, fangs foremost. Nemo saw that their ragged teeth moved independently in addition to the jaws' movement of them—mouths that worked more like shredders than scissors. The rabid schools milled insistently, their red, poisoned eye-clusters flashing with their sharp, snakish turns. Nemo racked the scythe and took down one of his three rifles. He began to pump explosive shot into the haggle-toothed mouths. Outside the orb, at the fringe of its dome just behind where he stood, something huge moved. It was a trio of Polyphemus's feeder-tentacles, beginning to elongate yearningly outward, toward the stubborn bait-raft. Nemo kept firing.

When he had killed perhaps a dozen, he found he was kindling unhoped-for havoc among these blinded sensories. Each one hit, as its head ruptured, went into spasms that snarled the coordination of its pack. Each, as it thrashed, scribbled the ichor with ribbons and wraiths of its blood, waking the appetites of the squadron it jostled. The cannibal frenzy spread as the blood got thicker and made every beast smell like food to its fellows. It was, apparently, some visual cue that normally inhibited this kind of accident—the taste of cannibal food itself certainly did not.

Two other of Polyphemus's feeder tentacles had gone out toward its recalcitrant prey. So far none had reached it, but all showed a slow, inexorable extensibility that was not yet exhausted. Nemo scanned the red uproar beneath his feet. His goal was now the basal stratum, and he sought a window to it through the fanged turmoil. He saw one down along a major strand of the kelp, turned the ignition of the motor on his back, and dove in, rifle first.

They had seen Helion's still-masked face remain unaffected after his engulfment, while Jax's had soon begun to bloat and corrode, but, curiously, it was in his face that Nemo dreaded first feeling some caustic leakage, rather than his hands, which had been left fairly thinly gloved for the manipulation of his weapons. The stalk he followed was as thick as his body, and he kept it just above his back, to force any attacker into a frontal approach.

Down where the stalks coalesced toward their common rootage, while there was still room to navigate between them, he branched off to his first task, where the wreck lay.

The hulk's cable had supported it against complete subsidence. It was sunk in a turgid half-liquid zone just above a more solid neural mulch. Its fractured hull offered many places where the coils of cable he had brought could be threaded through its chassis. Firmly and intricately, he wove the wreck to several major kelp stalks. Yesterday's bait had now set its hook in the prey that had swallowed it. Yesterday's bad luck—that Polyphemus should not flee in panic at its blinding, but feed regardless and wait to feed again—was today's good luck. "Take me down now if you want to," Nemo hissed in the smothered silence of his helmet.

Now came the task that probed luck's spiderweb. They had observed three distinct basal zones in which the sensories' neuro-umbilici attached. Now Nemo sped to the nearest of these and, trying to stay ahead of his fear, charged into it, scything through tethers in broad sweeps. He found a lateral branching of kelp to stand on and cut his motor.

As the squids came down, he shot them. They rained toward him with the erratic dodging movement of moths or snowflakes, and he shot them as they applied their caudal tips to the mulch to regenerate their tethers. The inner explosions tended to split them lengthwise, and several, in dying, vomited upward from their beaks little clouds of eggs like those found in the skull.

Nemo scythed the remaining tethers. Overhead, the silvery interface of ichor with open sky was visible in patches through the churned gore of the sharks, and Nemo saw it shattered by the impact of one of Sarissa's grappling hooks. The bait-raft's tether must be near breaking. He worked faster, darting upward from his ambush now to meet and kill those that were slow in descending. At least half of the tethers he cut must have been those of sharks, but few of these came down except in bleeding tatters, more mulch for the undiscriminating titan, which now dined upon its own senses.

And then Nemo was on to the second zone. Here he swept zigzag through the field and mowed it all at once. Panic was big in him, trying to split from within the shell of his self-command. His compromise was to push the very limit of recklessness. He stood in the center of the mown patch and fired directly overhead, accelerating his motor periodically against the muddy tug of Polyphemus's appetite at his feet. The sensories came dodging down through the veiny gloom, while from the smoky plane of the higher turmoil shark-meat drizzled ever more continually, trailing wisps of torn tissue. He saw Sarissa's second hook hit the interface and glide toward its purchase in the giant's mouth-corner.

The rent and ragged molluscoidal shapes piled in little drifts around him. When the weapon's fifty-shot magazine gave out, he dropped it and snatched down another rifle. And then no others descended. He waited two seconds, five, then launched himself toward the third attachment zone.

In the same instant that he did so, the floor of his little ocean tore itself from under his feet. In the inertial shock that followed, Nemo sprawled helpless in the turbid boil. He collided with a stalk and hugged it, and then the giant was still. A moment later, the silver ceiling of this living cosmos exploded a third time. The bait-raft, its snapped cable fluttering behind it, dug an effervescent shaft down toward him. Nemo accelerated toward the last of the sensories' anchorages.

Those on shore saw him raise his scythe, dart forward—but then check his swing and pull up just short of the umbilical thicket. There, at the edge of the webwork, the scaly little man-shape paused and, from his place in the orb's deepest murk, seemed to gauge how far the thicket towered over him.

"What's he doing?" Japhet called to Sarissa from the beach. She didn't take her eyes from Nemo, and her answer to Japhet was spoken only to herself, almost whispered:

"He's thinking how to kill them from higher up. Yes. Get near the exit before you do it—get near as you can!"

The scaly shape probed the kelp adjoining the thicket and separated out from it a slender side-stalk perhaps fifty meters long. Nemo grasped this by the tip and began to drag it in a gradually rising spiral round the thicket's perimeter. He tightened the spiral as he rose, gathering the lower parts of the neural tethers into a sheaf. When the stalk ran out, he tied it to a more massive growth and found another, higher branching one.

Orson Waverly had extrapolated rather extensively from what the previous day's test had shown them: "I think it fell back immediately on a more primitive feeding taxon, probably geared for motile but armored or shelled prey. Maybe it feeds on some of the pseudobrachiopoda—there's some big bathic ones just been found.

"But it's the implications of this behavior that are most significant to us. Totally blinded, and no panic reaction. I think these saprophytes, during their evolution, have maintained a very separable, interruptible kind of sensory feed-in with their host. After all, with tethers routinely broken, that kind of reaction wouldn't be very productive for Polyphemus. But, still, the complete deprivation of an important sensory input? My guess is that as long as the sensories are alive and maintain attachment, they transmit a steady flow of 'white noise,' random neural firings, to the host. It doesn't experience a disruption of sensation so much as a kind of zero-information state, such as it might experience on a dark night, or very deep down.

"I *am* convinced that as the sensories are killed, Polyphemus will feel a cumulative encroachment of sensory deprivation—a state of 'total blank' as opposed to one of 'no news,' and it seems to me this must produce a violent reaction of some sort. Now understand that from this point I'm only guessing, but it's often the case that creatures as primitive as Polyphemus is, when you consider it apart from this startling adaptive turn it has taken—that such creatures can be relatively insensitive to extensive physical disruption. For my money, Nemo should have a good chance of killing at least a majority of the sensories before any radical sense of anomaly begins to dominate the giant's behavior."

Now Nemo repeated Orson's words in a snarl—"for my money"—and began firing on the sensories his ploy had aggregated into a desperate snarl no more than twenty-five meters from the titan's mouth. He was prodigal of shot, perforated the bloody, frantic mass from every angle. When his magazine emptied, he let the rifle drop and grabbed his last. After a moment—during which the redundant butchery had him in a kind of vengeful trance—he realized his work was done. It was then that the giant moved again.

It filled Nemo with awe, as Polyphemus's previous lurching movement had not done, for this was an immense concerted muscular effort of the biocosmos that held him. The pressure of the ichor increased upon him as the entire orb tautened and strained to pull itself offshore, out to deeper waters. The message of darkness had at last definitely reached the titan's murk-shrouded ganglia. The giant was alarmed.

And on finding that a quintuple thickness of cable opposed its withdrawal from shore, alarm became the plainest panic. Nemo, who had felt so huge and blatant during his soaring approach to the enemy, now felt he was reduced to a jot of foam in the raging prow of a tidal wave. His motor's effort mouthward, skyward, seemed a ludicrous trivium. Polyphemus had a very powerful—awesome, even—capture-resistance taxon. It had sought to move and found that painful stasis opposed its murky will. It tried again, and a fang of pain on a scale that it could feel was sunk into its core as its efforts to flee tore loose the roots of its own most central nerves. And now Polyphemus was an earthquake. Volcanic clouds of its black blood roiled up from the wounds of its self-violated ganglia. Pain could not vie with the blind will to escape that it had kindled in this colossus—unmolested, no doubt, through centuries of easy gluttony. Polyphemus strove, and an ink storm arose from its tearing entrails.

And when they tore free and the boat, trailing broken trees of nerve cord, came vomiting, rocketing mouthward, Nemo knew he would be trapped in the ichor's inertia—would fall with Polyphemus and join him in his dark retreat, if he failed to reach the boat before it erupted free. He gave up vertical striving and fought to intercept it.

As it erupted he saw he was missing it, was a helpless half-second too slow, but mindlessly he sustained his drive after the craft had passed him. A trailing nerve stalk clubbed his belly, and he hugged it with both arms and legs, while all the fluid volume of Polyphemus strove to strip him off and flush him down. The boat, the stalk, and then Nemo, were into the sky.

The sudden surge into free-fall tricked Nemo out of his grip on the stalks. He could see he was falling free of the sinking feeder-tentacles, but that he was going to dive into the cilium-field sluggishly following the giant's subsidence. He fought to straighten for a sharp hands-first entry so that he could pull the dive shallow as soon as he struck. He hit the vipered foam and arched his back strongly as he entered. As he surfaced, he felt himself pulled short. A fibril had snarled in the screw of his motor.

The field was retiring laterally before it sank under—Polyphemus was pulling its skirts, so to speak, off of the midshallows they had overlain.

Nemo threw his feet in the air to flop backward where he could get a grip on the cilium. He just managed this, but was too awkwardly folded, legs flailing, to get a scythe free from his snarled rack. A red shock of pain ruptured his left foot.

An instant passed before he had the wit to seize hold of his foot and grab the line of the harpoon that pierced it. He wrapped it round his arm, feeling nothing so much as a vivid embarrassment and indignity in his position as he fought for his scythe with his free hand. He had been dragged past the littoral drop-off before he had it out and went under.

For a brief eternity he expected Polyphemus's full weight to haul against his steel-wound arm, and then he got the scythe tip under the fibril and pulled mightily.

Jones lay on the beach the expedition had first set out from. Japhet had brought the medical kit from the sand-hog and waited at a discreet distance while Sarissa cleaned and bandaged Nemo's foot. She finished the bandage and patted his thigh, smiling absently with an unconscious appraisal and satisfaction in her eyes, such a gaze as a breeder might bend upon his prize beast, knowing it safe after some hazard.

"No artery hit," she said, "a few of the metacarpals broken, I think. At the worst, you'll have a slight limp and that won't make you any the less active."

Nemo nodded gravely and didn't answer at once. "I love you all the more for your . . . determination to save me," he said at last. "No doubt you had an agonizing moment there as you fired, dreading that the shot might be . . . a little off."

"Not the slightest." She said it fiercely. Her large black eyes came up and bull's-eyed his; a distinct frost of impugned expertise gave them added bite. "I knew it before I even saw exactly what kind of fix you would get into: there was no way I was going to miss *you,* Jones."

Nemo nodded. "I see." He looked at the lake and smiled.

Down in its waters, their enemy still pursued its ponderous retreat.

Deep in the lake's root, the cold and lightless magmatic shaft, it sought the realms that were the ancient nursery of its evolution. Its encounter with the vertebrate bipeds had reft it of the fruits of five million years' development. It had found the butcherwork of these midgets far cannier than its own, and so it stumbled back down to the night of its origin.

Fill It with Regular

1

It was just past 3:00 a.m. An all-night gas station stood on its lonely little asphalt atoll, a delta bordered by two convergent country roads. Not far beyond this confluence, the two-lane blacktop passed under a freeway. Up there, along 101's unsleeping corridors, big semis boomed and groaned, their frequency abated at this hour, but still clocklike. Down here on ground level, however, below the imperial elevation of that viaduct, all was country darkness, country silence full of crickets. The black shapes of the roadside trees shrank and islanded the station's light between them, big, half-naked oaks, crooked against the stars.

The attendant stood by one of the pumps. His khaki jacket—with "Al" stitched in red over one pocket—was thin, but he stood relaxed, even slack-armed, in the chill air. In fact, in the absence of muscle tone from his sharp-nosed face, there was something faintly moronic.

A pair of headlights sank down the freeway off-ramp and approached. Al shifted slightly on his feet and worked his fingers. An old, dented blue Maverick sighed on worn tires up to the pumps. The driver was a large, rather drunk-looking man. His horn-rims, one hinge sutured with black tape, sat on his nose a shade askew. Two or three of his lower teeth were missing, and his chin stubble was gray in patches. His air was cordial.

"A glad good evening to you! Just fill this puppy to the brim with regular!"

Al nodded eagerly. Still, an uncertainty entered his manner after he unholstered the gas nozzle. The drunk blinked, smacked his forehead.

"Ach! Where's my *mind?*"

He hauled himself from the car, and an empty Rainier Ale can followed him out and tap-danced briefly on the asphalt. Dragging out his keys and moving sternwards, he unlocked his gas cap, set it on the trunk lid, and returned to his seat, all with a kind of staggery flourish.

Al filled the tank. A gush of excess foamed down the Maverick's tail, making a clean stripe across the dirty license plate. Al released the trigger. Still hesitant, but moving hopefully now, Al reholstered the nozzle. The drunk, squinting at the gauge, hoisted his hip for money—his unseen feet, shifting, raised the musical jostle of bottles. Peeling open a distorted lump of wallet, the drunk poked inside. He rummaged. He blinked. He raised a look heavenward and sighed as at some relentless, long-known enemy, now plaguing him anew.

"Will you *believe* this, man? Will you fuckin' believe this? I've only got a ten here! I should have looked! I should have fuckin' looked before I told you to fill it! But hey, listen. Look here. I don't live far off. Over that way somewhere. Take this now, and I'll bring you back the other two fifty, if not tonight, then first thing in the morning."

Al was watching him with a kind of raptness. He kept nodding nervously, as if in sign of noting important information. The drunk beamed.

"You're an ace, man! An ace! Just stick that in your pocket, and before another moon rises, I'll be back with its two little buddies! God bless!"

Looking genuinely moved, the drunk cracked another beer and sipped it as he drove off, dribbling gas at the stern. As he dipped the driveway, his gas cap tumbled off the trunk and rolled to the gutter as he accelerated away.

Al resumed his position by the regular pump. Then a thought seemed to strike him. He went into the office, and through its connecting door into the locked garage. Here the legs of a man on a mechanic's under-dolly thrust out from beneath a station wagon with its hood up. Al got some wrenches from one of the shelves along the back wall and laid them on the pavement beside the dolly.

Standing again by the pump, Al seemed less catatonic than he had.

His hands were more restive, task-ready, and his lips moved faintly, as though rehearsing words. From the freeway, another pair of headlights sank toward the empty corridors of oak shadows. A big new Cadillac slid its flawless, dark cream paint job up to the pumps.

It held a middle-aged couple, the Fennermans. They had been dining with their friends the Crosses and were in a pleasant mood. Fred Cross, who also ran a new car dealership, had let slip to Ted enough about his business to make Ted realize that his own lot had been doing pretty damn well lately by comparison. Gail Fennerman, for her part, had been deeply pleased by the enchiladas Muriel Cross had made, and no less pleased by the seven margueritas she had washed them down with. Al marched to the window as Ted rolled it down. He looked hopeful now, determined.

"Hi! Fill it with regular?" His energy bordered on the intimidating. "Oh, no!" Ted Fennerman chuckled uneasily. "Supreme! It's supreme all the way with these babies, right?"

"Ah!" said Al, seeming crestfallen. He brightened at a thought. "Want to give me your keys?"

"Right," said Ted, separating out his gas key so that the rest hung from it, and putting it between Al's fingertips. Al marched back, unlocked the cap, laid it on the trunk. He got the hose, which he handled now with increased panache. He began to fill the Caddy's tank.

"What a strange man," Gail Fennerman said.

"I'll say. I guess, though, that you'd have to be some kind of a loony to take a job like this in the first place. The boredom would drive a sane guy nuts."

"Teddy?"

"Yeah?"

"Isn't he filling us with regular anyway?"

"Hey! Hey! Stop that!" Ted thrust almost half himself out the window. "Cut that out!"

"Right," said Al. Even then the overflow puddled beneath the plate. "What the hell is *wrong* with you?" keened Ted. "Didn't I tell you *su-*

preme? Didn't I tell you that *specifically?*"

Hanging up the nozzle, Al gave a thoughtful nod. "You *did* say supreme specifically. Yes." He tucked the Fennermans' keys into the pocket containing the drunk's ten-dollar bill.

"Hey!" Ted half-erupted again. "Gimme back my keys!"

"Oh," said Al blinking. Returning the keys, he cleared his throat. "It's okay if you just give me ten dollars. You can bring the rest by later tonight, or first thing in the morning."

"I don't understand you," Ted Fennerman said slowly, astonishedly. He forgot even to contest payment. "Here's my credit card."

"Oh," said Al. He inspected the card carefully, and then put it in his pocket with the ten-dollar bill.

"What the hell are you doing?" Ted sounded hushed, awed. "Give me back my goddamned credit card!"

Al—perplexed, mouth ajar—returned the card. Pocketing it, Ted Fennerman hesitated only an instant over the legal risk of leaving without paying—then he fired up the car and pulled out. Gail's head turned, she spoke, and the Caddy lurched to a stop just short of the driveway. Ted popped out. Keeping his hands on the car, as if for cover, he hurried astern of her, replaced the gas cap, dove back inside, and slid the car up into the darkness between the star-hung trees.

Al walked to the driveway, picked the drunk's gas cap from the gutter, and gazed at it, nodding owlishly. He pocketed it and returned to the regular pump. Unholstering the nozzle, he put its tip to his mouth and triggered himself a couple of hearty gulps. Smacking his lips, he seemed to judge the savor. He went into the office and came out with a small, dark sack.

He went to one of the brass-hatched intake valves whereby the trucks fed the station's cisterns. He keyed it open, dug from the bag a handful of black dust, and dropped it in. He shut the hatch, returned the bag to the office. He resumed his post at the regular pump. Again his lips seemed to practice, voicelessly, and his eyes looked around at the country darkness environing his little wedge of light.

2

Next morning around eight, Ted Fennerman started siphoning the gas from his tank into a pair of cans from the garage. The engine had gotten detectably shuddery in just the few miles home from that miserable station. There had seemed a kind of juvenile-delinquent fun in the siphoning just at first, but his first draw was too prolonged, and he got a mouthful that soured the whole thing. He cursed the oil company whose logo had crowned that station, a seeming oasis down in the shadow lands, as seen from 101, which they had crested so serenely at sixty-five. Why hadn't he kept going? It was his own fault for being so compulsive about keeping the tank full. He called his local station to send out a tow truck with some supreme.

With tepid breakfast coffee, he rinsed the fumes from his mouth. When the tow truck arrived, he recognized the kid driving it—slight and pimply, but peppy. Today, though, he was so vague and slothful in his actions that Ted took the can and poured the gas into the Caddy himself. When Ted tipped him a buck, the kid didn't seem to know what to do with it. What the hell was happening? The Caddy thrummed and pinged all the way in to his car lot in Santa Rosa. He ground his teeth and swore as he drove. He might as well not have bothered changing the gas at all. He got to his desk around ten in a foul mood. He realized that, unmistakably, he had the beginnings of a sore throat.

It was a little after eleven when the drunk, an artist named Ken, got up. He had a good reason for getting up so early: he had to go see Dale and borrow a hundred dollars from his academic friend. Starburst Paperbacks still owed Ken six hundred on his last cover, but far be it from them to speed payment. He washed his face. He warmed up some pizza and poured a beer. He hummed between sips, waiting for the cheese to remelt. It was a nuisance having to borrow money, but afterward they could drink and bullshit and watch cable TV—Dale got all the channels.

He went out to his car around noon. He threw his traveling sketch pad—for ideas that obtruded themselves upon his drinking time—in through the passenger window and circled round the car. Feeling an odd crackliness to the asphalt underfoot, he paused, looked down—and noticed he lacked his gas cap.

"Shit!" he said.

He drove back to the gas station, trying to keep all his accelerations smooth. It hadn't seemed that cold last night, certainly not now, yet the roadway still felt faintly crisp under his tires. He pulled into the station. The garage's overhead door was now up, displaying someone on the floor dolly half under a station wagon. Al was standing near the regular pump. Ken got out.

"Hi, Al!" he cried, noting only now the red-stitched name. "Say, did I leave my gas cap here last night?"

"You sure did!"

"Ah, great! That's a relief!" There was a smiling pause. "Well," Ken prodded. "Can I have it back?"

"Why don't I get it for you? It's in the office!"

"Great idea!" Ken hung around the doorway of the garage while Al went in. Al seemed more sure of himself, much brisker today. On the other hand, Ken realized, he hadn't seen the guy under the car move very much at all.

"Ha!" he offered. "Great place for a nap, hey?" The guy didn't move or answer. Ken shrugged. Some assholes just didn't have a sense of humor. Al brought him his cap and smiled.

"Fill her up with regular for you?"

Ken laughed. "I didn't lose *that* much. Thanks anyway. So long! Inwardly he sighed, driving off—the two-fifty was forgotten. He'd scrounged up only two dollars anyway, and now he could get a sixer of Buckhorn with it. He slid on down Old Redwood Highway—which stretched bright, almost silvery before him—and smiled skyward at the fresh fall sunlight.

Gail Fennerman awoke numb, feeling nibbled away around the edges, at 12:30. Before moving, like a swimmer who chooses the bit of distant coast he will strike toward, she determined two of the things she would do today. First, have a sauna at the gym. Second, have a flame-broiled patty-melt at the Fern 'n Burger. The first would atone in advance the second, for Gail equated sweating with calorie loss.

She rose. She reached the shower, her legs feeling of unequal length. In the kitchen, her protein smoothie whirled strenuously in the blender, growling aggressively. Swallowing it was an act of grim will, such as she imagined it must take to lift weights, or learn French.

Confronting her mirror to make up, she asked it sarcastically: "Do you think you can drive? See? It really makes you look forty-three, every day of it!" She didn't even like the smell of alcohol, but these delicious cocktails, like Bloody Marys or margueritas, were her downfall. Last night she had, self-mockingly, kept mental count of her margueritas, but, perversely, this only enhanced the pleasure of the indulgence. Ted was partly to blame—he didn't even *go* to the gym anymore, even just for the Jacuzzi. His getting so paunchy, after he'd promised, undermined her own resolve. Not much past two o'clock, she locked the front door and crunched down the driveway to her Buick.

Crunched? On firm asphalt? She paused. The sun, sloping past zenith, delicately shadowed a kind of translucent fur, perhaps a quarter-inch deep, covering most of the drive, with an especially thick circular patch just behind where Ted always parked the Cadillac. She scuffed at the stuff with the tow of her designer track shoe. It was crackly, but seemed to be giving rather than breaking under the prodding. She shook her head. As a SoCal girl, she had always deplored the creepy growths that northern California's lushness fostered. She fired up the Buick and turned on the Montonavi tape she had left in the deck. She sped down the silvery highway—it *was* rather glittery today, wasn't it?

At the gym the strangest thing happened. With two other women, one of whom she knew slightly, she was sitting in the sauna. Tina Claymore, who managed a boutique in Coddingtown Center, was saying to Gail:

"Boy, this dry heat can sure get to your nose and throat sometimes, can't it?"

"Yeah. Mine really feels scratchy, too. What's that on your legs, Tina?"

Both bent to inspect Tina's pallid thighs, flattened to ovoids on the sweat-dark bench. Her thighs looked dusty. A vanishingly fine, faint soot besprinkled them. Tina brushed at it, but it smeared into her sweat. "Look!" the third woman told Gail. "It's on *your* arms and legs, too!"

"Yow! And yours, too!"

For a moment the three ladies twisted and splayed themselves to present all their surfaces to the weak, sulfurous light—patting and spanking at their limbs, till all at once the scene they made struck them and they all shakily laughed and trooped out.

They were in the showers, soaping lustily, when the instructress got back to them. She pushed her twenty-year-old T-shirted upper half into the room and told them brightly:

"I was right! Rod says it's just a little soot—the gas heaters have been burning a little sooty today!"

The girl's sunny self-approval vexed Tina Claymore, to whom soap-suds gave clownishly exaggerated breasts, as though some grotesque lichen had overgrown them. "Well that's just peachy! Peachy! Why didn't you *tell* us?"

"I haven't been in the sauna today," the girl said, looking stung. "Rod just forgot, I guess. It'll wash right *off,* won't it?"

"But it still *itches.* And what about my nose and throat? They're scratchy, too!"

Gail privately agreed that her skin also felt a bit prickly, but she didn't detain herself to make an issue of it. Purposefully, she dried and dressed. It was patty-melt time at the Fern 'n Burger.

From there she called Ted at four, to see if there were any errands that needed running before things started closing. Ted didn't feel like talking. He had "a goddamned sore throat." He said he'd meet her at eight at The Cattleman's for dinner, and hung up. Just as she returned to her table, her food arrived. It was exquisite, except that the meat had an odd extra crispness and very faint, so discreet as to be rather pleasing—a slight bitterness.

3

Dale was an entomologist out at Sonoma State. He had bought one of the little motor courts—proto-motels of thirties vintage—still to be found decaying along Old River Highway, which had been the 101 of the pre-freeway era. The office and the first two cabins were built of a piece, and this structure Dale had inhabited. By knocking out the connecting walls, he had created a single large living space with three bedroom cubicles, the office kitchen, and the old registration desk left standing by the office door, the only one Dale made use of.

A Charlie Musselwhite tape raunched and wailed roomfillingly. Near the entry the TV, sans sound track, beamed the Playboy Channel, which Ken, a great lounger and sprawler, watched from the couch. He had a Buckhorn in one hand, the remote control in the other, and in his thoughts the hard truth, ever less ignorable, that they were out of beer. Dale was more of a pacer and an arm waver, and he was near the rear of the room. Here were the bookshelves and dart board, and here he liked to do much of his ranting and raving while throwing darts. A blown-up photo of an ant, pinned to a corkboard, was his target. Big and shambling though Dale was, and eruptive with his restless thoughts, time and again the patterns of six darts he threw came incredibly close to pinning all the insect's feet— Ken glanced over and checked now and then. Dale had paused in his monologue, and Ken sighed.

"So come on, man! Money me! We need some more beer—you've been pecking at that one can for the last hour."

"It was the only one I got my hands on in your whole sixpack!"

"Wait," said Ken, palm raised. There was a wet T-shirt contest on the screen, and the guy with the bucket had finally gotten to the brunette. Ken watched her get it. "So?" he resumed. "All the more reason to get some more."

"It's amazing!" Dale grinned, poking another dart into the air. It landed in the ant's upper right tarsus. "How routinely, with such minimal effort, you get money out of me! A few solicitational gestures—a bow, a tap of the antennae, a nudge to the gullet—and I disgorge a big, fat drop of my hard earned nectar. Just like *Atta texana*."

"Don't be an asshole. You *know* you have it, you *know* you'll get it back, you *know* in the meantime I'll buy beer and enchiladas with it, and you *know* you're going to lend it to me in the end!"

"That's it exactly!" Dale crowed. "I'm going to do it! And I seem to have no more power over regurgitating this sugary blob of monetary energy than the poor insect does!"

"You're a scientist, Dale! Energy is collected in nature only to be utilized, dispensed, dissipated—converted into some other form, beer, in this case."

Dale, not listening, smiled at his own thought:

"And I let you sap me, you see, of that sugary blob, for one reason alone, one that should make all scientists humble. Because even the smartest of them—why, even *I*—even I am no more essentially free of my nature than the lowly bugs I study!" He threw a dart, which lodged a quarter inch off the mid-right tarsal claw. Ken regarded Dale.

"I think that's just incredibly humble of you, Dale."

Dale took up his beer. He began his professional patrol of the big room, pacing comfortably, causing for Ken two regular eclipses of the TV screen as he orbited. He said:

"It's a fact! A fact made banal by the facile affirmation of the heedless! You, Kenny, though only an artist, might guess at the arrogance that can go with a little knowledge among scientists. However much we know and can do, we mustn't swagger through the cosmos. Inevitably, some form exists that's perfectly adapted to exploit us in spite of all our technical furnishings."

Ken, musing, laughed. Dale's length of limb, the seemingly erratic emphasis of his movements, *were* antlike. "I have to buy that image, Dale.

I'd like to draw you that way—as an *Atta* worker disgorging your wallet from gaping mandibles."

Dale was nodding as he paced, assenting not to Ken, but to another dawning insight of his own. "Look here, Kenny. You've always confessed that my erudition gives you graphic inspirations. So to hell with this piddling parasitism—a hundred here, a hundred there. Let's get a real mutualism going." Dale's orbital speed increased as he warmed to the idea. "I'll ape that noble scale insect so famous for her fungal parasite. I'll be industrious *Chionaspis corni,* pumping the sap of learning from my academic branch. You, of course, will be *Septobasidium,* the fungus whose spores I ingest and that sprouts from the interstices of my dorsal sclera. At first, you see, I house you, and I feed your *oeuvre* from my brimming brain. Soon you're making real bucks in the art racket, and the tables turn. You house *me* grandly, as the embowering fungus doth the bug! Muriel moves in, we mate and reproduce and live as your coddled tenants from then on. The analogy's not perfect, of course. *Septobasidium* sterilizes its living plant pot. It's her sisters' offspring that the fungal tenement roofs and feeds with its plump sporangia. In our case, my *own* reproduction would be fostered by the setup—all the better for science, of course."

"I dunno, Dale, I can't quite picture this one. Me growing out of the cracks in your dorsal sclera and all. Suppose I think about it, and meanwhile you give me the fucking money so we can get some beer?"

Still smiling in the afterglow of his ironic vision, Dale tossed Ken his wallet. "Finally!" Ken said. He plucked the money and tossed the wallet back. "So let's make it a ride—take Reibli through the hills a ways. Bring the Ry Cooder tape."

Dale took the tape from the rack. "Time's a-wastin', Sonny!" he said, following Ken out the door. He paused to lock it, and turned as Ken was firing up the Maverick. Where the exhaust boiled against the drive, Dale thought he saw an odd glitter, but he was impatient to ride out and take the sun, and just got into the car.

Their windows overflowing Cooder's *Trouble,* Dale patting time on the doorsill with his jutting elbow, they roared down Redwood, up Mark West, and swung onto Reibli, which meandered along the hills just under their crests. In a pause between cuts, Ken asked:

"What's that? That crackling, hear it?"

They pulled onto the shoulder and got out. What they found shocked them. They saw it best when they squatted on the shoulder and looked at the road surface along the angle of incidence of the latening sunlight: a fine, translucent furriness perhaps a half-inch deep, all over the asphalt. It was finer, really, than the finest fur, yet its countless fibrils were made opulently distinct by the glints of diffraction their innumerable curvatures shed. The friends gaped at each other, poked and pinched the stuff.

"As far as you can see!" Ken said—"the whole road!"

"It's *tough,* Kenny! The tires don't crush it! It springs back! And these little droplet formations all through it. Like sporangia. Damn if it doesn't look like some incredible mold mycelium."

"Road-eating mold?"

"What can I say? There's a mold that eats creosote, I've heard . . ."

"Let's keep going." They drove on, without music. Only occasionally could they see its faint flash, but the frosty noise of it was continuous, though it wove easily into the susurration of a moving car. And didn't it intensify noticeably as they took more trafficked streets into Santa Rosa? They tried to see if other motorists were noticing it—and then they turned onto a broad, westbound street that dropped through the center of town. Now the crush of it was louder still, its slight resistance to their tires grew palpable—and this asphalt laneway to the sinking sun was laddered with ghostly smears of rainbow no one could miss. Now cars flowing in both directions were carrying people who were pointing out the roadway to each other. Ken swung north, and pulled in at Pap's Liquors on Mendocino Avenue.

Inside, with his twelve-packs and quart of Jack Daniel's on the counter between them, Ken asked the woman at the register:

"What's with this stuff on the streets? Has it been like this all day?"

"You know, for the last hour or so *everybody's* been asking that. I couldn't tell what the heck they were talking about at first. You can really see these, like, flashes of color off it now, can't you?" She mused on her view of the street, as though it were a picture in a travel brochure, or a telecast. "Oh dear!" she cried. "There's another one!"

"Another what?"

"Poor doggie! We saw one just a little while ago, and I asked this man was in here if it could be, you know, mad, but he said no, when they were mad they just foamed at the *mouth.* Oh dear!"

The dog, a mixed shepherd, flinched away and cantered down the sidewalk when Dale, newly amazed, went out and tried to coax the animal to hand. It was as if the dog felt some particular humiliation in its affliction—to have its all-questioning nose so strangely furred with a grayish thistledown that it could neither sneeze nor rub away.

Driving back up Redwood, Ken said, "I know it's got our attention now and all, but I'd swear it wasn't this thick an hour ago. We'd have heard it through the music."

"Park right where you were, Kenny. There was something I saw under your tail pipe."

This proved to be a patch of markedly thicker and taller roadgrowth. "When you first came over, you idled here a little before killing your engine."

"I was listening to the last part of a cut."

Dale nodded. "So . . . diffusion by automotive exhaust?" Both men gazed up and down the roadways. "I'm going to make some phone calls," Dale said, "and I think I won't be the only one doing it."

"Good idea. I'll wash us out a couple of glasses."

4

Ted Fennerman sat at his desk, his chair clicked back at its rest angle. From his window he looked across his lot, over the enameled candy colors of mint-new car tops, at the sky. Its dusky blue was turning purple as gradually as Ted imagined wine must ripen in a vat, or whatever they made wine in.

When business had been good, this was always an hour Ted savored, like a liquor sipped privately. He watched the arc of 101 that wrapped the south end of his lot, watched the dinnerbound traffic's headlights coming on like stars. He pictured, individually, the day's sales, each shepherded singly from his corral of glossy stock, and frisking with their new owners out to graze on 101's long pasture and raise the happy roar of their vitality.

Not so this evening, though business had been very good. Tonight, bone-weary and naggingly sore of throat, he couldn't taste the tang of it all. He'd told his secretary hours ago that he was out to calls; it seemed such an effort just to talk. He'd sat and fought his way through desk work, but at last ground to a halt. Lines of text had grown vague and slippery like snowed-under road; his pen lurched with a balky clutch, or lost it on the curves.

What kind of wimp was he? he asked himself bitterly. A simple god-damned sore throat, and bam—he was belly-up on the canvas. It was galling to feel too weak to strike when the iron was hot. He had promised himself that he would go in on that new franchise with Clark Mannheim if things stayed even half as good as they'd been going. Clark wasn't going to stand around waiting to be kissed forever—he'd find someone else. Ted thought of all those TV ads where tired businessmen bungled big deals for lack of the right antihistamine-and-aspirin compound—dumb, though there was a grain of truth. You feel just a little off your feed, and it could cost you some important moment.

Ted shook himself groggily, to wake his will. He snapped his chair up to its no-nonsense angle. He breathed deeply and punched Clark's number. When the receiver clicked open, he again drew breath for a hearty greeting. Clark's voice said:

"Yes?"

"Gullub!" Ted boomed. "Glarg?"

"What? Who is this?"

Ted, as shocked as Clark sounded, gaped at the phone. He clapped it back to his head and cried: "Glarg!? Gellub?!" Now fear raked his heart. He slammed the phone down, jumped up. Clicking on his washroom light, he saw his mouth loom gaping up to the mirror over the sink, as if to devour it. An eerie, pale fur thronged his throat and flourished from his gums. He moaned, watching his shaggy tongue shudder in its weedy pit, like some hibernating monster tormented by a dream. Ted Fennerman headed for the hospital without further attempts on the phone.

When Gail, after waiting through half an hour and two piña coladas at a table at The Cattleman's, called the lot, she learned that Ted had left long before without a word to anyone. So she went back and ordered her sirloin and a third colada—a double.

The drink seemed spiritless, but it did soothe a touch of soreness in her throat—Ted's bug no doubt—and help numb a general itchiness that had persisted since the sauna. See the cycle? she asked herself. Get hung over, get lowered resistance, get sick, and then you wind up having more cocktails for relief. But she couldn't seem to care, and ordered another double when the steak came.

The restaurant seemed to promote her lassitude. Usually thronged, it was rather empty tonight; and in spite of this, it was short-staffed, too— her waitress had apologized in advance, saying they were not only lacking table help, but were short on cooks, too. Gail ate. Even with plenty of horseradish, the steak entertained her dulled palate only mildly. She finished it, though well before the last bite she was beginning to feel almost drugged, as though she had ingested an anchor that tried to drag her head after it as it sank.

To hell with her thoughtless bastard of a husband. He'd forgotten her, gone home, was already resting. Thanks to him, she'd been stranded here to overeat and overdrink, but she'd waste no more time waiting on him. She'd get home and get off her feet. Slowly but decisively, Gail wiped her lips, rose, and walked out.

She stood in the parking lot. Out on Montgomery the mid-evening traffic looked pretty heavy. Did it sound extra screechy? More brakes and horns than usual? There! That tow truck nearly piled into that station wagon there at the light. She'd have to be very careful driving home.

"Mrs. Fennerman!" It was her waitress. The girl looked worried as well as tired. She seemed to stare a bit at Gail's face as she said: "You forgot your coat. And the check . . . ?"

"Oh dear! I'm sorry! I feel so *woozy* tonight . . ." The girl was looking at her face, strangely, as they went back inside. Gail smiled self-deprecatingly at the cashier as she extended the woman her credit card. The cashier gasped, and Gail, seeing what made her do so, felt her head wobble at the shock as though lightly punched: her own forearm and hand, all silkily befurred with an exquisite lawn of pallid fine filaments a quarter-inch long, like freshest, tenderest shoots of spring.

5

The windows, long gray with dawn, were turning buttery with sunrise. "Jesus Christ!" Ken said, keying down the newscast's volume. He and Ken sat in a kind of information trance, stunned by nightlong revelations. "I feel like a kid," Ken said. "After a sugar whiteout, my brain gorged with weird images, coming out into an afternoon sun so bright it hurts. I knew—I *knew* I should've stocked up better yesterday. I mentioned it, right? And now, God rot me, I've got to drive into town before it's too late—before it's *three* inches deep."

Dale shook his head and gestured at the screen. "Didn't you see how traffic's starting to slip and slide?"

"It still looks steerable to me. There won't be much traffic on Redwood. It's now or never."

"Well, if you break down, stay off the road walking back. And get some food. Something in cans, and eatable cold. Chili or stew."

Ken rose, scattering empty beer cans, loath to be reminded of the fungus's capacity for rooting in flesh. Shutting the door after him, he looked with hate at the drive, where the fungal mat was now a lush two inches deep. He did a lumbering ballet across it, his soles cringing from the contact, and hauled himself into the Maverick. He feared his ill-tuned engine stalling, so he idled till it was good and warm. It mortified him that in doing this he was feeding his world's new enemy, helplessly stoking the biological conflagration that had somehow, overnight, embraced it. The suspicion nagged him that this would be just how evolution's fallguys, the adaptively overtaken breeds, always exited the stage; by a droll, inadvertent suicide, mechanically revving up their long-sacred tricks of survival that the upstart, by some dire new ingenuity, has turned to death traps. He gunned onto Old Redwood Highway's long mycelial lawn.

It was supple. Its slick toughness made the curves tricky. At least he was rolling—his tires could have been fused with the road. It had happened to thousands of vehicles left parked overnight on heavily trafficked urban streets, which had been superabundantly seeded with exhaust-born spores. This lush crop's greedy upreach was answered by the germination of a second form of spore, the strictly wind-born kind produced by the road surface growth, and with which the treads of *all* cars that had been driven the day before were packed. By the time, two hours ago, the earliest commuters stepped out to their mounts, many found them crouched on crumbling flats that were already half digested by this devil grass growing from beneath and within. Ken, at some risk, stayed near forty, knowing his own venerable retreads must already be dying from within.

Maneuver proved little worse than on a slushy, half-snowed road, but in fact—wasn't the fungus beginning to look wet here and there? What was this, some new wrinkle? Should he call it in? The thought, an instant later, forced a laugh from him. Oh yes, report it! Add his jot of awe and stupefaction to the general delirium! Since TV's Tribal Eye first squinted at the streets on last night's six o'clock news, and blinking anchormen—raising uncertain voices above the rush-hour road—had affirmed the infestation, the municipal, technical, and military sectors of the area had been caucusing with state authorities. They had clashed and conferenced throughout the night, all consensus eluding them. Information-pooling switchboards were quickly formed and publicized, and the data for a sketchy etiology of the ecoplague were soon gathered. But as long as continued observation showed the roads to be drivable, all involved willingly shunned the contemplation of their clearest countermeasure—the interdiction of all public thoroughfares. So vast an arrest of circulation, assuming it could even be brought off, seemed itself a cataclysm, a mortal shock that must produce unguessed-at mayhem among the bottled masses. They flooded the media with advisories, put troops and cops on alert, and waited. And with the dawn, people started trooping out to their usual commutes, also waiting to see what would happen; as though the simple wonder of the thing had universally captured people's curiosity, the sheer scope and unity of it. A fungus, stunningly proliferative, that thrived on hydrocarbons of every kind.

Gasoline and some municipal supplies of natural gas were thought to be its initial vector, at least in California and others of the heaviest-hit states. The mechanisms of its continuing diffusion were no mystery. The fungus's omniperipheral advance, by mycelial branching, was incredibly rapid in itself, of course, through any food matrix. But with the combustion of the matrix, the mycelium it contained underwent a fusion and a heat-triggered concentration of genetic material, and resolved itself into a gust of exceedingly small and numerous spores. Hence the roadways were only the first of many zones that those first vectors had seeded, since most of a tailpipe's tillage went aloft to haunt the troposphere. *There* was the real scope of this thing, and it made Ken shiver slightly, imagining that global microsnow, that sooty seed like a gauze-fine, wide-flung shroud settling right now—softly, softly—down upon them all. What could anybody do but drive out to business as usual through this awesome newness that had been laid upon the world?

At the liquor store he called the hot line on the pay phone. The wet spots on the mold weren't news to the tired-sounding woman he got. "Enzyme puddles, they think," she said bleakly. "Stay off the roads, especially the freeways."

"Yeah," said Ken, who could hear 101's roar a quarter-mile from where he stood. He went in and got two cans of stew, two twelve-packs of Buckhorn, and a half-gallon of Jim Beam. Reapproaching his car, he saw two black smears matching his tires' path, and seeming to melt into the mold even as he watched. Further provisionings must surely be made afoot, and the imbalance of his supplies bothered him. He went back in and got another half-gallon of Beam.

He drove fast, as the few other cars on Redwood were doing, slewing and screeching. His tires were spongy now, taunting him with collapse. He rolled past vineyard and pasture, trailer parks and sprawled junkyard country houses. Fine fungal lawns toupéed all asphalt-shingled roofs— white lawns where antennas stood like stark, futuristic trees. Furred garden hoses lay in yards like feathered snakes in the grass. The pallid fuzz outlining window frames baffled him till he realized the monomers composing most caulks were hydrocarbons. On one porch he saw a shuddering puffball shape—just discernibly a dog, on its back, fighting to breath, its paws kneading the air. Ken's rear left tire gasped, and sagged, and started jouncing. He braked, the brakes locked, the Maverick came assaround, crossed the shoulder, dropped its rear in a rain ditch, and blew the tire on the right.

Raging, he got out hugging his bag, hotfooted across the sporulating mat, and jumped the ditch. He landed ankle-deep in sweet, sane, earthy grass—and partly in cowpat. He roared some nouns and gerundives, found and flung an illogical rock at his car, whose front left tire sank with a wet cough. Ken broke out a beer and strode north, hurrying not to hear the last tire go. He stooped through the wire and straddled the wooden fences, and tiptoed the highway only where berry-choked streams compelled it. The space he moved through now was that magnified space into which everyone emerges from a failed car—full-scale space, toilsome and time-swallowing, where to reap one aim or object, you had to plow across acres for hours. "I should've stocked up better," Ken muttered. He shifted his burden and cursed the weight of the stew.

Dale was where he had left him, but sitting straighter, rapt in the newscast again. "Enzyme slicks, Kenny! Like a sudden digestive *assault.*"

"What is it, near nine? Look there!"

"Man! That's 101 north of Novato?"

"Yup! Just where the southbound backup always starts—and I think its being rush hour's saved a lot of lives. From there on down, no one was going very fast when the fungus came on."

They watched an aerial view of confluent freeways where, at this hour, San Francisco–bound traffic routinely braked to join a creeping clog twenty miles long. Today the free-flowing traffic had come up on the clog at lower than usual speeds, though generally drivers had managed to maintain a cautious, coping flow over this invader of their path. They came in slower, but the enzyme sweat was brutally sudden in its increase, and their tires had turned greasy in their swift liquefaction. Brakes jammed fruitlessly. With seeming abandon—some with fey, balletic half turns—cars skied into the phalanxed bumpers of the idling backup.

Now the clog sat unmoving on twenty miles of flats, smoke penciling up here and there from the rivered vehicular jigsaw. South of the crazed skewing of the pileup zone, the jumbling of the derelict armada was less severe, though everywhere were sideways chromeboats with crumpled corners, ram-welded pairs of tailgating muscle-cars, and jacknifed semis pillowed on luckless imports. Diced safety glass, like a sugar spill, everywhere jeweled the prickly vigor, the pubic wetness of the mold.

The network's helicopter caught four others in its scan, two winching up wounded. The anchorman's voice-over announced his own craft's return south to base to be refurbished for rescue work. Thereafter, his shakily improvised script tended to relapse to a formula, an awed dirge:

"And of course here we're seeing 101 as it approaches San Rafael . . . And this of course is 101 climbing past Marin . . ." Already most of the vehicles were abandoned, while the people in their tens of thousands, in four streams choppy with contrariety, trudged along both sides of the freeway's two corridors, as clotted in this progress as they had been in their cars. As an image, Ken found it very moving. As if he viewed an epochal event—mankind at last abjuring some vast, ambiguous enterprise, a millennial pilgrimage frozen in its tracks by a cataclysmic unison of doubt, and abandoned at long last, all dismounting, all returning their myriad of separate ways. Their sun-blazoned fleet, while it roared, had seemed aimed, an army. It looked now like an aborted stampede.

"The shine of it! Christ!" Dale almost enthused. "It's almost *puddled* with enzymes."

"Tell me about it. Did you hear my car pull in? It's ass-in-a-ditch two miles back on four flats. Have a beer."

"And food?"

"In the bag. You know I just can't buy it, any kind of Russki gene-engineering angle. Why conquer a place so you can't get around in it once it's yours? They'd make something that went for the people primarily."

"This stuff doesn't do so bad on people," Dale said from the kitchen, plying a can opener.

"Yeah, but you've got to practically gargle or smoke spores to get it going."

Dale found a fork and came back to his chair. "It's not Russki, of course. It's off-world, obviously." He began gobbling stew. Ken nodded readily, but found he had to clear his throat.

"Right. Designed by another environment. And damn if I can imagine what kind of setup could produce . . . *this.*"

Dale sat forking, musing. His forking slowed a beat or two, and he interlaced it with conjectures. "Biologically hot world? Teeming? Epochs of floral/faunal explosion. Organic sumps capped. With limestone by shallow seas, like here? Vast petrochemical deposits, in any case. But lots of venting to the surface. By vulcanism? Other seismic events? So plenty of tar pools, asphalt seeps, burning vents of natural gas." Dale forked up the last muddy lump, dropped his fork in the empty can, belched, and sighed. Ken, though bleakly, had to laugh.

"Somehow, I see *you,* Dale. A titanothere of that alien Tertiary, shuffling to a flaming tar pit, munching the sludge."

"The flaming vents," added Dale composedly, "would promote the evolution of combustive sporulation, of course."

It sobered them a moment, this naming of that most frightening fungal trick. The ragged carbon microshells that their seemingly destructive birth created for the spores made them infinitely responsive to air currents, amazingly invasive and adherent once in contact with a food matrix. Was there even now a just perceptible tickle in their fall through the air? They sat feeling the noise and stir of this new day rising around them, the unimaginable bawl of mired commerce, of eighteen-wheel giants who lay half devoured by the very paths they trod.

6

Near the close of that same day, Sheri Klugman, Gail Fennerman's younger sister, blinked away tears, turning her face for a moment to the windows and the honey-and-roses light of dusk. Roy Hummer sat with his eyes commiserately downcast. He was experienced in the resurgences of grief his clients suffered in these interviews, but he was also exceedingly tired. This was his twelfth transaction since noon—all twelve of them involving loved ones in the Fennermans' condition.

"I'm sorry," Sheri said, resettling with a sigh the burden of composure on her shoulders. "It's just this awful *suddenness* of everything . . ."

"Please. You have our entire sympathy. And I know it's a terrible added burden, this time limit for disposal—*disposition* of your loved ones."

"Yes . . . well, I guess it's lucky that we live close enough to attend . . . Midnight tonight does feel so . . . *hurried,* though."

"Yes, of course, we're terribly sorry." Watch that tone of voice, Roy told himself. "It's certainly never been *our* way of doing things, this tactless hurry. But you can see that from a sani—a *medical* viewpoint . . . ?"

Grief resurged in Sheri, overflowing as plaintiveness. "Do you really think that an open-casket ceremony isn't . . . ?"

"No, that's quite definite, I'm afraid." Roy paused, and warned himself again. "You see, with this thing there's just nothing we can do. It's too tough to be, ah, shaved off. Even if it could be, there is a considerable, an extensive amount of *shriveling,* frankly—do you follow me?" He saw that Sheri, with the inattentiveness of sorrow, was looking out the window again. Roy felt frayed and gritty. He wanted a shower. He wanted to sleep. Sheri's eyes were full again. The woman was plainly dazed, powerless to leave alone the few futilities remaining of her sister. With the helpless iteration of bereavement she said:

"They were just both so *definite*—whenever it came up, I mean, about both wanting to be cremated—"

"No way," Roy Hummer snapped. "That's all there is to it. We're respecting the emergency ordinance one hundred percent. So please just take it or leave it, Miss Klugman."

7

"Screw the whole effort. Why struggle?" Ken asked, though he didn't stop working. It was the following afternoon. He was encasing his shoe and ankle in an aluminum foil bootie, crinkling it on sheet by sheet, securing it round the ankle with rubber bands. Dale already had his booties on. He tossed Ken a paper particle mask and stowed others, left over from his remodeling, into one of the two knapsacks lying readied on the counter.

"Hunger and thirst," he answered. "Curiosity."

"Boy. Look at that, Dale." The TV's copter-born eye scanned down over an oil tanker docked at Long Beach. The voice-over was saying:

"As you can see, the fittings of those off-load hoses are densely covered with the mold, and as I say, the samples from what's still in the tanker as well as what's now in the offshore tanks have both been tested positive for infestation. You can see, too, how these pipelines to the holding tanks in the hills are also covered. Officials have told us that this is merely a surface growth on a bituminous cover that's put on all gas pipeline to protect it from corrosion and weathering . . ."

"Christ!" Dale said. "What's it matter? That tanker was half off-loaded before they stopped! Three-quarters of a million barrels!"

"Know what they said last night, while you were asleep?" Ken asked, booting his other foot. "Seems they inject natural gas into the ground—to force up the pressure of crude they're pumping? So it turns out a lot of this natural gas also tests positive for infestation."

"Hoo boy," Dale said quietly. The newsman was now narrating a fly-by of one of the Long Beach refineries. It belonged, he said, to one of the first of the big oil companies to comply with the federal immediate shut-down order, acting within twenty-four scant hours of receiving it. The furnaces beneath, and burn-off pipes above; its fractioning towers had been quenched for several hours now. Every valve and juncture in its py-thon's nest of pipes was muffed with mold. Gaskets everywhere however thick, sandwiched at whatever pressures, were digested to monomers to feed the alien biopolymer, and wherever gas drizzled in result, the myceli-um grew in ghastly whiskers, along the undersides of pipe, in streamers trailing down to puddles, like moss dusting every secret little creek of leakage woven through the installation. And of course, as the hills and graded bluffs the storage tanks stood on were all capped with asphalt, the whole plant was environed with sweeping pastures of the pale predator.

"Think of it, Kenny." Dale still sounded subdued. "Those burn-off pipes just shut off this morning. Giant spore nozzles, pumping the atmos-phere full like it was just another giant tank."

The voice-over, having discoursed on gaskets, was saying:

"Chuck, I think, was pointing out earlier that here in L.A., the infes-tation layer has made airborne infestation of petroleum products in general an especially severe problem. Crated TVs still in the factory warehouses have been opened, and the insulation of their wiring found infested. And that, in fact, is why we're going to have this intermission in our telecopter report, because we're very concerned to have our copter return to base for regular checks of the fuel line. That's why you see us turning around right now, and that's why it's back to you now, Chuck."

The studio anchorman appeared, conjured by his name. "Right, Dave, and thank you. And you'll be back on the air about noon for continued coverage of the Long Beach area?"

"That's right, Chuck. I . . . Ah, it seems I'll have to sign off a little quicker than . . . the pilot says we have a sudden loss of fuel pressure that—MY GOD, THE ENGINE'S STOPPED!"

The studio men had cut back to the copter's video transmission, but the camera, being aimed out the copter's windshield, was half eclipsed by Dave's panicked profile. Some movement of the man's terror had killed the sound. He turned a blind stare, mouth moving, to the camera, then back to the view before them all. This now tilted and—shockingly—rushed upward.

The studio, with quick cannibalism, cut to the video from a second copter, clearly fleeing the scene as it recorded Dave's craft smashing to fire against the mossy, gas-rilled grounds. Smoke welled up. Flame bloomed, branched, and probed rootlike through the jungled steel, and then the fleeing copter cut transmission and the studio anchor team was back on screen, so stunned that Chuck actually gave an astonished laugh. "That really happened!" he said.

"I mean . . ."

Dale and Ken put on their packs, but stood waiting till a ground crew cut in transmission from a hilltop a mile from the refinery. There was a raving note in the reporter's voice left from the fury he had just seen. He told of the storage tanks' explosion moments before. The pair watched the black upward avalanche, the new hosts of spores storming up to mingle with their fellows under the inversion layer. Ken cracked the last beer, made room in it for bourbon, and spiked it. "So let's go," he said.

They left the TV on—an irrational, magical measure against its failure with the inevitable loss of electrical insulation—but there was relief in the firmness with which Dale shut and locked the door on its global window. They now marched—resolute, if shaky—into their local piece of the catastrophe, a share that seemed more manageable. The day was cloudless. Golden light waxed the blackish branches of the oaks and drenched the fields flanking Old Redwood Highway, while through these fields a fair number of folk trudged, townward or back. Dividing them, the translucent luxuriance of the roadway was riverlike, something that made the people on either side more separate than could the gap alone. They all walked through a country silence never known here with the freeway running so near. They looked rather dwarfed in their unshelled littleness—by the green acres they had always zipped past. They traded calls here and there, in voices also dwarfed by the big, breeze-whispery trees. Many of them wore bandanas like silent-Western stickup men, and some wore masks like Ken's and Dale's.

Both, as they walked in their bright-booted guise, felt a touch of unmeant circus gaiety in the spectacle. Now dozens of cars, mired within a half-hour of Ken's mishap, were derelict on the ermined asphalt—whimsically angled, or half in ditches, or squared off in the disarray of impact. All were richly bearded on their greased underbellies; the interiors of most, those with plastic upholstery, were lavishly robed. There was something of Mardi Gras in the long, disjointed rumba line of them.

"Floats in the Fungus Bowl Parade," Ken said. "Aborted due to lack of tires." The flanking power lines with their tufted insulation suggested streamers, while a service station just ahead offered racks of furry tires, like festively frosted doughnuts. Dale gave a laugh that was half a groan.

"I tell you, Kenny, we're doomed! Look at those sporangia. I mean, as if the combustive spores aren't enough, we're getting this incredible ground crop in just three days! I mean, this stuff is *fast*. We either hit the bush, head for the unpaved hills, or we've had it. And you know, all the time it keeps nagging at me: how the hell did this stuff *get* here? I mean, did it just blow across space?"

"How the hell do I know? Here." Ken took the bottle from his pack and tilted some bourbon in under his mask, and Dale followed suit. "Once we pick up some more beers at Larkfield, we'll both feel better," Ken advised.

There was a crowd at Larkfield, and beer's price had gone up sharply.

They proceeded with three more twelve-packs, Ken grumbling. They gingerfooted on their silver feet through the shopping center—all paved—and across Mark West Road. After that there were fields to walk on again. Lifting their masks often to swallow beer, they climbed the highway's gradual rise to an overview of 101, which swept near at this point, just above town.

The freeway's curve, the outward surge of it, acted as their TV had done, brought home afresh the continental scope of this plague, the wheels of trade and travel locked in this hoarfrost coast to coast. They paused to ply the bourbon, hundreds of captured vehicles visible from here. All the sunlight, and the beauteous diffractions of the sporangia, made them seem numinous things, crude Elder Gods overtaken by an exuberant cosmos of simpler, more vigorous beings: a tow truck, its oily boom so bearded it seemed some exotic sailbacked being; a toppled bus like a giant bug cocooned or spider-shrouded—

"Hey. Look there," Ken said. "That Rolls behind the bus? It's *idling. Christ, you'd think the jackass could've—*"

"No, there's a guy there that just leaned in and started it up! Look, there he is, moving up to that green van, see?"

"Jesus Christ! That's Al! Guy that works in a gas station up the road. What the hell's he *doing?*"

Al's awkwardness and odd hesitations of three days ago were gone. He was a man of experience now. He grasped the van's door handle as surely as its owner might. The van yielded what he sought—the keys—for he geared it to neutral, fired it up, warmed it, and then left it idling on what remained to it of fuel.

Al surveyed the way he had come, and then the way he was headed. He looked up at the sun and seemed to come to a decision. He sat down on the step-up of a big semi's cab. He settled back with an odd completeness, so the stepwell and door received and propped him fully. Then he opened his shirt. Dividing his chest and stomach was a vertical red scar. Al grasped the flaps of this seam as briskly as he had his shirt, and spread open a slick chasm from which a multi-legged blackness, about a small dog's size, came nimbling down across his lap, and sprang thence to the fungal lawn. The hands that freed it fell slack as its last leg was plucked from the incision.

The thing was glossy and quick. There was much of the insect about its structure, about its scissoring, multiple mouthparts, with which it now began to gorge on the sporangia that sparkled everywhere around its stilting legs. It wandered out to graze the jeweled laneway, while slump-headed Al stared empty-eyed.

"Ah yes," Dale said in a slow, strange voice. "A biologically hot world indeed. Full of remarkable forms. You know what, Kenny? See the pickup in that guy's driveway over there? See the gun racks? Let's go borrow a rifle, or bring him over here."

"There must be thousands of them, man. All over."

"Yeah. But we can *get* this one."

This seemed to waken Ken a bit. "Right on," he said.

Ghost

The sun was sinking fast, as Monk walked down a mean-looking street in South Boston. Even big streets here felt narrower and colder to him than the ones he knew in L.A. or Frisco. It felt a little ancient and weird here, actually, maybe because everything was made of bricks like fairytale towns.

What the hell was he doing down here? This was as far from San Francisco as you could get. Kathleen was why, of course. The thought of her spun his mind, and turned his heart on a pivot of grief.

Here came a couple guys. They looked local and tough, fedoras on longish slicked-back hair, white T-shirts on under open jackets, one leather, one denim. As they drew closer he saw that the taller one had some scar tissue dividing his left eyebrow, and his partner had a chunk missing from one of his cheeks. Leather turned and said something to denim, and Monk saw a shared intent flicker between them.

A slippery slope here, but he was already committed, trading stares with them. Just what he needed, some stupid confrontation . . . But now, something odd entered their faces. Their eyes seemed more baffled than combative, as if they were trying to decide what they saw in him.

They passed each other. Monk was relieved, but not relieved. He looked back and caught them still staring after him. What was that all about?

Maybe they saw him and knew, simply by looking at him, that his lover had just dumped him. Maybe there was a certain Look that everyone could see except the guy who wore it.

But he had to put Kathleen out of his mind for a while. He'd been chewing on that bitter lump of pain for months, and he had to give his heart a rest from it. Right now he was headed for a gym they'd told him about at his hotel. He needed to sweat out some of his misery before he went to see her—went, without much hope, to try to persuade her back into his life.

OK, here was his right turn . . . another mostly empty, mean-looking stretch, lots more old brick four-stories . . . The sun at his back pushed his ink-black shadow in front of him. It made him feel really alone, something about his long, sharp outline stretched out on this empty street. Like, there was his soul in front of him, walking through its time on earth, its outline gradually growing crookeder with the years, till finally the body that cast it would crumble under its weight of days, and nothing would remain of him to block the light and print itself upon this planet . . .

Whoa. Where did *that* come from? Morbid! He was brooding too much, thinking too much about Kathleen lying under Guy Brandon, that purse-proud lump of meat. Kathleen not his love any more, no longer his. He'd already said goodbye to her in San Francisco. He shouldn't even *be* on this side of the continent.

The thing was, he just had to tell her what he sensed about Guy, because Monk had been getting these feelings about him, nagging, awful feelings. It wasn't just jealousy, he was sure it wasn't. He *felt* jealousy, of course. But these sensations were something else, were a squirm of dread and loathing that seemed to push itself up into his mind out of nowhere; a sense of danger, of murderous intent in the man.

And this just wasn't like him. Monk didn't *get* "feelings" about people. Feelings that seemed—bizarre though it was—to hover around him, like circling eels, and then to dart into his spine.

Be strong, fool! You'll see her soon enough. You'll tell her you're afraid for her, you'll admit you can't explain it, but that you just had to tell her face to face, to show her how urgent you felt it was.

So. For right now, get back into your body and try to sweat some of this shit out. Do some light weights, take a sauna. He wouldn't think another thought about Kathleen, until he faced her across her doorstep, her *new* doorstep, in fucking Boston.

Now he saw his destination halfway down the next block: Rainey's Gym, flaking gold-and-black letters in a half-circle across a grimy window. Looked to be a big place. Could he actually *smell* it from here? A cold, swampy whiff of old tiled showers, stained faint green with mold . . . ?

There he went again. Bizarre, these vivid feelings he was getting since stepping out into this city. And those two guys, acting like they were seeing not him, but someone really threatening. Is there some contamination in the air here? These East Coast cities, with their dark Industrial Revolution streets, and factories, had been putting complex toxins in the air for a hundred-fifty years . . .

As he crossed the street toward Rainey's, his long shadow was already across it, was rising up the front of the gym, his shadow-head sprouting from the sidewalk and gliding like Nosferatu up the bricks, up across the dusty glass . . . and there was a *face* in that shadow-head of his.

He stumbled. Stood staring. For an indelible instant it was right there, a horror: the gaping mouth a tarry hole, the jaw a hinge of naked bone, the eyes two onyx knobs whose gaze was purest hunger.

Monk stood teetering there . . . and then beheld just his shadow, his shadow pure and simple on the dusty window.

He willed his heart to stop hammering. OK. These last couple months he'd been stressed. Granted. But why should he start going bat-shit today, here in South Boston? He just *wasn't* somebody who hallucinated.

Go into the gym, for chrissake. Take a goddamn sauna. Sit there in the heat and let the sweat river down. Sweat out the poison of brooding and worrying about Kathleen.

Alas. It turned out there *was* no sauna. Rainey himself was very emphatic about it. He looked like he had to be Rainey—he was ancient and monolithic, an old Mick so mountainous that his sagging frame wholly eclipsed whatever little piece of furniture it was he sat on in his cage.

"Sauna!" he echoed Monk's courteous query. He seemed, deep in his folded face, to relish the word. "No sauna, no way, son! A *steam-room,* that's what we got! An' while I'm at it, I hafta disappointcha about station-ary bikes an ski-machines too! An we got no wine-an-froot-smoothie-bar, either! You get thirsty, there's a beer-joint down the street."

"What?" asked Monk mildly. "You don't have a Bud-machine in the locker-room?"

You could almost see in Rainey's millennially seamed face that he liked this crack. He took Monk's twenty and slid him two towels with a key on top that looked like it had been dipped in acid, or lain undersea for a generation or two. "Towels more'n two are fifty cents each—there's a stack in the locker."

It said "Locker" above two battered swing-doors at the end of a long dim hall. He glanced back on his way down, but the cage hid Rainey. Was this whole place empty? Not a sound anywhere—until the hinge of the door wheezed as he pushed it.

There were long, narrow, butt-bruising benches between banks of bat-tered lockers. It swept Monk back to high school, but the darkness and dankness here were bigger, maybe because they were so empty. The whole place felt ancient. "The locker-room of an extinct civilization," he mut-tered—and then was startled to realize there *was* another man in here, sari-ed in a towel, elbows on knees, on the far end of the bench to Monk's left.

"How's it going?" he asked. "How's the steam-room? I'm new here."

The man raised his head, and his face surprised Monk. He had a big old nose broken to a slant, and an over-large, loose mouth. The guy looked at him a moment. "You'd be new anywhere." His voice was old and gritty. "Look at you. Got another thirty good years ahead of you, with luck."

"Well . . . thanks for that encouraging thought."

The guy hung his huge head, done with talk.

Monk switched into his sweats. The void around him still felt like an archaeological dig, but one where some of the ancient inhabitants had been fossilized too, and spoke like oracles from its shadowed corners . . . He glanced at the guy as he dressed: a short, thick brute he was, dense white hair matting his chest.

Empty though this place was, it wasn't exactly quiet. There was an echoey something, as if the emptiness faintly muttered and groaned. Like some ghostly reverb of all the people who'd toiled and sweated here through the decades—hints of their vanished voices along with the smell and the breath of them . . .

There he went again. It had to be Kathleen weirding him out like this, like a big planet tearing a smaller one apart, like what Jupiter did to that planet that was now the asteroid belt. If she were just absent, that would be better. It was that her absence was *with* him: Kathleen living with Guy. All her invisible doings with him tugging and tearing at his mind.

He guessed what the weight room would be like, and smiled to find it much as he'd expected. A bunch of lift benches padded with tattered canvas, wall-racks of hand-weights, a heavy bag and two fast bags, and several of those pulley-weights fighters use to train punching-muscles. It didn't smell like sweat, though. The walls, the concrete floor, the stained ceiling—they all gave off an old stone-and-concrete scent of long endurance through East Coast winters.

Monk put a hundred pounds on the bench-press. He was lying under it, had just gripped the bar, when the door flapped open and a gaunt old black man came in. He drifted over to the wall and started wiping hand-weights with a rag. He had an expressive way of doing it, grabbing each one with contemptuous skill, wipe-wipe with the rag, tucking it back quick but with scarcely a clink, snatching the next one, wipe-wipe. . . . Meanwhile his dark narrow face lived in a much slower time. His eyes were old and dazed, his narrow jaw hung slack, and his little lips showed tobacco-stained teeth.

Monk, resting from his set, watched him, and the man caught him at it. He held Monk's eyes, but kind of absent-mindedly, as if Monk was someone he knew, but couldn't place. It irked Monk.

"You know," he said smiling, "I kind of wonder"—and he swept his eyes around this empty iron warehouse—"just how many people have *used* these things. I mean, what sweat was on em long ago must be turned to dust by now." He felt witty and sly. Maybe he was just pumped from the set. But the old man's eyes opened right up, and now you saw some glee there.

"All due respect an all," the old man answered, "but you fulla shit." His voice was deep, but hit raspy shoals, as if a shriller, more scarred man shared his body. "You know how many generations done sweat this aaarn? You can't wipe it off, you can't wipe it *outta* the metal, boy. You know you like every young man walkin! You can't *see* what you walkin through. You can't even *smell* it." His tight little lips twisted in a leer. Monk suddenly saw there was a lot of ugly laughter in this skinny old dude, in his dirty-looking bloodshot eyes. "But maybe you *can* smell it. Smell all those people come an gone in here . . . ?"

And the man came over, slowly, wiping his hands on the rag he wiped the weights with. "The thing is, m'man—you mind if I call you m'man?" Paused here, a yard or so away. Monk's "Sure" caught a little in his throat. The question seemed oddly momentous.

The man came the rest of the way over, so he towered above the bench Monk lay on, and Monk sat up not to feel so overtopped. "Thing is, m'man, you walkin anywhere, not just here, you walkin down a street you walkin by the river you walkin in a field you walkin cross a *bridge* . . . every step you take, you walkin through the *ages*. Thing to remember in this world is, you part of somethin' *big*."

The weird little sermon dazed Monk a bit. Hadn't he already been feeling something like this on the streets? How this East Coast was so much older, and how many more human bones lay under its pavements, a great jumble of them surely, cages of ribs, jawbones grinning at remembered lives . . . ? Out of his depth in all this dark echoey funk of Rainey's Gym, out of his depth on the streets where the hoods looked spooked when they looked in his eyes, where his own shadow showed him a monstrous face?

He nodded at the old man, as if comprehendingly. But then said, "Well . . . what about the steam-room? Will the Ages be in there with me? Or can I have a little time by myself in there?"

The man grinned, looked really tickled for the first time. "I *highly* recommend the steam room! It'll he'p you relax. Open your eyes."

It opened his eyes all right, because the place was a blind swamp of hot fog. But oddly, the fog felt *big*. Once he'd shut the door behind him, he had no sense of where the walls were, except that they felt a lot farther apart than they should be.

The heat was a little strange too, not frankly baking him like a good sauna, but stroking at him, touching him now here, now there, as if in the wraiths of mist there were fingers that explored him. He shuffled carefully across the slick tiles, and at last he encountered a two-tiered bench of sodden black wood slats . . . It felt cooler to his butt than he'd expected it to be.

He wasn't used to sitting in this kind of haze. The place felt huge one moment and claustrophobic the next. And then he saw someone else looking back at him.

It startled him, the opposing bench so much closer than he'd expected. Startled him too because he saw only the eyes, intent as a hawk's, and nothing else of the face regarding him. These eyes were dark, intent, and close-set eyes—perhaps, he suddenly thought, a *woman's* eyes. Their gaze focused him fiercely as a hawk's—looked *angry* too, the way hawks do.

. . . And something else. A feeling in those eyes, layers of feeling like concentric pools, anger and something else . . . it was longing, an indescribable *longing* shining there too, and grief.

Suddenly he was seized by his shoulders from behind. Someone was pulling him backwards, back and back . . . and he was *falling*.

There was no bench, was *nothing* under him, just hot fog he fell through. But fall was just half of what he did, because he also *ricocheted,* deflecting like a bullet from face after face that he knew—faces he *felt* he knew but which were none of them from his own past.

Down he plunged through foggy winds that blew in braided currents, each current a suite of faces, of touches, and tellings, and feelings, each current a thread of what *felt* like his past but which he knew was someone *else's* past . . .

Plunged zigzag through memories, a big-city life that steered vehicles down crowded streets, down freeways, that rode packed subways, that typed fast-fingered on computer keyboards, that lifted a rollicking voice in smoky, convivial bars . . .

And streaming through these days and nights, Monk understood them as the landscape of his Taker's own life, of whoever it was who had seized him, and they were streaming past because they were the path to his Taker's urgent destination.

Where was Monk's *body?* How could he be experiencing all this without it? This was precisely insanity, wasn't it? To fall into a life entirely different from the one your body was really living?

Here he was, where his abductor wanted to bring him. She was a young woman—he knew this because he was facing a mirror, and there she was in the mirror, brushing her hair. A thin, pretty, red-haired woman wearing a blue dress . . .

She was *seized* from behind by a man who was only fragmentarily reflected in the mirror she faced as he snatched her back off her feet and flung her down.

But then this man was more fully seen, seen through stars by the woman's dazed eyes, as she looked up at him from the floor where he'd thrown her. The man was holding a knife blade-down for stabbing, and looking down at her with a strange, calm impassivity, wearing a vague expression like that of someone who was just idly gazing out of a window . . . And then she saw him bringing the knife down in a blur of speed, and felt that knife driving into her chest.

Now there was brief chaos in his young woman, a spike of shock so numbing to her heart that it seemed for a long, stunned while that she dreamed, that she only dreamed the repeated stabbings that followed. After which she died, almost calmly, while her killer's face, itself still calm, hung above her looking absently down at her, as her sight darkened out.

And just before it did darken out, as Monk looked up out of her dimming eyes, it dawned on him that he *knew* this hawk-eyed killer's face.

Knew him only from a photo, but a photo vivid to him for all the brevity of the look Kathleen gave him at it: this man was Guy, her new lover.

Darkness fell on Monk like a ton of bricks, the darkness his own body returning to him all at once, the suddenly heavy meat and bone of him, enveloping him so densely for an instant that it felt like burial alive, felt as if the black mass of his regained flesh would snuff out his life like a candle.

The steam room again. He lay slack on the wet slats. Touching his will to his body seemed risky, like waking a possibly dangerous beast. With some effort, he raised his long-limbed frame back up to a seated posture. Heaved a breath of hot fog. His right hand, gripping the slats of the bench, felt something much more viscous than damp wood.

He raised his palm before his face and through the steam's pallid obscurity, saw that it was smeared with blood.

With a muffled yelp he dismounted from the bench and thrust his face to the bench he'd touched . . . and found nothing at all like blood there. Found nothing like blood on his hand either. Oh Lord, where had he just *been?*

He staggered to the steam room's heavy glass door. And as he thrust it open before him, he saw that three words had been written in the fog on its inner surface: BRING HIM HERE.

Someone must have come in while he was so strangely passed out. What the hell was *happening* to him today?

Now the locker room was completely deserted. Showering, dressing, he was jumpy as a cat at the echoes he woke all around him. Vividly felt the whole building enclosing him, as lifeless as a tomb, yet felt sure that some of those echoes were of noises not his own.

When he came out, he found Rainey still in his cage watching TV.

"Where's that older guy that works here?"

"Who knows? He comes an goes."

"That steam-room—you ever use it?"

"It's been a while."

Monk looked in the man's little flinty eyes, trying to read them. Was he laughing in there? Daring him to say something? *Did* Monk want to speak? To say that he'd just *died* in that steam-room in the body of a young woman he'd never seen before? Ask old Rainey if *he'd* ever done something like that in there?

Monk stepped out of Rainey's Gym with a shudder, like someone who shrugs off a foul old coat. Started walking again, who cared where? People he passed steered left and right of him—saw at a glance that this guy wasn't walking on the same street they were.

Many blocks later, the sun getting low now, he went in a small bar and ordered a draft beer. Not much of a drinker, he rarely went into bars. This one was . . . a relief. A middle-aged couple gave him a glance and returned to quiet talk. The bartender was the only other person here, a thin young woman with a blue-tooth, who after serving him resumed her murmured phone talk.

He found himself quite thirsty, drank the beer off in two breaths. Then sat embarrassed at his gulping. The bartender, alert within her soft conversation, came over. Almost smiled.

"Another?"

Monk's laugh was a bit croaky. "Yes, please. I was in a steam-room."

This declaration echoed ludicrously in his own ears: the opening statement of a simpleton preparing to tell her the stickiest details of his life. Now she did smile. She had a grave face and thoughtful eyes, her hair in black quills like a wet bird. "Were you at Rainey's?"

"How did you know that?"

Her smile grew. "Well, I didn't *know* of course, but it's just down the block."

He'd walked at least five miles. He laughed a bit better than he had before. "I was walking for a long time, and I must have circled back around without realizing it. I'm an out-of-towner."

"Really," she said, with some gentle irony—but then had to smile again. "I almost said, No shit, Sherlock."

He laughed. "So I *look* really . . . out of town?"

"Maybe just . . . somewhere else?"

Which took him there, back into the steamroom, but now suddenly seeing *Kathleen* there in some dark hypothetical room, with Guy lifting his knife above her.

Guy, standing back from the window a ways in the shadows of his living room, trained his field glasses down on the coffee shop across the street. There at a sidewalk table, yet again, sat Kathleen's ex, gazing up at his window.

He'd had a chance to study good old *Monk's* face for several days now. At first he'd just seen jealousy in it, that odd vacillation between anger and fear that he had grown acquainted with in other men. But now he'd begun seeing something odd in the man's look, a kind of objectivity, a musing quality there, as if the guy were weighing options. It was the look of a man who was trying to figure out *how* to do something he'd already *decided* to do.

And this was very interesting indeed.

Guy's gift for reading eyes was key to his success with women. When younger, he'd been amazed at how flagrantly people's faces declared their thoughts and feelings. It had taken him some time to realize that most people didn't see nearly so much in others' faces as he did. He remembered this dawning on him in his teens: that compared to him, most people lived in glass houses with all their motives on display.

Quite interesting. Look at the man's expression: just a hint there of self-awe, as if he couldn't quite believe his own thoughts or intentions. The man—gazing up at Guy's window—was trying to get his mind around something he hadn't contemplated before. The anxious fixity of his eyes, as if he sought to focus something almost too far off to see . . . it suddenly recalled to Guy his *own* gaze lingering in a similar way, weighing the sublime act of murder, determining for this or that prospect if it could be pulled off, gauging the optimum moment and manner of its execution.

My goodness! Could that be it? Was this man thinking of killing him?

Now here, by God, was a fascinating possibility.

Fascinating in what it implied. Many people, including discarded lovers, "wanted to kill someone" now and again, but that fleeting impulse never frightened them, because they never really believed they were going to do it.

But this Monk down here—awed and uneasy—was plainly convinced that he would. And what that meant, inescapably, was that the man knew that Guy himself was a killer—knew that Kathleen's life was in imminent danger.

How on earth could he *know* that?

Guy set about brewing himself a nice pot of dark roast. This was a solemn and an exciting moment. He had never doubted the perfection of his methods. Time had proven the absolute untraceability of the nine murders he had performed in the last seven years. Not one of them could be known to this man, or to anyone at all. How could this plodder have found him out? A college instructor, a mild, bookish type . . .

He raised the binoculars to his eyes again—but it was no field of vision he beheld. Another pair of eyes met his, magnified eyes that filled his sight. Violet-brown eyes, unmistakable eyes, for he had watched them, relished the dying light in them, as they had rolled back in death above his own strangling hands not quite three months ago. He was seeing *Sheila's* dying stare once more!

His hands ejected the binocs as if they'd turned red hot, and in his sudden backwards lurch his heels snagged in the carpet and he fell, just barely managing to break his fall with back-thrust arms.

For Guy, aggression was an inbred response to terror. Scrambling to his feet, he snatched the instrument back up. With the absurd logic of a dream, he turned their primary lenses toward himself, and saw in them—of course—only two reflections of his own face.

Except that . . . Jesus!

And he dropped the instrument again.

Because his two reflected faces showed no eyes, showed only empty black holes beneath his brows!

He stood swaying as if drunk, looking down across the street. Monk sat sipping coffee as before, but his gaze kept slanting back up to Guy's window, and damnably *knowing* glances these seemed, telling Guy that Monk knew he was there, oh yes . . .

He picked up the binocs again. Now both primary lenses had branching cracks from rim to rim, so that either lens was split into three ragged triangles. And in all six of these glass fangs, Guy's six smaller faces looked back at him *still* with black holes for eyes, but now— Oh my God now, *within* those black voids were little icy-white frecklings of stars! No mistake! All those eyes of his were filled from lid to lid with little night skies full of blazing stars!

Awe and something more than awe filled him: it was a swiftly kindling blaze of joy. He stood steadily beholding this impossible vision, and it never wavered, never flickered. He stood confronting the supernatural, placed like an omen squarely in his hands, to make of what he could.

Guy stood dazed. He had always felt the conviction that every time he killed, he thrust his strangling hands into Eternity, tore through mortality's suffocating shroud, and *exempted himself* from the fate he was inflicting.

And here now was something very much like *proof* of this! Here was a miracle of cosmic vision blazing in his sight. Fields and wheels and clusters of countless stars in the little black gulfs of his eyes! Proof that by his daring, his bold destructions of *others'* mortality, he had vaulted beyond his own, and galaxies of galaxies now blazed within his gaze.

He had felt his cosmic stature growing, unfolding its titanic limbs within an ever-widening sphere of space with every soul he crushed between his hands. When, on a midnight three months ago, he'd taken Sheila's strangled body, wrapped in sixty pounds of chain, far out into the harbor and heaved her overboard, her collision with the sea had seemed to swell his body explosively. As the deeps gulped her down, he stood towering above his tiny craft. It seemed impossible the little boat should bear his hugeness, should not sink straight to the bottom beneath his godlike stature.

His cell chirred. Kathleen. His gaze still fixed on Monk down across the street, he put a smile on his face (to put one in his voice) and said,

"Hey, Cupcake! What's up?"

"Hon, I just have to ask. I know I've brought this up before, but could you *please* call Monk? I'm texting you his cell. I'd feel so much better if you two guys could just get together for a beer or something. I mean, since he's out here now, if you could just be friends? He's really a great guy, and it would make me feel so much better!"

"Well of course *I'm* amenable! I'll do it right now, Cupcake. Call you later."

Guy watched Monk pull out his phone. If he saw his caller's I.D. on his display he gave no sign of it—leaned back and gazed down the street as he answered: "Hello?"

"Hi, Monk. Guy here."

"Hey, how you doing?"—tone cordial, but still no slightest bodily acknowledgment that they were right across the street from each other. The man's relaxed slouch in his chair seemed perfectly natural. He might have been talking to someone miles away.

"Well, I'm doing fine, thanks. You know, Kathleen's made a suggestion which I think is actually pretty good. She thinks you and I should meet somewhere. Talk things out a bit. She'd like us all to be friends, and frankly, so would I."

Monk sat there, smiling slightly and nodding, gazing at the cerulean sky. He seemed to be weighing this proposition. Something strange about his expression in that moment—a touch of fascination? Unease? He smiled again. "There's an old gym up the street. Rainey's? Why don't we meet there around six? It won't be crowded."

"Deserted's more like it—I know the place. I think that's a good idea. Six then."

Guy stood looking at the shabby façade of Rainey's Gym from across the street. He was smiling very faintly at himself. In ten or fifteen minutes he would be sitting naked next to Monk in a welter of steam, almost as if *they* were intimates.

Ah! Mon Dieu! If anything was a *danse macabre,* it was the Mating Game, was it not? Would this spurious intimacy arouse him to kill Monk as well as his ex? No—he lacked the homo-erotic gene. Still, the dark comedy of such an act drew him.

Like the amateur he was at power-games, Monk was here first. He stood up from an armchair in the gym lobby to greet Guy and was the first to extend his hand . . .

But when their hands were clasped, Guy felt directly, like electric contact from Monk's eyes, that this man *knew* him for a killer. It quite astonished him. So searing was his spinal certainty that Guy performed a frantic inner scan of seven decaying female corpses moldering in deep earth, or rolling bones—all skinless now—on silty seafloors up and down this coast . . . All those deaths *obliterated.* All those obliterations *buried* in the earth or the sea, *buried* in the years, eternally masked from human eyes . . .

"I got you a locker right next to mine," Monk told him. He smiled saying this, but his eyes were almost somber, dreamy. "I bought you some shorts too—most people don't like to press their flesh to the sweat-soaked benches."

Monk stripped quickly—had his shorts on under his jeans. He sat smiling at Guy as he caught up, and then led him to the foggy door of glass and chrome. He paused before it, gazing at the blind gray glass. His fixity in this moment struck Guy; the man seemed to Guy to scan the foggy glass like a text.

"You first," Monk smiled. "Sit on the highest bench, the steam rises. I've sweated once today—I'm sitting lower down."

They took their seats within the cottony air. The vapor drenched their pores and probed them like hot tiny tongues. Its wet heat whispered— faint, far exhalations seemed to stir its foggy hush. Guy felt a shiftiness within this cottony damp, like vague vaporous brutes stirring in their misty den. When Monk's voice came again, it seemed strangely far away.

"Do you know who I saw in here a few days ago?"

"Who?"

"A skinny pretty little redhead. You know what she was doing?"

"What?" The word came out harsher than Guy meant it to.

"She was dying of multiple stab wounds."

"What the fuck are you talking about?" It was like tripping in the dark and falling down a short flight of stairs, the way Guy felt these words come snarling out of him. It seemed his guilt, all sticky with blood, jumped right out with the words.

"Well, it only stands to reason she was dying. You were stabbing and stabbing and stabbing her in the chest. It would just stand to reason she was dying, wouldn't it?"

The narrow planks that formed the inner walls of the steam-room were three inches wide. One of these directly behind Guy emitted a crack as sharp as a gunshot, and its upper half sprang out from the wall just as Guy jumped to his feet in shock at the noise, impaling his back on the down-angled wooden blade. It slid in between his back ribs and seven inches deep into his lung.

Monk leapt backwards in mindless reflex from this brute material assault as Guy writhed, screaming in a whisper, pinned like a bug from behind. The sprung plank left a narrow black void in the carpentered wall, and out of that slot of darkness thrust two clusters of black roots.

No! Thrust *two skeletal hands of blackly mummied flesh on knobby bone.*

These corpse-hands gripped and pulled, and two great sections of the steam-room's wall buckled outward with a shriek of snapping lumber. Buckled outwards and fled in fragments into an absolute and empty blackness that was thus revealed.

Then those same hands of bone and leather seized both of Guy's shoulders and hauled him howling after into the outer dark.

The buckled walls groaned and sprang back in place. The one shattered plank leaked a scent of ice and putrescence into the room for six, seven heartbeats more, and then the smell of steam and harmless human funk again prevailed.

Monk looked about the little wooden chamber. "Are you still here?" he asked the emptiness. "Are you . . . avenged?" He could not know if he was heard, or if he was, by what. He spoke to what he *thought* she was, groping for exactly what he wanted to tell her.

"I thank you. You've saved someone dear to me. If you can find some comfort from me—some kind of . . . *company*—I give it gladly."

Was that the lightest *touch* he felt against his cheek?

Or did he just want it to be?

The Autopsy

D r. Winters stepped out of the tiny Greyhound station and into the midnight street that smelled of pines. The station's window showed the only light, save for a luminous clockface several doors down and a little neon beer logo two blocks farther on. He could hear a river. It ran deep in a gorge west of town, but the town was only a few streets wide and a mile or so long, and the current's blurred roar was distinct, like the noise of a ghost river running between the banks of dark shop windows. When he had walked a short distance, Dr. Winters set his suitcase down, pocketed his hands, and looked at the stars—thick as cobblestones in the black gulf.

"A mountain hamlet—a mining town," he said. "Stars. No moon. We are in Bailey."

He was talking to his cancer. It was in his stomach. Since learning of it, he had developed this habit of wry communion with it. He meant to show courtesy to this uninvited guest, Death. It would not find him churlish, for that would make its victory absolute. Except, of course, that its victory would *be* absolute, with or without his ironies.

He picked up his suitcase and walked on. The starlight made faint mirrors of the windows' blackness and showed him the man who passed: lizard-lean, white-haired (at fifty-seven), a man traveling on death's business, carrying his own death in him, and even bearing death's wardrobe in his suitcase. For this was filled—aside from his medical kit and some scant necessities—with mortuary bags. The sheriff had told him on the phone of the improvisations that presently enveloped the corpses, and so the doctor had packed these, laying them in his case with bitter amusement, checking the last one's breadth against his chest before the mirror, as a woman will gauge a dress before donning it, and telling his cancer:

"Oh, yes, that's plenty roomy enough for both of us!"

The case was heavy, and he stopped frequently to rest and scan the sky. What a night's work to do, probing pungent, soulless filth, eyes earthward, beneath such a ceiling of stars! It had taken five days to dig the ten men out. The autumnal equinox had passed, but the weather here had been uniformly hot. And warmer still, no doubt, so deep in the earth.

He entered the courthouse by a side door. His heels knocked on the linoleum corridor. A door at the end of it, on which was lettered NATE CRAVEN, COUNTY SHERIFF, opened well before he reached it, and his friend stepped out to meet him.

"Dammit, Carl, you're *still* so thin they could use you for a whip. Gimme that. You're in too good a shape already. You don't need the exercise."

The case hung weightless from the sheriff's hand, imparting no tilt at all to his bull shoulders. Despite his implied self-derogation, he was only moderately paunched for a man his age and size. He had a rough-hewn face, and the bulk of brow, nose, and jaw made his greenish eyes look small until one engaged them and felt the snap and penetration of their intelligence. In the office he half filled two cups from a coffee urn and topped both off with bourbon from a bottle in his desk. When they had finished these, they had finished trading news of mutual friends. The sheriff mixed another round and sipped from his, in a silence clearly prefatory to the work at hand.

"They talk about rough justice," he said. "I've sure seen it now. One of those . . . patients of yours that you'll be working on? He was a killer. Christ, 'killer' doesn't half say it. A killer's the least of what he was. The blast killing *him,* that was the justice part. Those other nine, they were the rough. And it just galls the hell out of me, Carl! If that kiss-ass boss of yours has his way, the rough won't even stop with their being dead! There won't even be any compensation for their survivors! Tell me—has he broke his back yet? I mean, touching his toes for Fordham Mutual?"

"You refer, I take it, to the estimable Coroner Waddleton of Fordham County." Dr. Winters paused to sip his drink. With a delicate flaring of his nostrils he communicated all the disgust, contempt, and amusement he had felt in his four years as pathologist in Waddleton's office. The sheriff laughed.

"Clear pictures seldom emerge from anything the coroner says," the doctor continued. "He took your name in vain. Vigorously and repeatedly. These expressions formed his opening remarks. He then developed the theme of our office's strict responsibility to the letter of the law, and of the workmen's compensation law in particular. Death benefits accrue only to the dependents of decedents whose deaths arise *out of the course of* their employment, not merely *in* the course of it. Victims of a maniacal assault, though they die on the job, are by no means necessarily compensable under the law. We then contemplated the tragic injustice of an insurance company—*any* insurance company—having to pay benefits to unentitled persons, solely through the laxity and incompetence of investigating officers. Your name came up again, and Coroner Waddleton subjected it to further abuse. Fordham Mutual, campaign contributor or not, is certainly a major insurance company and is therefore entitled to the same fair treatment that all such companies deserve."

Craven uttered a bark of wrathful mirth and spat expertly into his wastebasket. "Ah, the impartial public servant! What's seven widows and sixteen dependent children, next to Fordham Mutual?" He drained his cup and sighed. "I'll tell you what, Carl. We've been five days digging those men out and the last two days sifting half that mountain for explosive traces, with those insurance investigators hanging on our elbows, and the most they could say was that there was 'strong presumptive evidence' of a bomb. Well, I don't budge for that because I don't have to. Waddleton can shove his 'extraordinary circumstances.' If you don't find anything in those bodies, then that's all the autopsy there is to it, and they get buried right here where their families want 'em."

The doctor was smiling at his friend. He finished his cup and spoke with his previous wry detachment, as if the sheriff had not interrupted his narrative.

"The honorable coroner then spoke with remarkable volubility on the subject of Autopsy Consent forms and the malicious subversion of private citizens by vested officers of the law. He had, as it happened, a sheaf of such forms on his desk, all signed, all with a rider clause typed in above the signatures. A cogent paragraph. It had, among its other qualities, the property of turning the coroner's face purple when he read it aloud. He read it aloud to me three times. It appeared that the survivors' consent was contingent on two conditions: that the autopsy be performed *in loco mortis,* that is to say in Bailey, and that only if the coroner's pathologist found concrete evidence of homicide should the decedents be subject either to removal from Bailey or to further necropsy. It was well written. I remember wondering who wrote it."

The sheriff nodded musingly. He took Dr. Winters's empty cup, set it by his own, filled both two-thirds with bourbon, and added a splash of coffee to the doctor's. The two friends exchanged a level stare, rather like poker players in the clinch. The sheriff regarded his cup, sipped from it.

"*In loco mortis.* What-all does that mean exactly?"

"'In the place of death.'"

"Oh. Freshen that up for you?"

"I've just started it, thank you."

Both men laughed, paused, and laughed again, some might have said immoderately.

"He all but told me that I *had* to find something to compel a second autopsy," the doctor said at length. "He would have sold his soul—or taken out a second mortgage on it—for a mobile X-ray unit. He's right, of course. If those bodies have trapped any bomb fragments, that would be the surest and quickest way of finding them. It still amazes me your Dr. Parsons could let his X-ray go unfixed for so long."

"He sets bones, stitches wounds, writes prescriptions, and sends anything tricky down the mountain. Just barely manages that. Drunks don't get much done."

"He's gotten that bad?"

"He hangs on and no more. Waddleton was right there, not deputizing him pathologist. I doubt he could find a cannonball in a dead rat. I wouldn't say it where it could hurt him, as long as he's still managing, but everyone here knows it. His patients sort of look after *him* half the time. But Waddleton would have sent you, no matter who was here. Nothing but his best for party contributors like Fordham Mutual."

The doctor looked at his hands and shrugged. "So. There's a killer in the batch. Was there a bomb?"

Slowly the sheriff planted his elbows on the desk and pressed his hands against his temples, as if the question had raised a turbulence of memories. For the first time the doctor—half hearkening throughout to the never-quite-muted stirrings of the death within him—saw his friend's exhaustion: the tremor of hand, the bruised look under the eyes.

"When I've told you what we have, I guess you'll end up assuming what I do about it. But I think assuming is as far as any of us will get with this one. It's one of those nightmare specials, Carl. The ones no one ever does get to the bottom of.

"All right, then. About two months ago, we had a man disappear— Ronald Hanley. Mine worker, rock-steady, family man. He didn't come home one night, and we never found a trace of him. OK, that happens sometimes. About a week later, the lady that ran the laundromat, Sharon Starker, *she* disappeared, no trace. We got edgy then. I made an announcement on the local radio about a possible weirdo at large, spelled out special precautions everybody should take. We put both our squad cars on the night beat, and by day we set to work knocking on every door in town collecting alibis for the two times of disappearance.

"No good. Maybe you're fooled by this uniform and think I'm a law officer, protector of the people, and all that? A natural mistake. A lot of people were fooled. In less than seven weeks, six people vanished, just like that. Me and my deputies might as well have stayed in bed round the clock, for all the good we did." The sheriff drained his cup.

"Anyway, at last we got lucky. Don't get me wrong now. We didn't go all hog-wild and actually prevent a crime or anything. But we *did* find a body—except it wasn't the body of any of the seven people that had disappeared. We'd taken to combing the woods nearest town, with temporary deputies from the miners to help. Well, one of those boys was out there with us last week. It was hot—like it's been for a while now—and it was real quiet. He heard this buzzing noise and looked around for it, and he saw a beeswarm up in the crotch of a tree. Except he was smart enough to know that that's not usual around here—beehives. So it wasn't bees. It was bluebottle flies, a goddamned big cloud of them, all over a bundle that was wrapped in a tarp."

The sheriff studied his knuckles. He had, in his eventful life, occasionally met men literate enough to understand his last name and rash enough to be openly amused by it, and the knuckles—scarred knobs—were eloquent of his reactions. He looked back into his old friend's eyes.

"We got that thing down and unwrapped it. Billy Lee Davis, one of my deputies, he was in Viet Nam, been near some bad, bad things and held on. Billy Lee blew his lunch all over the ground when we unwrapped that thing. It was a man. Some of a man. We knew he'd stood six-two because all the bones were there, and he'd probably weighed between two fifteen and two twenty-five, but he folded up no bigger than a big-size laundry package. Still had his face, both shoulders, and the left arm, but all the rest was clean. It wasn't animal work. It was knife work, all the edges neat as butcher cuts. Except butchered meat, even when you drain it all you can, will bleed a good deal afterwards, and there wasn't one goddamned drop of blood on the tarp, nor in that meat. It was just as pale as fish meat."

Deep in his body's center, the doctor's cancer touched him. Not a ravening attack—it sank one fang of pain, questioningly, into new untasted flesh, probing the scope for its appetite there. He disguised his tremor with a shake of the head.

"A cache, then."

The sheriff nodded. "Like you might keep a pot roast in the icebox for making lunches. I took some pictures of his face, then we put him back and erased our traces. Two of the miners I'd deputized did a lot of hunting, were woods-smart. So I left them on the first watch. We worked out positions and cover for them, and drove back.

"We got right on tracing him, sent out descriptions to every town within a hundred miles. He was no one I'd ever seen in Bailey, nor anyone else either, it began to look like, after we'd combed the town all day with the photos.

"Then, out of the blue, Billy Lee Davis smacks himself on the forehead and says, 'Sheriff, *I* seen this man somewhere in town, and not long ago!'

"He'd been shook all day since throwing up, and then all of a sudden he just snapped to. Was dead sure. Except he couldn't remember where or when. We went over and over it, and he tried and tried. It got to where I wanted to grab him by the ankles and hang him upside down and shake him till it dropped out of him. But it was no damn use. Just after dark we went back to that tree—we'd worked out a place to hide the cars and a route to it through the woods. When we were close, we walkie-talkied the men we'd left for an all-clear to come up. No answer at all. And when we got there, all that was left of our trap was the tree. No body, no tarp, no Special Assistant Deputies. Nothing."

This time Dr. Winters poured the coffee and bourbon. "Too much coffee," the sheriff muttered, but drank anyway. "Part of me wanted to chew nails and break necks. And part of me was scared shitless. When we got back, I got on the radio station again and made an emergency broadcast and then had the man at the station rebroadcast it every hour. Told everyone to do everything in groups of three, to stay together at night in threes at least, to go out little as possible, keep armed and keep checking up on each other. It had such a damn-fool sound to it, but just pairing-up was no protection if half of one of those pairs was the killer. I sent our corpse's picture out statewide, I deputized more men and put them on the streets to beef up the night patrol.

"It was next morning that things broke. The sheriff of Rakehell called—he's over in the next county. He said our corpse looked a lot like a man named Abel Dougherty, a mill-hand with Con Wood over there. I left Billy Lee in charge and drove right out.

"This Dougherty had a cripple older sister he always checked back to by phone whenever he left town for long, a habit no one knew about, probably embarrassed him. Sheriff Peck there only found out about it when the woman called him, said her brother'd been four days gone for vacation and not rung her once. He'd hardly had her report for an hour when he got the picture I sent out, and recognized it. And *I* hadn't been in his office more than ten minutes when Billy Lee called me there. He'd remembered.

"When he'd seen Dougherty was the Sunday night three days before we found him. Where he'd seen him was the Trucker's Tavern outside the north end of town. The man had made a stir by being jolly drunk and latching onto a miner who was drinking there, man named Joe Allen, who'd started at the mine about two months back. Dougherty kept telling him that he wasn't Joe Allen, but Dougherty's old buddy named Sykes that had worked with him at Con Wood for a coon's age, and what the hell kind of joke was this, come have a beer old buddy and tell me why you took off so sudden and what the hell you been doing with yourself.

"Allen took it laughing. Dougherty'd clap him on the shoulder, Allen'd clap him right back and make every kind of joke about it, say, 'Give this man another beer, I'm standing in for a long-lost friend of his.' Dougherty was so big and loud and stubborn, Billy Lee was worried about a fight starting, and he wasn't the only one worried. But this Joe Allen was a natural good ol' boy, handled it perfect. We'd checked him out weeks back along with everyone else, and he was real popular with the other miners. Finally Dougherty swore he was going to take him on to another bar to help celebrate the vacation Dougherty was starting out on. Joe Allen got up grinning, said goddamn it, he couldn't accommodate Dougherty by being this fellow Sykes, but he could sure as hell have a glass with any serious drinking man that was treating. He went out with him, and gave everyone a wink as he left, to the general satisfaction of the audience."

Craven paused. Dr. Winters met his eyes and knew his thought, two images: the jolly wink that roused the room to laughter, and the thing in the tarp aboil with bright blue flies.

"It was plain enough for me," the sheriff said. "I told Billy Lee to search Allen's room at the Skettles' boardinghouse and then go straight to the mine and take him. We could fine-polish things once we had him. Since I was already in Rakehell, I saw to some of the loose ends before I started back. I went with Sheriff Peck down to Con Wood, and we found a picture of Eddie Sykes in the personnel files. I'd seen Joe Allen often enough, and it was his picture in that file.

"We found out Sykes had lived alone, was an on-again, off-again worker, private in his comings and goings, and hadn't been around for a while. But one of the sawyers there could be pretty sure of when Sykes left Rakehell because he'd gone to Sykes's cabin the morning after a big meteor shower they had out there about nine weeks back, since some thought the shower might have reached the ground, and not far from Sykes's side of the mountain. He wasn't in that morning, and the sawyer hadn't seen him since.

"After all those weeks, it was sewed up just like that. Within another hour I was almost back in Bailey, had the pedal to the metal, and was barely three miles out of town, when it all blew to shit. I *heard* it blow, I was that close to collaring him. I tell you, Carl, I felt . . . like a *bullet.* I was going to rip right through this Sykes, this goddamned cannibal monster . . .

"We had to reconstruct what happened. Billy Lee got impatient and went after him alone, but luckily he radioed Travis—my other deputy—first. Travis was on the mountain dragnetting around that tree for clues, but he happened to be near his car when Billy Lee called him. He said he'd just been through Allen's room and had got something really odd. It was a sphere, half again big as a basketball, heavy, made of something that wasn't metal or glass but was a little like both. He could half see into it, and it looked to be full of some kind of circuitry and components. He hadn't found anything else unusual. He was going to take this thing along with him, and go after Allen now. He told Travis to get up to the mine for backup. He'd be there first and should already have Allen by the time Travis arrived.

"Tierney, the shift boss up there, had an assistant that told us the rest. Billy Lee parked behind the offices where the men in the yard wouldn't see the car. He went upstairs to arrange the arrest with Tierney. They got half a dozen men together. Just as they came out of the building, they saw Allen take off running from the squad car. He had the sphere under his arm.

"The whole compound's fenced in, and Tierney'd already phoned to have all the gates shut. Allen zigged and zagged some but caught on quick to the trap. The sphere slowed him, but he still had a good lead. He hesitated a minute and then ran straight for the main shaft. A cage was just going down with a crew, and he risked every bone in him jumping down after it, but he got safe on top. By the time they got to the switches, the cage was down to the second level, and Allen and the crew had got out. Tierney got it back up. Billy Lee ordered the rest back to get weapons and follow, and him and Tierney rode the cage right back down. And about two minutes later half the goddamned mine blew up."

The sheriff stopped as if cut off, his lips parted to say more, his eyes registering for perhaps the hundredth time his amazement that there was no more, that the weeks of death and mystification ended here, with this split-second recapitulation: more death, more answerless dark, sealing all.

"Nate."

"What."

"Wrap it up and go to bed. I don't need your help. You're dead on your feet."

"I'm not on my feet. And I'm coming along."

"Give me a picture of the victims' position relative to the blast. I'm going to work, and you're going to bed."

The sheriff shook his head absently. "They're mining in shrinkage stopes. The adits—levels—branch off lateral from the vertical shaft. From one level they hollow out overhand up to the one above. Scoop out big chambers and let most of the broken rock stay inside so they can stand on the heaps to cut the ceiling higher. They leave sections of support wall between stopes, and those men were buried several stopes in from the shaft. The cave-in killed *them.* The mountain just folded them up in their own hill of tailings. No kind of fragments reached them. I'm dead sure. The only ones they *found* were of some standard charges that the main blast set off, and those didn't even get close. The big one blew out where the adit joined the shaft, right where, and right when, Billy Lee and Tierney got out of the cage. And there is *nothing* left there, Carl. No sphere, no cage, no Tierney, no Billy Lee Davis. Just rock blown fine as flour."

Dr. Winters nodded and, after a moment, stood up.

"Come on, Nate. I've got to get started. I'll be lucky to have even a few of them done before morning. Drop me off and go to sleep, till then at least. You'll still be there to witness most of the work."

The sheriff rose, took up the doctor's suitcase, and led him out of the office without a word, concession in his silence.

The patrol car was behind the building. The doctor saw a crueller beauty in the stars than he had an hour before. They got in, and Craven swung them out onto the empty street. The doctor opened the window and hearkened, but the motor's surge drowned out the river sound. Before the thrust of their headlights, ranks of old-fashioned parking meters sprouted shadows tall across the sidewalks, shadows that shrank and were cut down by the lights' passage. The sheriff said:

"All those extra dead. For nothing! Not even to . . . *feed* him! If it was a bomb, and he made it, he'd know how powerful it was. He wouldn't try some stupid escape stunt with it. And how did he even know that globe was there? We worked it out that Allen was just ending a shift, but he wasn't even up out of the ground before Billy Lee'd parked out of sight from the shaft."

"Let it rest, Nate. I want to hear more, but after you've slept. I know you. All the photos will be there, and the report complete, all the evidence neatly boxed and carefully described. When I've looked things over, I'll know exactly how to proceed by myself."

Bailey had neither hospital nor morgue, and the bodies were in a defunct ice-plant on the edge of town. A generator had been brought down from the mine, lighting improvised, and the refrigeration system reactivated. Dr. Parsons's office, and the tiny examining room that served the sheriff's station in place of a morgue, had furnished this makeshift with all the equipment that Dr. Winters would need beyond what he carried with him. A quarter-mile outside the main body of the town, they drew up to it. Tree-flanked, unneighbored by any other structure, it was a double building; the smaller half—the office—was illuminated. The bodies would be in the big windowless refrigerator segment. Craven pulled up beside a second squad car parked near the office door. A short rake-thin man wearing a large white Stetson got out of the car and came over. Craven rolled down his window.

"Trav. This here's Dr. Winters."

"'Lo, Nate. Dr. Winters. Everything's shipshape inside. Felt more comfortable out here. Last of those newshounds left two hours ago."

"They sure do hang on. You take off now, Trav. Get some sleep and be back at sunup. What temperature we getting?"

The pale Stetson, far clearer in the starlight than the shadowface beneath it, wagged dubiously. "Thirty-six. She won't get lower—some kind of leak."

"That should be cold enough," the doctor said.

Travis drove off, and the sheriff unlocked the padlock on the office door. Waiting behind him, Dr. Winters heard the river again—a cold balm, a whisper of freedom—and overlying this, the stutter and soft snarl of the generator behind the building, a gnawing, remorseless sound that somehow fed the obscure anguish that the other soothed. They went in.

The preparations had been thoughtful and complete. "You can wheel 'em out of the fridge on this and do the examining in here," the sheriff said, indicating a table and a gurney. "You should find all the gear you need on this big table here, and you can write up your reports on that desk. The phone's not hooked up—there's a pay phone at the last gas station if you have to call me."

The doctor nodded, checking over the material on the larger table: scalpels, postmortem and cartilage knives, intestine scissors, rib shears, forceps, probes, mallet and chisels, a blade saw and electric bone saw, scale, jars for specimens, needles and suture, sterilizer, gloves . . . Beside this array were a few boxes and envelopes with descriptive sheets attached, containing the photographs and such evidentiary objects as had been found associated with the bodies.

"Excellent," he muttered.

"The overhead light's fluorescent, full spectrum or whatever they call it. Better for colors. There's a pint of decent bourbon in that top desk drawer. Ready to look at 'em?"

"Yes."

The sheriff unbarred and slid back the big metal door to the refrigeration chamber. Icy tainted air boiled out of the doorway. The light within was dimmer than that provided in the office—a yellow gloom wherein ten oblong heaps lay on trestles.

The two stood silent for a time, their stillness a kind of unpremeditated homage paid the eternal mystery at its threshold. As if the cold room were in fact a shrine, the doctor found a peculiar awe in the row of veiled forms. The awful unison of their dying, the titan's grave that had been made for them, conferred on them a stern authority, Death's Chosen Ones. His stomach hurt, and he found he had his hand pressed to his abdomen. He glanced at Craven and was relieved to see that his friend, staring wearily at the bodies, had missed the gesture.

"Nate. Help me uncover them."

Starting at opposite ends of the row, they stripped the tarps off and piled them in a corner. Both were brusque now, not pausing over the revelation of the swelled, pulpy faces—most three-lipped with the gaseous burgeoning of their tongues—and the fat, livid hands sprouting from the filthy sleeves. But at one of the bodies Craven stopped. The doctor saw him look, and his mouth twist. Then he flung the tarp on the heap and moved to the next trestle.

When they came out, Dr. Winters took out the bottle and glasses Craven had put in the desk, and they had a drink together. The sheriff made as if he would speak, but shook his head and sighed.

"I *will* get some sleep, Carl. I'm getting crazy thoughts with this thing." The doctor wanted to ask those thoughts. Instead he laid a hand on his friend's shoulder.

"Go home, Sheriff Craven. Take off the badge and lie down. The dead won't run off on you. We'll all still be here in the morning."

When the sound of the patrol car faded, the doctor stood listening to the generator's growl and the silence of the dead, resurgent now. Both the sound and the silence seemed to mock him. The afterecho of his last words made him uneasy. He said to his cancer:

"What about it, dear colleague? We *will* still be here tomorrow? All of us?"

He smiled, but felt an odd discomfort, as if he had ventured a jest in company and roused a hostile silence. He went to the refrigerator door, rolled it back, and viewed the corpses in their ordered rank, with their strange tribunal air. "What, sirs?" he murmured. "Do you judge me? Just who is to examine whom tonight, if I may ask?"

He went back into the office, where his first step was to examine the photographs made by the sheriff in order to see how the dead had lain at their uncovering. The earth had seized them with terrible suddenness. Some crouched, some partly stood, others sprawled in crazy free-fall postures. Each successive photo showed more of the jumble as the shovels continued their work between shots. The doctor studied them closely, noting the identifications inked on the bodies as they came completely into view.

One man, Roger Willet, had died some yards from the main cluster. It appeared he had just straggled into the stope from the adit at the moment of the explosion. He should thus have received, more directly than any of the others, the shock waves of the blast. If bomb fragments were to be found in any of the corpses, Mr. Willet's seemed likeliest to contain them. Dr. Winters pulled on a pair of surgical gloves.

Willet lay at one end of the line of trestles. He wore a thermal shirt and overalls that were strikingly new beneath the filth of burial. Their tough fabrics jarred with the fabric of his flesh—blue, swollen, seeming easily torn or burst, like ripe fruit. In life Willet had grease-combed his hair. Now it was a sculpture of dust, spikes and whorls shaped by the head's last grindings against the mountain that clenched it.

Rigor had come and gone—Willet rolled laxly onto the gurney. As the doctor wheeled him past the others, he felt a slight self-consciousness. The sense of some judgment flowing from the dead assembly—unlike most such vagrant fantasies—had an odd tenacity in him. This stubborn unease began to irritate him with himself, and he moved more briskly.

He put Willet on the examining table and cut the clothes off him with shears, storing the pieces in an evidence box. The overalls were soiled with agonal waste expulsions. The doctor stared a moment with unwilling pity at his naked subject.

"You won't ride down to Fordham in any case," he said to the corpse. "Not unless I find something pretty damned obvious." He pulled his gloves tighter and arranged his implements.

Waddleton had said more to him than he had reported to the sheriff. The doctor was to find, and forcefully to record that he had found, strong "indications" absolutely requiring the decedents' removal to Fordham for X-ray and an exhaustive second postmortem. The doctor's continued employment with the Coroner's Office depended entirely on his compliance in this. He had received this stipulation with a silence Waddleton had not thought it necessary to break. His present resolution was all but made at that moment. Let the obvious be taken as such. If the others showed as plainly as Willet did the external signs of death by asphyxiation, they would receive no more than a thorough external exam. Willet he would examine internally as well, merely to establish in depth for this one what should appear obvious in all. Otherwise, only when the external exam revealed a clearly anomalous feature—and clear and suggestive it must be— would he look deeper.

He rinsed the caked hair in a basin, poured the sediment into a flask and labeled it. Starting with the scalp, he began a minute scrutiny of the body's surfaces, recording his observations as he went.

The characteristic signs of asphyxial death were evident, despite the complicating effects of autolysis and putrefaction. The eyeballs' bulge and the tongue's protrusion were, by now, as much due to gas pressure as to the mode of death, but the latter organ was clamped between locked teeth, leaving little doubt as to that mode. The coloration of degenerative change—a greenish-yellow tint, a darkening and mapping-out of superficial veins— was marked, but not sufficient to obscure the blue of cyanosis on the face and neck, nor the pinpoint hemorrhages freckling neck, chest, and shoulders. From the mouth and nose the doctor scraped matter he was confident was the blood-tinged mucous typically ejected in the airless agony.

He began to find a kind of comedy in his work. What a buffoon death made of a man! A blue pop-eyed three-lipped thing. And there was himself, his curious solicitous intimacy with this clownish carrion. Excuse me, Mr. Willet, while I probe this laceration. What do you feel when I do this? Nothing? Nothing at all? Fine, now what about these nails? Split them clawing at the earth, did you? Yes. A nice bloodblister under this thumbnail, I see—got it on the job a few days before your accident, no doubt? Remarkable calluses here, still quite tough . . .

The doctor looked for an unanalytic moment at the hands—puffed dark paws, gestureless, having renounced all touch and grasp. He felt the wastage of the man concentrated in the hands. The painful futility of the body's fine articulation when it is seen in death—this poignancy he had long learned not to acknowledge when he worked. But now he let it move him a little. This Roger Willet, plodding to his work one afternoon, had suddenly been scrapped, crushed to a nonfunctional heap of perishable materials. It simply happened that his life had chanced to move too close to the passage of a more powerful life, one of those inexorable and hungry lives that leave human wreckage—known or undiscovered—in their wakes. Bad luck, Mr. Willet. Naturally, we feel very sorry about this. But this Joe Allen, your co-worker. Apparently he was some sort of . . . cannibal. It's complicated. We don't understand it all. But the fact is we have to dismantle you now to a certain extent. There's really no hope of your using these parts of yourself again, I'm afraid. Ready now?

The doctor proceeded to the internal exam with a vague eagerness for Willet's fragmentation, for the disarticulation of that sadness in his natural form. He grasped Willet by the jaw and took up the postmortem knife. He sank its point beneath the chin and began the long, gently sawing incision that opened Willet from throat to groin.

In the painstaking separation of the body's laminae Dr. Winters found absorption and pleasure. And yet throughout he felt, marginal but insistent, the movement of a stream of irrelevant images. These were of the building that contained him, and of the night containing it. As from outside, he saw the plant—bleached planks, iron roofing—and the trees crowding it, all in starlight, a ghost-town image. And he saw the refrigerator vault beyond the wall as from within, feeling the stillness of murdered men in a cold yellow light. And at length a question formed itself, darting in and out of the weave of his concentration as the images did: Why did he still feel, like some stir of the air, that sense of mute vigilance surrounding his action, furtively touching his nerves with its inquiry as he worked? He shrugged, overtly angry now. Who else was attending but Death? Wasn't he Death's hireling, and this Death's place? Then let the master look on.

Peeling back Willet's cover of hemorrhage-stippled skin, Dr. Winters read the corpse with an increasing dispassion, a mortuary text. He confined his inspection to the lungs and mediastinum and found there unequivocal testimony to Willet's asphyxial death. The pleurae of the lungs exhibited the expected ecchymoses—bruised spots in the glassy enveloping membrane. Beneath, the polyhedral surface lobules of the lungs themselves were bubbled and blistered—the expected interstitial emphysema. The lungs, on section, were intensely and bloodily congested. The left half of the heart he found contracted and empty, while the right was overdistended and engorged with dark blood, as were the large veins of the upper mediastinum. It was a classic picture of death by suffocation, and at length the doctor, with needle and suture, closed up the text again.

He returned the corpse to the gurney and draped one of his mortuary bags over it in the manner of a shroud. When he had help in the morning, he would weigh the bodies on a platform scale the office contained and afterward bag them properly. He came to the refrigerator door, and hesitated. He stared at the door, not moving, not understanding why.

Run. Get out. Now.

The thought was his own, but it came to him so urgently he turned around as if someone behind him had spoken. Across the room a thin man in smock and gloves, his eyes shadows, glared at the doctor from the black windows. Behind the man was a shrouded cart, behind that, a wide metal door.

Quietly, wonderingly, the doctor asked, "Run from what?" The eyeless man in the glass was still half-crouched, afraid.

Then, a moment later, the man straightened, threw back his head, and laughed. The doctor walked to the desk and sat down shoulder to shoulder with him. He pulled out the bottle and they had a drink together, regarding each other with identical bemused smiles. Then the doctor said, "Let me pour you another. You need it, old fellow. It makes a man himself again."

Nevertheless his reentry of the vault was difficult, toilsome, each step seeming to require a new summoning of the will to move. In the freezing half-light all movement felt like defiance. His body lagged behind his craving to be quick, to be done with this molestation of the gathered dead.

He returned Willet to his pallet and took his neighbor. The name on the tag wired to his boot was Ed Moses. Dr. Winters wheeled him back to the office and closed the big door behind him.

With Moses his work gained momentum. He expected to perform no further internal necropsies. He thought of his employer, rejoicing now in his seeming-submission to Waddleton's ultimatum. The impact would be dire. He pictured the coroner in shock, a sheaf of pathologist's reports in one hand, and smiled.

Waddleton could probably make a plausible case for incomplete examination. Still, a pathologist's discretionary powers were not well defined. Many good ones would approve the adequacy of the doctor's method, given his working conditions. The inevitable litigation with a coalition of compensation claimants would be strenuous and protracted. Win or lose, Waddleton's venal devotion to the insurance company's interest would be abundantly displayed. Further, immediately on his dismissal the doctor would formally disclose its occult cause to the press. A libel action would ensue that he would have as little cause to fear as he had to fear his firing. Both his savings and the lawsuit would long outlast his life.

Externally, Ed Moses exhibited a condition as typically asphyxial as Willet's had been, with no slightest mark of fragment entry. The doctor finished his report and returned Moses to the vault, his movements brisk and precise. His unease was all but gone. That queasy stirring of the air— had he really felt it? It had been, perhaps, some new reverberation of the death at work in him, a psychic shudder of response to the cancer's stealthy probing for his life. He brought out the body next to Moses in the line.

Walter Lou Jackson was big, six feet two inches from heel to crown, and would surely weigh out at more than two hundred pounds. He had writhed mightily against his million-ton coffin with an agonal strength that had torn his face and hands. Death had mauled him like a lion. The doctor set to work.

His hands were fully themselves now—fleet, exact, intricately testing the corpse's character as other fingers might explore a keyboard for its latent melodies. And the doctor watched them with an old pleasure, one of the few that had never failed him, his mind at one remove from their busy intelligence. All the hard deaths! A worldful of them, time without end. Lives wrenched kicking from their snug meat-frames. Walter Lou Jackson had died very hard. Joe Allen brought this on you, Mr. Jackson. We think it was part of his attempt to escape the law.

But what a botched flight! The unreason of it—more than baffling—was eerie in its colossal futility. Beyond question, Allen had been cunning. A ghoul with a psychopath's social finesse. A good old boy who could make a tavernful of men laugh with delight while he cut his victim from their midst, make them applaud his exit with the prey, who stepped jovially into the darkness with murder at his side clapping him on the shoulder. Intelligent, certainly, with a strange technical sophistication as well, suggested by the sphere. Then what of the lunacy yet more strongly suggested by the same object? In the sphere was concentrated all the lethal mystery of Bailey's long nightmare.

Why the explosion? Its location implied an ambush for Allen's pursuers, a purposeful detonation. Had he aimed at a limited cave-in from which he schemed some inconceivable escape? Folly enough in this—far more if, as seemed sure, Allen had made the bomb himself, for then he would have to know its power was grossly inordinate to the need.

But if it was not a bomb, had a different function and only incidentally an explosive potential, Allen might underestimate the blast. It appeared the object was somehow remotely monitored by him, for the timing of events showed he had gone straight for it the instant he emerged from the shaft—shunned the bus waiting to take his shift back to town and made a beeline across the compound for a patrol car that was hidden from his view by the office building. This suggested something more complex than a mere explosive device, something, perhaps, whose destruction was itself more Allen's aim than the explosion produced thereby.

The fact that he risked the sphere's retrieval at all pointed to this interpretation. From the moment he sensed its presence at the mine, he must have guessed that the murder investigation had led to its discovery and removal from his room. But then, knowing himself already liable to the extreme penalty, why should Allen go to such lengths to recapture evidence incriminatory of a lesser offense, possession of an explosive device?

Then grant that the sphere was something more, something instrumental to his murders that could guarantee a conviction he might otherwise evade. Still, his gambit made no sense. Since the sphere—and thus the lawmen he could assume to have taken it—was already at the mine office, he must expect the compound to be scaled at any moment. Meanwhile, the gate was open, escape into the mountains a strong possibility for a man capable of stalking and destroying two experienced and well-armed woodsmen lying in ambush for him. Why had he all but ensured his capture to weaken a case against himself that his escape would have rendered irrelevant? Dr. Winters watched as his own fingers, like a hunting pack round a covert, converged on a small puncture wound below Walter Lou Jackson's xiphoid process, between the eighth ribs.

His left hand touched its borders, the fingers' inquiry quick and tender. The right hand introduced a probe, and both together eased it into the wound. It was rarely fruitful to use a probe on corpses this decayed; the track of the wound would more properly be examined by section. But an inexplicable sense of urgency had taken hold of him. Gently, with infinite pains not to pierce in the softened tissues an artifactual track of his own, he inched the probe in. It moved unobstructed deep into the body, curving upward through the diaphragm toward the heart. The doctor's own heart accelerated. He watched his hands move to record the observation, watched them pause, watched them return to their survey of the corpse, leaving pen and page untouched.

External inspection revealed no further anomaly. All else he observed the doctor recorded faithfully, wondering throughout at the distress he felt. When he had finished, he understood it. Its cause was not the discovery of an entry wound that might bolster Waddleton's case. For the find had, within moments, revealed to him that, should he encounter anything he thought to be a mark of fragment penetration, he was going to ignore it. The damage Joe Allen had done was going to end here, with this last grand slaughter, and would not extend to the impoverishment of his victims' survivors. His mind was now made up: for Jackson and the remaining seven, the external exams would be officially recorded as contraindicating the need for any external exam.

No, the doctor's unease as he finished Jackson's external—as he wrote up his report and signed it—had a different source. His problem was that he did not believe the puncture in Jackson's thorax *was* a mark of fragment entry. He disbelieved this, and had no idea why he did so. Nor had he any idea why, once again, he felt afraid. He sealed the report. Jackson was now officially accounted for and done with. Then Dr. Winters took up the postmortem knife and returned to the corpse.

First the long sawing slice, unzipping the mortal overcoat. Next, two great square flaps of flesh reflected, scrolled laterally to the armpits' line, disrobing the chest: one hand grasping the flap's skirt, the other sweeping beneath it with the knife, flensing through the glassy tissue that joined it to the chest wall, and shaving all muscles from their anchorages to bone and cartilage beneath. Then the dismantling of the strongbox within. Rib shears—so frank and forward a tool, like a gardener's. The steel beak bit through each rib's gristle anchor to the sternum's centerplate. At the sternum's crownpiece the collarbones' ends were knifed, pried, and sprung free from their sockets. The coffer unhasped, unhinged, a knife teased beneath the lid and levered it off.

Some minutes later the doctor straightened up and stepped back from his subject. He moved almost drunkenly, and his age seemed scored more deeply in his face. With loathing haste he stripped his gloves off. He went to the desk, sat down, and poured another drink. If there was something like horror in his face, there was also a hardening in his mouth's line and the muscles of his jaw. He spoke to his glass: "So be it, your Excellency. Something new for your humble servant. Testing my nerve?"

Jackson's pericardium, the shapely capsule containing his heart, should have been all but hidden between the big blood-fat loaves of his lungs. The doctor had found it fully exposed, the lungs flanking it wrinkled lumps less than a third their natural bulk. Not only they, but the left heart and the superior mediastinal veins—all the regions that should have been grossly engorged with blood—were utterly drained of it.

The doctor swallowed his drink and got out the photographs again. He found that Jackson had died on his stomach across the body of another worker, with the upper part of a third trapped between them. Neither these two subjacent corpses nor the surrounding earth showed any stain of a blood loss that must have amounted to two liters.

Possibly the pictures, by some trick of shadow, had failed to pick it up. He turned to the investigator's report, where Craven would surely have mentioned any significant amounts of bloody earth uncovered during the disinterment. The sheriff recorded nothing of the kind. Dr. Winters returned to the pictures.

Ronald Pollock, Jackson's most intimate associate in the grave, had died on his back, beneath and slightly askew of Jackson, placing most of their torsos in contact, save where the head and shoulder of the third interposed. It seemed inconceivable Pollock's clothing should lack any trace of such massive drainage from a death mate thus embraced.

The doctor rose abruptly, pulled on fresh gloves, and returned to Jackson. His hands showed a more brutal speed now, closing the great incision temporarily with a few widely spaced sutures. He replaced him in the vault and brought out Pollock, striding, heaving hard at the dead shapes in the shifting of them, thrusting always—so it seemed to him—just a step ahead of urgent thoughts he did not want to have, deformities that whispered at his back, emitting faint, chill gusts of putrid breath. He shook his head—denying, delaying—and pushed the new corpse onto the worktable. The scissors undressed Pollock in greedy bites.

But at length, when he had scanned each scrap of fabric and found nothing like the stain of blood, he came to rest again, relinquishing that simplest, desired resolution he had made such haste to reach. He stood at the instrument table, not seeing it, submitting to the approach of the half-formed things at his mind's periphery.

The revelation of Jackson's shriveled lungs had been more than a shock. He had felt a stab of panic too, in fact that same curiously explicit terror of this place that had urged him to flee earlier. He acknowledged now that the germ of that quickly suppressed terror had been a premonition of this failure to find any trace of the missing blood. Whence the premonition? It had to do with a problem he had steadfastly refused to consider: the mechanics of so complete a drainage of the lungs' densely reticulated vascular structure. Could the earth's crude pressure by itself work so thoroughly, given only a single vent both slender and strangely curved? And then the photograph he had studied. It frightened him now to recall the image—some covert meaning stirred within it, struggling to be seen. Dr. Winters picked the probe up from the table and turned again to the corpse. As surely and exactly as if he had already ascertained the wound's presence, he leaned forward and touched it: a small, neat puncture, just beneath the xiphoid process. He introduced the probe. The wound received it deeply, in a familiar direction.

The doctor went to the desk and took up the photograph again. Pollock's and Jackson's wounded areas were not in contact. The third man's head was sandwiched between their bodies at just that point. He searched out another picture, in which this third man was more central, and found his name inked in below his image: Joe Allen.

Dreamingly, Dr. Winters went to the wide metal door, shoved it aside, entered the vault. He did not search, but went straight to the trestle where Sheriff Craven had paused some hours before. He found the same name on its tag.

The body, beneath decay's spurious obesity, was trim and well muscled. The face was square-cut, shelf-browed, with a vulpine nose skewed by an old fracture. The swollen tongue lay behind the teeth, and the bulge of decomposition did not obscure what the man's initial impact must have been—handsome and open, his now-waxen black eyes sly and convivial.

Say, good buddy, got a minute? I see you comin' on the swing shift every day, don't I? Yeah, Joe Allen. Look, I know it's late, you want to get home, tell the wife you ain't been in there drinkin' since you got off, right? Oh, yeah, I hear that. But this damn disappearance thing's got me so edgy, and I'd swear to God just as I was coming here I seen someone moving around back of that frame house up the street. See how the trees thin out a little down back of the yard, where the moonlight gets in? That's right. Well, I got me this little popper here. Oh, yeah, that's a beauty, we'll have it covered between us. I knew I could spot a man ready for some trouble—couldn't find a patrol car anywhere on the street. Yeah, just down in here now, to that clump of pine. Step careful, you can barely see. That's right . . .

The doctor's face ran with sweat. He turned on his heel and walked out of the vault, heaving the door shut behind him. In the office's greater warmth he felt the perspiration soaking his shirt under the smock. His stomach rasped with steady oscillations of pain, but he scarcely attended it. He went to Pollock and seized up the postmortem knife.

The work was done with surreal speed, the laminae of flesh and bone recoiling smoothly beneath his desperate but unerring hands, until the thoracic cavity lay exposed, and in it, the vampire-stricken lungs, two gnarled lumps of gray tissue.

He searched no deeper, knowing what the heart and veins would show. He returned to sit at the desk, weakly drooping, the knife, forgotten, still in his left hand. He looked at his reflection in the window, and it seemed his thoughts originated with that fainter, more tenuous Dr. Winters hanging like a ghost outside.

What was this world he lived in? Surely, in a lifetime, he had not begun to guess. To feed in such a way! There was horror enough in this alone. But to feed thus *in his own grave.* How had he accomplished it— leaving aside how he had fought suffocation long enough to do anything at all? How was it to be comprehended, a greed that raged so hotly it would glut itself at the very threshold of its own destruction? That last feast was surely in his stomach still.

Dr. Winters looked at the photograph, at Allen's head snugged into the others' middles like a hungry suckling nuzzling to the sow. Then he looked at the knife in his hand. The hand felt empty of all technique. Its one impulse was to slash, cleave, obliterate the remains of this gluttonous thing, this Joe Allen. He must do this, or flee it utterly. There was no course between. He did not move.

"I *will* examine him," said the ghost in the glass, and did not move. Inside the refrigeration vault, there was a slight noise.

No. It had been some hitch in the generator's murmur. Nothing in there could move. There was another noise, a brief friction against the vault's inner wall. The two old men shook their heads at one another. A catch clicked, and the metal door slid open. Behind the staring image of his own amazement, the doctor saw that a filthy shape stood in the doorway and raised its arms toward him in a gesture of supplication. The doctor turned in his chair. From the shape came a whistling groan, the decayed fragment of a human voice.

Pleadingly, Joe Allen worked his jaw and spread his purple hands. As if speech were a maggot struggling to emerge from his mouth, the blue tumescent face toiled, the huge tongue wallowed helplessly between the viscid lips.

The doctor reached for the telephone, lifted the receiver. Its deadness to his ear meant nothing—he could not have spoken. The thing confronting him, with each least movement that it made, destroyed the very frame of sanity in which words might have meaning, reduced the world itself around him to a waste of dark and silence, a starlit ruin where already, everywhere, the alien and unimaginable was awakening to its new dominion. The corpse raised and reached out one hand as if to stay him—turned, and walked toward the instrument table. Its legs were leaden, it rocked its shoulders like a swimmer, fighting to make its passage through gravity's dense medium. It reached the table and grasped it exhaustedly. The doctor found himself on his feet, crouched slightly, weightlessly still. The knife in his hand was the only part of himself he clearly felt, and it was like a tongue of fire, a crematory flame. Joe Allen's corpse thrust one hand among the instruments. The thick fingers, with a queer simian ineptitude, brought up a scalpel. Both hands clasped the little handle and plunged the blade between the lips, as a thirsty child might a Popsicle, then jerked it out again, slashing the tongue. Turbid fluid splashed down to the floor. The jaw worked stiffly, the mouth brought out words in a wet ragged hiss:

"Please. Help me. Trapped in *this.*" One dead hand struck the dead chest. "Starving."

"What are you?"

"Traveler. Not of Earth."

"An eater of human flesh. A drinker of human blood."

"No. No. Hiding only. Am small. Shape hideous to you. Feared death."

"You brought death." The doctor spoke with the calm of perfect disbelief, himself as incredible to him as the thing he spoke with. It shook its head, the dull, popped eyes glaring with an agony of thwarted expression.

"Killed none. Hid in this. Hid in this not to be killed. Five days now. Drowning in decay. Free me. Please."

"No. You have come to feed on us, you are not hiding in fear. We are your food, your meat and drink. You fed on those two men within your grave. *Their* grave. For you, a delay. In fact, a diversion that has ended the hunt for you."

"No! No! Used men already dead. For me, five days, starvation. Even less. Fed only from need. Horrible necessity!"

The spoiled vocal instrument made a mangled gasp of the last word—an inhuman snake-pit noise the doctor felt as a cold flicker of ophidian tongues within his ears—while the dead arms moved in a sodden approximation of the body language that swears truth.

"No," the doctor said. "You killed them all. Including your . . . tool—this man. *What are you?*" Panic erupted in the question that he tried to bury by answering himself instantly. "Resolute, yes. That surely. You used death for an escape route. You need no oxygen perhaps."

"Extracted more than my need from gasses of decay. A lesser component of our metabolism."

The voice was gaining distinctness, developing makeshifts for tones lost in the agonal rupturing of the valves and stops of speech, more effectively wrestling vowel and consonant from the putrid tongue and lips. At the same time the body's crudity of movement did not quite obscure a subtle, incessant experimentation. Fingers flexed and stirred, testing the give of tendons, groping the palm for old points of purchase and counterpressure there. The knees, with cautious repetitions, assessed the new limits of their articulation.

"What was the sphere?"

"My ship. Its destruction our first duty facing discovery." (Fear touched the doctor, like a slug climbing his neck; he had seen, as it spoke, a sharp spastic activity of the tongue, a pleating and shrinkage of its bulk as at the tug of some inward adjustment.) "No chance to reenter. Leaving this body takes far too long. Not even time to set it for destruct—must extrude a cilium, chemical key to broach hull shield. In shaft was my only chance to halt my host."

Though the dead mask hung expressionless, conveyed no irony, the thing's articulacy grew uncannily—each word more smoothly shaped, nuances of tone creeping into its speech. Its right arm tested its wrist as it spoke, and the scalpel the hand still held cut white sparks from the air, while the word *host* seemed itself a little razor-cut, an almost teasing abandonment of fiction preliminary to attack.

But the doctor found that fear had gone from him. The impossibility with which he conversed, and was about to struggle, was working in him an overwhelming amplification of his life's long helpless rage at death. He found his parochial pity for Earth alone stretched to the transstellar scope this traveler commanded, to the whole cosmic trash yard with its bulldozed multitudes of corpses; galactic wheels of carnage—stars, planets with their most majestic generations—all trash, cracked bones and foul rags that pooled, settled, reconcatenated in futile symmetries gravid with new multitudes of briefly animate trash.

And this, standing before him now, was the death it was given him particularly to deal—his mite was being called in by the universal Treasury of Death, and Dr. Winters found himself, an old healer, on fire to pay. His own more lethal blade tugged at his hand with its own sharp appetite. He felt entirely the Examiner once more, knew the precise cuts he would make, swiftly and without error. *Very soon now,* he thought and coolly probed for some further insight before its onslaught:

"Why must your ship be destroyed, even at the cost of your host's life?"

"We must not be understood."

"The livestock must not understand what is devouring them."

"Yes, Doctor. Not all at once. But one by one. You will understand what is devouring you. That is essential to my feast."

The doctor shook his head. "You are in your grave already, Traveler. That body will be your coffin. You will be buried in it a second time, for all time."

The thing came one step nearer and opened its mouth. The flabby throat wrestled as with speech, but what sprang out was a slender white filament, more than whip-fast. Dr. Winters saw only the first flicker of its eruption, and then his brain nova-ed, thinning out at light-speed to a white nullity.

When the doctor came to himself, it was in fact to a part of himself only. Before he had opened his eyes he found that his wakened mind had repossessed proprioceptively only a bizarre truncation of his body. His head, neck, left shoulder, arm, and hand declared themselves—the rest was silence.

When he opened his eyes, he found that he lay supine on the gurney, and naked. Something propped his head. A strap bound his left elbow to the gurney's edge, a strap he could feel. His chest was also anchored by a strap, and this he could not feel. Indeed, save for its active remnant, his entire body might have been bound in a block of ice, so numb was it, and so powerless was he to compel the slightest movement from the least part of it.

The room was empty, but from the open door of the vault there came slight sounds: the creak and soft frictions of heavy tarpaulin shifted to accommodate some business involving small clicking and kissing noises.

Tears of fury filled the doctor's eyes. Clenching his one fist at the starry engine of creation that he could not see, he ground his teeth and whispered in the hot breath of strangled weeping:

"Take it back, this dirty little shred of life! I throw it off gladly like the filth it is." The slow knock of boot soles loudened from within the vault, and he turned his head. From the vault door Joe Allen's corpse approached him.

It moved with new energy, though its gait was grotesque, a ducking, hitching progress, jerky with circumventions of decayed muscle, while above this galvanized, struggling frame, the bruise-colored face hung inanimate, an image of detachment. With terrible clarity the thing was revealed for what it was—a damaged hand-puppet vigorously worked from within. And when that frozen face was brought to hang above the doctor, the reeking hands, with the light, solicitous touch of friends at sickbeds, rested on his naked thigh.

The absence of sensation made the touch more dreadful than if felt. It showed him that the nightmare he still desperately denied at heart had annexed his body while he—holding head and arm free—had already more than half-drowned in its mortal paralysis. There, from his chest on down, lay his nightmare part, a nothingness freely possessed by an unspeakability. The corpse said:

"Rotten blood. Thin nourishment. I had only one hour alone before you came. I fed from my neighbor to my left—barely had strength to extend a siphon. Fed from the right while you worked. Tricky going—you are alert. I expected Dr. Parsons. The energy needs of animating this"—one hand left the doctor's thigh and smote the dusty overalls—"and of host-transfer, very high. Once I have you synapsed, I will be near starvation again."

A sequence of unbearable images unfolded in the doctor's mind, even as the robot carrion turned from the gurney and walked to the instrument table: the sheriff's arrival just after dawn, alone of course, since Craven always took thought for his deputies' rest and because on this errand he would want privacy to consider any indiscretion on behalf of the miners' survivors that the situation might call for; Craven's finding his old friend, supine and alarmingly weak; his hurrying over, his leaning near. Then, somewhat later, a police car containing a rack of still wet bones might plunge off the highway above some deep spot in the gorge.

The corpse took an evidence box from the table and put the scalpel in it. Then it turned and retrieved the mortuary knife from the floor and put that in as well, saying as it did so, without turning, "The sheriff will come in the morning. You spoke like close friends. He will probably come alone."

The coincidence with his thoughts had to be accident, but the intent to terrify and appall him was clear. The tone and timing of that patched-up voice were unmistakably deliberate—sly probes that sought his anguish specifically, sought his mind's personal center. He watched the corpse—over at the table—dipping an apish but accurate hand and plucking up rib shears, scissors, clamps, adding all to the box. He stared, momentarily emptied by shock of all but the will to know finally the full extent of the horror that had appropriated his life. Joe Allen's body carried the box to the worktable beside the gurney, and the expressionless eyes met the doctor's.

"I have gambled. A grave gamble. But now I have won. At risk of personal discovery we are obliged to disconnect, contract, hide as well as possible in the host-body. Suicide in effect. I disregarded situational imperatives, despite starvation before disinterment and subsequent autopsy being all but certain. I caught up with the crew, tackled Pollock and Jackson microseconds before the blast. I computed five days' survival from this cache. I could disconnect at limit of my strength to do so, but otherwise I would chance autopsy, knowing the doctor was an alcoholic incompetent. And now see my gain. You are a prize host. Through you I can feed with near impunity even when killing is too dangerous. Safe meals are delivered to you still warm."

The corpse had painstakingly aligned the gurney parallel to the work-table but offset, the table's foot extending past the gurney's, and separated from it by a distance somewhat less than the reach of Joe Allen's right arm. Now the dead hands distributed the implements along the right edge of the table, save for the scissors and the box. These the corpse took to the table's foot, where it set down the box and slid the scissors's jaws round one strap of its overalls. It began to speak again, and as it did, the scissors dismembered its cerements in unhesitating strokes.

"The cut must be medical, forensically right, though a smaller one is easier. I must be careful of the pectoral muscles or these arms will not convey me. I am no larva anymore—over fifteen hundred grams."

To ease the nightmare's suffocating pressure, to thrust out some flicker of his own will against its engulfment, the doctor flung a question, his voice more cracked than the other's now was:

"Why is my arm free?"

"The last, fine neural splicing needs a sensory-motor standard, to perfect my brain's fit to yours. Lacking this eye-hand coordinating check, only a much coarser control of the host's characteristic motor patterns is possible. This done, I flush out the paralytic, unbind us, and we are free together."

The grave-clothes had fallen in a puzzle of fragments, and the cadaver stood naked, its dark gas-rounded contours making it seem some sleek marine creature, ruddered with the black-veined gas-distended sex. Again the voice had teased for his fear, had uttered the last word with a savoring protraction, and now the doctor's cup of anguish brimmed over; horror and outrage wrenched his spirit in brutal alternation as if trying to tear it naked from its captive frame. He rolled his head in this deadlock, his mouth beginning to split with the slow birth of a mind-emptying outcry.

The corpse watched this, giving a single nod that might have been approbation. Then it mounted the worktable and, with the concentrated caution of some practiced convalescent reentering his bed, lay on its back. The dead eyes again sought the living and found the doctor staring back, grinning insanely.

"Clever corpse!" the doctor cried. "Clever, carnivorous corpse! Able alien! Please don't think I'm criticizing. Who am I to criticize? A mere arm and shoulder, a talking head, just a small piece of a pathologist. But I'm confused." He paused, savoring the monster's attentive silence and his own buoyancy in the hysterical levity that had unexpectedly liberated him. "You're going to use your puppet there to pluck you out of itself and put you on me. But once he's pulled you from your driver's seat, won't he go dead, so to speak, and drop you? You could get a nasty knock. Why not set a plank between the tables—the puppet opens the door, and you scuttle, ooze, lurch, flop, slither, as the case may be, across the bridge. No messy spills. And in any case, isn't this an odd, rather clumsy way to get around among your cattle? Shouldn't you at least carry your own scalpels when you travel? There's always the risk you'll run across that one host in a million that isn't carrying one with him."

He knew his gibes would be answered to his own despair. He exulted, but solely in the momentary bafflement of the predator—in having, for just a moment, mocked its gloating assurance to silence and marred its feast.

Its right hand picked up the postmortem knife beside it, and the left wedged a roll of gauze beneath Allen's neck, lifting the throat to a more prominent arch. The mouth told the ceiling:

"We retain larval form till entry of the host. As larvae we have locomotor structures, and sense buds usable outside our ships' sensory amplifiers. I waited coiled round Joe Allen's bed leg till night, entered by his mouth as he slept." Allen's hand lifted the knife, held it high above the dull, quick eyes, turning it in the light. "Once lodged, we have three instars to adult form," the voice continued absently—the knife might have been a mirror from which the corpse read its features. "Larvally we have only a sketch of our full neural tap. Our metamorphosis is cued and determined by the host's endosomatic ecology. I matured in three days." Allen's wrist flexed, tipping the knife's point downmost. "Most supreme adaptations are purchased at the cost of inessential capacities." The elbow pronated and slowly flexed, hooking the knife bodyward. "Our hosts are all sentients, ecodominants, are already carrying the baggage of coping structures for the planetary environment we find them in. Limbs, sensory portals"— the fist planted the fang of its tool under the chin, tilted it and rode it smoothly down the throat, the voice proceeding unmarred from under the furrow that the steel ploughed—"somatic envelopes, instrumentalities"— down the sternum, diaphragm, abdomen the stainless blade painted its stripe of gaping, muddy tissue—"with a host's brain we inherit all these, the mastery of any planet, netted in its dominant's cerebral nexus. Thus our genetic codings are now all but disencumbered of such provisions."

So swiftly that the doctor flinched, Joe Allen's hand slashed four lateral cuts from the great wound's axis. The seeming butchery left two flawlessly drawn thoracic flaps cleanly outlined. The left hand raised the left flap's hem, and the right coaxed the knife into the aperture, deepening it with small stabs and slices. The posture was a man's who searches a breast pocket, with the dead eyes studying the slow recoil of flesh. The voice, when it resumed, had geared up to an intenser pitch:

"Galactically, the chordate nerve/brain paradigm abounds, and the neural labyrinth is our dominion. Are we to make plank bridges and worm across them to our food? Are cockroaches greater than we for having legs to run up walls and antennae to grope their way? All the quaint, hinged crutches that life sports! The stilts, fins, fans, springs, stalks, flippers, and feathers, all in turn so variously terminating in hooks, clamps, suckers, scissors, forks, or little cages of digits! And besides all the gadgets it concocts for wrestling through its worlds, it is all knobbed, whiskered, crested, plumed, vented, spiked, or measeled over with perceptual gear for combing pittances of noise or color from the environing plentitude."

Invincibly calm and sure, the hands traded tool and tasks. The right flap eased back, revealing ropes of ingeniously spared muscle while promising a genuine appearance once sutured back in place. Helplessly the doctor felt his delirious defiance bleed away and a bleak fascination rebind him.

"We are the taps and relays that share the host's aggregate of afferent nerve-impulse precisely at its nodes of integration. We are the brains that peruse these integrations, integrate them with our existing banks of host-specific data, and, lastly, let their consequences flow down the motor pathway—either the consequences they seek spontaneously, or those we wish to graft upon them. We are besides a streamlined alimentary/circulatory system and a reproductive apparatus. And more than this we need not be."

The corpse had spread its bloody vest, and the feculent hands now took up the rib shears. The voice's sinister coloration of pitch and stress grew yet more marked—the phrases slid from the tongue with a cobra's seeking sway, winding their liquid rhythms round the doctor till a gap in his resistance should let them pour through to slaughter the little courage left him.

"For in this form we have inhabited the densest brainweb of three hundred races, lain intricately snug within them like thriving vine on trelliswork. We've looked out from too many variously windowed masks to regret our own vestigial senses. None read their worlds definitively. Far better then our nomad's range and choice than an unvarying tenancy of one poor set of structures. Far better to slip on as we do whole living beings and wear at once all their limbs and organs, memories and powers—wear all these as tightly congruent to our wills as a glove is to the hand that fills it."

The shears clipped through the gristle, stolid, bloody jaws monotonously feeding, stopping short of the sternoclavicular joint in the manubrium where the muscles of the pectoral girdle have an important anchorage.

"No consciousness of the chordate type that we have found has been impermeable to our finesse—no dendritic pattern so elaborate we could not read its stitchwork and thread ourselves to match, precisely map its each synaptic seam till we could loosen it and retailor all to suit ourselves. We have strutted costumed in the bodies of planetary autarchs, venerable manikins of moral fashion, but cut of the universal cloth: the weave of fleet electric filaments of experience that we easily reshuttled to the warp of our wishes. Whereafter—newly hemmed and gathered—their living fabric hung obedient to our bias, investing us with honor and influence unlimited."

The tricky verbal melody, through the corpse's deft, unfaltering self-dismemberment—the sheer neuromuscular orchestration of the compound activity—struck Dr. Winters with the detached enthrallment great keyboard performers could bring him. He glimpsed the alien's perspective—a Gulliver waiting in a Brobdingnagian grave, then marshaling a dead giant against a living, like a dwarf in a huge mechanical crane, feverishly programming combat on a battery of levers and pedals, waiting for the robot arms' enactments, the remote, titanic impact of the foes—and he marveled, filled with a bleak wonder at life's infinite strategy and plasticity. Joe Allen's hands reached into his half-opened abdominal cavity, reached deep below the uncut anterior muscle that was exposed by the shallow, spurious incision of the epidermis, till by external measure they were extended far enough to be touching his thighs. The voice was still as the forearms advertised a delicate rummaging with the buried fingers. The shoulders drew back. As the steady withdrawal brought the wrists into view, the dead legs tremored and quaked with diffuse spasms.

"You called your kind our food and drink, Doctor. If you were merely that, an elementary usurpation of your motor tracts alone would satisfy us, give us perfect cattle-control—for what rarest word or subtlest behavior is more than a flurry of varied muscles? That trifling skill was ours long ago. It is not mere blood that feeds this lust I feel now to tenant you, this craving for an intimacy that years will not stale. My truest feast lies in compelling you to feed in that way. It lies in the utter deformation of your will this will involve. Had gross nourishment been my prime need, then my grave-mates—Pollock and Jackson—could have eked out two weeks of life for me or more. But I scorned a cowardly parsimony in the face of death. I reinvested more than half the energy that their blood gave me in fabricating chemicals to keep their brains alive, and fluid-bathed with oxygenated nutriment."

The corpse reached into its gaping abdomen, and out of its cloven groin the smeared hands pulled two long skeins of silvery filament. The material looked like masses of nerve fiber, tough and scintillant—for the weave of it glittered with a slight incessant movement of each single thread. These nerve skeins were contracting. They thickened into two swollen nodes, while at the same time the corpse's legs tremored and faintly twitched, as the bright vermiculate roots of the parasite withdrew from within Allen's musculature. When the nodes lay fully contracted the doctor could just see their tips within the abdomen—then the legs lay still as death.

"I had accessory neural taps only to spare, but I could access much memory, and all their cognitive responses, and having in my banks all the organ of Corti's electrochemical conversions of English words, I could whisper anything to them directly into the eighth cranial nerve. Those are our true feast, Doctor, such bodiless electric storms of impotent cognition as I tickled up in those two little bone globes. I was forced to drain them just before disinterment, but they lived till then and understood everything—*everything* I did to them."

When the voice paused, the dead and living eyes were locked together. They remained so a moment, and then the dead face smiled.

It recapitulated all the horror of Allen's first resurrection—this waking of expressive soul in that purple death mask. And it was a demon-soul the doctor saw awaken: the smile was barbed with fine, sharp hooks of cruelty at the corners of the mouth, while the barbed eyes beamed fond, languorous anticipation of his pain. Remotely, Dr. Winters heard the flat sound of his own voice asking:

"And Joe Allen?"

"Oh, yes, Doctor. He is with us now, has been throughout. I grieve to abandon so rare a host! He is a true hermit-philosopher, well read in four languages. He is writing a translation of Marcus Aurelius—he was, I mean, in his free time . . ."

Long minutes succeeded of the voice accompanying the surreal self-autopsy, but the doctor lay resigned, emptied of reactive power. Still, the full understanding of his fate reverberated in his mind as the parasite sketched his future for him in that borrowed voice. And it did not stop haunting Winters, the sense of what a *virtuoso* this entity was, how flawlessly this mass of neural fibers played the tricky instrument of human speech. As flawlessly as it had puppeteered the corpse's face into that ghastly smile. And with the same artistic aim: to waken, to amplify, to ripen its host-to-be's outrage and horror. The voice, with ever more melody and gloating verve, sent waves of realization through the doctor, amplifications of the Unspeakable.

The parasite's race had traced and tapped the complex interface between the cortical integration of sense input and the neural output governing response. It had interposed its brain between, sharing consciousness while solely commanding the pathways of reaction. The host, the bottled personality, was mute and limbless for any least expression of its own will, while hellishly articulate and agile in the service of the parasite's. It was the host's own hands that bound and wrenched the life half out of his prey, his own loins that experienced the repeated orgasms crowning his other despoliations of their bodies. And when they lay, bound and shrieking still, ready for the consummation, it was his own strength that hauled the smoking entrails from them, and his own intimate tongue and guzzling mouth he plunged into the rank, palpitating feast.

And the doctor had glimpses of the racial history that underlay the aliens' predatory present. Glimpses of a dispassionate, inquiring breed so advanced in the analysis of its own mental fabric that, through scientific commitment and genetic self-sculpting, it had come to embody its own model of perfected consciousness. It had grown streamlined to permit its entry of other beings and its direct acquisition of their experiential worlds. All strictest scholarship at first, until there matured in the disembodied scholars their long-germinal and now blazing, jealous hatred for all "lesser" minds rooted and clothed in the soil and sunlight of solid, particular worlds. The parasite spoke of the "cerebral music," the "symphonies of agonized paradox" that were its invasion's chief plunder. The doctor felt the truth behind this grandiloquence: the parasite's actual harvest from the systematic violation of encoffined personalities was the experience of a barren supremacy of means over lives more primitive, perhaps, but vastly wealthier in the vividness and passionate concern with which life for them was imbued.

The corpse had reached into its thorax and with its dead hands aided the parasite's retraction of its upper-body root system. More and more of its livid mass had gone dead, until only its head and the arm nearer the doctor remained animate, while the silvery worming mass grew in its bleeding abdominal nest.

Then Joe Allen's face grinned, and his hand hoisted up the nude, re-gathered parasite from his sundered gut and held it for the doctor to view—his tenant-to-be. Winters saw that from the squirming mass of nerve cord one thick filament still draped down, remaining anchored in the canyoned chest toward the upper spine. This, he understood, would be the remote-control line by which it could work at a distance the crane of its old host's body, transferring itself to Winters by means of a giant appa-ratus it no longer inhabited. This, he knew, was his last moment. Before his own personal horror should begin and engulf him, he squarely met the corpse's eyes and said:

"Goodbye, Joe Allen. Eddie Sykes, I mean. I hope he gave you strength, the Golden Marcus. I love him too. You are guiltless. Peace be with you at the last."

The demon smile stayed fixed, but, effortlessly, Winters looked through it to the real eyes, those of the encoffined man. Tormented eyes foreseeing death, and craving it. The grinning corpse reached out its viscid cargo—a seething, rippling, multinodular lump that completely filled the erstwhile logger's roomy palm. It reached this across and laid it on the doctor's groin. He watched the hand set the bright medusa's head—his new self—on his own skin, but felt nothing.

He watched the dead hand return to the table, take up the scalpel, reach back over, and make a twelve-inch incision up his abdomen, along his spinal axis. It was a deep, slow cut—sectioning, just straight down through the ab-dominal wall—and it proceeded in the eerie, utter absence of physical sensa-tion. The moment this was done, the fiber that had stayed anchored in the corpse snapped free, whipped back across the gap, and rejoined the main body that now squirmed toward the incision, its port of entry.

The corpse collapsed. Emptied of all innervating energy, it sagged slack and flaccid, of course. Or had it . . . ? Why was it . . . ? That nearer arm was *supinated.* Both elbow and wrist at the full upturned twist. The palm lay open, offering. *The scalpel still lay in the palm.*

Simple death would have dropped the arm earthward, it would now hang slack. With a blaze, like a nova of light, Winters understood. The man, Sykes, had—for a microsecond before his end—repossessed himself. Had flung a dying impulse of his will down through his rotten, fading muscles and had managed a single independent gesture in the narrow interval between the demon's departure and his own death. He had clutched the scalpel and flung out his arm, locking the joints as life left him.

It rekindled Winters's own will, lit a fire of rage and vengefulness. He had caught hope from his predecessor.

How precariously the scalpel lay on the loosened fingers! The slightest tremor would unfix the arm's joints, it would fall and hang and drop the scalpel down farther than Hell's deepest recess from his grasp. And he could see that the scalpel was just—only just—in the reach of his fingers at his forearm's fullest stretch from the bound elbow. The horror crouched on him and, even now slowly feeding its trunk line into his groin incision, at first stopped the doctor's hand with a pang of terror. Then he reminded himself that, until implanted, the enemy was a senseless mass, bristling with plugs, with input jacks for senses, but, until installed in the physical amplifiers of eyes and ears, an utterly deaf, blind monad that waited in a perfect solipsism between two captive sensory envelopes.

He saw his straining fingers above the bright tool of freedom, thought with an insane smile of God and Adam on the Sistine ceiling, and then, with a life span of surgeon's fine control, plucked up the scalpel. The arm fell and hung.

"Sleep," the doctor said. "Sleep revenged."

But he found his retaliation harshly reined in by the alien's careful provisions. His elbow had been fixed with his upper arm almost at right angles to his body's long axis; his forearm could reach his hand inward and present it closely to the face, suiting the parasite's need of an eye-hand coordinative check, but could not, even with the scalpel's added reach, bring its point within four inches of his groin. Steadily the parasite fed in its tapline. It would usurp motor control in three or four minutes at most, to judge by the time its extrication from Allen had taken.

Frantically the doctor bent his wrist inward to its limit, trying to pick through the strap where it crossed his inner elbow. Sufficient pressure was impossible, and the hold so awkward that even feeble attempts threatened the loss of the scalpel. Smoothly the root of alien control sank into him. It was a defenseless thing of jelly against which he lay lethally armed, and he was still doomed—a preview of all his thrall's impotence-to-be.

But of course there was a way. Not to survive. But to escape, and to have vengeance. For a moment he stared at his captor, hardening his mettle in the blaze of hate it lit in him. Then, swiftly, he determined the order of his moves, and began.

He reached the scalpel to his neck and opened his superior thyroid vein—his inkwell. He laid the scalpel by his ear, dipped his finger in his blood, and began to write on the metal surface of the gurney, beginning by his thigh and moving toward his armpit. Oddly, the incision of his neck, though this was muscularly awake, had been painless, which gave him hopes that raised his courage for what remained to do.

When he had done the message read:

ALIEN

IN

ME

CUT

KILL

He wanted to write goodbye to his friend, but the alien had begun to pay out smaller auxiliary filaments collaterally with the main one, and all now lay in speed.

He took up the scalpel, rolled his head to the left, and plunged the blade deep in his ear.

Miracle! Last accidental mercy! It was painless. Some procedural, highly specific anesthetic was in effect. With careful plunges he obliterated the right inner ear and then thrust silence, with equal thoroughness, into the left. The slashing of the vocal cords followed, then the tendons in the back of the neck that hold it erect. He wished he were free to unstring knees and elbows too, but it could not be. But blinded, deaf, with centers of balance lost, with only rough motor control—all these conditions should fetter the alien's escape, should it in the first place manage the reanimation of a bloodless corpse in which it had not yet achieved a fine-tuned interweave. Before he extinguished his eyes, he paused, the scalpel poised above his face, and blinked them to clear his aim of tears. The right, then the left, both retinas meticulously carved away, the yolk of vision quite scooped out of them. The scalpel's last task, once it had tilted the head sideways to guide the blood flow absolutely clear of possible effacement of the message, was to slash the external carotid artery.

When this was done, the old man sighed with relief and laid his scalpel down. Even as he did so, he felt the deep inward prickle of an alien energy something that flared, crackled, flared, groped for, but did not quite find its purchase. And inwardly, as the doctor sank toward sleep—cerebrally, as a voiceless man must speak—he spoke to the parasite these carefully chosen words:

"Welcome to your new house. I'm afraid there's been some vandalism—the lights don't work, and the plumbing has a very bad leak. There are some other things wrong as well—the neighborhood is perhaps a little *too* quiet, and you may find it hard to get around very easily. But it's been a lovely home to me for fifty-seven years, and somehow I think you'll stay . . ."

The face, turned toward the body of Joe Allen, seemed to weep scarlet tears, but its last movement before death was to smile.

Tollbooth

Manny springs it on Tara during brunch on the foredeck lounge of the houseboat, which is anchored in a tranquil lagoon rimmed by lush walls of mangrove. Manny's meal is a Bloody Mary and a couple fat rails of 'lumbo flake on a little monogrammed crystal chopping block. Tara is having coffee and yogurt. At present her angry-nostriled Jewish face is a study in outraged intelligence.

"Two experienced soldiers?" she protests. "Just on this . . . jungle bum's say-so? Are you going through some kind of mid-life crisis here, Manny? Is this early Alzheimer's?"

Benny chooses this worst possible moment to bring a message from the old *brujo* Doc Tolteco; the guy is asking for another bag of flake. "Take him *two* bags," Manny says quickly, shooing Benny off.

"Give him all the blow you want, Manny," Tara tells him. "It's your money. But your *people,* for shitsake? You're being an idiot, Manny. This is your hired Brain talking, doing what you pay her for: attention! You are being an idiot."

Manny knocks back his Mary and honks his rails with a monogrammed silver straw. "Tara. Sweetie. Please shut the fuck up. I hear you. Just take it for now, I've got *reasons.* Just tag along, help me through this, and I'll explain. Okay?"

A hydroplane lands in the lagoon. Two of Manny's soldiers, Trini and Deke, disembark into the little motored inflatable Manny keeps moored to the landing buoys, and come chugging over to the houseboat.

"Deke! Trini! Amigos!" He hugs them, thwacks their meaty shoulders. "Go down to the green room! There's some brewskis and 'lumbo you'll love!"

They go down and Manny calls Benny. While Manny builds a second Mary and Tara smokes a cigarette in ironic silence, Benny gets two flat packets from a locker near the aft rail. After a few minutes Manny checks his watch, rises, and the three of them go down to the Green Room, the main below-decks lounge.

Deke and Trini, given drugged blow, already sprawl unconscious over the glass table. Two other buttons—Chad and Ratón—who welcomed them and helped them to the lines, now rise to drag them clear of the table. Benny unscrolls his packets; they are body-bags. The three conscious soldiers bag Deke and Trini.

"Tolteco says it's important they're awake," Manny explains. "Cold beer might do it." Their faces, the only part of them not zipped in, are doused with beer. They blink and sputter. Manny gestures and Chad hands him his nine-millimeter automatic. "Check these out," he tells Tara enthusiastically. "Kevlar body-bags! Just shoot 'em right in the bag, no spatter, no slug frags!" He looks at Deke and Trini. "Sorry, guys," he tells them amiably. He puts a bullet in each, shooting downward through the hollow of the throat, nailing the heart from above.

Manny slips Tara a quick kiss to the cheek as they head astern to the cabin where Doc Tolteco has been put up. "Still friends?" he coaxes.

She's not having any. "What bothers me is that you know this is crazy and you go for it anyway. I've gotta know, Manny, are you losing it on me?"

Uncharacteristically, he lets some anger show, holding a stiff forefinger in her face. "You keep quiet and make nice in there. Please. And when we come out I'll tell you something, make you understand, Okay?"

Tolteco, whom Manny's Bolivian agents have gone to great lengths to locate and engage, is a half-naked, coffee-brown man wrapped in ropy old muscle. He sits crosslegged on the bed; his coke-pipe fumes and the air is dim with its haze. Their pulses rise merely from the act of sharing the old man's air. The old man's deep-carven nostrils are huge and hungry. His whole face might be carven from mahogany, his eyes from obsidian. Manny makes an awkward, ingratiating gesture. "All taken care of, Doc, the two, ah, attendants you requested."

Stoically, Tara translates this. *"Todo hecho como dijiste; los dos matados."* Her Spanish is crude, but it is not Doc Tolteco's first language either. Manny waits, visibly tense. He plainly regards the old man-witch as an inspired simpleton. Doc Tolteco gives him back obsidian eyes, and then gives him rusty, guttural words:

"Pura te. Rapido. Viene Otro. Otro 'sta muy acerca."

"He says hurry," Tara translates to Manny. "The Other is coming. The Other is close now." Her face is a bland mask, but to Manny's ear, who knows her, her voice is aquiver with irony.

Doc Tolteco lights another bowl of flake with a little brass blow-torch, inhales endlessly, exhales endlessly, and adds, *"Los dos chóferes, ellos también. La vida del Otro valga muchas vidas."*

This widens Tara's eyes. "He says that he wants the two drivers also, that the life of the Other is worth many lives."

It hangs there between them, Tara staring fascinated now at the question of how far Manny is going to be willing to go in this madness. Already he has agreed to a Funeral Offering, a quarter-ton of flake to be driven down from New York—driven, mind you, in a "dignified vehicle," a black Continental. And now he is visibly weighing the order to have the two buttons driving this insane offering added as human sacrifices, to join Deke and Trini.

And Manny's answer? He's smiling, giving a little what's-a-trifle-between-friends? shrug. "Okay, why not, Doc? As soon as they arrive! I gotta say, this isn't a cheap cure we're running here. I realize, of course, that El Otro was big, big medicine . . ." And now he is trying to sound contrite, trying to sell this savage with a tattooed face on his regret for El Otro's death. Tara translates this in halting Spanish, incredulous. Doc Tolteco nods once, and relights his pipe.

*   *   *

Rudy and Nolo are driving down an absolutely empty turnpike. It's Saturday morning, the sun not up yet, but emptiness like this is unnatural. Recent transplants from L.A. and its never-sleeping freeways, they are confirmed in their dislike of the East by this uncanny desolation.

Rudy says, not for the first time, "I just hate the whole idea of this fucking run! You don't *drive* product! Nobody fucking *drives* product." Rudy's face is scarred by early acne. He's an anxious over-eater with an acid stomach. Weaselly, wiry Nolo at the wheel is calmer and wiser. "Well, at least we're not likely to get shook down, look at it that way, *Ese.* Jesus Christ, you realize we haven't seen one other car in . . . how long?"

"I tell ya, man, I don't like this whole fucking little mission here."

"Look there—no one in 'em." He means the toll plaza they now approach—all the booths are lighted but empty.

But then a shape rises within the booth they glide up to. Dark and lean in the dirty glass. Nolo, pulling up to the coin bucket, gives the shape in the booth a smile. He can see now that this is a very gaunt old guy with white stubble on his jaw. "It's hell, this rush-hour traffic, isn't it?" Nolo offers, still smiling. Debonairly he tosses a handful of quarters in the bucket.

Dark fluid splashes back from the coins' impact and spatters the sleeve of Nolo's sportsjacket. He is stunned, but before he can react, the guy in the booth leans forward and tells him in a foghorn voice, "You didn't pay enough." The voice sounds utterly unused, like rusted iron pried open. Now Nolo registers that the thick spattering on his sleeve is gore—and that the air reeks of blood. "The fuck?" he asks, voice breaking in astonishment.

The toll guy is gaunter than ever, seems to be shrinking even as he answers. "You didn't pay enough for what you're carrying back there." Nolo peers back at the trunk where the toll-taker's gaunt hand is pointing. A red mess is drizzling out of it, spattering on the pavement—the trunk lid is copiously leaking blood all around its rim. Nolo flings open his door and gets out, while nervous Rudy steps out his door but stays behind it, his sawed-off twelve-gauge held down out of sight. Nolo goes back to the trunk and watches the reeking blood drizzling, falling in a comblike formation to spatter and puddle on the asphalt.

"Nolo!" screams Rudy. Nolo straightens to see the toll-taker—but what is happening to his *skin?* His skin is alive with worms now, and where are his eyes?—to see the toll-taker taking a bead on him with a big .45 automatic. Then Rudy's wad of double-aught sprays the toll-taker's carrion head away. The barrier arm of the gate pops up, as if homicide is the coin that works it.

"Throw him in back!" shouts Rudy. "Don't leave a stiff behind us!"

Still the turnpike is utterly empty. They roar through its void. "Find a fucking turnoff, we're leaking blood!"

"No! Look back there! No trail!"

"Find a fucking turnoff, we've got a stiff here!"

"Do you *see* a fucking turnoff? I'm *looking.* Calm down—this ain't happening! It's fumes from the shit in the trunk—we're freaking!"

"No way—flake don't do *this* to you!"

"You see any blood back there now?"

"Find a fucking turnoff!"

"I'm trying!"

Now bushes screen them from the little county two-lane they have finally found. They have pulled onto a little dirt spur off the road, and now have the back doors open and from opposite sides are looking into the Connie's back seat, which is utterly empty of the toll-taker's body, and unsullied by the least smutch of gore.

"Something's freakin' our brains," Nolo says at last. "It's gotta be what's in the trunk."

"If it is, it ain't product that's doin' this to us, Nolo."

"Let's look in the trunk."

Out in Long Island last night they loaded the truck with bricks of flake neatly taped in black plastic. But now the trunk does not contain a single one of these black plastic bricks. Instead it is occupied by the naked corpse of a dark-skinned old man. The corpse is folded fetally on its side. It shows them its profile, a carven jungle face with faint blue tattoos near the eye.

"Jesus Christ," whispers Rudy. "He looks like that witch-doctor Manny's been puttin' up."

"Doc Tolteco. It's not him, though."

"No, but this guy looks like he's in the same racket. Jesus Christ, what the fuck are they *doing* to us here, Nolo? Is Manny havin' us on? Is it inside guys fuckin' with our load somehow?"

"When could they have switched it? We've been drivin' all night! And why would they? Some kinda frame?"

"I say we dump this fuckin' thing—fuck figurin' it out!"

"Right on. We abort, get clean of this. Grab his ankles."

At the first touch of Rudy's fingers a little lightning bolt blows the air to pieces, and the shock throws Rudy straight back ten feet through the air.

Poking the corpse with a heavy bough leaves them with a charred and splintered branch, and Nolo with a sprained arm.

"We drive to the nearest fuckin' major airport," Nolo says, "we ditch this fuckin' ride, we take a plane to L.A. and disappear."

"Jesus Christ, Nolo," Rudy whimpers. "The finger I touched him with—there's like a worm in the tip of it!"

The worm is plump and pallid, a vigorous maggot in fact; the attempt to dislodge it from the meat of Rudy's finger with a pocket knife makes him half pass out with pain, and after they've dug at it, they find that not one, but two maggots are now busily at work in the flesh. Rudy pulls on a glove and straps it tight around the wrist as a containment measure. They swing the Lincoln out on the road and burn rubber toward the nearest, biggest airport.

Manny takes Tara to the jacuzzi room; she knows he likes the covering-noise and intimacy of the jacuzzi for particularly serious talk. "The long and short of it," he tells her, when they are both neck-deep in the fizzing heat, "we had some growers in the mountains. We had what you might call a contract dispute, they had what we felt was a paid obligation, and suddenly they were telling us they weren't obligated any more. Seems there was some guy advising them—I mean these were all really simple mountain types, easily influenced etcetera—so here I'm told this troublemaker is stirring them up, and so I order him taken out. See, things weren't accurately reported to me, and I made a hasty order, and the guy was taken out. But the thing was, the guy was no adviser, he was a *brujo*. He was a medicine man, a very big medicine man, El Otro. Now see, even I had heard that name, once I got the full and correct story. El Otro was maybe the oldest, with the biggest ju-ju, in that whole part of the mountains."

There is a pause. Tara looks at Manny's sweating face floating on the seethe, like some luckless missionary in a cannibal's pot, sees him struggling with how to put this, then deciding just to plunge ahead. "When I was working with Desi? My apprenticeship, you might say? Well, I walked with the mules in that operation, I got up country—Desi really wanted his people to be plugged in . . ."

"I know the background, Manny, you're always talking about your days 'up-country.'" She senses he wants to slide off the subject, delay. "Just cut to the chase."

He is stung, but it works. "Well, there's one thing I didn't tell you," he growls. "This one day, late in the day, I'm in the high country with my guide, Garcia. We're following a ridge line way up, and way in. So we come up on these two Indians heading toward us on the trail. Garcia takes one look and steps off the trail into the brush and pulls me off the trail with him. Then he goes down on one knee, like you might do in church, and makes me do the same. I do it but I'm too amazed to bow my head like he's doing. And these two Indians walk past us, moving real slow, like there's all the time in the world. The first one is a brujo, got the tattoos round his eyes, walking with a staff all carved with the witch-signs. Then behind him comes this other Indian who's got all the brujo's loads on his back. And this guy's eyes, Tara, are *sewed shut.* Sewed shut! But that's not even half of it! The light's really strong remember, slanting right down on them both, and there's no way on earth I didn't see what I saw. This guy carrying the load has a big ragged red drippy hole in his chest, and like an empty red wound where his heart should be! I looked right at it ten feet away, looked two, three, four of my heartbeats. The guy had a hole in his chest, and no heart in it. And afterward Garcia explained it to me. I mean, he was scared, but he wasn't surprised, he was like matter-of-fact. That guy had insulted the brujo, and the brujo had zombied him and made him his slave."

"Made him his attendant," corrects Tara. Her eyes are calm but remote. "That's how the Doc here refers to all the soldiers you're killing for him—they're supposed to be Otro's *attendants* as he crosses over into the land of Death where you sent him. His is a great life and he must have enough attendants to suit his stature."

Manny looks into the unblinking brightness of her eyes. "You just don't believe me, Tara. You can't. I understand, I really do, but it's a fucking shame. If you'd seen what I saw, you wouldn't . . . quibble like this about a few, like, precautionary investments. You fight fire with fire, it's that simple."

Entering the vast airport parking structure, Nolo and Rudy drive up to the entry booth. The guy in the booth stands with his back to them and doesn't seem aware they're there waiting for their ticket. Nolo struggles to stay cool, gives a polite little honk, not wanting to draw notice here. Still the guy doesn't even turn around. He shouts over his shoulder, "Go on! You don't need a ticket. Your toll's taken care of!" And the barrier arm goes up. Nolo doesn't quite like this strangeness, but there is a van behind him honking with impatience. Nolo drives in. He and Rudy want only to leave the car somewhere and get as far from it as possible.

Nolo heads automatically for a lower level, his instinct being to bury the corpse they are carrying. As they cruise through the second tight turning of the down-ramp, they both notice that the battered gray van from the entrance is still behind them.

"You see the guy drivin'?" asks Rudy. "You get a feelin' you know him?"

"I do, man, I do. And I don't like this shit, Rudy."

The van stays right with them through the third and fourth levels, too. Nolo pulls out across the fourth level, accelerating but not quite fleeing, looking for another ramp up out of this level, and looking to see if the van is still following.

It is still following, and suddenly the power dies in the Lincoln. It's like the engine suddenly vanishes, and the car becomes a creaky, coasting chassis. Nolo works the steering wheel but the Connie drifts unresponding into a dark corner, the new radials crackling delicately on the gritty concrete. Both men have their hands on their door handles but sit tranced, movement far from their thoughts, because now the hood of the car is opening soundlessly. "Look at that," says Rudy in awe. The hood is opening sideways, like a cellar door, or casket. White swamp mist coils up as it rises. No engine is revealed. Just the corpse of the old Indian they found in their trunk.

But this time the Indian sits up, allowing them now to note the large chunk of skull missing from the back of his head. The mummied Indian stands and with a casual gesture, like a man moving a branch from his path, rips the hood from its hinges and flicks it aside; it spins floatingly away, light as a dead leaf.

The corpse leaps down, light and limber as a gymnast, though his mummied tendons audibly creak. He says, *"Son viajeros conmigo. Ven."* His breath is a black gust of fungus, his voice the brutal thrust of gnarled root in earth. There seems to be grave sadness in his seamed mouth as it speaks. Now Nolo and Rudy hear the rhythmic growl of an engine idling behind them, and the bang of doors. Rudy, holding his forgotten twelve-gauge, finds someone he knows standing by his door: Sal, a Bolivian mule, a co-worker in Manny's operation. But what has happened to Sal? He is drenched and stinking, fungus sprouting through his suit, his body a rotting floater's, obesely bloated with broken wire manacles embedded in the cheese of his wrists and ankles. "'Ey, Rudy," Sal says in a leaky, sloshy voice. "El Otro says you travel with him, like us."

Rudy looks with sudden horror at his gloved hand. The glove is bulging, all its fingers swelling and rippling furiously. "The worms!" he gasps. "Sal, I think I'm—"

"Yeah, you are," Sal gargles. He reaches in and plucks Rudy's head off, the neck's pliant stalk of bone and meat surrendering with an indescribable *pop*. El Otro touches Nolo's shoulder and waves a gnarled hand toward the van. It is full of faces Nolo knows. Co-workers' faces, living men last Nolo knew, but all now staring waxy-eyed, torn, putrescent faces. El Otro says to Nolo, *"Tu puedes manejar."*

Sal is carrying Rudy—with one part in either hand—back to the van; he pauses to tell Nolo, "He says you can drive."

Manny and Tara watch a fine sunset from the after-deck lounge. When Nolo and Rudy arrive with the blow and are bagged and shot, the whole offering will be ready; then bodies and product are to be loaded on a raft, and towed out to sea.

"Decisiveness is everything in this business," Manny tells Tara, sipping his piña colada. "You get an expert to tell you the price, you pay the price, and you're done with it."

Tara sighs. "I'll be honest with you, Manny. Apart from all this being pure insanity, I've had this, like, instinct about Doc Tolteco. From day one. Just this gut feeling that inside, he's *laughing* at you."

"Laughing, huh? You can read that face of his?"

"No. It's just my instinct. That's it, now. We'll just drop it."

Manny shrugs this off, but after a bit he begins to get fidgety. He tells Tara he's going to check on the old Indian.

His knock is unanswered. He eases the door open on a dense white haze. Never has the pipe fog been like this. He steps inside; the carpet feels wrong underfoot—feels cold and clayey, like soil. There is the strangest smell of . . . open space, as if this were one misty segment of a whole fog-shrouded mountainside. His knees must actually bump against the bed before he finds it.

Doc Tolteco is a tiny, half-sized thing of sticks and parchment; he is a mummied dwarf, light as a leaf when awed Manny prods his shoulder. His eyes are centuries gone.

Manny runs and gets Tara; he does not get truly scared until he sees her fear of the thing. "It could be theater," she says grimly, "but I'll tell you, it scares the shit outta me."

Manny nods decisively. "We're outta here. My spine says cut and run. Fuck who or what—they can't get us if they don't know where we are."

In five minutes Eric is out warming up the Evinrudes on their fast little runabout that will take them to their car at the estate on the mainland, and in fifteen minutes they are skimming through the swell. The dying sun bleeds profusely on the jungled coast. "I feel like we're riding a wave; like a shockwave, that hasn't burst yet," Tara tells him, musing on the dying sun. Manny says nothing, is silent all the way to their little dock. But when he gets behind the wheel of their Jag he lets the car speak for him; it's a wild ride that calls on all his considerable gifts as a driver. They can just make a nonstop to Heathrow—an ideal place to get lost from—if they drive like the damned. Manny does.

They run down the cyclopean corridors at the airport. They are both expert short-notice travelers, their carry-ons stashed with major cash and multiple IDs and credit cards. They are shrewd, nimble souls, Manny is thinking, decisive and quick off the mark in a game where life depends on being both. "We're gonna make it," he tells Tara. She nods, but is that fear that flashes in her eyes?

Their boarding-lounge seems endlessly distant past countless identical lounges; while still far they see that it is empty, that a lone woman in the airline's livery is stacking papers at the pass-taking podium. "Wait!"

Manny trumpets. The woman raises a pert face with very red lipstick and honey-colored hair. "Go right on board!" she yoo-hoos with a neighborly smile. "You've just made it! Your seats are waiting for you, and the toll is paid." She plucks, with startlingly red-nailed hands, the passes Manny proffers, rushing past. As they burst through the double doors her words echo oddly in their ears, but they are intent on rushing down this carpeted tunnel that will funnel them utterly out of this menacing part of the world.

They rush through a turning, and suddenly the light is dim and the corridor is much too steeply pitched, and it is carpeted with something most unlike carpet—more like slick, squishy moss. Their feet squirt out from under them. They slam down on the steep muck and skid sledding smack down into knee-deep swamp.

They are kneeling waist-deep in stinking black water, kneeling at the brink of a black lagoon, where a huge, shabby, amphibious plane floats. A barge crowded with charnel figures waits, its sputtery motor idling, to ferry them to the plane.

Two huge escorts, one a shotgunned Bolivian, the other, torched by gasoline, indeterminate, stand flanking Manny and Tara. "We're gonna eat it now, Tara, honey," Manny quavers. Reality has fallen into place around him. He knows where they really are now—where they have been for how long? "Look up there in the cabin," he says pointing up at the plane.

Framed in the glass, a gaunt Indian profile wears a pilot's cap. The apparition looks down at them, its regard a twin amber glow in the shadow of the cap's bill. The plane's prop coughs, twitches, and starts to spin, soundless and slow, churning the endless fog surrounding them.

"Crossing over," Manny whispers. "We're crossing over."

The Angel of Death

A young man named Engelmann, out late one night, entered a phone booth and pretended to search for a number in the book. He savored the booth's little island of light, and his own prominence in it, like a lone glass-cased museum exhibit on the dim street.

Displaying himself thus made him grin with irony, for he knew his rarity and power would not be perceived by anyone who passed. Here, O street, was the man the city lived in fear of! His very shape and substance! Behold, and fail to see! He lifted the receiver, deposited two dimes, dialed a local prefix and then, randomly, four more digits.

He got an old man's voice. "Who is it?" A little angry-edgy, as if to an unexpected knocker outside his door. There was a TV on in the background.

"Hello, sir," Engelmann cried, hearty as an emcee. "I'm glad you tuned in, sir, because, once again, it's Angel of Death time!"

A pause. Just enough to show the name had struck, registered. "What? Is this some radio call? I never listen to the radio."

"No, sir! This is a *hot tip.* I'm letting you and only you know that it's Angel of Death time, brought to you by that ol' Guy in the Sky, the Angel of Death himself, *my*self!"

Now the pause echoed unmistakably with the old man's awareness. "Who is this? Who are you calling?"

"But I'm calling you! And I know you're ecstatic, 'cause only I can satisfy, right? Only I can make 'em die!"

"You're crazy! Who do you want? Leave me alone!"

Engelmann positively shimmied with contained laughter, for the old man didn't hang up! He waited, as if for the reply of Death itself. He waited to argue for mercy, for exemption, as if Engelmann hovered some-where above his roof and clutched his very fate in angelic talons.

"Oh, but, sir—*you're* not my Mystery Guest tonight. I'm just calling to *tell* you. You must know about me—how I go light-foot, smoother than smoke, or growl along in my powerful car. I'm that devilish, cleverish, fe-verish Angel of Death, that snooper and swooper and brain-outscooper. This is a *tip,* sir! I picked you out of the air! Take this down."

The old voice came back, half-begging, half-barking: "You shouldn't be bothering people that don't do you any harm! Is this a joke?"

"Just take this down please, sir. Don't you see it's a newsworthy *tip?* You can send it to that Jimmy what's-his-name. Is it Scheiss-kiss? The guy who writes the column. Ready now? Take this down:

> "*Those sniggering bitches*
> *Out scratching their itches—*
> *All steamy and sticky,*
> *All teases and twitches—*
> *I shatter their skulls into*
> *Spatters and tatters—*
> *I slug and I slug them*
> *To jumbled red matter!*"

Engelmann hung up crisply and left the booth. He strolled back the way he had come. His body was plump and tall, and he moved with a kind of stately drift—a secret pomp. He was a visiting potentate, again at large in the Cosmos. Tonight, in fact, he was stepping down from his Citadel and into the city's Time and Space, for the eighth time.

During his intervals up in his eyrie (where he lay in timeless power, watching TV) he was also down here among men, of course. Their un-flagging vigilance and dread enshrined him everywhere, night after night. He was a Presence here even between those times when he chose, accord-ing to the long sweet tidal shiftings of his will, to descend in the flesh.

And now, for the eighth time, he had descended, and moved among men. Even unto his angelic car he moved, and entered it, and woke the vigor of its engines.

At this point a remarkable coincidence—the first, in fact, of a series—occurred. At the very hour of the Angel's descent into the space and time of mankind, another transcendent individual made a similar entry. That is to say, he plunged from space into the warm, rich atmosphere of Earth.

It wasn't only the timing that made this remarkable. For as the newly arrived entity braked his plunge and extruded an umbrella of rigid cilia so that his sphericity, hanging beneath, began to drift smoothly like a giant thistledown—as he performed these adjustments, he immediately initiated a sensor-probe of relative psychic concentrations throughout the biosphere. And in doing this he quickly identified as his nearest promising target a huge concatenation of vitalities that was none other than the city through which Engelmann then moved.

Engelmann was driving at that moment, gliding down lamplit corridors of parked cars. Humorously, he had chosen a street that was just on the margin of what the press generally designated as his "territory." As he drifted past, his eyes ransacked the cars, front seats and back. Eerie emptiness! Nine months before, a street like this would have offered a dozen pairs of greedy mammals, hutching up, for here was the only escape for the ache of young blood in the crowded apartments everywhere. And it had been he, Engelmann, who, like a scouring wind, had cleansed these streets.

But there was something here. He sensed it. He almost felt the secret rocking, the muffled titter aimed precisely at himself, a snigger of triumph at duping the Angel of Death. He turned and came back down the block. There was a van ahead that, just perceptibly, had moved, or had it? As he passed, his senses crowded up to it, embraced it, passionate for any faint clue of hot, hidden grapplings. And, by his fierce angelic eyes, it moved! The van rocked slightly!

He parked around the nearest corner. His hand, stark and gorgeously remorseless like an eagle's talon, grasped his weapon and plunged it deep in his jacket's side pocket. Ah, the luscious tang of imminence in the night air! They in their grunting swinish scorn of him, thinking themselves safe. To know he could creep near them, pluck off their nasty shell of secrecy, smash to putty their sneering softnesses till they bled and dribbled, swooning and collapsing in exquisite agonies of remorse and futile repentance!

He stepped out, feeling the swell and tug of mighty wings at his shoulders, and wing-buoyed he moved, his heels treading in creamy silence the would-be-betraying pavements.

He stood at the van's cab door. There were curtains behind the front seat, and even as he stared at them, they shivered. He shuddered, their undulation smoothly continued in his flesh; and looking down with casual sovereignty, he saw that the lock button stood tall and silver within the rolled-up window, obedient to his will.

Then he moved, knowing his own speed and clarity compared to the dazed flesh-tranced time he was thrusting into: he, a celestial falcon; they, groggy and a-blush with blood, like vermin too gorged even to flinch. He seized the handle, thumbed home the button, pulled wide the door, and vaulted up to jam his knees into the driver's seat. He swept aside the curtain, and two matted heads popped up from the broken pane of streetlight that fell and shattered on two bodies. The Angel of Death squeezed out a bullet from his Magnum and felt the delicious lurch of its velocity jump from him and plunge through the skin and domed bone of the smaller head. With splendid fluid flexions of sinew and talon, with leisurely largess, he hammered both those skulls repeatedly, distributing the roaring gouts of lead to follow his dying targets through their spasms of recoil.

Engelmann drove home wanderingly, whimsically. He went to an all-night market for a six-pack of root beer, doubled back to buy a newspaper at a liquor store, went to a drive-through taco stand, and after elaborate polite discussion with the woman behind the clown-faced intercom, ordered a vanilla shake. These movements were his way of relishing his almost dizzying freedom—freedom to prowl these streets, or to quit them, to pull up and, in one smooth climb, to exit them, whenever he chose.

Meanwhile, that intercosmic tuft of thistledown was drifting over the very neighborhood that Engelmann had just visited with his wrath. This being had, among his colleagues, a complex personal designation that involved simultaneous articulations in a multiple of electromagnetic frequencies. The phonetic aspect of this designation was, roughly, "Siraf."

Siraf, then, just as Engelmann was ordering his vanilla shake, selected the rooftop of a tall and partly disused building as a covert in which to pass his inert phase. The Archives required that all field-workers, upon entering an alien sphere, lie passive for a time, before engaging in research on the indigenous life-forms. By this tactic the worker could gain some assurance that he had entered a sufficiently stable configuration, before expending valuable research energies on mimicry and transactional involvement. Each worker could carry only limited quanta of metamorphic power, and even in the best circumstances, only brief investigations were possible. Hence the care taken to telepalp the surroundings thoroughly for any sign of disruptive local phenomena that might abort the worker's researches.

Siraf adopted a spherical shape and rolled himself against the tarry brick parapet of the rooftop. He immediately initiated telescans of the nearest lying indigenes. Although most of these seemed to be dormant, and all were in any case too distant for fine-focused observations, the young scholar was able to add much to the morphological program provided him by the Archives for this race. That program had been in truth the merest sketch, and Siraf improved the hours of inertia by fleshing it out with studious encodements of the data he was able to gather.

But of course, this kind of preparation could only go so far in alleviating the inevitable obscurity and confusion of alien interactions. He could expect to assimilate most of the physical structure, locomotor routines, much vocabulary, and so be able, on emerging from dormancy, to mimic and to initiate transactions with the autochthones. But it would only be *during* that brief and energy-exorbitant period of mimicry and close-range interaction that he could fine-tune his observations.

For example, Siraf had soon enzymatically recorded much of the local

speech. But when it came time actually to effect relationships with the natives, he would still have no clue to the motile and behavioral patterns that
this vocabulary served. He would know how to express many concepts,
but would have no guide to what concepts it was appropriate to express
under what circumstances. A field-worker could come onstage in perfect
costume, so to speak, but with no hint of his role, or even, in many cases,
of what kind of thing a role might *be.*

It should give some sense of Siraf's excellence as a scholar to report
that within a few busy hours of assimilations and inferences he had arrived
at a closely reasoned choice of form. Of the two sexes, it appeared that the
larger, the "male," enjoyed a significantly greater degree of mobility and
social initiative than did the "female." (For example, the dreams of several
nearby dormant females were full of this very theme.) To this finding he
added the fact that the sexual drive of this race seemed remarkably dominant among its impulses—a circumstance that boded well for his chances
of getting much valued insights into its reproductive rituals. Altogether, a
young male with high mating potential seemed indicated for a maximum
probability of successful interaction. The specifications he arrived at were,
in the native units: height, 6′ 4″; weight, 215 lbs.; age, 24 years; muscular
and vascular systems highly articulated; features, Nordic; hair, blond.

Siraf was aware that many of his colleagues would condemn this
choice by reason of its exceeding the norms of size, strength, and general
aesthetic appeal by local standards. They would point out that an abnormal
individual was not likely to elicit normative reactions. His atypicality
would distort his findings.

But Siraf's heuristic methods were the reverse of conservative. He reasoned that there was no such thing as "situational purity." To experiment
at all was to disrupt, distort. And since there was no way around it, why
not *use* slight disruption? Let the fieldworker agitate a bit the hive he vis-
its. Not traumatically, but to a degree that might intensify and multiply the
scholar's involvements in his all-too-brief time for probing.

Throughout those hours when Siraf lay conceiving himself, it happened that Engelmann was doing very much the same thing. He was in his room on the top floor of an old apartment building. He lay on his mattress before the TV, propped to a half-sitting posture by pillows. He was alternately watching the tube and writing in a spiral notebook that he held against his raised knees.

"Freedom!" (he wrote) "It's a joke/miracle, a staggering simplicity! You just dare to take justice, and the daring alone fills you with power. The mere daring-to-fly *is* the power of flight. I *can* fly. I *have* power over life, and freedom from death. Even if the Insect-Squads eventually do take me—"

A Jacuzzi ad came on and he stopped writing to watch it, having seen it twice already. It would repeat throughout the program, a late movie on a local channel. Two big-breasted girls in bikinis—one on the edge of the pool paddling her legs, one sitting in the water—laughed with a young man. He was neck-deep, and his trendy mustachioed head bobbed on the bubbles just at the submerged girl's breast level. There was a voice-over pitch, and addresses of the company's outlets rolled across the scene. When the ad was over, Engelmann had to reread what he had written before he could go on:

"I won't be taken to the Poison Room. Oh, no! I'll go to the shining halls of Medicine. I'll be given soul-upholstering drugs. For my freedom itself protects me. It's too 'unreal' for the Little Folk. The very horror of what I do classifies it past the reach of punishment."

He stopped to watch the movie for a while. It was sci-fi, and there were spaceflight shots with starry backgrounds that exalted him. The ad returned. He watched it closely, and afterwards he wrote with a heat and fitfulness he had not shown:

"I do what I will. I paint the world as I will. Your skulls are my paintpots, bitches! I empty them with my rude and potent brush. I splash out frescoes of my revenge. Your cheating sneering little world is my palette. I'll make my masterpieces and lay them out to dry. And I'll have them displayed in the press as if it were no more than paint I splash around. And so it is! And so it is! I make it so, and so it is!"

Engelmann laid aside his notebook. He found that he ached to go down again, to swoop for another kill. That lovely blind red impetus had returned to him, his heart was engorged with it as with some bodily fluid.

It caused him a painful division of feeling. He had always loved to savor each deed both ways in time, first through a long anticipation, and after, to relish its echo through the expectant desolation of the city's renewed terror. Especially in this latter period he felt his tread to reverberate, gigantically, through the city. Then, spectral, huge, he lived in the hearts of seven million.

But desire was great upon him, and he lusted for a fierce, unparalleled abundance that would fill the air with the red debris of his redundant rage. After brief hesitation, he made the pact with himself to take further vengeance the following night.

Engelmann did not fall asleep until the afternoon of the next day, and he was still in the depths of his sleep when, at dusk, Siraf terminated his dormancy.

He rolled out from the brick parapet to a clear space on the tar and gravel. There, again in compliance with Archivist tradition, Siraf uttered the Field-worker's Vow prior to transmorphing. The articulation involved a phonetic aspect that sounded like lush, melancholy flute solos. Its cognitive content was, roughly:

> *Having sworn to be a foundling through the stars,*
> *I lie on yet another threshold.*
> *I will remember, though I travel far.*
> *As treasure I'll store up all I behold.*

He extended his mass into a slender ellipsoid six and a half feet long, and transmorphed.

He had perceived that the fiber-envelopes universally adopted by the indigenes were pretty widely available and thus did not warrant the energy expenditure that would be needed to fabricate them from his own substance. He found, as he lay making detailed adjustments of his new material apparatus, that the pebbles of the rooftop painfully disrupted the curvature of his dorsal dermal surface. He sat up and brushed the little stones off the pale ridgings of back and shoulder muscle. His length of limb stretched his sinewing to gothic gauntness. He stood up and did a brisk dance of acquaintanceship with arms, legs, lungs. Then he walked to the parapet, leaned on it, and looked consideringly over the city.

Profitable as his dormant scanning had been, he now faced a demanding struggle for comprehension. The race was a complex one; close-range involvement with it was going to be a matter of frantic ad-libbing, a swift juggling of known variables with the always bewildering influx of new data. A local parallel for his plight would be a man running dizzily ahead to keep a crazy stack of dishes balanced in his hands. Siraf smiled, practicing the facial contortion that would be deemed appropriate to this image.

His first goal must be clothing. He had foreseen that if his stature was unusual, so would commensurate enfiberments be, but he was counting on the abundance of the population to ensure that an appropriate envelope could be found fairly readily. He scouted now for the nearest considerable center of vital activity.

Siraf happened to be in a largely residential neighborhood, but it was a Saturday night, and three streets away was a very thriving stretch of bars, discos, dirty bookstores, and rib joints. It was invisible to him, even from his thirty-story elevation, but he telepalped the psychic concentration, noting that high emotive levels seemed to prevail. The area should offer a rich field of options, at least. He picked out an alleyway route that would bring him to the middle of the block. Then he found the shadowiest side of the building and walked down the wall, risking this anomalous gravity-orientation because dark had fallen and it saved time.

The last alley Siraf followed debouched on the activity zone. He crouched behind some big packing crates just inside the alley mouth. Across the street he could see an adult bookstore and an Italian takeout stand. Within five seconds of his pausing in this covert, an individual pulled up to the curb in front of the bookstore, and he was not only amply clothed, but just about Siraf's size as well!

Surely this was one of those rare assignments where the field-worker and his target cosmos were in a strange harmony, and luck blessed the scholar's labors. This convenient individual was of a darkly pigmented species that Siraf had rejected as a mimicry choice when he perceived that it enjoyed more limited options of social interaction than the paler ones. The man wore a broad-brimmed leather hat, a pirate shirt of maroon silk, leather pants, and calf-high Peter Pan boots. He also wore a gold watch and a gold pendant and several fat gold rings. The Eldorado he sat in, all burnished chrome, glowed on the pavements. He waited behind the wheel, and after a few moments two brightly and scantily dressed young women sauntered up to speak to him through his half-open window.

The psychic effluvia that flooded these neon-starred blocks were those of highly stimulated organisms. In all directions he detected the perceptual blur and latent vulcanism of alcohol-saturated brains. Even a highly disruptive act, if swift and decisive, should be slow to engender any organized response in such surroundings. Siraf deemed some initial traumatizing of the natives permissible, if it was strictly localized in its impact and if it facilitated entry into full interaction with them elsewhere. He began to increase the density of his hands and arms.

It took several moments to achieve a massiveness sufficient to deal with the glass and steel of the Cadillac. The girls strolled off again. The statuesque black man in the colorful enfiberments sat adjusting his tape deck. Siraf gauged him to be perhaps an inch taller and twenty pounds heavier than himself. He realized that when the man's enfiberments had been removed, he would experience the atmospheric temperature as a great discomfort. The large boxes behind which the scholar crouched were full of shredded wood, and he decided they should answer nicely for insulation.

His arms were ready. He straightened up and strode toward the Eldorado.

There was a fair number of people on the sidewalks, but all at some distance. The nearest were the two girls. Both gave amazed shouts, and one of them made a merry, obscene gesture of admiration. The well-dressed man became aware of Siraf a fraction later than his two employees. He was, however, like most successful pimps a quick-thinking man. He took in the nude stranger's sheetings of stomach muscle, the machine-like power of his thighs, his dreamy and absorbed gait—and he locked both doors and twisted the key in the ignition.

Siraf, telepalping the mechanism, inhibited the spark. He plunged his hands through the window glass, took a crushing grip on the steel of the door, and ripped it entirely out of its snug frame. He placed it as neatly as possible on the roof of the car. Then he reached inside for the man, who was just then crawling through the farther door, and seized him by shoulder and thigh. He spoke several reassurances that he had prepared in advance:

"Come along now," he said soothingly. "Nothing to worry about. This won't take a minute, and you'll be plenty warm afterward."

The man gave him a long, horrified glance. Siraf found pressure points in shoulder and leg that canceled resistance and allowed him to lift the man out. "Outsy-daisy," he said, uncertain of the expression. He hoisted the man straight-arm over his head and carried him to the sidewalk. There he sat him down, leaned him against the wall, and started to remove his clothes. A fascinated crowd was forming, at a respectful distance. Siraf took and donned the hat, the shirt, the trousers, and, last, the boots. He left the jewelry on the man.

When he was dressed—and it was done in moments—he picked up the still-quiescent donor and carried him to the alley mouth. There Siraf bedded him snugly amidst the shredded wood in the largest packing crate. He tucked the insulator around him till only the head lay visible, like a set jewel, or shipped fruit, in the midst of the excelsior. Since he had already grossly violated behavioral norms, he took his leave of the crowd, after an amicable salute, by running straight up the wall of the nearest building and disappearing over the top, eighteen stories above.

He knew that the indigenes' communication system was relatively swift and efficient, and so he traveled several miles, overleaping streets, when he had to, at the darkest points and most carefully chosen instants. He did not think a concerted pursuit likely in a place not only populous but rife, as far as he could gather, with transactions of the most intense and violent kind. He fled on nevertheless, conscientiously safeguarding his researches, and it so happened that as he fled across one particular roof, his passage sent down an eerie drumbeat into the sleep of that other alien, Engelmann, the Angel of Death.

Just then he lay in the dense webbing of a lustful nightmare where ghastly sprawling spiders envenomed and sucked away his flesh. The hammering of those feet kicked through and scattered the nightmare like gusts tearing up a sluggish ground mist and sent sad, turbulent dream-reverberations through him. He felt that desperately vital news, cosmic tidings, were being sped by messenger to a distant city, where there would be a vast rejoicing. And meanwhile he, Engelmann, lay in a living grave upon some giant plain, and saw the runner pass him with that news, and struggled to rise and follow, and could not, could never reach that far, vast rejoicing.

As for Siraf, about a mile beyond this new coincidence he slowed and found a high building for reconnoitering. He decided that his entry point would be a park some blocks distant, and when he had approached it and studied it from a new rooftop perch just across the street, he felt fully confirmed in his decision. Singles bars, cabarets, movies fringed the leafy square, whose pathways and benches were as lively as the surrounding sidewalks.

Long unmoving, he spied that scene. With his fine-spun nets of telepulses he trawled and seined the swarming lagoon of psychic life below. His investigative powers were cruelly limited by distance, but such was the emotive unanimity of the crowd that he could read much from its sheer ambience. It was overwhelmingly obvious from what he saw—pairing rituals, symbolic self-exhibitions, musical mimicry of copulatory contortions—that the place was a hotbed of mating-related activities. It seemed the luck that had clothed him was not faltering.

In the Archives, mating transactions were highly prized as data, for among sexed organisms they often provided a key to many other emotive patterns and social rituals in a given race's repertory. At the same time, they were recognized as the trickiest exchanges for a field-worker to mimic, since cuing behavior and display symbolism were likely to be very subtly elaborated in such crucial interactions. But Siraf resolved that his daring would match his luck. He would take mating for his immediate aim. He adjusted his hat and took the stairs down to the street.

He followed the sidewalk for a short time before crossing over to the park. With every step he modulated more precisely his posture and gait to those prevailing and achieved a fuller acquaintance with the local vocalization system by rummaging in the vocabularies of those he passed. He accomplished, in a few hundred yards, great refinements in the facial and bodily techniques of confronting and moving among others. He also satisfied himself that most of the active pairing was going on in the park, and, accordingly, he soon crossed over.

It happened that a tall, exhilarated grad student named Jeannie Kudajzinsky had entered the park not long before Siraf did. Prior to doing so, she had enjoyed three stiff Bloody Marys at the Elevator DiscoBar while watching the dancers with increasingly droll approval. She had spent the last five days, ten hours a day, in the library stacks preparing for her doctoral exams in anthropology. And now she lounged in the park, watching the passersby with a jaunty smile, indulging in what she thought of as "contemporary anthropology," an amused survey of current styles in self-decoration and self-preservation. Her overall feeling was that the night was splendid and anything might happen.

It was from Jeannie that Siraf received his first unmistakable lead in the tangle of fleeting ideations he was combing through as he strolled the paths. He noted among her cerebral events his own image undressed and subjected to various erotic attentions. He circled round to pass her again in a few moments.

She wore body-emphasizing courting finery. Her mammary and gluteal bulges appeared precisely to fulfill the normative ideal, but her stature was sufficiently norm-excessive to make it likely that she was deprived of interaction and thus probably the more motivated toward it. She would stand about six feet tall. Fighting that inevitable pang, that forlorn sense of ignorance every investigator felt as he prepared to grapple closely with alien phenomena, Siraf stepped up to her bench and opened with an expression that he felt fairly sure was appropriate:

"Hello, my dear. You're looking lovely tonight."

Jeannie laughed. Her first disbelief at the approach of this beautiful Nordic pimp became a giddy sense of *savoir-faire,* and she promptly countered him:

"You say that like you know how I look other times. You've been following me around, right?"

"Oh, no. I only just now picked you out. Does your appearance change radically with the passage of time?"

"That's putting it mildly. Think how I'll look in forty years!"

Siraf was about to clarify that he meant over short periods, but Jeannie laughed with such gusto at her own retort that he was cued to discount the whole exchange. The image of himself sitting by her on the bench was recurring vividly in her cerebrations, attended by strong though ambiguous affect. Siraf sat down with a reassuring smile. He was aware of a verbal routine apparently designed for such a situation as this, and so he ventured it: "I was just passing, and I thought I'd stop by for a while and see how you are."

The woman's new laughter informed him that the formula did not apply. "Well, that's wonderful," she gasped. "We don't get to see you much out this way." Jeannie was going to elaborate the joke when she was taken with a guilty awareness that, in her excitement and anxiety, she had done nothing but laugh at the man. "Listen," she said, "are you a foreigner? Your accent is perfect, I mean you have no accent at all, but your . . . your idioms are a little funny—Christ! That doesn't sound like I'm putting you down, does it?"

"I'm not the slightest bit put down. In fact, I am a foreigner. I'm Norwegian." Jeannie's turn of speech had given him his cue, and as he spoke he read the nationality in her expectations.

"You certainly look it," she said. "I mean that as a compliment."

"Oh, yes," said Siraf, adopting a grave manner and feeling with new keenness his ignorance. He decided it was safest to answer tautologically and countercompliment: "A compliment is a very pleasant thing to receive. Thank you. You are a very desirable woman. I mean that as a compliment in return."

Jeannie could find no sign in his face that he was joking, and as she smiled incredulously at him, he went on, developing the seemingly gratifying theme of her physical form:

"For instance, something the observer immediately notes about you is the abundant development of your breasts and your posterior. Your face has a delightful symmetry. It is . . . foxlike." He caught a clear suggestion from her here, as he hesitated. "Moreover I see that you are unusually large, and I thought this a wonderful coincidence, because I too am abnormally large-bodied."

From resurgent hilarity, Jeannie had subsided to bemused attention. All shadings of irony or affront were missing from the man's impossible words. There was an honesty, a tender objectivity in them such as she had never heard in a man's voice. An Innocent? A Noble Savage? If this was illusion, as the whole man seemed illusory in his perfection, she decided to rise to it, as on a dare, and take it at face value. Had she only been pretending to believe that anything might happen tonight?

"You are very sweet to tell me the things you do," she answered. "You have this marvelous sincerity. I hate that word, but it's what you have. Furthermore, you're beautiful, physically I mean, as far as I am concerned. What do you say to that?"

She smiled in his eyes, half humor, half suspense. She did not know what to expect, as if she were Baucis in the myth and had just given a nudge of collusion to one of the disguised gods in her house. Siraf, finding no clue, returned her own formula:

"You are very sweet to tell me."

"Most men wouldn't react that way," she said.

Siraf had a swift fear that the woman was objectively rating the credibility of his performance—knew him to be a performer, in other words, though he found no such image in her. "They would not?" he asked, trying to express innocent, grave alarm. It made Jeannie laugh again in spite of herself.

"Don't be so shocked! It's beautiful that you answered that way. See? Again beautiful. See how you're racking up points?"

The game metaphor, which he had noted as a common turn of mind, locally, oriented him, and he recognized that performance here was humorously commented on without signifying doubt of the performer's genuineness. He laughed, and Jeannie felt a burst of *déjà vu*. Long ago, in high school, before she had become (as she liked to phrase it) "a certified giantess," she had often sat in a car with a certain basketball player. There had been in him a similar ease of acceptance, and with him she had felt an exhilarating, unthreatened freedom of thought and body. He would always start by inviting her for a burger and a Coke . . . "Well," said Siraf, "how about driving out for a burger and Coke?"

This almost eerie echoing of her reverie at first made her stare and then made her jump up, as if to throw off bodily the last encumbrances of cynicism and disbelief. She snuffed the night air appreciatively, and said:

"Wonderful! I'd love a drive! I'd love a hamburger!"

They walked down the paths to the sidewalk. The curb was parked solid, and Siraf was confident that an adequate vehicle could be procured. As they passed, he telepalped each car for fuel and performance levels and settled on a new black Cadillac halfway down the block. He probed its ignition and, as they approached it, started it up. Jeannie's surprise told him that the performance was anomalous. Hastily he searched out a reassuring tag for such occasions:

"Oh, you know how it is. It sometimes does that."

"Oh, yes," Jeannie nodded emphatically. "I know what you mean. Sometimes they just get eager to get going."

He now made out the proper sequence from her anticipatory ideations and, springing the locks with telepulses, opened the passenger door and let her in.

At just about this time, Engelmann was slowly awakening. He had left the TV on, and its rising to the more hectic pitch of prime time was what gradually wedged him out of his sleep. He stumbled to the bathroom, came back to his mattress only slightly less groggy, and plunged his hand into a cardboard box on the floor near the bed. From amidst candy bars, cheese-'n'-cracker packs, bags of chips, and boxes of cookies, he drew out several packages of cupcakes, some rolls of miniature doughnuts, and a quart of chocolate milk, which he liked warm.

He breakfasted. Some of his mind followed the beloved food down to his insides; some of his mind carefully watched the backgrounds of the tired cop-series for streets and locales he knew; but most of it peered queasily back into the dream-tangle he had just crawled out of.

All those Things That Should Not Be—all that spiderous, bristly grappling. Granted, such things squirmed eternally behind the veil of nightmare. But why should he plunge so often into them? Why should his thought so tirelessly conceive the worst it could? Wasn't it after all only the price of his greatness, his terrible freedom? Engelmann licked his fingers and, with a musing air, took up his notebook.

"Lo!" (he wrote) "I've burst from the shadow-show called Human Action. That pantomime! It's all cringing, all shying-away-from, all writhing-to-please! So I've torn free—I've swung at those shadow-manikins and smashed them to tatters, to rags and lust." He paused, corrected "lust" to "dust," and sped on.

"But just for this reason, the shadow-dimness no longer protects me. I see the real infinity of possibility, infinite possibility both dark and light.

That's why so many nightmares come with freedom!"

He stopped to savor this high pitch of understanding for a moment, and the feel of archangelic overview quickened his heart to full wakefulness.

"Oh, yes, I pay!" (he wrote) "Power isn't free! It's not just given away! Dues? I guess I know about paying dues!"

He shook his head here with a wry smile of self-admiration.

"Oh, there will be rest at the end! I admit I've had that consolation to stiffen me against the nightmares. Everyone earns a rest, and for me there'll be the long hours of protection and nourishment. Institutional life! All shining and brilliant with the lovely psychic varnishes of drugs!

"But for now, there is still the struggle! I'm not so ready to give up the power of flight—not so fast, whatever it costs! So for now let the dues be reckoned, and I'll just pay up on demand."

All the latent feeling of the nightmare was dispersed now, and the Angel of Death was fully himself, voluptuously stretching out the wings of his oversoaring irony. And, like the splendid sun-burnished cock in the fresh morn, he suddenly craved to tread some squawking, fluster-feathered she-bird and hammer the heat of his blood into her pleasure-devastated flesh.

So the Angel of Death took up the image of his beloved and laid her in a shadowy place behind his eyelids. He laid her so that the shadows concealed her head. Her body cringed and shivered under his taloned regal feasting. She rolled her dark-smeared head with her cherished agony. And her clutching, penetrated flesh—aided by Engelmann's deft right hand—tugged and tugged on the root of his pleasure and at last, powerfully, quite plucked it out of those divine loins.

The Angel of Death rose and washed and changed his clothes. He began to clean his gun, and as he did so, fell to musing again on the ease and quietude of a mental institution. This line of thought shortly led him to so piercing-sweet a mirth that he dropped his work and snatched up his notebook again. He wrote:

"It's like being a giant that no one sees rightly. The doctors will come up to me, and they'll talk to my knees, thinking they see me. I roar down to them: 'Here I am up here, you sniveling jerks!' They nod compassion-ately to my knees and answer: 'Yes, these inflated ideas—they are your punishment as much as your pleasure. Tragically for others, you've been led to cherish these ideas of exaggerated potency and now you are com-pelled to enact them.'

"I boom back jovially: 'Doctors! My exaggerations are made true by your sons' and daughters' blood. I *am* gigantic with it. Up here, Doctors! Up here I am!'

"'Yes,' they say, 'that is the horror of your condition—your utter sepa-rateness. You're trapped in a void where others are no realer, no more comfort to you, than furniture.'

"How answer to be heard? This dogged, blind, idiot compassion is of course only the child of fear. Everyone on Earth uses others like furniture, cautiously at first, then abusively, once familiarity sets in. I have made grosser and more daring uses of them and admit it's for my whim, and through this I've reached another order of being, another order of happi-ness. I could roar out louder than an H-bomb, and they'd still be straining their ears at me to catch the nuances. It's just this simple: I'm the crazy guy who happens to *be* Napoleon. I *am* the Angel of Death."

Engelmann read what he had written, reread it, and at length, took up the gun again. When it was cleaned and reloaded he got up and turned off the TV. He pulled on a jacket and stuffed his Magnum into one pocket of it. Into the other he shoved three candy bars from his cardboard box and turned off his light.

Fearlessly he walked down the dark flights and fearlessly out into the gusty night. He stabbed and twisted with his key, and his deep-chested car came to life. The Angel of Death was again on the city, and he meant to hover wheresoever he would—to stand and stoop with Olympian ran-domness wherever the covert stirred beneath his eye.

Siraf, for much of their drive, was absorbing navigational procedures and signals, while following Jeannie's ideations closely for clues to his route.

Simultaneously, of course, he was encoding everything, for in this he never ceased. Jeannie talked about herself, luxuriating in a sense that she could say anything that came to her, and yet only half attending to what she did say. For her sense of sexual-fantasy-come-true had not faltered. The very turnings of the car had a dreamlike congruence with her desires. All the shopping districts and showpiece streets of the city that she loved to see at night streamed past them now, while through it all Siraf sat stately, beautiful, and grave, receiving the details of her life with his odd, earnest answers. The sensation of unreal rightness peaked when he steered them into one of the few old-fashioned drive-ins still operating in the city. In her high school days they had been the norm, before the coming of the drive-through.

Siraf handled the opening meal transactions fairly smoothly, using his foreigner's prerogative to ask for details of procedure when he failed to palp clear indications. He watched her handling of the food when it arrived, and aped it.

"How did you start the car from outside?" Jeannie asked. He read her back the hypothesis she mentally rehearsed in self-answer.

"Remote control," he said and, on a further hint, significantly tapped his empty pocket. He bit into his cheeseburger, far too hard. It ejected a gout of sauce through its greasy diaperings and splattered the chest of his shirt.

When Jeannie laughed, he joined her, causing her to apply her napkin with guilty solicitude and turn on the lights to bring the carhop. She was an older woman. Pointing to his shirt, Siraf told her:

"The cheeseburger squirted it."

"Look, sir. We make them all the same," she said. "They don't squirt other people."

He nodded. "I see. Perhaps I bit it too forcefully."

The woman stared, and seeing his candid gaze, her brow darkened. "Then, again," he offered, "it is possible that I was holding it incorrectly."

Jeannie leaned forward quickly.

"Could we just get some water, please?"

She helped him wipe the silk clean, pressing her free hand against his chest to tauten the fabric. The tactile influx she experienced awakened a complex image in her that Siraf noted.

Precisely here—in Siraf's notice and misunderstanding of Jeannie's mental image—was demonstrated an insidious and incorrigible blind spot affecting the judgments of all the Archives' field-workers in their readings of highly evolved conscious forms. Jeannie's image—to which her mind had reverted throughout their meal—was one of copulation in the backseat of a car on a breezy night. The car was parked on a street canopied by big broad-leaved trees and lit by old-fashioned streetlights.

Siraf took this ideation as a simple, projected goal, though Jeannie did not clearly visualize her partner in it. The assumption was reasonable, on the grounds of the image's consonance with their actual situation: it was night, there was a light breeze, they had a car.

In fact, Jeannie was savoring a fantasy. The spilled sauce, the heat of skin felt through a thin shirt, had renewed certain memories of her basketball player. They had never parked in such a place as she pictured, however—the street was added from childhood walks in another city, where she had lived for a time with an aunt. This sensual nostalgic compound, mixing memory and desire, was in no sense a project. Jeannie feared the Angel of Death as much as anyone.

On the theoretical level, the Archives fully recognized the inevitability of such errors. But in the field, the urgent thing was always to identify the subject's dominant psychic configuration. The less articulated strata of consciousness that this emerged from must often be neglected, for simple lack of time to analyze them; the interaction must be kept going above all else, and of course there were the field-worker's ongoing anatomical investigations and his monitoring of the larger environment to be sustained simultaneously as well.

In the present instance, Siraf was lucky. His proposal that they "drive to a tree-lined street, and park there," did not elicit the alarm it might well have done. His unfailing closeness to her thought so emphasized his magic aura that she could not simply recoil in fear from a suggestion that would have to be called insane, in this place and time, coming from anyone else. Coming from Siraf, this offer of her erotic dream made real had the character of one of those crucial choosings offered the heroes of so many of the myths she studied. To the daring, this mythic choice offered revelation. To the daunted, drab endurance. Jeannie, aglow with three Bloody Marys and dawning lust, decided that here was a critical challenge to her faith and recklessness. She must dare to choose enchantment over safety.

And, after she had assented to his proposal—with a grand "Why not?" and a sweep of the arm that scattered a few drops of her Coke on the lap of his trousers—a further, somewhat shabbier, reflection occurred to her that made the risk seem less. After a moment she brought it out, to confirm it to herself:

"I know it's morbid, but you get to where you calculate, you know? I mean about this Angel of Death character. The week just after one of those killings is statistically the safest time, right? Ghoulish way to think, I guess, but there it is."

Siraf was preoccupied with internally reviewing the sexual apparatus he would shortly have to employ, for he palped high oxygen concentrations nearby and guessed they were approaching heavily treed neighborhoods. He gathered, distractedly, that the "Angel of Death" awakened strong avoidance reactions and that he was a kind of public figure. His name was not associated in her with any clear facial or bodily image, but rather with written accounts too elliptically evoked to admit piecing out.

Jeannie had quelled her own fear. Thus easily was this phantom vanquished, whose only reality to her was a series of news photos of meaningless curbsides with police and stretchers. But as fear dwindled to insubstantiality, she was pleased to poke at it with little jabs of theory, noticing the while that Siraf was experimentally stiffening his procreative member. (He was astonished at the rigidity that the flaccid protuberance was capable of attaining.)

"It's really amazing to think that what that character does is essentially a substitute for, you know, sex. It's a classic pattern, I mean apparently it pops up at the time—I mean *all* the time. You've heard of it, the weapon's the symbolic organ, right? He's displaying his potency to the woman by killing her. There's the equation of sex and pain, death is the orgasm he causes. I guess sometimes you feel vengeful, but what's the point of killing someone like that? It would be just as cruel and pointless as what he does to others."

Just then Siraf was busy appreciating for the first time what a powerfully engrossing phase of experience sexual engagement was for this race. As he tested the relevant aspects of his neural apparatus—that is to say, almost all of it—he saw that he faced a turbulent adventure. Perhaps a fit image for this stout spirit, as he faced the strange cerebro-neural uproar that would shortly engulf him, would be that of a beginning swimmer facing huge waves that he must, for the first time, ride.

Nevertheless he was, in a half-attending way, fascinated by this strange ritual variant of the mating pattern that Jeannie was so glibly describing. It appeared to be a cultural institution that was abhorred, but of sufficient permanence to generate a theoretical tradition. That he was dealing, on this planet, with a highly symbolic sentience, he had seen immediately.

But a symbolic system that could substitute death for the process of insemination would be a startling oddity to add to the Archives' store. Then Jeannie's train of thought became strongly and unequivocally mating-directed. He sought, amidst towering leafy sycamores and old-style streetlights, a place to park.

Thus it was that Jeannie Kudajzinsky became a point of intersection, of convergence, for the two starry nomads abroad in that night. Unburdened by all sense of antecedent and consequence, she enjoyed fluid and explosive embraces and intermittences of warm enclaspment, during which she watched the gold-brown sycamore leaves where the sparse lights splashed them with visibility. Of the two who converged on her, Engelmann, even in the instant of his actually seeing her, possessed her only as an abstraction, while Siraf was so busily encoding her (and his own) electrochemical activity that he almost ceased to perceive her simple bodily presence at all.

Between these two potencies, she lived her dream of love alone.

Siraf, for his part, was humbly amazed at the extreme aesthetic capacities that were being revealed to him. Their copious, spasmodic exchanges of fluids he found to be among the most dynamic transactions he had ever observed to fall within the repertory of a race's routine behaviors. So desperately focused was his attention that the brief impingement of a strong psychic source outside that focus came as a slight shock to him. The signal he caught, as the pair of them rested, was a very intense ideation of a faceless pair coupling in a car. Siraf found the coincidence striking. The ideator was moving at a vehicular rate and passed from range almost as soon as Siraf had identified his thought. Then Jeannie's slow, rocking demands recommenced.

Siraf reentered the labyrinth of his borrowed form. Jeannie, splendid and abandoned, rode his lap until, all at once, she drove herself greedily to climax. He followed suit.

She lay against him. She spoke thickly into his chest. "It's astonishing. Having exactly what I want so easily. But then you're like a dream. A wet dream."

"A wet dream. Is that an idiom?"

She sat up and laughed. "I don't think so, dear. I don't know what else you call them. Nocturnal emissions, I guess, would—"

The light in the car came on. It was Siraf's doing, and what had moved him to do it had gone unnoticed by Jeannie, so that at first all her startlement was at the sudden illumination. Then, following Siraf's eyes, she saw the gun and squinting face behind it just outside the window. She saw this through the image of herself and Siraf mirrored on the glass— saw how she straddled him and gaped, saw how her gape began to become a scream—all these last readings of the world she took before the gun fired. When it did, alarm had activated only the slightest muscular resistances in her, and the slug's impact snatched her off the scholar's thighs and flung her slack as a doll against the farther door.

For both the superhuman wanderers who were thus brought together face-to-face for the first time, this was a moment almost impossibly charged with meaning. On Siraf's side, so surprised had he been that he was still scrambling along a nanosecond behind the attacker's cerebral flow. He had hit the light in a reflexive attempt to maximize data of the transaction he suddenly realized was at hand. During the first shot, and Jeannie's falling, and the subsequent instant that the eyes stared over the gun at him through the hole in the glass, his mind sprinted to get abreast of developments: (a) Jeannie was dead. (b) This was beyond doubt precisely the mating variant, and the practitioner of it, she had spoken of. (c) He himself was just sufficiently entangled with her legs to inhibit by a critical instant his extricating himself. (d) The man was now squeezing the trigger again, and the slug would surely reach Siraf's skull. (e) Therefore, he must of necessity again exceed behavioral norms, to preserve the viability of his mimicked apparatus.

The confrontation found Engelmann likewise somewhat stunned. There had been that sudden blooming of light within the car, just as he was stealing near, infernal yellowish light falling on those splendid lengths of limb, those heroic loins all notched and knotted with the goatish strength of lust; there had been her Atlantean breasts nosing like lilies from the rumpled calyx of her pushed-up clothes, and his Luciferian face. Engelmann felt that he had stumbled upon the very archetype of the crime that it was his divinity to scourge. He had uncovered daemons, or demigods, at the coupling. Here was the two-backed beast itself, the Enemy, divine, in its way, as the Angel of Death was. Here was the test, and he would meet it. Exalted, he raised his massy Magnum at her staring not-yet-fearful eyes, and bravely, steadily, mightily, he smote her with fire and ruin. And lo, she was hurled down by the power of his tool and cast below in blood and darkness. And then Engelmann swung that godly tool on the goatish colossus. Here, for an instant, the Angel of Death bore with his naked eyes the stare of the enemy. In that hawk-browed gaze the Angel saw no fear, only a bright unreadable concentration. Then the Angel of Death gave battle, fearing not, the song of supreme combat in his ears. He pumped out roaring destruction into the eyes of the Enemy.

This was the beginning of the Angel's ordeal. Here commenced That Which Should Not Be. The range was close, and the shot sprayed what seemed to be the whole back of the man's head against the black tuck-and-roll and the windshield behind him. But even as Engelmann turned to flee his triumphant work, that spray of pulverized bone and brain leapt off the upholstery, jumped off the glass, leaving it unmarked save for the bullet's exit hole, and sped back, recohering in air like a convergent beeswarm, to reconstitute the gold-haired spheroid of the titan's head.

Seeing that face reknit, and the dark shattered eyes resume their stare— seeing this ruptured the very soul of the Angel of Death. A vital tissue of belief, a deep and unsuspected faith, was torn in him. His mind bled horror that flooded thought and swept it down dreadful channels that had long been dug in him and lain waiting. The Angel of Death ran, flinging away his gun, and making water in his chaotic muscular exertions to escape.

He hauled himself behind the wheel of his car, left idling a half block down the street. He loosed the brake and grabbed the stick shift and . . . waited.

He could not flee, plunge off into the madness now alive in him, as long as a hope remained that he had dreamed. If that black car in his rear-view did not stir, if the moments lengthened and nothing happened, he had hallucinated and was free. If not, Engelmann knew with an eerie certainty what would happen: that *thing*, only temporarily a man in form, would burst through the very steel of the car, surge out, and, with a roar of Ragnarök, sprint after him. He waited, the gunfire utterly forgotten. That, and the police it might have summoned, existed in another world, to which he could never return if he did not prove now to himself that only corpses lay in that black car.

Siraf was ready for immediate pursuit but sat still throughout Engelmann's sprint back to his car. He longed to give chase. On this lucky excursion, jackpot on jackpot of data was falling to his lot, and he meant to seize on this second homicidal subject in any way he could, if only by getting a verbal report from the individual on the full meaning of his rite's bizarre symbolism.

But the female, Jeannie, had clearly abhorred in the abstract the fate that had now actually stricken her. Siraf very much wanted to fix her while it was still possible. He touched her long calves, still across his thighs, hating the wastage. The Archives' most fundamental traditions abjured him not to do it—not at the cost of the new data and not when the first subject's loss was completely fortuitous. Siraf's ambition, and his dedication to the Archives, showed him necessity, but he could not bring himself to move until absolutely the last moment, when the other's car should start to move and he must run it down before it lost him.

And, then, it did *not* move! The aggressor waited down the street, visualizing a bizarre form of pursuit by Siraf, ideating with such intensity that the image came through clearly even at that range. Siraf was being invited into the ritual. What an amazingly flexible acceptance of the (to him) impossible on the part of this attacker! For he was now playing the game of retreat and coy pause, and waiting to be chased by his victim!

There would be time then, after all. He began increasing his bodily density. Simultaneously he sought out by thermal palp every least fragment of Jeannie's head throughout the car's interior. The finer fluids had cooled quickly on the glass and metal, but all retained critical traces of warmth. The reassembly was telekinetic, his body motionless in its process of mass- gain. He referred to his enzymatic record for his exhaustive readouts of her cranio-cerebral morphology. It was a work of delicate correlations, electrically swift. The chips and tissue-shreds each had to be minutely cleansed and neatly relodged in the dense three-dimensional puzzle. It took twenty-seven seconds. He sanitized, sutured, and sealed the countless seams with thermal telebeams, infinitely fine. When he saw her eyes open and struggle for focus, he was content, and as, just then, his density had reached its peak, he propped her on the seat, pulled up his trousers, and hurled himself against the car door.

For Engelmann, the healing seconds of silence and inactivity had almost closed his horror's wound. He breathed deeply and pulled the car into gear, scarcely yet daring to believe he had been delivered from a mythic retribution, delivered from the Impossible. Then in the mirror he saw the Cadillac's side bloom outward and the giant emerge from the tattering steel and spraying glass amidst a roar of Ragnarök. With a howl of acceleration his deep-chested car fled away.

Now inexorably That Which Should Not Be came to pass. Precisely as he dreaded, the giant began to sprint after him, and though Engelmann shortly hit fifty, his Enemy gained. He drove at and beyond the limit of control, sliding and careering through turns that ought by all odds to have destroyed him. The giant gained. The Angel of Death was Phaethon now, dragged broken-limbed among the stars, a mortal suddenly seized by real gods.

"Real Gods!" He screamed it aloud. "No!" Had he not then believed his own godhead? Yes. No. Yes—but *not like this.* It was partly a *game!* Only the deaths had been real—ordinary deaths. His divinity had only been . . . poetic!

But there was no holding on to this late truth, for it was truth no more. He had flown upward on real wings, had for a fact soared up to where the Impossible lodged. For here it was a dozen strides back of him, its face an image of mythic calm while its legs and arms drove it forward as furiously as the connecting rods on a locomotive's wheels. The Angel of Death had been just angel enough, had had just power enough, to damn himself, to bring down on himself a truly divine avenger. At home there was a machine gun, and to that poor scrap of potency, the limit of his defense, Engelmann now bent all his thoughts. He threw a left turn too fast, sideswiped a parked car, and roared on, dribbling glass and clattering with popped chrome.

Siraf stopped. He had by now returned to normal mass, but even so he found that the effort required to maintain this speed would shortly do serious damage to his adopted anatomy. He had read a clear destination in his attacker's thoughts, including a map thither that the latter had fleetingly rehearsed to himself. The distance remaining to be covered was not great.

So the young scholar settled to an easy jog, husbanding his forces. He had received premonitory glimpses of his quarry's desire—of the scenario that the man waited to play out when Siraf joined him in his room. He foresaw that new mimicries would be required, and that this investigation would almost surely exhaust his research energies—hardly a misfortune, considering the choice insights he had been granted. Especially this second find. Could a rarer, more paradoxical and self-destructive rite exist, than this his recent attacker flew to consummate?

And at length, when Siraf stood in the vestibule of Engelmann's apartment building and read him clearly where he lay seven stories above, the scholar found in full what he had guessed at, an astonishing necroerotic ritual with himself as co-celebrant. He was indeed expected to transform his body—and how could the man have educed so unerringly his power to do so? More, how could he so smoothly accept it, beyond the capacities of his kind though it was, and incorporate it in his passionate fantasies? Not for the first time in his career, Siraf acknowledged with awe in his heart the endless creativity of consciousness as he had met with it throughout its polymorphic, transgalactic sprawl. He deactivated the lights of the stairwell and caused his form to melt into several smaller ones. Slowly these climbed the carpeted stairs, with a whispery prickly noise, mounting multiply to probe this second earthly mystery.

Could a more dreadful, even tragic, misunderstanding be conceived? It was lunatic expectation, not desire, that powered those intense imaginings of Engelmann's! But how could Siraf, speed-reading his impossibly involved text, be blamed? The Angel's visions sprang from his real (and all too unreal) encounter, but the grafting where hallucination sprouted from fact was missed by the scholar. And since the half-sexual terror that now flooded the man's nerves was not grossly different from the half-sexual rage of his initial assault, here too Siraf saw continuum and concentrated on reading his scripted role in the rite. Repugnance he surely felt, but professionalism squelched it. He had already gathered that no kind of emotional violence should surprise him, coming from this turbulent species.

Somewhat later, near the stillest hour of the night, Jeannie Kudajzinsky stepped through a great hole of shredded steel and stood on asphalt and broken glass, an alien in this ended and continued world. It might have been one of those ritual womb-symbols that she emerged from, she thought, for she found herself reborn—into the Impossible.

She walked along the sidewalk, very slowly. All was emptiness, holocaust hadn't raised a single siren. Had she died in fact, and were all these buildings crypts? An hour and more she had sat in the ruined car, remembering, and no one had passed.

She decided that the most terrible aspect of it all, the thing that could conceivably drive her mad, was that there should be nothing more, that she should now have to walk back into her life and simply resume it. She looked at the big sycamore leaves applauding the wind. Like vile arthritic hands they covetously rubbed the brass-nippled streetlamps. Panic began to radiate from a point-source in her stomach's pit. Just then she was spoken to—distinctly, voicelessly:

"Jeannie. Be comforted. This is Siraf. I am an extraterrestrial and your experiences were simple realities, every one."

She looked straight up—from instinct, as the telepulses bore no directional trace. Ten feet above her, under a vaulting of branches, hung that tuft of transcosmic thistledown, Siraf's traveling shape. Jeannie gazed. After a long and chaotic moment, she *was* comforted. Softly she said:

"You were . . ."

"In a human shape. We mated. The sexual homicide—his name was Engelmann—killed you. I repaired you. Then I indulged Engelmann in his fantasies. He is dead, my dear. Barring the energy I need for my return, I am utterly depleted, and there was no fixing him. But from Engelmann I learned—too late for him—the proneness of your race to psychic trauma, and so I've taken care to explain these things to you. Do you understand?"

"Yes," she said. "But why . . . ?"

"Scholarship. Please accept my thanks for your time and cooperation. I apologize for the inconvenience involved."

"I'm a scholar too!" she blurted. Sadness, and the lone discoverer's exaltation, stretched her heart between them, while through all else and amazing to herself, she felt a piercing envy.

"Yes," Siraf responded. "And you have taught me much. Goodbye."

He was gone. "Goodbye," she said, an instant too late. And then once more, in a shout, the better to project her voice across the light-years: "Goodbye!"

After a moment she spread her arms and did a sprawling, not to say gargantuan, pirouette under the sycamore trees. She whooped with laughter, and at the quiet, coward streets where gunshots and fury had not raised a single stir of protest or of aid, she shook her fist and shouted: "Revelation! Great! But what the hell can I *do* with it?"

Engelmann sat on his mattress with his back against the corner he'd shoved his bed into, after bolting his door. He had the machine gun across his thighs and the TV on. He couldn't watch the TV, however—only the door, whose terrible flimsiness was like an ongoing horror show that the tube could not compete with. That Which Should Not Be, was. Effortlessly, irresistibly, It took Its being and did Its will on man. Not any man. On *him* alone. Engelmann wept and ground his teeth together.

What was there not? What unspeakabilities, glimpsed in dreams, were not proven now? For he knew the true form of that which chased him. It was a trinity, three-in-one. Eight-legged things from the sniggering dark, come scuttling down from the poisonous cobwebby stars. But he had not flown up there! Not truly! Why should they come down? That dreadful three-in-one—one for his face, one for his heart, one for his loins. He'd had no wings, not really! Only a costume made of others' blood, only a god-costume. Was that his crime, blasphemy? What wall, what puny dike of Possibility, was left to stand between himself and chaos now? All the rest of the world was safe in its fortress, only he—*was that a movement outside the door?*

Back inside the Fortress! Back inside! O World, let Engelmann back within the walls! Engelmann wants back in, dear world! Things are coming, things that will pierce his pitiful skin and corrode his precious heart with poisons!

Was that a bulging of the panel of the door?

Oh, here is Engelmann, alone and naked! Take him in, he begs you; he is helpless, his water flows; oh, pick him up and cradle him out of harm! Momma! Not death! Not pain and death!

But something was piercing the door, soundlessly, as if it were clay, or cheese. And a blister was swelling from the ceiling, and another from the wall. Three tarantulas, big as German shepherds, hatched through wood and plaster; their shaggy legs whispered as they came tender-footing toward him. One for his face. One for his heart. One for his loins. The gun, as they do in nightmares, failed to fire.

Feeding Spiders

The kid was eleven. In the long lonely summer days he'd developed his own little science in his big backyard, an experiment he also practiced in the front lawn and garden facing busy Washington Boulevard, where the traffic noise was echoed back at the house off the high unbroken wall of the MGM Studios across the street.

The backyard was big, four or five times bigger than any other kid's that he knew of. It was entirely fenced in. It was walled on one side by the two-story pink stucco flank of a big old furniture store. At its rear his old man's study-shed and the garage beside it sealed it off from the back alley—the garage a barn-shaped building with a domed half-story loft built, like the house, in the Twenties.

And all along the other side of the yard ran a six-and-a-half-foot plank fence, no gaps between the planks. The invisible neighbor on that side of the kid's house was an auto wrecking yard—a big gravel lot full of broken cars all crashed and smashed.

With that fence, the kid's old man had perfected a real privacy back here: an unusually big backyard with a swing and climbing bars the old man had made of pipe and stout lumber, with a big pen for the tortoise and guinea pigs and rabbits, with four trees—two orange (their fruit abundant and all lemon-sour), a big silk oak, and a tall gingko—and with lots of room to run around in.

The hard part was that the kid was commanded to stay in this yard during the long summer week-days when the old man was at work. In the last year or so the old man had relaxed his standing order to the point where it was understood between them that the kid could also go out to the front lawn, which was unfenced from the busy street, and somewhat more tacitly it was understood that he might, as well, occasionally go play a bit among the wrecked cars in the lot next door. This last concession was *strictly* tacit, because some of those wrecks were pretty bad. In fact, if his old man realized in detail how bad some were, the kid figured he would probably ban him from going in there again.

But the kid couldn't go out there too often—that was their tacit deal. Not more than a couple days a week. The kid tried to keep this covenant. He scouted the backyard for new diversions, and in his eleventh summer he came to develop an accomplishment—an art you might say—all his own.

It had begun with his loathing of the fat summer flies. The four cats and the dog had between them three different clusters of plates and pans they ate and drank from in different corners of the yard. These drew the summer flies. And in the wire-fenced pen where the tortoise, the guinea-pigs, and the rabbits lived, there always lay baking in the sun a litter of *their* food: old veggies culled from the supermarket's produce dumpster. The kid couldn't long sit on his swings or perch in his monkeybars before these fat flies found and tormented him once he'd played up a sweat.

On the old pet food the flies would form a thick crust, and the kid had developed a way to strike a counter-blow against them. Scooping a handful of the yard's light-gauge gravel, he learned how to edge close to a buzzing plate of them and pelt them, stunning half a dozen flies literally at a stroke, so they stayed still for the killing and could even be picked up by their disjointed wings and brought close for a detailed inspection of their exquisitely jointed little legs all treading the air. . . .

There was a good number of spiders in the yard as well, and these jewel-bright web-spinners had captured a lot of his attention in their own right. He would go and study now this one, now that one, through the long summer days. There were in particular several gold-and-black orb-spinners in the yard's sunnier corners. These were big spiders that he gazed on with awe, their incredible architecture fixed still as stone, all etched by the sun.

The first time the kid carefully snagged the legs of one of these flies into the weave of the biggest orb-spinner, he utterly surprised himself, and then suddenly felt that he'd been thinking about doing it for the longest time.

The suddenness of the spider's waking was a revelation. The perfect traction of its scuttle across the weave, the lightning seizure of its caliper legs! The short, sharp hooking of the fangs one, two, three times! A stroke of simultaneous capture and kill, precisely calibrated.

The kid stood watching. The devouring, its exquisite precision, proceeded. The spider's inner legs turned the bound fly daintily against the lathe of its fangs.

This long, grotesque transaction between the light-footed spider and the pinioned prey—it was like naked magic.

From that afternoon, on through the summer, the kid honed his technique. He quickly got good at this little miracle. Learned that a slightly higher gauge of the gravel yielded more stunned flies. Learned also that an oblique throw improved yield, flies' reflexes quickest—it seemed—against assaults from directly overhead . . .

It was like sorcery to be able to unveil this treasure of exquisite detail, of small living machines feeding and dying.

Not perfect machines. Spiders recoiled from too vigorous prey. Took forever cringing around the struggling captive, and only dared to dart in when it hung exhausted. . . .

Then the spider nailed and froze it up. Then the spider settled down and tucked into the prey. Then came peace, and the spider's long-protracted, daintily studious appropriation of the bug's life.

This little back-yard biological machine cranked reliably on through the summer. In the fly-hunting phase the kid's motive was always vengeance on the flies—big, bright solid sweat-suckers that fed on *his* sweat when he'd been swinging in his swing, their prickly feet all over his skin and their pointy mouths poking it. Their landings on him always scared him an instant before they enraged him. And then he would go hunting for spider-prey.

But always when it came to the feeding phase he was awed and a little afraid. The fly was a victim now, and the spider a dire carnivore. Part of what awed him when he watched it was knowing that this incredibly detailed devouring was happening everywhere all by itself, and had been happening forever before he was born. Millions of this kind of trap were set all over the world. The kid had just happened to *spring* this one.

Just a couple weeks off from his twelfth birthday, the kid was a month into his second summer at this sport. He'd already fed the backyard's orb-spinners to obese proportions—was flirting with the thought that it was a little scary how fast they grew on the food from his fingers, and grinning edgily at the notion. What were their limits, obese as they already seemed?

He decided he'd feed one of his smaller pets—his biggest funnel spider. These were like wolf-spiders—their abdomens trim oblongs carried on hairy wolvish legs—big-fanged, these, leaping on and nailing prey in one move. Like wolf-spiders save that they ran strictly across their own broad parabolic sheets of silk—silk whorled in a horn of knit fabric, a tidy trampoline of gauze upon which nothing moved as fast as they.

But these too were skittish monsters. A snared bug's weight and mass determined whether they were fierce assailants or cowardly cringers.

The kid weighed getting a cockroach from under the trash out in the back alley—something big and strong enough to stand the spider back, tear up its funnel some, perhaps. . . .

In the end he did get a cockroach. But a smallish one—quick and strong, but not quite as massive as this funnel spider. He wanted some collision. See how tough this spider was.

Half its legs snagged, the roach listed sharply to port, but its three free legs winnowed the air with a power the spider cringed from.

But the kid had fed this spider big as well, though the web-wolf was lean compared to the orb-giants. Its cringe was precisely calibrated. It back-leapt just half its own length from roach's free-flailing legs, and poised tensing on its curved silk sheet. Feinted once and recoiled. A second feint. Then it leapt.

It had the wolf-spider's exaggerated fangs (real sabers compared to the big orb-spinner's nasty little hooks), and these it sank through the roach's dorsal sclera, crisp amber-colored plates that yielded brittle as candy to the black hypodermics.

Throughout the studious feeding, the kid felt . . . discontented. When he went into the kitchen for a snack late at night, he hated the roaches that scattered when light flooded the cupboard.

But this spider was like the orb-spinner. It was *pampered.* How big and lethal would it be on its own, without the kid's help? He wondered if there was a way to feed this spider itself to something else. A big preying mantis would eat it, but where could he get one?

At length the kid turned away. He had to grant that this had been a good feeding. The spider was in top form, and the kid had been skillful in putting it through its paces. Good work, he granted it, but somehow found himself unwilling to follow it with its usual sequel: a feeding of the spiders out front.

Out front, feeding spiders was a different matter. For one thing, there were all the cars out on Washington Boulevard rushing right past, their noise echoing back off the high wall of the MGM Studios on the street's other side. The half of the lawn where his spiders lived was pretty well screened from this traffic, but not from its noise, and he always felt edgier feeding out there.

But his screening off from the street was pretty good. His grandmother's real estate office—like a miniature house with a shingled roof—stood right next to the lawn, and her sign, big as a fence, was mounted on that half of the grass. Abbreviations and numbers filled its slotted streetward face, and behind it the kid was fenced off from the street.

And just behind the sign stood their big sycamore tree—which roofed the grass over in leaves. The kid could concentrate just fine on his feedings out here, but the traffic-hiss persisted at his back like a threat.

And an equally powerful distraction lay right beside the lawn: the graveled lot where wrecked autos lay in dozens. His grandmother owned this lot too, and leased it to the wreckers. All the ruptured, accordioned car-corpses—their starred glass and dusty mirrors, the stains on their seats.

The kid loved his grandmother, Nanny, the mother of his long-gone Mom. He got a faint thrill at this strange degree of potency in her: that it was Nanny's ownership that had brought all those battered car-corpses to lie right next to his house, and that she drew support from those corpse-cars' paid rent. The kid also knew that his grandmother shared that support with his old man and him.

The call of this frozen traffic-jam lying right next door to him was strong on the kid, who snuck over there to play with his friends when the chance offered. He didn't quite like going over there to play alone, though. . . .

The wrecking lot was fenced off from kid's place by a six-foot plank fence. The fence stopped short of his grandmother's real estate office, and the kid could jump down from his lawn's slight elevation right onto the gravel of the lot.

But the kid still didn't quite like going over there to play alone.

The kid loved Nanny. He was sure she didn't think about the cars themselves at all. She had almost certainly never crawled around inside any of them, as the kid had, and seen what was in them. . . .

The kid's spiders lived in a long, narrow, heavily planted strip be-tween the fence and the flank of the house. Shrubs, flowers, tall plants, and small trees—a gingko among them—jammed the space except for a thin footpath down the center. The kid stepped into that narrow jungle.

The spiders were bigger here, where the lush greenery lavished bugs on them. A couple of the orb-spinners here in their big wheel-webs dwarfed the ones in the back yard. These were a bit more gorgeously col-ored too: their obese abdomens white and golden with black frecklings, their legs just detectably bristly with their delicate fur.

The feeding was definitely creepier out here. He felt much more in Spiderland. The wrecked cars next door with all their crumplings and dents looked like big bugs, spider-food corpses. When he'd had friends over and they'd played in them, they pretended car-crashes, wrenching at their steering-wheels and making screeching and smashing noises.

The feeding out here on the lawn was also different because it was a little more his *own* doing, and less Nature's. Out here the kid knew he was crueller than Nature was, because here what he fed the spiders was something they never caught on their own. This food was easy catching and was everywhere on the leaves and fronds of all the plantings.

Little green caterpillars, smooth as skin. As easy to hang in one of the orb-webs as a tiny Christmas ornament.

Once hung, the caterpillars would writhe strenuously. Struggling to get all their stubby caterpillar feet on a smooth surface like their native leaves. Like the flies, they sent out a vigorous signal, but because they did not present the struggle of legs or wings against the spider's advent, their twistings invited its instant assault.

The kid watched these feedings much more solemnly. Sometimes he felt someone was *watching* him do it. Watching, but keeping his mouth shut.

Here now. He confronted the biggest of the garden spiders; its abdomen was near as big as the ball of his thumb. It was gorgeously upholstered in its gold and black. The kid expertly pinched up a caterpillar, possessing but not damaging its softness. He hung it in the web.

The caterpillar, its whole front half unsupported, began waving and wagging its length. The spider erupted toward it.

It seized the caterpillar by its tail-end and *bit . . . bit . . . bit.*

It seemed to paralyze only the tail end of the caterpillar, the rest of which kept twisting while the spider settled down to feed on the paralyzed part. The kid had read how spiders ate. They injected a solvent that liquified the bug's insides, and then drank in the liquid.

He could see this plain as day here. Part of the caterpillar's bitten end changed color, got blackish, and then began to crinkle and shrink. Meanwhile its fore-part, its questing head, and purchaseless little feet kept patiently probing the air for something to grip. It was still completely alive at that end and trying to escape, and it was already eaten at the other end, the shriveled part slowly growing toward the struggling fore-part.

Anger took the kid by surprise. It was like there was someone standing beside him whenever he did this, a partner who never spoke, but who now suddenly lost patience and took over. He tore a small branch from the bush behind him and slashed the web with it, web, spider, and prey all vanishing completely.

And then he jumped to see the spider struggling vigorously on the ground right beside his sandaled foot. He raised his foot and crushed it, twisting and twisting, feeling it pop like a grape and still grinding it, grinding it out.

He'd surprised himself utterly. He felt like . . . there was a new power in his body that filled him but wasn't quite his. For three scared heartbeats he had no idea what to do with it.

And then he did. He would go, by himself for the first time, into one of the wrecked cars. Go without a friend with him for the first time into one of the two *worst* ones.

He went to the fence's end and jumped down from the lawn onto the graveled lot next door. His legs were a little wobbly jumping down, but the jolt of landing steadied him somewhat.

One of the two worst cars was the old green-over-blue Plymouth. A fire had half gutted the interior and stained everything with greasy black smoke, smutting the inner windshield so it looked like a dimly translucent blackboard. Above the steering wheel was a partial hand-print of clear glass. There were several of these now where he and his friends had proved to themselves that the original handprint had been made by someone like them long after the accident. But that first handprint had something much . . . realler about it. He couldn't look at it long before he *knew* it was made by the driver as he was burning alive.

But that was really just the *second* worst wreck. Steeling himself, the kid threaded his way toward the *worst* one, carefully not picturing its interior as he so easily could. He went over to the black Buick.

It slumped there, its front wheels pigeon-toed, struts crushed by a frontal collision that had buckled the long black hood into a crumpled steel tent.

He thumbed the door button. Paused, thinking maybe this time the door wouldn't swing free, might not let him in—but it came free smoothly as it always did, its mass swinging creamily out.

Now he had to get in and sit behind the wheel. He could see the wheel plainly from where he stood outside the door here, but that wasn't the same as sitting dead-center behind it.

He had to do that, or he wasn't really taking the dare.

He got in behind the wheel and hauled the door shut on himself—massive in the first instant, then slamming home with a creamy thunk.

Here now. Here it was. Here he was alone with it for the first time.

Seriously smashed though the front of the car was, by far the worst thing about it was right in here. Was the steering wheel and the steering column.

The steering wheel was an ivory-white plastic. Concentric inside it was a double horn ring, chrome bright.

Both the steering wheel and the horn-ring had been *pushed down* over the steering column. They encircled it neatly, with almost a foot of the column now sprouting forward from their recessed calyx. The brutally blunt end of the column, capped with the Buick logo, was crusted and smeared with a brownish stain.

"It—" The kid had to clear his throat. "It punched right through his chest," he said.

"It . . ." But this he said only in his mind: *It crushed his heart.*

Sitting here, thinking this, was as close as the kid could get to it. This was the best he could do. And he wasn't close at all. He was *alive.* He hadn't died here. Somebody else had.

He was *going* to die. His old man had said so, and look at everything else, everyone else that was dying.

He searched for something, for some kind of answer. And found something else of the old man's he thought he could use: what the old man said—smiling—when he'd had a few.

"Fuck it!" the kid said.

It didn't quite work.

He tried again, trying for the cheerful tone his old man used: "*Fuck* it!"

That came out much better, and the kid smiled.

Upscale

From where Frank was working in the garage of Dave's Chevy-Geo, unscrewing the old plugs from a customer's pickup, he could look out the rear window, over the back fence, across the patio of Wine 'n' Cheez 'n' Stuff, across the next street, and into the tastefully furnished Le Bistro, an upscale bar with a picture window. While his hands tuned the Chevy, he was trying to project himself astrally into a window seat in Le Bistro, where he would sip a beer and a bump—no, you didn't order a beer and a bump in that kind of place, let's say a Manhattan—where he would sip a Manhattan and watch the yuppies arriving for their after-work wind-down.

It was pushing six, Frank was working alone and still looking at another three hours in the garage. Tomorrow was Saturday, but it would be the same. Frank had just come back from a week's bass fishing, meaning a few mornings bass fishing and most of a week's poontang hunting up in the bars of Lake County. Now good old Dave, the owner, was getting it all back in overtime—he'd even left his Mercedes over the weekend: "Throw a tune on 'er for me when you get a spare minute, Frank. I won't need 'er till Monday."

Right, Dave. Why don't I just do that? You're the guy with the car lot, I'm the chimp with the spark plug wrench, so why not?

Frank tightened plugs with his physical hands, while he tried sipping his second Manhattan with his astral hands. It was tricky work, especially since he was trying to look suave as he sipped, look like a power player, catch the eye of some slick yuppie 'tang.

Like that one there, pulling up in a black Mercedes, opening the car door and planting a glossy pair of black, high-heeled pumps on the pavement.

242

What followed this promising beginning fulfilled the promise in spades: legs clear up to here, the thighs sheathed in something black and supple and mere inches longer than an out-and-out mini-skirt; a kind of a pirate blouse, cream-colored, loose and silky but hugging a major pair of headlights the way cream hugs strawberries; a face like a cross between Kim Basinger and Daryl Hannah, honey-colored hair in a French knot, and a coolly lascivious walk as she cruised into Le Bistro. She took a window seat. Thank you, God.

She sat there quite a while, sipping something now and then, improving the quality of life for Frank. Somehow she put so much *into* just sitting there. Traffic zipped up and down the street, people came and went in the Wine 'n' Cheez patio, but it was all just foreground static. She was the reallest thing for blocks around. When she touched her glass to her lips it made Frank swallow, and it seemed he could almost taste her drink. He jockeyed the cars he had to work on into the slot in front of the window so he could keep watching her.

Then it got even better. As dark was coming on a bright red Mercedes parked behind her black one. Frank had noticed it cruise by twice before—perhaps scoping her in the window? So it seemed, for the guy who popped out, an upscale stud of about Frank's age in an Armani suit, went into the bar and a moment later appeared by her table. His smile said: *Just cut me a minute here.* His gestures said: *Just check me out—am I not cool?* Frank liked the way she took him in, like someone idly channel-surfing who pauses to check out a movie that maybe she's seen before but found mildly amusing. The upshot was, Mr. Armani sat down, and a drink was brought him.

Now this was entertainment. Armani irked Frank—a competitive instinct, Frank guessed—but he also interested him. How did the Mercedes set play it? After all, he and Armani were just fellow marathoners in life's great poontang chase.

It was so interesting it began to interfere with Frank's work—he had to redo a distributor that he'd gapped way wrong. Finally he just put down his tools and watched. How often did you get a window on little real-life dramas like this? In the lit window they were like video. She was so vivid though she scarcely moved, and when she did her moves were slight, graceful, slow. Meanwhile Armani was moving too much, talking too much, and talking about himself, Frank could tell by the modest gestures, the suave shrugs: *Ah well, I'm something, aren't I?—Which reminds me of another fascinating thing about me . . .*

"You're getting it wrong, Chump," Frank murmured. "You talk about *her*. You act like you're lost in her." He felt he had a right to talk, last week up in Lake County a case in point. Granted that Frank had been working the RV-and-pickup crowd, but a guy who scores three nights out of five anywhere knows what he's doing.

Then lo and behold, the pair of them got up and strolled out of Le Bistro together! They both got in her car, and she drove off, just like that.

Frank finished the rig he was tuning and knocked off—he couldn't concentrate. He went over to Wine 'n' Cheez 'n' Stuff, a fruity place he hated, and had a carafe of Port out on the patio. There was Armani's red Merce parked right across the street. What could be more blatant? They'd zipped off to her place to do the hot trot. Was she a pro, then? Every instinct he had said she wasn't. A pro radiated a subtle tension, however classy—on some band she broadcasted: *Hey. You.* A pro had to advertise—life was too short. But this one beamed out no such signal. And anyway, would a pro with her assets be working bars for pick-ups?

Maybe he was reading this wrong. Maybe it was standard for yuppies to go for spins to check out each other's Merces—*O hey, you've got to take a ride in mine!*

He finished his wine and the red Merce was still there. He went back to Dave's and got his Dodge Ram, which in the five years he'd owned it had come to look as if it had been rammed into every hillside in three counties. Normally he was proud of its funkiness inside and out—it was battered but *individual,* god damn it! Tonight it just depressed him. He drove to the Eight Ball and drank for a couple hours, and thought about hitting on one or two of the honies present, and didn't. All he picked up, at a nearby liquor store, was a pint to drive home with. He went out of his way to pass Le Bistro going home.

And it happened that he turned onto the far end of the block just in time to see the cream-colored Mercedes drive off, one shapely hand giving a casual wave from the driverside window, which Armani, standing in the street beside his own car, answered with a more vigorous wave.

Frank pulled over to watch. Armani fumbled his keys out and had a little trouble unlocking the car door; he seemed both jaunty and dazed. Frank decided the dude had definitely had his horns well trimmed. Squinting in the dim streetlights, Frank just made out the letters of the red Merce's sissy plate before it pulled out: POCKT CHG. Pocket Change. Rich and proud of it, are we?

Saturday afternoon, when Frank lifted the hood and leaned over his first engine of the day, his thirty-pound head almost fell in and pulled the rest of him after. His breakfast aspirins were taking forever, so he chased them with some blow from the phial in his sportscoat. His sportscoat and slacks hung in the cab of his pickup. For no particular reason he'd decided to hit some of the more uptown bars tonight.

The blow helped his efficiency, but not his mood. Some part of his mind was standing back and quietly sneering at him as he worked: *Hey, grease-monkey.* His eye kept going to the window, and in its frame the more distant window of Le Bistro played a ghostly re-run of yesterday's little soft-porn video.

He shifted his work-station away from the window, though the new spot was darker and he had to depend more on the trouble light, and walk back and forth for things he needed from the tool rack. Grimly he plugged away, going back to his sportscoat from time to time for moral support. On one of these trips, which took him past the window, he looked out and saw the cream-colored Merce outside Le Bistro, and the creamy babe inside at her window table.

Some part of him had been expecting it—only this could explain how smoothly he now moved. He shed his coveralls, cleaned his hands with the lanolin gel, changed his clothes, and hopped into Dave's Mercedes . . . in less than fifteen minutes he was parking it behind *her* Mercedes. Tan and cream-colored, the two cars harmonized. And there she was, smiling at him from the window as if she thought so too.

And moments later he was standing right there by her table, making his pitch. Being here was like dreaming of jumping into a river on a hot day, and then actually doing it—the feeling was both blissful and a little shocking in its vividness. She was dazzling! Talent rises to challenges, though—the words, the gestures came easy and flawless: "Excuse me but, you know, I've seen you here before. And the last time I saw you I made myself a promise. I promised myself that I'd buy you a drink if you'd let me."

He hid his awe as he spoke—she was a phenomenon of sexiness. This near her, he felt sunk in a lagoon of magical waters; his nerves sparkled in his skin as if the air around her were a stimulant. Was it her perfume? Or something more tenuous? A kind of aura? He felt wrapped in sorcery. Her voice had a musical echo when she answered, smiling languidly up at him: "Why not?" He sat down hastily, feeling himself beginning to sprout a major woodie even as he stood there.

He soon understood Armani's talkiness yesterday. This was a woman of few words. He told her he was an acute judge of character, a born guesser of people's lifestyles from their appearance, yet she had him utterly baffled. She smiled. He told her he was in banking himself, commercial property loans, and that he sensed a particular brand of cool intelligence about her that made him think maybe she was in the same racket. She smiled. He began manufacturing talk about himself to fill the silence.

Not in desperation, though. With each second he sat by her, he grew more certain—he *knew:* he was going to be pronging his brains out with this woman in very short order.

Then a red Mercedes pulled up outside, making three in a row at the curb, and Armani got out and, from the sidewalk, aimed an uncertain wave at the woman. The look of stone she gave him back foretold the rest, but he came in anyway.

Decidedly dazed: that was the only way to describe the guy. Frank gave him a brief smile, briefly returned his awkwardly offered handshake. The guy's name was Jules. "Well, I was just driving by," Jules said to her, "I happened to notice you, thought I'd say hi . . ." There was disorientation in his shaky smile, his eyes edging here and there but always snapping back to hers, which were dead and cold as glass to him. She sat there giving him her blank face, letting him wind down and finally wander back out. Jules was stiff in his movements, confused for sure. He pulled out without looking, nearly got tail-ended, and drove off in a blare of horns. Pitiful. This woman must have fucked his brains out. Frank looked at her and knew it for a fact. Her eyes were not stones to him, but pools of hot honey.

"Shall we?" she asked. "We'll take my car."

"Absolutely."

A townhouse in an upscale development. Frank's oaken boner tented his slacks following her across the somewhat shaggy lawn, and he hobbled after, not giving a damn. Going through the front door he kicked a pile of unopened mail on the floor, but never paused. They beelined across the living room, past dusty-looking furniture and dead houseplants, into a bedroom where she turned and dropped backwards onto a kingsize bed, spreading her unbuttoned blouse from which erupted her big tits tautly brassiered in sheer pink. She stabbed her spike heels deep into the mattress and spread her legs wide; down at the crux of the sharp-kneed 'M' of her legs, the swollen rose-and-plum mollusk of her sex was wet and ready in the lace-trimmed aperture of pink split-crotch panties. Frank dropped his pants, fought his way out of his boner-snagged briefs, and dived in.

Each plunge of his phallus peeled red velvet layers of delight from his nerves, each stroke stripping him down to a hotter and brighter core of bliss. Her hands gripped his buttocks as ivy grips stone and planted him, planted him, planted him home. He clutched the hot loaves of her tits, sucked her nut-hard nipples through her bra, and, hilted in her cunt's snug suction, geysered, geysered, and geysered, blowing star-bursts out his eyeballs.

She never undressed, she never spoke a word, but, rolling him onto his back, with an air of the preliminaries being over, she went to work on him with a dreamy half-smile on her face. Laying a gentle finger to his lips when he made as if to speak, she got all his clothes off him and began to massage him: left leg, right leg, left arm, right arm . . . it wasn't exactly massaging, more a kind of complex stroking really, but as she worked from each extremity up toward his body, she seemed to be concentrating energy toward his center, and already his cock was beginning to stiffen again.

Was the magic in her hands, or was it in the scent that welled from her with each move she made? An utterly novel, ethereal perfume—so elusive!—that teased him right down to the brainstem. Was there even an erotic hypnosis in her voice? For she hummed, almost inaudibly, a strange, meandering air as she stroked him. No matter, *all* of her was magic. Now it was his chest she was stroking, and cascades of neural fire were pouring into his groin. His dick stood quivering sixty degrees above his stomach—he hadn't been this hard since adolescence. She straddled him and socketed his glans. Her molten love-muscle sank slowly down the length of him, inflating his balls drum-tight with ready seed.

As she ratcheted him up toward climax, his nerves knew dawning awe at the megaton orgasm he approached. His hollowed-out excitement was, for long heartbeats, indistinguishable from terror as he inched inexorably up to the brink of joy's abyss. He gripped her pantied buttocks, the nylon like an electric haze exhaled directly from her skin; she hung her sheathed teats lower till their hot, blunt kisses swallowed up his face, and then her hips shoved down the plunger that blew the dynamite lodged within his loins. She hauled an endless, ice-hot rope of come from him that started in his spine and stretched for miles up toward her undiscoverable center, and while it joined them, this timeless jism juncture, it seemed to him a fixed link, a charged cable through which her energy flowed into him as much as his into her.

Frank's head lolled on the headrest as she drove them back to "his" Mercedes. Never had he known such fulfillment—or emptiness. When absolute, they were the same, no?

He realized she was done with him, now and forever—as done with him as she had been with Jules. It wasn't just her silence, her total attention to the road, that told him this; it was the absence of her subtler output, that magical wavelength she had beamed. That marvelous aura of hers was switched off now. The air between them was empty.

How strange she was!—the thought cruised slowly through Frank's mental lassitude. Leaving, he'd bent to pick up and place on the (very dusty) coffee table some of the mail he'd kicked coming in, and had glimpsed that it was all addressed to a Robert someone. Indeed, when he thought of it, the place had seemed a single man's. In one corner of the bedroom there'd been an exercycle with some very stale-smelling, man-size sweats heaped on the carpet beside it; from a distance in passing he'd glimpsed a bare, unused-looking kitchen. But when he thought of asking her a few casual questions—her name, for instance—he felt himself recoiling from the mere idea, so palpable was her closure to him, the void she'd effortlessly opened between them.

She pulled up beside Dave's Merce and Frank got out. It actually dizzied him slightly to stand. She waved once, a brief smile on her lips, her eyes stones. Frank fumbled more than a little getting his key into the car door. He had to smile. Wasn't the *woman* supposed to feel like this? Swept off her feet, humped and dumped? Not that his heart was crying lover-come-back—he'd just come five times in less than two hours, and the bare thought of further sex made his heart race with something very like fear. But by god, he'd certainly been the fuckee in this little afternoon, hadn't he? In spades! And had she come at all? That closing of her eyes she did, that long deep hiss of breath exhaled each time he popped his rocks . . . why did he feel it had nothing to do with orgasm?

He dropped off Dave's Merce and drove his Ram back to his shabby apartment complex. Dark was falling. The taco burners downstairs had rap music blaring, the students next door were pounding out heavy metal, and the toothless tattoos who sold crank from the house across the street were having a Hog-revving contest, but Frank dropped onto his couch and was dead asleep in ten seconds.

He woke to Dave's voice talking to his answering machine. Afternoon light bathed the couch. ". . . just *had* a vacation if I'm not mistaken. 'Preciate a call-back here, Frank, 'cause you got us backed up real good here right now." The receiver clicked, not quite slammed down. Frank lay struggling with the implications of Dave's call. He listened to the traffic noise outside. Definitely weekday afternoon noise-levels. This was *Monday* afternoon, not Sunday!

Sitting up proved it past whatever doubt remained—his body had the stiffness of the long-entombed. He groaned aloud with the pain of moving.

He tottered to the fridge and cracked a beer. He drained it in two breaths and cracked another. It made his arm ache just to hoist the can. Dear Christ, had she given him some raging disease? Syphilis? Galloping AIDS? Alarmed, he marshaled heavier medicines. He splashed four fingers of Jack Daniel's on some rocks and knocked it back; he sat at the kitchen table and honked a five-inch rail of blow. His veins began to come unkinked; his muscles thawed a bit, and panic subsided.

Truly, he had been screwed as never before, fucked down to his footsoles. He'd been deeply rummaged around in and he felt strange emptinesses inside him even as he sat there, felt bird-light, hollow-boned. But a woman like that, a fuck so perfect you couldn't even have thought her up on your best night—well, you had to pay the piper, right? When you made whoopee on a revolutionary new scale, you had to expect a Morning After.

He drank and snorted a bit more, then washed and shaved, beginning to feel human again. But as he went downstairs to his truck he realized that fear had not completely left him, that he was headed, not for work, but for Le Bistro. Why? Not from lust—the bare thought gave him a full-body shudder. Why did he need to go back there? Was it to be sure she existed? Was it because, even reamed-out as he felt, he could not shake the conviction that he had experienced a hallucination, an impossibility?

The bar's window was empty of her, and there was a pang of relief in the fact, in not beholding those remorselessly beautiful eyes. But there, parked across the street from the bar, was the red Merce with the POCKT CHG plates. Frank pulled to the curb. Here was a piece of the dream, real and solid, Jules sitting at the wheel. Why not see what he did, where he went next?

Perhaps Jules had been dozing, for after a few minutes he straightened slightly and seemed to shake himself. He then fired up and pulled out without even a glance behind him. Frank followed. It was easy. Jules drove at a smooth, sedate pace, never varying it, his head tilted slightly, as if he were musing.

Jules parked at the B of A downtown and was inside for almost an hour. Frank sat in his truck. He'd brought the JD along and sipped it placidly now and then. Only gradually did he begin to wonder at this surveillance of his, his patience at it. What was this? How could that empty red Mercedes there radiate such a fascination that he could sit watching like this, completely absorbed? Jules was his predecessor in a strange adventure, sure, but what was Frank expecting to *see,* after all?

When Jules came out he drove straight to another bank. Again Frank followed, and again sat waiting half a block away. When Jules came out of the second bank, he got back in his car and just sat there. And Frank sat watching him, less and less troubled by thoughts, letting the sights and sounds of the busy street move through his senses. He saw the sun on the trees that lined the street go from honey-yellow to burnt gold to fiery rose. In slow-dawning astonishment he grasped that perhaps two hours had passed.

He made himself get out of the truck. See? He could move if he wanted. At first his legs were unsteady, until a core of energy seemed to come alight in him, and his movements grew smooth. He was close to the Merce now, feeling a tug at his guts toward Jules as he got nearer, as if a kind of gravity were at work between them. As he passed, scanning Jules as if idly, Jules looked back at him. He had melty-dark Italian eyes. The total alertness of his look, from a man who sat so utterly at rest, was a bit scary somehow. There was no sign of recognition. Jules's eyes were empty of intent, waiting.

Frank crossed at the next light and walked back to his truck on the other side of the street. Again they sat in their rides until, night coming on, the Merce fired up and pulled out.

It drove to a Safeway and parked in the farthest corner of the lot. Frank parked four rows off and sat waiting. He sat there while the worn-down moon moved from the zenith almost to the horizon. He sat there until around them there was only empty asphalt, with a faint glaze of streetlight thrown across it, and on every side the city lay asleep. He sat there utterly still, as if under a spell cast by the stillness of his quarry, until, finally, he saw movement in the Mercedes.

Once more Frank got out of his truck. He crossed the asphalt, feeling hollow and light. He was not himself, the work of walking showed him this beyond a doubt now. He'd caught some unknown bug from Her. Equally unknown to him was what he meant to say to Jules, if anything— his only certainty was that the time had come to face him.

Frank stopped quite close to the driver-side window. Jules, oblivious to him, was undressing. His peaceful face gazed upward through the windshield while he disrobed, peeling off shirt and coat, skillfully contorting in the tight space to shuck down pants and briefs. His sky-aimed face was rapturous but also taut and masklike, as if the skull had grown within it. His nakedness was bright with sweat, and he trembled delicately. And what was that stacked on the seat beside him? Neat packets of twenty-dollar bills. A hefty stack—tens of thousands in cash.

Jules's trembling suddenly increased; a gush of sweat foamed out of every square inch of him, like juice from a squeezer. His face split lengthwise, this throat cracked open like a cloven stump, his chest burst open like a stove-out cask.

He was only a thick glove of skin and meaty pulp, a sodden envelope. The woman sat in Jules's stead, shedding him as he had shed his coat. She shifted, shucking him down to her ankles as he had done his pants.

Her breasts swayed with her struggles, though they were veiled, sheathed in a billowy, milky gauze. Already this was shrinking, drying like butterfly wings, the pink bra crystallizing first, and then the creamy pirate blouse stabilizing, growing opaque around it. With her fingers she stroked her garments into final shape, stroked her face, making brows and lashes dark, lips glossy red.

Her eyes cut once to Frank's, and then indifferently away. She tilted the rearview to check her face, a simple, womanly gesture, spine-chillingly true. The key hung ready in the ignition, and she twisted it. Frank stepped back politely as she pulled away.

Frank's hatching refuge, some twenty-four hours later, proved to be a semi-rural cul-de-sac dead-ended by one of the new freeways, a spot which he was already unsure who—himself or Her—was choosing as he drove there. Already the inward process was accelerating, a full-body sensation of compression, an attenuation of his thoughts as if his brain were a balloon slipping its tether. Still, even at this point, he managed a thought completely his own. Picturing his shabby, battered truck, its torn upholstery, its cracked windshield, the shriveled burger wrappers scattered on its floor—picturing too the $67.53 sitting on the seat beside him, there was enough of his own self left to smile a little: *Boy, was She going to be surprised.*

Water of Life

As the sun goes down, a lot of the skid-row trade goes to A-Rab's Liquors. They come out from the alleymouths where they've been loitering, out from the shadows between the legs of billboards; they drift in a slow, faltering, tidal way as the dark comes on. A-Rab's never opens till dark.

A-Rab is bulky and Mediterranean-looking, with big, dark eyes. His torso is twisted; he wears a steel back-and-shoulder brace and moves with a labored, rolling gait. He has a smiling, mocking manner and a kind of rapport with the winos, even a soft spot for them. The local winos form a slow, fuddled line, inching toward the register.

"Ninety-six, ninety-seven . . . you need another fifteen cents, Sammy . . . OK, next time. But don't forget. That's your one break I give you this week, don't fuck up. So Ernie, is it Popov tonight? Remember now, you guys can can take the first few pokes in my alley, but then move on. I don't want Grand Central out there, got it? Hey guys!"—this to the men pondering their decisions by the cooler—"think it over, but keep the aisle clear while yer thinking, awright?"

His place is crowded with the night's first trade, but on one customer in particular A-Rab keeps a subtle eye. This guy is a booze-shrunk fifty, once powerfully built. His clothes are shabby, but a cut above a hard-core wino's filth. He steps up for his turn and A-Rab asks him, "The usual, Cal?"

"You got it. Quart and a chaser." A-Rab's oil-black eyes hold Cal's sardonically as he raps down the quart—cheap bourbon—and the chaser, a miniature of Jack Daniel's. Though no one else notes it, A-Rab has not drawn this miniature from the regular rack of miniatures, but from under the counter instead.

Outside, Cal holsters his drinks, small and large, in the side pockets of his tough old corduroy sports jacket. He turns his collar up; the night is obscured by a thin fog, and the air has a bite in it. He walks briskly, gets four or five blocks away from A-Rab, and starts looking for a spot.

A gaunt wino moves down the sidewalk. His deflated jowls are prickly with white stubble. His clothes aren't bad—gray slacks and sportscoat just recently acquired from a Mission thrift shop. He lights a smoke, teetering slightly when he stands still. Someone is sitting in that doorway just ahead of him. There's the glint of a bottle being tilted upwards. The gaunt wino shuffles up to the drinker in the doorway. "Y'ain't a smoker, are ya, Bo? I got some Humps here for a poke a that. I sure could use it to shut out this chill. Whatcha got, whusky?"

"Yep," Cal smiles, "usqua-baugh as the Celts called it. Water of Life. Take two pokes, pilgrim—this quart's young."

"Mmmmmm! Hooo! My God, that come outta the right bottle! Sure, I know that stuff, like Aqua Vita in Italian, water of life. I knew all that stuff, hadda education an' everything!"

"Well by God," says Cal, lighting his cigarette and sucking down a drag, "if you're an educated man that likes the ancient art of conversation, let's get outta the cold a little an' share this bottle and that pack a Humps!"

They sit on pads of folded cardboard between two dumpsters in an alley, and they feed twisted scraps of cardboard to a little fire between them. The wino's name is Dan. "I mean ta tell you, Cal," he's saying, "there was nothing with wheels under it I couldn't sell. I should be ashamed of myself! I sent hundreds of rubes off drivin' stinkers you wouldn't believe!" Dan cackles. Cal smiles at him with an irony that has grown more naked the more Dan has drunk.

Dan gets up and staggers across the alley to piss. Cal drinks down the remnant of the quart till less than an inch remains. Then he unpockets the miniature, empties it into the larger bottle, and throws the miniature bottle away. Seeing Dan's back still turned to him, Cal holds the quart bottle up to the firelight. He studies a little knot of transparency, no bigger than a tequila worm, which is visible only as an elusive, twisting glimmer in the whisky's amber. In his eyes both disbelief and loathing can be faintly read.

Dan resumes his seat and takes the bottle that Cal offers him. Dan is meditative, almost smiling. "I love cosyin' down by a fire with a bottle! S'what I loved about sales. Not cars, after that. Insurance. I loved takin' the prospects to a bar an' grill. Cocktails all around, be wintertime, winter's best for selling people insurance, people see the gloomy side. Sittin' there, cocktails all around, some barbecue, knowing we'd eat hearty an' I'd make the sale . . . Boy, I had my pitch cold in those days!"

"You got the butt end of the bottle there," Cal says. "Go on and kill it off, Dan."

Dan salutes him debonairly with the bottle, sockets its mouth in his, and hoists it. In the instant of swallowing, he freezes in this posture. His mouth tightens on the glass, all his facial muscles knotting furiously. Then, while still frozen in this chugging posture, he begins to shudder powerfully, and a great bulge moves up and down the taut line of his throat.

Dan continues in this racked paralysis. Cal feeds up the fire for more light. He watches Dan with horror and a resolute attention; he is still trying to fully comprehend this bizarre, predatory enterprise that he has become a part of. Soon now . . . It is always so fast once it starts . . . Now! Now Dan's face, neck, and arms start to shrivel, blacken, and crumple. At the same time a bulge begins to form within his chest, pushing his shirt out taut.

Still Cal cannot believe how fast it happens. Dan shrinks within his clothes to half his size. He is a husk, a dark mummy. Cal takes his lockback knife, jaw clenched; the whisky he has just drunk helps him now. He spreads Dan's jacket and shirt from the bulging chest and pokes the knife into the fissured skin. The skin looks like scorched leather, but cutting through its crispness is easy—Cal thinks, shuddering, of pie-crust. He cuts a square around the central bulge. Before he pries off this lid of flaky skin and bone, he takes a large Zip-loc bag from one of his pockets. Now his blade lifts the hatch of cut crust.

Nested in the mummy's chest-socket is a smooth, rosy fatness. Its shape suggests an engorged tick's, but its color is translucent crimson, and it is as big as a pint-bottle. Appended to the great fuselage of its abdomen is a small, delicate head, like an insect's.

Now comes what has always been the hardest part for Cal: slipping on a rubber glove and plucking this firm but gelatinous sac from its socket, and slipping its warm wobbliness into the Zip-loc bag.

Dan's corpse he folds up in its clothes, the crisp limbs flattening like cardboard to a bundle no bigger than a crouching child, which is handily hidden under the debris in one of the dumpsters.

In the wee hours, A-Rab is in the back room of his liquor store. At a knock on the alley door, he hastens cumbersomely to open it, his distorted body rolling side to side. Cal steps in and holds out the bulging Zip-loc, pinching its top between thumb and forefinger in a way that delicately signals disgust. A-Rab takes the bag, bows sardonically, and hands Cal a packet of hundred-dollar bills.

A-Rab goes to a stainless steel sink where a little silver press stands ready on a tripod, an empty wine bottle under it. "How about it, Cal?" he asks. "Will you stay and have a real drink with me tonight?"

Cal smiles thinly, as at an automatic jest, and watches as A-Rab slips the creature out of the bag with his naked hand. The egg-shaped silver socket of the press fits neatly around the parasite's abdomen. A-Rab brings down the lever of the press. A flood of clear fluid the tint of dark burgundy gushes into the wine bottle. A-Rab corks the bottle and takes up a felt-tip pen and the bottle, which bears a blank label. "What was his name?"

"Dan was all I got."

A-Rab writes it. "You're working out splendidly, Cal, you know that. Why not drink with me? The job's so much more meaningful when you know what you're doing."

"I find myself curious, A-Rab." Cal's voice is grainy, worn ragged at the edges by years of cigarettes and eighty-proof. "Why would someone quit a job like this? I'm curious about my predecessor. Where did he go?"

"It's the most astonishing thing." A-Rab has shelved his new bottle in a little wine-rack, where he now seeks an older one, and as he speaks he turns to Cal a face of amazement. "He killed himself! I'd made him practically rich. Of course he was an aging alcoholic, like yourself, and no doubt had a depressive streak, but it still puzzles and mortifies me! Sit with me at least while I imbibe, won't you? Have some whisky to keep me company?"

"OK. Why not?" Cal watches A-Rab tidy up. He opens a little slot in the side of the press and extracts the "ferret" he has just milked. It is once more a little viscous jot of movement. He slips it into a fresh miniature bottle and puts it in the refrigerator. "Our little ferret here," A-Rab obligingly explains, "is native to a system colder than yours, though its toughness and tolerance are great. Indeed, we have never seen one die, and we have never seen one reproduce. They are, as far as we know, immortal."

"How do they . . . or why do they . . . ?"

"We are equally ignorant of the process of their alimentation. Whatever the cycle involves, the waste it excretes is neither more nor less than the concentrated essence of the prey's total conscious experience." A-Rab re-locks the heavy padlock on the refrigerator's massive door.

They drink out in front, at a coffee table A-Rab has installed behind the counter. A pair of armchairs flank the table, where the pair settle comfortably, walled round by the gemlike glint of bottles in the one low lamp that burns. Cal stoically sips his whisky while A-Rab decants a glassful from his chosen bottle. "Merely, your predecessor, wouldn't try this for the longest time. He put it off too long, in my opinion, until his depression already got the upper hand. But even he granted the joy, the miracle it was to taste this vintage."

Cal's face subtly steels itself for what he knows is coming. And here it comes, sure as death: A-Rab drinks. With an expression of self-abandon—an exquisite little elevation of his shaggy dark brows—A-Rab thrusts his face upon the wineglass. From his mouth erupt two black, bristly insect mouthparts—prickly, clubbed horrors that thrust deep into the glass and empty it in one noisy slurp.

"Forgive me," A-Rab says, deeply sighing, himself again after a long tranced moment of inward voyaging. "But I cannot dissemble my delight. But now, may I say something without offense? I have a feeling about you. I sense that, were one to taste the waters of your life, one might detect a thrilling murder or two. Years ago, of course." Cal gives him an utterly blank stare. "Lighten up, Cal! It's a joke! You've lived, is all I mean! You've taken risks and discovered things for yourself. So what puzzles me is how can you be so . . . timid now? I can't believe you've—what's the jargon?—wussed out in your recent years."

Cal's eyes give back a glint of irony, but his jaw is knotted, the barb has lodged. A-Rab, with a coy smile, brings out a second wineglass he has been hiding. He sets this before Cal and pours him his own glass of the life-waters. "You're such an entertaining race," A-Rab teases. "Such a mix of motives within any of you! You won't be disappointed, Cal. Taste!"

Cal is a man who has seldom refused a dare in his life, and even more seldom refused a drink. He takes up the glass and sniffs it. He blinks, and amazement dawns in his eyes. He takes a sip.

Cal has been drinking A-Rab's water-of-life every night for a week now. Tonight he sits under a railway overpass, sharing his quart with a black wino named Rufe. They have a fire of twigs and weeds going, and Rufe is very drunkenly feeding it, half falling in, giving the flames more of his fingers than of fuel. They are very far down the bottle. Cal watches Rufe raptly, with a slight, constant shifting of the eyes, as if the sight of Rufe was rich; as if the old scarecrow was auraed with epics.

"You've hung a lot of years on you, Rufe. Don a lot of deeds. Seen a lot of sunrises."

Rufe pauses, looks at him with wobbly surprise. "I guess I have," he says, "Mostly, though, I don't remember 'em now, the things I done, thank the Lord."

Cal swigs off most of the inch left in the bottle. "Whoops," he says. "Lucky I got this." He empties the miniature JB into the bottle. "You can kill it with a touch of class," he tells Rufe, but doesn't hold out the bottle all the way, and still looks at Rufe with busy eyes.

Rufe, not shy, reaches a little extra and takes the bottle. "But just think," urges Cal, "if you remembered them, the things you've lived, then you could—" But Rufe, not one to waste time, has locked mouths with the bottle and hoisted it.

Was there perhaps some unguessed-at depth to this man? For the ferret seems to find an unusual feast in him. Long after Rufe has shrunken to a mummy, he trembles and thrashes, his wrinkled lips gripping the glass spout, his dwarfed arm locked in hoisting. There is no need to cut the ferret from his husk. The chest bulges and splits, and the ferret's distended sac extrudes, more swollen than Cal has ever seen it.

Clearly the alien has found feeding past its norm in Rufe. Cal studies it, amazed. Its little head, reminiscent of a termite queen's, is twisting, its jaws working. Is this a swelling just behind its head? Where its tough abdominal material flares out from its neck, at this narrow point of junction, a long blister has formed—is growing before Cal's eyes.

The blister begins to split. Is this something wriggling free? Cal leans close, rapt.

Cal and A-Rab are in their easy chairs behind the counter. Cal lingeringly sips from his wineglass. "Its just . . . stupefies me! How much of the world someone can hold. All the days in them, all the skies and landscapes, rainstorms and blizzards and gales on the open sea! And it's all my world of course, but at the same time it's a new one. It . . . enlarges my universe."

"How well you put it," A-Rab smiles. "There's no entertainment like it!"

Cal has not heard. "What you said about my having . . . killed? It's true. And it astonishes me to think how big those lives were that I ended."

"Yes," says A-Rab, sipping now, which involves only the briefest and most delicate thrusting forth of those barbed horrors which are his true mouth. "Human life is so rich and so delightfully cheap at the same time! I knew you were a man to appreciate that delicious paradox. So. What do you think of Bruce Barker here?" He gestures with the wine bottle before refilling their glasses. "Did you discover yet his youthful surfing? He was quite good! Those twenty-foot tubes? And those sandy beach-bunnies, eh?" A-Rab laughs. When his delight is genuine, his laughter takes on more-than-human notes: something like the shrilling of crickets comes in-to it, and the chirring of chitinous wings.

Cal has found a hollow beside a railway embankment. Beyond the weeds, factory walls give their backs to him. Up on the tracks he hears the crunch of feet on the cinders. He hoists up the bottle in a swig so the firelight glints off it. A pause above, then a courteous query. "That looks heavy, man. Need help?"

"Step down and belly up!" calls cheery Cal.

"Name's Nolan, 'cher service." A lean wino with a silver-gray ponytail hanging out of a broken fedora comes skidding fairly nimbly down the gravel embankment.

"Well, Nolan, I *was* kind of thinking how nice it would be to share this bottle with someone who hasn't forgotten the fine art of conversation."

Nolan smiles. He touches his stomach and speaks eyes-averted, as if to his own interior: "Liver? You hear me in there, liver? You gimme this one more, all right?"

"The Tet offensive . . ." Cal muses. "Just some newsprint to me but to you a whole world you could fill a hundred newspapers trying to describe." He drinks. Two inches left in the bottle.

"S'funny," says Nolan, "there's probably not a day goes by it doesn't cross my mind, but I almost never sit down and really remember it, recon-struct it."

262 THE AUTOPSY: BEST WEIRD STORIES OF MICHAEL SHEA

"Really getting back into it is like surfing inside yourself. You ever surf?"

"Nah. You?"

Cal realizes that in strict truth, he hasn't. He falters. Nolan politely disattends. "Only thing like surfing I did," he offers, "was go down with a lung. Saw some incredible reefs in the Gulf and the South Pacific. In the jungle there's a lotta life, but you gotta catch sight of it." Already Cal has taken out the miniature, and he adds its contents to the larger bottle's without concealment. But Nolan is distracted by remembering. "Down in those reefs, though, you're surrounded. It teems. You're just one of the crowd, in flat rubber clown-feet. It's . . . Darwinian! You feel like one more soldier in the Great March of life as it stomps its way across the Cosmos. God, how could it be so long since I even remembered those times?" Nolan takes the bottle from Cal. Cal's heart gives a sudden jump, Nolan hoists the bottle high.

Cal's hand darts forward to detain him.

A-Rab is in the back room of his store during the small hours. He is tense. Cal didn't come back last night, and tonight he didn't show up when the liquor store opened. A-Rab moves around in a way that can't quite be called pacing—his misshapen bulk writhes in its complex brace like something that wants to get down on the floor and scuttle or slither. But now there comes a light knock on the alley door.

It is Cal, with a bloated red baggie in hand. "No takers on Thursday, so I called it a night. I think you'll find this tasty. Call it Doug, no last name."

"You might have phoned this evening." When A-Rab gets testy, something shrill and dry and unsettling creeps into his voice.

"I've got a life of my own, A-Rab. And since you bring it up, I've been thinking long and hard." At this preamble, A-Rab nods with a bitter knowing little smile that Cal misses. "I frankly don't think, A-Rab, this is the best line of work for me."

A-Rab sighs, apparently prepared for this. "Have, at least, a last glass of the waters with me. Do you think you're the first person to quit my employ—I mean before your melancholic immediate predecessor? I want to talk you out of quitting, of course. Decency demands that you at least have a glass with me and give me the chance."

Soon they are comfortable in their armchairs, walled in by the warm glint of bottles. Cal smiles, strikes a genial note, leans and takes the evening's vintage from A-Rab's hand and insists on pouring it himself with a hostly flourish. A-Rab beams, finding much comedy in human manners. Both sniff their glasses without drinking, the first phase of what has become their ritual. "We are boon companions," Cal proclaims. "We are friends by the only real measure of friendship, which is how much experience you've shared. Think of it! We've spent what's almost a life together. That's why I want to be completely honest with you about my feelings toward this job."

"Of course we're friends, Cal! And let me clear the ground by saying that I will unhesitatingly double your present salary to persuade you to stay in my employ. Is this merely about wage? If so, don't let that detail stand between us."

"Sorry, A-Rab. It's a mental thing. It's . . . philosophical, I guess. Mmm! You should taste this!" Cal has taken the first sip of his waters. "This guy was in some kind of war. Astonishing visuals!"

A-Rab laughs unpleasantly, ignoring his own glass. It is beginning to emerge in his manner that he is more vexed with Cal than he has let on. "You are such a—forgive me, but you are such a clownish race! You are philosophical—oh, solemnly so! Like Fletch, the idiot before you— philosophical to the hilt, and at the same time you blow each other to rags in wars that are vast orgies of cannibal slapstick! You are so . . . infantile! You are sentient, crudely intelligent, yes, but whole orders of complexity in sentience escape you utterly. For instance, the lives we sip? They still live in their bottles! They know themselves! And when we consume them, they know us as we know them. What terror it must be to them to enter my memories, eh? Like entering a vast alien Hell." A-Rab, while saying this, has slowly leaned forward. His face is now a foot from Cal's. He holds up his glass between them, though still he does not taste of it. Its bloody glint is repeated in his eyes, and his smile is barbed with cruelty.

Cal sips his own glass, looking unmoved. Down here behind the counter there is little room for movement, and he is sunk awkwardly deep in his chair. "Well, A-Rab," he says mildly, "I've always had the feeling that you had a complicated sense of humor."

"How well you put it," A-Rab says. He is still leaning too close. "This is a good time to tell you that I have not been entirely honest with you, Carl. It was more an omission than a lie really. My last collector did kill himself. But all his predecessors, well, I terminated them myself."

"You killed them."

"I ate them. Unavoidably, that killed them." A-Rab does not move his fleshy body—still holds up between them his untasted wineglass—but two sharp peaks stretch the shoulders of his shirt. Cloth tears, and two black, jointed legs sprout out and seize with pincers the sides of Cal's chair, jailing him.

"Well," Cal says, "I sure am sorry things have come to a point where you feel called upon to tell me that." His voice is shaky at first, but gains strength. "I'd say your frankness bodes ill for my own immediate future. Well, since that's the case, I've got nothing to lose by giving you my true opinion of you, have I?"

"You mean you haven't been wholly sincere with me, Cal?" asks A-Rab archly.

"I'm afraid not. But hey, why should I fake it anymore? You come on like you've got this deep alien mind, but in essence—I'm sorry to have to say this—you're just a fat, candy-ass couch potato! You're just a watcher and a guzzler, not a doer! And for that reason, just one short muddled human life like that one"—he points to the glass A-Rab holds—"outweighs and outclasses your life a thousand to one. It's more real than you, it's more significant than you—"

"Allow me to refute you without a word, Cal," A-Rab interrupts. A strange yellow light glows through the human eyes he wears; his grin is pure hate. "Behold this wondrous life's utter impotence, its perfect triviality; it is a cheap confection I imbibe at a whim!" He extrudes his oral apparatus and slurps the glass empty at a noisy stroke.

When the seizure takes him it is volcanic. He straightens epileptically and knocks the table over: the straps that bind him to his body-brace snap and he lies on the floor, a twisting shape of shuddering limbs. There is a moment there when his tremoring face turns to Cal a look that might be read as astonished inquiry.

"I've found out how your ferrets reproduce!" Cal explains. "After a particularly heavy feeding, perhaps one that offers them a richer than usual fund of experience, they bud. They form this little blister, and this little copy of themselves pops out. That's an offspring you've just swallowed. How's it doing?"

But already A-Rab is shriveling. Oddly, both his flabby human envelope and the thing inside it shrivel. Cal is grateful that a human similitude continues to mask A-Rab even in death.

It is near dark, and A-Rab's should open soon. One of the waiting winos is telling another, "Damned if I know. But Smalley said it was amazin' hooch, an' they jus' give it to 'im."

"Didn't Smalley just go on the wagon?"

"Did he? I dunno, I ain't seen him."

"'S what I'm tellin ya, he's been off the circuit a couple weeks already—"

The door of A-Rab's opens, and Nolan, Cal's last intended quarry, steps out. The old Viet-vet's silver ponytail now hangs out of a newer fedora, and the rest of his clothes are equally improved. "Remember we only take four guys a night," Nolan tells the men on the sidewalk, "but someone different every night. You'll all get a turn eventually. OK. So you, you, and you two. The rest of you try again tomorrow."

Nolan ushers the four men into a radically altered A-Rab's. (He and Cal have tasted of A-Rab's waters—just enough to discover the alien's awesome cache of currency.) Most of the shelves are gone; armchairs and an old couch have taken their places. After locking the front door, Nolan seats three of the winos in chairs. The counter looks almost like a bar now, with the displays cleared off and stools installed on the customer side of it. This is where Nolan seats the fourth wino, Lucius, a man he knows. Lucius moves totteringly and has a nasty, unhealthy-looking abdominal swelling. Cal is standing behind the counter. He and Nolan trade a look that acknowledges Lucius's terminal appearance.

"How's it goin', Loosh?" Cal asks.

Lucius answers in a faint, careful voice that saves its strength. "I'm bad off, Cal. Real bad off lately."

"Here. Taste this, Lucius. Just a sip to start—be careful."

Lucius tastes. His face grows quizzical. He tastes again. His jaw sags, and he sits astonished.

Nolan joins the other three customers while Cal sips a little to keep Lucius company. Their two little wineglasses prove to be hours deep. At one point Lucius finds enough voice to gasp, "Who is this? Who was this, Cal?"

"A man I never met, named Tom McGrath."

"Dear Christ, it makes me remember . . . so many things of my own."

Dawn isn't far off when Lucius sets the empty glass aside. "Boy, Cal!" he sighs. "It's always the way, isn't it? Too late smart. Now I finally get it, how to have my life—and I'm checkin' out any day now. Can't hardly walk, can't breathe."

Cal nods thoughtfully. "What if you could just shuck this body, but still remember your life? Could still remember it, and know the lives of other people?"

"I'd do it quicker'n spit."

Cal nods slowly. "Well, is there anybody you'd like to say goodbye to, Loosh?"

"No. No one left, Cal."

"Well, then, let's go into the back room, Loosh."

Nolan and the other three men have sat all night sunk in silences, alternating with quiet, awed talk. Not long after Cal and Nolan go in back, the sky begins to turn gray against the windows. Nolan sees the three winos to the door, where they linger in talk awhile and then drift, still dreaming, onto the dawning street.

Cal reenters as Nolan is locking the door. Cal sets a bottle and two glasses on the counter.

"Come bellyup to the bar, Nolan!" he calls. Nolan takes a stool, playing the customer. Cal pours an inch in each glass. They touch their glasses rim to rim, and then hold them up to the light, observing a contemplative pause before tasting that has become a kind of sacrament with them. "It's Lucius," Cal says. "He told me to tell you. Have one on me."

Acknowledgments

"The Angel of Death" was first published in the *Magazine of Fantasy and Science Fiction* (August 1979).

"The Autopsy" was first published in the *Magazine of Fantasy and Science Fiction* (December 1980).

"Feeding Spiders" is previously unpublished.

"Fill It with Regular" was first published in the *Magazine of Fantasy and Science Fiction* (October 1986).

"Ghost" is previously unpublished.

"The Horror on the #33" was first published in the *Magazine of Fantasy and Science Fiction* (August 1982).

"Polyphemus" was first published in the *Magazine of Fantasy and Science Fiction* (August 1981).

"Salome" was first published in *Cemetery Dance* (Summer 1994).

"Tollbooth" was first published in *Tomorrow* (August 1995).

"Upscale" was first published in the *Scream Factory* (1995).

"Water of Life" was first published in *Aboriginal Science Fiction* (Spring 1999).